Praise for The Vixen's Unlikely Marriage:

"Would absolutely give this story more than 5 star rating if I could... This author keeps you spellbound with her writing, just can't say enough about this book, the series and her." 5* Goodreads review

"I found myself totally immersed in the plot straight away and it kept me hooked right until the end. I find Ms Wakeford's writing style is fantastic, she includes such detail and depth to her stories and characters which I love to read.." 5* Goodreads review

"If you like captivating historical romance novels with virginal cinnamon roll heroes, bold vixens and lots of steam, you are sure to enjoy this book." 5* Goodreads review

"A delight to read! The story of Benedict and Grace is an unforgettable tale of love, devotion, daring, sacrifice, believing in miracles, and that there is no limit to what one will do to save the life of one's beloved." 5* Goodreads review

"Wonderful characters, sweet romance with much steam, concluding with an extremely beautiful ending." 5* Goodreads review

"A magnificent piece of work addressing a woman's sexuality... The twists and turns were incredible and surprising, evoking one's emotions." 5* Goodreads review

"A very sexy and romantic story. A+++++" 5* Goodreads review

"A wonderful story. Very entertaining." 5* Chirp review

THE STANTON LEGACY

Interconnected steamy historical romances set in England and America from the 1830s to the 1860s following two generations of the powerful and wealthy Stanton family.

Book 1: The Viscount's Scandalous Affair
An illicit affair set in late regency London between two unlikely lovers whose emotional and bumpy journey into love ends in a happily ever after.

Book 2: The Vixen's Unlikely Marriage
A steamy romance set in Victorian England featuring a marriage of convenience between two unlikely characters, a beautiful vixen and a virtuous clergyman, who nevertheless find themselves falling in love.

Book 3: The Bluestocking's Secret Obsession
A slow-burn but steamy friends-to-lovers romance set in Victorian England and America in the Civil War.

Book 4: The Viscount's Forbidden Love
An MM romance set in Victorian England with plenty of heart, angst and steam—and it does have a happy ending.

Spin-off novellas:

Mr Templeton Finds Himself a Wife
A steamy romance featuring two jilted lovers who find a second chance at love.

Miss Stanton Meets Her Match
A steamy age-gap, enemies-to-lovers romance.

THE VIXEN'S UNLIKELY MARRIAGE

A HISTORICAL MARRIAGE OF CONVENIENCE ROMANCE

THE STANTON LEGACY
– BOOK 2 –

M.M. Wakeford

DEDICATION

Dedicated to A.
my wonderfully nerdish other half,
who puts conventional men in the shade

STANTON FAMILY TREE

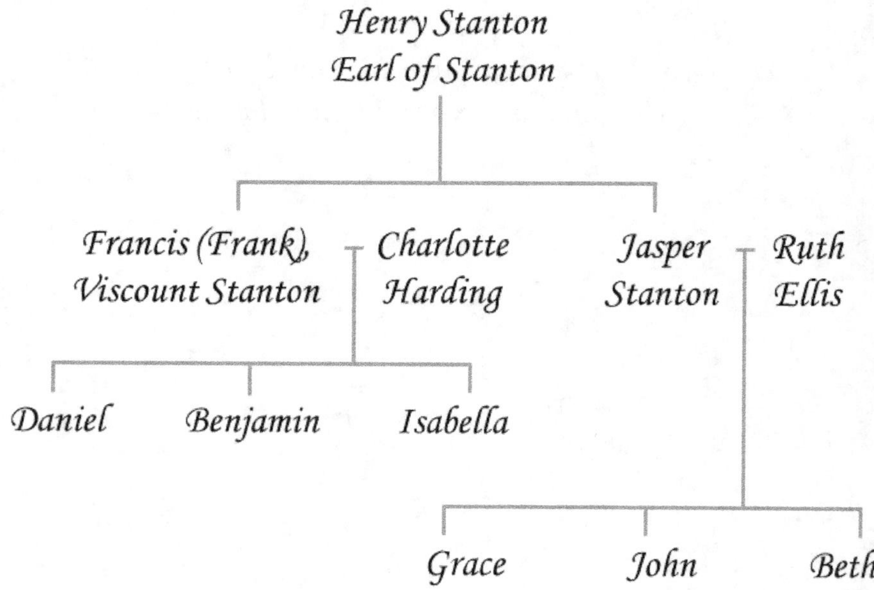

PREFACE

This is a historical novel written for a mature audience. There are sexual scenes that make this story unsuitable for anyone under the age of 18. Please also be aware that this novel includes scenes that describe the death of a close family member and scenes of a traumatic birth. As ever in my writing, the inclusion of such scenes is not for gratuitous purposes but because they are integral to the plot and character development. Please trust, however, that there will be a happy ending for the two main characters.

CHAPTER 1

Ohio, September 1860

SHE NUDGED OPEN the stable door and stepped inside. All was quiet except for the occasional snuffle of the horses. It was over an hour since they had been brought back into their stalls for the night. They had been rubbed down and fed, their water trough filled. Nobody would be coming back in here until morning.

Shutting the door quietly behind her, she carefully struck a match and lit the small oil lamp she had brought along, setting it atop an empty shelf so that it cast a dim orange glow throughout the stable. Then, very carefully, she stepped up the ladder to the hayloft. A brown woollen rug had been spread above the bed of hay in anticipation of her arrival. She smiled. *Good old Jimmy.*

She began to undress methodically, unbuttoning her dress and pulling it above her head. Beneath it, she wore only a shift and a pair of stockings held up by a garter. These she removed too, leaving her pale naked body gleaming like an alabaster sculpture in the dull light. It was a pert body, its youthful curves subtle yet noticeable. Her breasts were tipped by dusky pink nipples that tightened and pebbled in the slight chill of the evening. Dark blond curls nestled upon her mound, only a fraction darker than the curls on her head.

She lowered herself to the rug, leaning upon her elbows, and waited. Not two minutes later, she heard the stable door open and gently shut. "Grace!" whispered Jimmy's voice.

"Up here," she responded quietly.

She heard his boots cross the stable floor to the hayloft ladder and his quick steps climbing up. He paused as he reached the top, his eyes finding her spread naked on the rug. For a long moment, he simply stared at the wondrous sight.

"Oh my great Lord!" he declared in absolute awe. "How beautiful you are."

"Are you just going to stand there and gawp?" enquired Grace with an amused and pleased smile.

"No ma'am." In one bound, he was over the ladder and at her feet. His eyes stayed fixed on her luscious beauty while he hastily disrobed. The shirt flew over his head, revealing a thick, muscular frame. Work boots were kicked off and his pants pushed to the floor together with his undergarments. He stood above her, powerful thighs from years of training and riding horses, ruddy skin tanned by hours spent under the sun, and a thick cock jutting from a nest of sandy coloured curls.

She gazed at him appreciatively. *"Men are such interesting looking creatures,"* she thought, *"especially down there."* She noted the clear-coloured secretion that oozed from the dark-fleshed tip of his cock and the two plump sacs behind it that dropped down like low-hanging, succulent fruit.

A moment later, his body came down on top of hers and she felt that hardened shaft press into her abdomen as he sought her mouth for a kiss. She opened her lips to him, letting her tongue tangle with his. He tasted like Jimmy, an earthy male tang, with a hint of the beef stew he had just eaten for his dinner.

They kissed hungrily as hands explored whatever was within reach. He squeezed a breast with a palm, then brought his fingers to play with the pebbled texture of her nipples. They kissed some more.

Grace was familiar with his kisses. They had been fumbling around in darkened corners, snatching stolen moments to lock their lips together ever since she had turned fifteen—he a year older. Over time, their fumbles had become more intense, more curious, until two months ago, when, just shy over her eighteenth birthday, she had stumbled upon him swimming in the tree-sheltered shore of the creek lake. It had been a blisteringly hot day, and she had badly needed to cool off in the water. She had arrived at the lake, only to find Jimmy already there, presumably for the same purpose.

"Jimmy!" she'd called. "You have stolen a march on me. I came here to bathe. Now what am I to do?"

He'd swum towards her to stand up to his waist in the shallow end of the lake. "Why don't you join me?" he'd suggested with a cheeky grin.

At first, she had hesitated. Should she? Ma and Pa would definitely not approve, but there again, they would not approve of those delightful stolen kisses she had indulged in for the past three years either. What could a little more sinfulness matter in the grand scheme of things? She'd shrugged and called out to Jimmy, "Alright."

With hands that shook ever so slightly, she had undone the fastenings of her dress and slipped it over her head. Quickly, before she could lose her nerve, she had taken off her undergarments and run, fully bare, into the cool, welcoming embrace of the water.

Jimmy had watched her in astonished awe, not quite believing that she would follow through with his suggestion. For a while, they had circled each other, splashing about in delight at the wonderfully soothing caress of the water on their naked skin. Soon though, they had begun to swim a little closer to each other until Jimmy became emboldened and grabbed hold of her.

That afternoon had ended with Grace giving away her maidenhead, the blood of which was washed away in the calm waters of the lake. When finally she had dressed to go home, she had known that this one time would never be enough, and that she would seek every opportunity to lie with Jimmy again. In the past few weeks, the hayloft in the stable had become the place where they met in secret for their lovemaking. Each time,

Grace grew more hungry for the ache and release that Jimmy's body gave her. She could no longer imagine going through life without this.

Now, Jimmy's hand crept down her body to stroke the soft, hidden flesh at the pinnacle of her thighs. It was sticky and wet with her desire. He knew that a few more strokes would have her convulsing in sweet relief, but he wanted to feel those heavenly contractions on his cock. "Gracie," he said roughly. "I need to be inside you."

In answer, she guided his shaft to her opening. Taking this as his cue, he pushed forward, thrusting himself into her all the way to the hilt. They both sighed in pleasurable relief at the sensation of being joined so intimately. "Oh Jimmy, you feel so good inside me," Grace breathed.

"Not half so good as you feel to me." He began to thrust deep into her, slowly at first but soon building up a rapid rhythm as they both chased their climax. Ever since Grace had laid herself bare in wait for him, her body had been tingling with excitement at the deliciously forbidden things she was about to do. Her core had been pulsating to the rapid beat of her heart and leaking a sweet sticky dew. As his thick cock filled her tight passage, rubbing it pleasurably, it did not take either of them long to reach that state of bliss. Just in time, Jimmy remembered to pull out and shoot his seed on her abdomen. He had been careful, apart from that first time by the lake, not to come inside her, and so far, they had been lucky.

Having grown up on a farm, both knew well the reproductive facts of life, and neither relished the prospect of producing a child outside of wedlock. Grace also knew that Jimmy would never be more than a secret fling. Her father, Jasper Stanton, and her uncle, Frank Stanton—who back in England was a viscount—owned the extensive farm on which Jimmy worked as a stable boy, and they would hardly be likely to approve a match between herself and him. Of course, she was very fond of Jimmy, but their relationship was built on camaraderie and lust rather than love.

Gently, he rolled over until he lay on his back beside her, basking in the afterglow of pleasure. After a while, he murmured, "You had best be getting back, Gracie, before you are missed."

She stretched her arms luxuriously over her head and gave a sigh, followed by a yawn. "I know. Help clean me up."

He sat up and reached into the pocket of his pants for his handkerchief, using it to mop up the sticky mess that coated Grace's belly. Once she was clean, they both stood and silently dressed.

"You go first," Jimmy whispered. "Leave the lamp here. I'll take care of it."

"Goodnight," she whispered back, then climbed down the ladder and slipped out the door.

CHAPTER 2

THE FOLLOWING MORNING, which was a Sunday, saw Grace and her family attend service at their nearest village church. The day was bright and warm, showing no hint that autumn, and its chill breezes, would soon be upon them. The men rode on their horses alongside the ladies who sat in the buggy, the skirts of their best gowns billowing up around them.

Grace would have wanted nothing more than to ride on Willow, her beloved mare, but Ma had insisted she dress appropriately for church. As fashion dictated, her gown flared in a wide arc thanks to the crinoline she wore beneath it, an undergarment with metal spring hoops which she despised and which made it nigh on impossible to mount a horse. So on the buggy she travelled.

The journey was not long on the narrow road that cut through lush green pasture on one side, and fields of wheat and corn on the other, lined with banks of trees. To Grace, sitting in the confines of the buggy and gazing out, the flat landscape seemed endlessly vast and majestic.

Soon they came to a stop in front of the white clapboard church building with its pointed arched windows. Quickly, they secured the horses and made their way inside. They took their seats on a pew towards the back of the hall, reserving space for the rest of the Stanton clan—Uncle Frank, his wife Charlotte and Grace's three cousins, Daniel, Benjamin and Isabella—who all arrived with barely a minute to spare, sliding into their designated space. There was no time for anything more than smiles of greeting between family members before the service began.

Grace sat with a bowed head, to all appearances deep in holy reflection, though this was far from the case, for she heard very little of the sermon—something to do with fire and brimstone, no doubt. Instead, her mind was busy plotting her next encounter with Jimmy. She knew she had to be careful not to be missed when she slipped out for her trysts in the stable barn, which was no easy feat in her tightly knit family. Last night, she had retired to bed early, claiming a headache, then wisely waited for Ma to check in on her before she tiptoed out of her room and escaped through the back door. For her next tryst, she would have to think of another excuse. She could not claim to be unwell each time she met with Jimmy in secret—that would surely raise suspicion, or at the very least, questions she had no wish to answer.

Finally, the service was over, and they filed out of the church into the dazzling sunshine. "Well, thank God that's done!" muttered Jasper Stanton, Grace's father. "I vow the reverend gets worse every time. Can he not brighten the mood just once in a while? There are only so many dire warnings about hellfire that I can take!"

Ruth, his wife, put her arm through his. Grace's mother was small and slight in stature, though not in spirit. A plain-speaking woman with a will of iron, whose once fiery red hair had faded to a pale blond, she now said, "Never mind dear, it is done, and we may go home. Beth has baked a pumpkin pie specially for you."

Jasper smiled fondly at his youngest daughter, "Anything made by your hands, Beth, is sure to be perfection."

"That's what you say every time," laughed Beth, a freckled fourteen-year old with light-brown hair and large hazel eyes that gazed at the world with bright, innocent curiosity. "May I remind you, Pa, of the blackberry cobbler from two summers ago that I managed to char in the oven."

Jasper waved a dismissive hand. "The exception that proves the rule, my dear."

"I see the reverend looking our way, Pa," warned John, the middle child in the family—now at sixteen, more of a young man than a child. He was nearly his father's great height and shared his dashing good looks, though his frame had yet to fill out and match Jasper's broad, muscled build.

Jasper shuddered. "Then let us go quick, for I have no wish to converse with him."

They headed towards their buggy and horses, which were tethered to a nearby post. Ahead of them, his brother Frank and his family were climbing aboard their own vehicle and horses. It was a tradition among the Stantons that Sunday lunch was an extended family affair, with the location alternating between each brother's house every week. Today, it was Jasper's turn to play host at the large, grey-painted home he had built for Ruth all those years ago as a way to convince her to marry him.

Whenever Grace was told the story of how Jasper had wooed Ruth by building a magnificent house for her, much of it with his bare hands, she would feel a delicious tingle of heartwarming emotion at the evidence of her father's love for her mother. Now at the age of eighteen, she had no plans to fall in love quite yet. Like her mother, she was determined to keep her heart barricaded until a man proved himself worthy of breaking through its defences. In the meantime, there was no reason why she could not have a little fun with Jimmy.

MUCH LATER, AFTER the pumpkin pie was demolished with many a word of praise, Grace stood to help clear the dishes from the table, together with the other womenfolk in the house. Sunday was a day off for their housemaid, Rose, so they all stepped in to do the household chores. The girls may have had an earl for a grandfather back in England, but over here, nobody was considered too good to do honest manual labour. With so many helping hands, it was quick work anyway.

Grace dried her hands on a dish towel and prepared to leave the kitchen to join everyone in the main parlour. She was stopped, however, by her aunt Charlotte. "Grace, if I may have a word with you?"

Startled, Grace replied, "Yes, of course."

"Let us go sit at the table in the corner there by the back door, so we are not overheard."

Now more curious than ever, Grace did as she was told, taking a seat next to Aunt Charlotte, who was not only her uncle's wife but also her mama's childhood friend, as well as the village school teacher who had taught Grace her letters. Aunt Charlotte got straight to the point. "Grace, you know of course that the stable building is within view of my bedroom window. Last night, I had gone to draw the curtains when I noticed some movement outside. On closer inspection, I saw that it was you, coming out of the stable. Strange, I thought. Then lo and behold, the stable door opened again, and this time I discerned the familiar form of Jimmy walking out, looking very furtive indeed."

She paused and waited for Grace to respond. When Grace said nothing, Charlotte continued, "I can only assume, Grace, that you were meeting him there for some kind of assignation."

Grace nodded, but still did not speak.

Charlotte sighed, "How far has it got?" At Grace's questioning look, she added, "Have you lain with him, Grace?"

"Yes," mumbled Grace.

"Oh my dear Lord. I take it Ruth does not know of this?"

Grace shook her head vehemently. "No, Aunt Charlotte and please, she must not know."

"Ruth is my best friend. I do not keep secrets from her."

"Please, just this once. It would upset her terribly to find out."

"Yes, it would," Charlotte agreed. "A shotgun wedding to Jimmy is not what she has envisaged for your future."

"There won't be a need for that to happen, Aunt Charlotte, if we keep things between ourselves."

"And what if this results in you being with child? Have you considered, Grace, the risks you are taking?"

"We are being very careful."

At this, Charlotte snorted and moved her chair closer to Grace's. They were quiet for a moment, then she said with a wistful smile, "Grace, I do not believe I have ever told you this, but your uncle Frank and I had an affair in London, before we came to America and got married. It caused a small scandal at the time, because you see we were caught in an embrace at a society ball. It was why I decided to leave England and come here with your mother and uncle Robert. Then Frank followed me of course, and the rest is history."

Grace was staring at her aunt in surprise. "I never knew!" she breathed.

Charlotte chuckled, "Well, it is not something we go around talking about. The reason I am telling you now is because I want you to know that I understand, but also that you need to be very, very careful. If I discovered you, then who is to say someone else might not do so too? You heard the sermon in the church today. People here would not be understanding, and you would be branded a jezebel. It would cause an even greater stir than my scandal did back in London."

"I shall be very careful," Grace promised.

"What steps are you taking to ensure you do not become with child?"

Grace flushed. "We, erm, he does not complete inside me."

"Well, that is a start, but not enough. You still run too high a risk of becoming an unwed mother unless you do something more."

"What else can we do?" wondered Grace.

"You need to be very aware of your menses and note down the details of your cycle. On some days, when you are very fertile, you must avoid being with Jimmy altogether. The first seven days after you start bleeding should be safe, and the week before you are due as well, but the time in between is when you must be very careful."

Grace listened attentively, making a mental note of this extraordinary advice from Aunt Charlotte. "I will be," she promised again.

Her aunt observed her closely then sighed, "Very well, let us go back before we are missed."

They returned to the parlour with Grace in a pensive mood, thinking of the disgrace that would befall her should her affair with Jimmy ever be discovered. It was not quite enough to dissuade her from continuing with the affair. She could acknowledge privately to herself that it was its very illicit nature that made it so exciting. Unlike her staid cousin Isabella, Grace thrived on the thrill of danger, whether it was galloping on Willow a fraction too fast or slipping out at night for a lustful encounter with the stable boy. However, she was not foolhardy. She knew she would have to exercise a bit more care, for she could not imagine herself ever running away with Jimmy should they be found out.

CHAPTER 3

LIFE CONTINUED AS normal over the course of the following month. Grace, ever the fast learner, heeded her aunt's advice and redoubled her efforts not to have her dalliance with Jimmy discovered. It seemed she was successful, for there were no further difficult conversations to be had with any member of her family, and her monthly bleeding came reliably on time.

One late October morning, she was in the main parlour, in the company of her mother and sister, engaged in the never-ending needlework that was required to maintain all their clothing in good order. Through the window, they heard the sound of a horse clattering over the gravelled path to their house. A few moments later, there came a knock on the door, which was answered by Rose, the housemaid, who then hurried into the parlour holding a folded slip of paper in her hand. "This came for Mr Stanton, ma'am."

"Thank you, Rose." Ruth took the folded slip of paper. "It looks like a telegram," she mused.

They had never received a telegram before, but Grace had heard of the much vaunted new invention that facilitated communication across great distances.

"Who could it be from?" wondered Beth.

Ruth's mouth formed into a tight line. "I am very much afraid that it can only be news from England, and not anything good." She pondered a moment then came to a decision. "Grace, will you be a dear and go fetch your father. He said he would be in the wheat fields, supervising the harvest. Hop on your mare and get him quick."

"Yes, Ma."

Grace hurried out, stopping only to put on a warm riding coat and boots. Then she was out like an arrow, running to the stable. She found Jimmy there, cleaning out a stall with a broom. "Help me saddle Willow, quick," she called out. "I must get to Pa at once."

He put the broom down, startled, but rushed to do her bidding. "What's the matter?" he asked.

"A telegram has arrived. Probably from England."

Jimmy brought the horse round and, with quick, efficient movements, attached the saddle, bridle and reins. Grace went to stand on the block and lowered herself into the side-saddle position, placing her right leg bent in front and tucking her left leg behind. Once secured into position, she urged her mare forward. As soon as she had crossed the gravelled entrance to her house and was out on the narrow mud road, she bid her horse to speed up, galloping at a brisk pace towards the wheat fields.

She slowed down as she approached her destination, her eyes searching for her father in the distance. She finally spotted a group of men further down to her right, of which one had the distinctive, tall gait of Jasper Stanton. She nudged her horse to move at a canter towards them.

Hearing the sound of hooves, Jasper turned his head to observe her approach with a frown. As she stopped her horse beside him, he called out worriedly, "Grace, what is it?"

"Pa, you need to come home now. We have received a telegram for you."

Jasper reacted instantly. He turned to his foreman, Tom Shaw, giving him quick instructions, then strode over to his horse, tethered nearby. In a trice, he had mounted it and was urging it into a gallop. Grace followed, matching her father's pace on her own mare. Within minutes, they were both dismounting and handing over the reins to Jimmy before hurrying up to the house.

Ruth waited for them inside, the sealed telegram clasped in her hand. On seeing her husband, she went over to him. "It's addressed to you and Frank," she said, handing it over. With a frown, Jasper took it and quickly unfolded the sealed sheet of paper. He read it, then silently held the sheet out to his wife.

"What does it say?" asked Grace, impatient to know.

In a voice laced with worry, Jasper replied, "Father is gravely ill. He wishes us to return home as soon as possible."

"What will you do?"

Jasper stood still, thinking, his eyes on Ruth. She came to him, placing a soothing hand on his chest. "Ruthie, can you get us all packed and ready to leave by tomorrow?" he asked very softly.

"Yes." Ruth was firm, decisive.

Jasper inhaled sharply. "Very well. Let me go make the arrangements." Thinking things over as he spoke, he continued, "Tom can take over the running of the farm while we are away. He practically does it already. Frank's overseeing the transport of a grain consignment in Ashtabula today. I'll need to ride over and find him. While there, I'll see about booking our train passage to New York."

"I'll send word to Robert," said Ruth, speaking of her brother, who owned a large tract of neighbouring land. "He can help keep an eye on things here while we are away."

"Yes, good idea," murmured Jasper, running an agitated hand through his mussed hair.

Ruth held his eyes. "We could be at Stanton Hall within two weeks, at most three. We will do all we can to get there as quickly as it is possible. Beyond that, there is nothing more we can do except pray. What will be will be."

Jasper exhaled deeply, then drew his wife to him. He dropped a kiss to her forehead then pulled back reluctantly. "I had better get going," he sighed.

CHAPTER 4

Two weeks later

THE DESERTED READING room was deathly quiet apart from the creaking of the polished wooden floors with each sway of the ship. The furniture, fixed with bolts to the walls and floor, stayed firmly in place. It consisted of several tall shelves stacked with books, a large coffee table, two armchairs and the settee on which Grace sat, flicking listlessly the pages of the book she was trying to read.

For the past two days, stormy seas had confined all but the most hardy of passengers to their cabins. Her mother, father, uncle and aunt, together with her cousins and siblings, were all either lying prostrate in their beds or tending to the sick. She had escaped only an hour ago from the room she shared with her sister, Beth, who had finally managed to get to sleep after spending a miserable night retching into a bowl by her bedside. Grace had found her way here, to the reading room, in search of a book that would help her while away the time until she had to return to her nursing duties in the cabin.

They had been on board the RMS Persia, a steamship on the prestigious Cunard Line, for just under a week. In another few days she hoped, they would arrive in Liverpool, and from there make their way to Stanton Hall in Oxfordshire. For someone accustomed to the outdoors—whether it was tending to the kitchen garden back home or daily rides on Willow—she had found it hard to have her movements restricted, especially the last few days. The walls of her cabin had begun to press in on her, and she had needed to get away, if only for a short time.

Grace lifted her arms above her head and gave an inelegant stretch. As she did so, she felt the tips of her breasts brush against the fabric of her shift and pucker up at the contact. Taking advantage of the fact she was alone in the room, she gave each breast a little tweak with her fingers and exhaled in relief. They felt tender and needy. It had been over two weeks since she had last lain with Jimmy, and her body was craving his touch.

Not for the first time, Grace wondered whether she should find herself another lover to ease that ache. She was hesitant about it, though not for any sentimental attachment to Jimmy. Her hesitance was mainly out of concern for how she would go about finding a lover while maintaining the necessary discretion. Jimmy she had known since childhood and trusted, but a relative stranger? That would be too risky. As for any moral qualms, she consoled herself with the thought that anything that felt so good could surely not be sinful.

She stood with a sigh and put the unread book back on the shelf from which she had found it. The ship swayed beneath her feet, and the books on the shelf rattled alarmingly but stayed in place. Time to get back to the sick room and check on her sister. Poor Beth. She had not coped well with the swaying motion of the ship even before they had encountered this storm, whereas she, Grace, had not felt a single moment of queasiness throughout their journey so far.

Captain Gregory had been most approving at dinner yesterday when she had presented herself at the table deserted of its usual occupants. Of her family, only Uncle Frank had made it to the meal, the rest of them opting to stay abed. The captain had been full of praise for her admirable sea legs, hinting that perhaps there was a future for her as the wife of a seaman. To this she had smiled, without voicing a response. The captain had then turned his attention to her neighbour at the table, Mr Drummond, the ship's chief engineer. "Indeed, Mr

Drummond here can attest to the importance of having a wife that can withstand the rigours of a sea voyage."

All eyes had turned to Mr Drummond, a mild-mannered man in his early thirties, who had smiled self-deprecatingly and elucidated. "Captain Gregory is alluding to my wife's unfortunate attempt to accompany me on board the ship after I was first appointed chief engineer. Alas, she spent the entire journey laid up in bed, feeling extremely unwell. And therefore, much as she and I would have liked for her to join me on my work travels, it was not to be."

"It must be hard to endure such long separations from your wife," had murmured Grace.

"Yes, it is, but we are used to it now. It is not all bad though. My long absences mean I am treated like a king on my return and spoiled with my favourite dishes, receiving all the attention and care I could wish for."

To this, Uncle Frank had replied, "I take your point Drummond, but I must confess, no cosseting or special treats could ever compensate for the absence of my wife by my side."

Mr Drummond had nodded in acquiescence. "Viscount Stanton, you are quite right."

It was strange to hear her uncle addressed by his title. Back home, he was just Frank or Mr Stanton to everyone around. Grace was reminded how different things would be once they were in England. She had only been there once before at the tender age of eight, on a visit to her grandpa, the Earl of Stanton. She recalled the magnificence of Stanton Hall, the numerous servants and the stiff formality. It had not been to her taste, and she had longed for the visit to end so they could return to the familiarity and comfort of home.

Now aged eighteen, she wondered how this next visit would go, especially with her grandpa being so gravely ill. She hoped and prayed that they would not be too late. She was rather fond of the old earl. True, his manner was cold and imperious, but she had detected a faint twinkle in his eyes when no one else was looking. Refusing to be intimidated by such a great personage, she had sat beside him and quizzed him about the horses at Stanton Hall. He had been taken aback at first that an eight-year-old girl should display so little fear of him, but he had solemnly responded to all her questions. Over the course of that visit, she had gotten into the habit of going to sit with her grandpa in his study each day and regaling him with tales of her adventures. On her return to America, she had been excited to receive a letter from him, which had led to a regular correspondence between them over the years.

Bracing herself against another sway of the ship beneath her feet, Grace picked up the oil lamp she had brought with her and stepped carefully towards the door of the reading room, intent on returning to her cabin. She had nearly reached it when the door opened suddenly, and a man hurried in. He stopped in surprise upon seeing her.

"Miss Stanton, I had not expected to see you here," exclaimed Mr Drummond.

"I-I came to find a book to help pass the time, but I should be getting back now to check on my sister."

"Yes, of course." He stood aside to let her pass. In that moment, the ship swayed again, and she was thrown forward. Seeing her and the oil lamp in her hand about to fall, he lunged towards Grace, hooking an arm around her waist and pulling her back against his chest. "It's alright," he puffed. "I've got you."

The ship began lurching from side to side, and his arm tightened reassuringly around her. "What is happening?" she breathed worriedly.

"The eye of the storm, I'm afraid. It's going to feel a bit rocky for a while, but it is not anything to worry about, Miss Stanton." His arm was like a band of steel around her, and she sank back against him gratefully. In her ear, she heard him say, "I suggest you wait here until we are over the worst of it, before attempting a journey back to your cabin. Hold on to me and we'll go sit on the settee over there."

Slowly, he guided her towards it. Once they had sat down, he took the oil lamp from her and placed it on the side table, alongside the one he had been holding. The lamps were solidly built, their heavy metal bases anchoring them to the table. The ship continued to sway, alternately pushing Grace against Mr Drummond then pushing him towards her. After this had happened a few times, he spoke again. "Miss Stanton, I hope you will not take this the wrong way, but I think it would be best if I were to place my arms around you while the ship lurches in such a manner. It will help to keep us in one place."

"I—yes, of course," she murmured.

With great care, he encircled her with both his arms, letting her rest comfortingly against his side, her right cheek pressed to his shoulder. On her next inhale, she scented tobacco, cologne and the unmistakable aroma of a virile male. It sent her pulse racing. This was no overgrown boy such as Jimmy had been. This was a man through and through.

The ship rocked violently, but Mr Drummond held her tight, tucking her head under his chin and bracing his feet against the legs of the coffee table beside him to keep them both in place. She heard him exhale a gentle sigh above her. Very quietly, he said, "Pardon me for saying this, Miss Stanton, but it feels good to hold a female in my arms again. I have missed this greatly."

"How long has it been since you last saw your wife?"

"Just over a month. It feels like longer."

"It must be hard to be away for such long periods from a loved one. I wonder how you can bear it."

She felt his breath ruffle her hair as he said, "It is not easy. I hope to put a stop to it in a few years once I have saved up enough to invest in an engineering workshop I have plans to build. Until then, we manage as best we can. I am fortunate in that Lucy is a very understanding wife."

"How so? Because she treats you like a king when you return?"

He chuckled. "Yes, there is that too."

Intrigued, Grace probed a little more. "How else then is she understanding?"

He hesitated a fraction, seemingly unsure if he should go on. Then, softly, he said, "We have spoken of the problems that might arise from a long separation, and she has intimated that she would understand if I ever felt the need to seek solace in the arms of another, in the full knowledge of course that no one would ever replace her in my heart." He paused. "I hope I have not shocked you too much with such talk, Miss Stanton."

She was quick to allay his fear. "Not at all, Mr Drummond. I like to think I am conversant with the ways of the world."

"You are very young. Perhaps it was not my place to discuss such matters with you. Forgive me, Miss Stanton, the long night I have spent in the engine room must have addled my brain."

Instinctively, she rubbed her face against the fabric of his jacket and replied, "Please do not concern yourself, Mr Drummond. I may be young in age, but I have an old head on my shoulders. I am not so coddled as to be unaware of the realities of life. Your Lucy sounds like an admirable woman."

"That she is." The ship continued its rocking motion. His arms around her tightened a fraction before he continued, "So you see, Miss Stanton, she would not find fault with me for holding you so and finding comfort in it. I do hope though, that my proximity is not making you too ill at ease."

"On the contrary, Mr Drummond. I am glad to provide solace in such lonely and stormy seas, and to take comfort for myself. You see, it has been two weeks for me and already I feel like I may go mad with need."

She felt him go still and belatedly realised what she had inadvertently given away. Quickly, she blurted, "I am sorry. I should not have said that."

He nuzzled the top of her head. "One should never regret honesty, Miss Stanton. Am I to take it you have someone back home for whom you care greatly?"

"His name is Jimmy."

"Tell me about him."

"I have known him all my life. He is a stable boy at our farm. He gave me my first kiss when I was but fifteen. Then some months ago, things went further than just kisses. We meet after dark in the hayloft in the stable."

"I see."

"Please do not judge me too harshly, Mr Drummond. I know in many eyes what I have done is a sin, but I have felt such joy in his arms that I cannot believe it to be so."

He huffed out a breath. "I am the last person to judge, Miss Stanton. Before we married, Lucy and I would also meet in secret, though not in a hayloft. We would sneak out to a deserted barn on the edge of her father's estate." He laughed reminiscently. "I had it snug and cosy, with rugs and pillows and blankets."

"That sounds lovely."

"A little on the rustic side, but I have fond memories of that time."

They were quiet for several minutes, holding each other close, not just to combat the swaying of the ship. Grace wondered if perhaps she had been foolish to reveal such things about herself to Mr Drummond. She was interrupted in her musings by his gentle voice. "You say you may go mad with need, Miss Stanton. Tell me what it is you feel. Perhaps there is some way I can help you."

He sounded sincere. She decided to honour his question with an honest response. "Lately, it feels as if my whole body aches with need."

"Where do you ache most?" he asked, his voice husky.

With one hand, she pointed to her breasts. "Here." Then she pointed down to the juncture of her thighs. "And here."

"Grace, may I call you by your name?"

"Yes," she breathed.

"Grace, will you let me touch you there and ease your ache?"

"Please."

Ever so slowly, his hand travelled from her waist and up to cup one breast. He squeezed it gently, then pinched the tip with his fingers. Grace moaned.

He brought his other hand up to cup a second breast. For long, pleasurable minutes, he kneaded and squeezed and pinched, making her tingle all over. Eventually, his dexterous fingers made quick work of undoing the front buttons of her dress, opening it to expose her chemise. She had not worn a corset nor a crinoline this morning, deciding her comfort was more important than proprieties on a day such as this. His hand pushed the cotton fabric of the chemise aside to release one breast and then the other. He took a moment to admire the dainty, pink-tipped flesh, before cupping a breast in each hand and squeezing gently.

"Beautiful," he said reverently, and Grace moaned again.

"Please, Mr Drummond—"

"It's Alex," he murmured, his mouth nuzzling the sensitive column of her throat.

"Alex, please."

His mouth travelled down to her collar bone, then further down still. "Yes!" cried Grace.

A moment later, his lips clamped around an aching breast, sucking gently, while one arm steadied her against the swaying of the ship. "More!" demanded Grace, any shyness overcome by need. He sucked at her breast even harder, while toying with the tip of the other with his fingers. Grace slid her hands into his hair, holding his head firmly to her chest, lest he dare move it away—which he was not minded to do at all.

She felt him bite the tip gently, then go back to sucking it feverishly. She arched against him, wanting more. It was as if he understood, for soon he lifted glittering eyes to hers before reaching down to tug at her skirt. A moment later, he was diving under her petticoat, searching for the aperture in her drawers that would give him access to that most aching part of her body. With the experience of a man that had undressed a woman many a time, he drew the slit of her drawers apart and found the moist sensitive flesh he was looking for.

By now, Grace was breathing in shallow pants. Her heart pounded with excitement and fear at the risk she was taking in exposing herself so publicly. The thrill of what she was doing though, overcame any rational thought. When his fingers began to stroke her quivering centre, she cried out, the words incoherent. This! Oh yes this!

Alex stroked her expertly, finding the small, sensitive nub that swelled and throbbed under his ministrations. His mouth returned to her breast, licking and sucking as his fingers wove their magic down below. It was perfection. So wet was she with her desire that Alex's thick finger slid easily inside her slick passage. How was it he knew she needed to be filled, to have something solid to clench around? Alex's finger plunged in and out of her, while his clever mouth continued to drive her wild. At last it was too much. With a loud gasp, she felt her body convulse as she reached her peak.

Alex brought his hand back up and released the breast he had been suckling. A sudden sway of the ship had him catch her in his arms again. She rested her head against him, eyes closed, feeling languid and replete. Eventually, she regained enough sense to sit up and look at him.

His eyes burned with barely repressed desire as he took in the sight of her, breasts peeking out of her unbuttoned dress, the nipples puckered. "How is your ache now?" he asked, his voice sounding rough.

"Much better, thank you," she murmured.

He nodded, his expression tense. "Grace," he muttered. Then, rather than speak, he took one of her hands and laid it over the hardness straining beneath the fabric of his trousers.

"Grace," he repeated, his eyes pleading. "Will you let me? Please?"

In answer, Grace reached over to pull her skirt and petticoat up around her waist, exposing her drawers, the slit still gaping wide where his hand had been. Then, she looked into his eyes, nodding slightly. Needing no further persuasion, Alex pushed her gently to lie on the wide settee and parted her legs. With fumbling hands, he released his swollen cock from the confines of his clothes, pumping it a few times as he looked into her eyes, a mixture of need and gratitude in his. He bent down to claim her lips in a sweet, tender kiss. "Thank you, Grace," he mumbled, a moment before he positioned his shaft at her opening and drove in.

They both gasped together at the delicious sensation of their joining—and at the lurch of the ship which drove him deeper into her. He braced himself on his elbows and started to thrust, using the rocking motion of the ship to find a rhythm. Each forward motion of the vessel had him sink further inside her. Grace felt his penetration with every nerve ending in her body. She ached and throbbed, needing to reach that pinnacle once again. Her hands dug into his firm buttocks and urged him to plunge deeper and faster. She was so close, drunk on sensation and on the decadent thrill of rutting with a near stranger on a swaying ship, in a room where anyone could walk in at any moment. How wild she felt! How free! He must have sensed this, for he barked out, "Come, Grace. Come for me now!"

She gave a cry, her eyes going slack as she pulsed around his shaft. With a grimace of near pain, he pulled out just in time, releasing string after string of pearly cum over the bunched up fabric of her dress. Drawing heavy breaths, he brought his forehead to hers. "Thank you," he said again.

"No, it is I who should be thanking you," she panted.

He smiled against her mouth and kissed her. Then he became all business-like, pulling out a handkerchief from his breast pocket and using it to mop the mess on her skirt. Quickly, he restored his own clothing into proper order, then assisted her to a sitting position, buttoning up her dress with practised hands. She noticed dazedly that the ship had stopped swaying so violently. As if he could read her mind, he said, "It looks like the storm has blown over."

He stood and helped her to her feet, patting her skirt down to make sure she looked respectable again. She faced him, uncertain of what to say. Eventually, he murmured, "Despite what I said earlier, I do not make a habit of being unfaithful to my wife."

She glanced down at the floor, tongue-tied now the moment of hedonism was over.

"Thank you, Grace," he said, "for giving yourself so freely and bringing me the utmost pleasure. However, this will not happen again."

"Will you tell Lucy?" she asked.

He shook his head. "She would not want to know." With a sigh, he continued, "I am not one for regrets, Grace. What is done is done. And I will not lie and say I did not enjoy every delicious moment with you. But now, it is best to put it from our minds and to move on."

Grace nodded. "Good day, Mr Drummond," she said.

"Good day, Miss Stanton," he replied. He fetched the lamp and handed it to her, then went to open the door. With a small inclination of her head, she stepped out of the reading room and made her way back to her cabin.

Throughout the rest of the day, as she cared for Beth and checked in on the rest of her family, visions of what she had done flooded her mind, bringing a flush to her cheeks. Had she really made wild, abandoned love with Mr Drummond in the reading room? Even she could hardly believe it. Never had she imagined that she could do something quite as depraved as this. It was wicked, wrong, and yet it had felt so wonderfully good.

After much churning of her thoughts, she eventually came to the conclusion that this was a one-time occurrence that must never happen again, the memory of which she would treasure, like the guiltiest of secrets, until the end of her days.

CHAPTER 5

JUST BEYOND THE village of Stanton Harcourt in Oxfordshire lay Stanton Hall, the stately home of the Earl of Stanton. It stood proudly in thirty acres of rolling parkland, including ornamental and kitchen gardens, woodland and a small fishing lake. The grand house was reached via a long tree-lined avenue that began its path at the outskirts of the village. Towards the village end of the avenue, screened by a bank of tall oak trees, was Ivy Cottage.

A charming stone building with two good-sized drawing rooms, a study and three brightly-lit bedchambers, Ivy Cottage was home to Ambrose Cranshaw and his sister, Sarah. The tenancy of Ivy Cottage came as part of the job of manager for the vast Stanton estate, which stretched for several miles around and encompassed over ten thousand acres of farmland as well as several manor houses. Three years ago, Ambrose Cranshaw had been entrusted with the important job of managing the entire Stanton estate, taking over from the elderly Mr. Finlay, with whom he had apprenticed. Since then, he had acquitted himself well in the position, earning the respect and trust of the earl.

On this evening in the middle of November, two persons were having a lively conversation in the main drawing room of Ivy Cottage. A fire burned brightly in the fireplace, keeping the autumnal chill at bay. On each four walls, oil lamps had been lit, casting a warm glow over the simply furnished room.

"How about this one? Truro to Brixworth. Fastest route. I give you two minutes to work it out," said Sarah. In her hands, she held the latest copy of Bradshaw's Guide, that ultimate authority on the timetable of trains around the country.

Benedict Sedgwick scrunched his nose in concentration. He was a slim young man of average height and ordinary looks. His unremarkable face—earnest brown eyes set behind a pair of wire-rimmed glasses, a thin but longish nose, a well-formed mouth and a good set of teeth—was framed by a messy mane of light-brown hair that was in need of a cut. As the newly appointed curate of the parish, he had been too busy getting to know his parishioners and practising his sermon to schedule a visit to the barbers.

This was the end of his first week in Stanton Harcourt, and he had come to partake of dinner with his childhood friends, the Cranshaws. It was through them that he had been lucky enough to obtain this position. The elderly vicar of the parish had become too incapacitated to fulfil his church duties, and it was decided that a curate should be appointed to help out with the necessary work.

As the most powerful landowner in the area and the holder of the church living in question, the Earl of Stanton had a great deal of influence in the matter of who was appointed. So it was that in conversation with him, Ambrose Cranshaw had mentioned his childhood friend, Benedict Sedgwick, the youngest son of a gentleman of modest means, Oxford-educated and newly ordained. So warmly did he speak of his friend that the earl had been convinced to invite young Benedict for an interview, and then to appoint him as the new curate.

The position was poorly paid, a mere £60 a year, but it came with the provision of a small village house and the possibility of obtaining the living after the current vicar passed away. The earl, moreover, had it in his gift to bestow several other livings when they became vacant, so having him as a patron would be highly beneficial. Benedict had jumped at the chance. As the seventh born in his family, he had very little in the way of assets except for his education and good name. Thus he had arrived a week ago with a small trunk carrying all his worldly goods, which consisted mostly of books and a meagre wardrobe of frayed and patched up clothes.

Although it was early evening, Ambrose was not yet come home from his duties as estate manager, so it had fallen to Sarah to entertain her childhood friend. She did so by invoking an old game of theirs—find the fastest train route from one destination to another, all from memory, no cheating and looking it up in the book.

"Hmm," murmured Benedict. "Well, the simplest way would be to take the 8:15 from Truro all the way to London and from there go by way of Euston to Northampton, connecting on to Brixworth."

"That would be simplest way," agreed Sarah, "but is it the fastest?"

Benedict brushed back a shock of hair that had fallen across his forehead. "There is a faster way," he said, looking amused. "However, it does not quite follow the rules of the game as it requires a break in the train journey."

"All the same, let me hear it."

"Very well. I would take the 8:15 from Truro, but instead of then going by way of Euston, I would travel out to Market Harborough by way of Kings Cross. The Midland Railway has recently opened its new route that way, and I can thereafter connect to Brixworth. By taking advantage of this, I save time because the train from Euston to Northampton takes a meandering and agonisingly slow route."

"Hmm, but it does require a break in the train journey at Hitchin to rebook, so I am not minded to accept your answer."

Benedict laughed. "It was worth a try! How else could the journey have been accomplished?"

As Sarah went to answer this, they heard the front door open and slam shut, followed by heavy footsteps in the hall. A moment later, the door to the drawing room burst open and in walked Ambrose Cranshaw.

"Benedict!" he called out. "I am so sorry to have kept you waiting. I do hope Sarah has accomplished her duties well as hostess in my absence."

With a teasing smile, Benedict replied, "Sadly not, I'm afraid. You must have words with her about the drop in the standard of hospitality, for I have merely been offered a cup of tea. No biscuits or cakes. Not even a boiled sweet. What on earth is the world coming to?"

No sooner had he said these words than a cushion was thrown at his face. He caught it with a smile, just as Ambrose chuckled, "I see the two of you are back to your old tricks. Have you been playing that game with Bradshaw's Guide again?"

"Of course," boasted Sarah, "and I beat Benedict by two points to one, so that is why he is being so disagreeable about me."

"I do think the score should be an even tie," riposted Benedict.

"Now, now, children, let us not argue," said Ambrose, putting on a haughty voice. "Let me just go up and refresh my appearance, then we can sit down to dinner. I have news to share."

"Oh, do tell!"

"Wait until I return. I shan't be long."

True to his word, Ambrose was back in a few minutes, and the three friends adjourned to the dining room where a housemaid served them their first course of leek and potato soup. They ate hungrily and were quiet at first while they paid attention to their meal. At length however, Sarah bethought herself to ask her question again. "Ambrose, what is this news you wanted to tell us about?"

Her brother set down his spoon and gazed at her. "As you know, the earl requested I send a telegram to his sons in America, urging them to return. The poor old goat has been on tenterhooks the last few days, expecting their arrival. But frail as he is, the hope of seeing his loved ones again seems to have given him a little spurt of health. He was able today to leave his bed for a few hours, which is much more than he has been able to do in a long while. Anyway, when I got there earlier, I found out the sons, their wives and children had all arrived yesterday evening."

"What are they like?" asked Sarah eagerly.

"I only met them in passing, so it is too soon to judge. Their manners were easy, and there was no standing on ceremony, as one might expect after they have spent so long in America. The younger son, Jasper Stanton, was the friendlier of the two; the eldest son, the viscount, a little more reserved. However, both were perfectly pleasant. With the earl so frail, it is natural that I have wondered about his successor here and what this will mean for my position as estate manager. As I said, it is too soon to tell, but my first impressions were favourable."

"If the viscount inherits the estate, do you think he will stay here permanently or will he return to America and be an absentee landlord?"

"We shall have to wait for these and many questions more to be answered in due course," replied Ambrose.

"I suppose this will mean I must cultivate a relationship with my soon-to-be new patron," said Benedict. "And I have only just arrived and met the earl twice."

"All in good time," smiled Ambrose. "Let us not get ahead of ourselves. The earl, I hope, may recover from this latest illness and have many weeks or months ahead of him."

"He is in my prayers," murmured Benedict.

"And mine," said Sarah.

"There is one more piece of news," continued Ambrose. "The earl, in his joy at being reunited with his family, is keen to celebrate Christmas in style this year. He has asked me to procure a large tree and decorations, and he will be hosting a Christmas ball, inviting all the local folk. He has already sent orders to his kitchen staff for a half dozen large turkeys, as well as a wide range of delicacies. It is going to be quite the feast."

"That is certainly something to look forward to," said Benedict, who rarely saw such things in his frugal life.

"Indeed it is."

The three friends spent a convivial evening together, reminiscing about the past and making plans for the future. Sarah insisted that henceforth Benedict come dine with them every Friday evening. She reminded him to pay a visit to the barber before leading church service on Sunday, and noticing a tear in the elbow of his jacket, bade him bring it over the next day for her to mend.

There was a strong bond of affection between the three of them. Having been brought up close neighbours and played together all through their childhood, there was an ease and familiarity not often found in other friendships. It helped that Sarah, in a most unladylike fashion, shared many of Benedict's eccentric pursuits. From memorising train timetables, to helping him create models of his favourite locomotives, to stargazing with him on his telescope, she had shown an uncommon interest in science and engineering. Even better, as she grew into womanhood, she had not developed those missish tendencies that would have put a natural break on their friendship. There had been no budding romantic feelings on his side nor, thankfully, on hers.

Benedict was glad of this as such things had a tendency to make him extremely uncomfortable. He had no clue how he would ever go about wooing a female, and in any case, his penurious state made it unlikely he would have the means to court a lady for a very long time. At Oxford, while other fellows had engaged in the usual round of debauchery, he had concentrated on his studies, keenly aware that he was there on a scholarship and that his future depended on earning the most distinguished possible degree.

Thus he had reached the age of twenty-five still ignorant of the ways of women. That is not to say he was disinterested. A pretty face or figure, a tantalising scent or seductive voice, would naturally occasion in him a reaction—a second look at the lady or a flush to his pale cheeks. But that was usually as far as it went for Benedict Sedgwick. What would happen if he ever came across a lady who really tempted him, he was not sure.

CHAPTER 6

THE EARL GAZED in satisfaction at his family gathered around him. His had been a lonely life ever since his two sons had taken off for America twenty-five years ago. At first, he had been furious, raging for days against the wilful insubordination of Jasper and Francis. The life he had mapped out for his eldest son—an advantageous marriage and a distinguished political career—all up in flames because Francis had fallen for the dubious charms of a woman with questionable parentage. And then Jasper had to compound the foolishness by following his brother on this mad escapade across the ocean.

Once his anger cooled, the earl had decided to await their penitent return, for he had no doubt that they would soon come to their senses, realise the error of their ways and return to England begging for forgiveness. Alas, he was to be proved wrong in this. A year passed and then two. A steady trickle of letters from both sons updated him on their progress as they claimed a thousand acres of forested land in Ohio and set about clearing it. That his sons, brought up in the lap of luxury and refinement, were spending their days in hard, physical labour, had appalled him and upset all his sensibilities about what was right and proper. The shame of it! High society had been rife with gossip about the goings on of his family, and unable to bear it, he had retreated to his impressive but lonesome mansion, refraining from all but the most necessary of social duties.

More years passed. He heard tales of success, and of tribulations, as his sons set about establishing themselves as landowners in the brave new world. A house was built; a first harvest was celebrated; grandchildren were born. The letters kept coming, though the earl stubbornly refused to answer any of them. Slowly, so imperceptibly that he could not pinpoint when the change occurred, his feelings of shame and betrayal turned to grudging admiration and then to pride. That his sons were making a success of their lives was inescapable.

With each passing year, it also became clear to the earl that his sons would not be returning to England, and that he would need to make the first move to mend the breach between them. This was no easy decision to reach for a man as prideful as he. It took several years, but eventually, he booked a passage on one of the new steamships that had begun to operate across the Atlantic and made his way to visit his sons in Ohio. The emotional reunion of father and sons had led to an improvement in relations. The earl had stayed long enough to attend Jasper's wedding to Ruth Ellis, then bid them goodbye. There followed regular correspondence and occasional visits— two further trips by the earl to America, and a return visit by each of his sons with their family.

In between such visits, the earl had resigned himself to a life of duty, turning his attention to making improvements to his vast estate and taking an interest in the welfare of the people living under his care. Having witnessed the example of his own sons finding success across the ocean through their hard work and endeavours, the earl had been keen to provide opportunities for capable and ambitious men from more humble backgrounds to better themselves.

It was in this vein that the earl had chosen Benedict Sedgwick as the new curate of the parish. The young man, with few connections and little wealth, had impressed him with his erudition and earnestness. Not only that, but Benedict Sedgwick's remarkable intellect was accompanied by humility and great compassion for his fellow man—all qualities that made him admirably suited to his vocation as a clergyman. The earl was keen to follow Benedict's progress and, should the young curate acquit himself well in his parish duties, planned to reward him with a living when one became available.

This existence, one of duty tinged with loneliness, was unexpectedly interrupted when a debilitating illness had laid the earl up in bed for the better part of a month. For someone used to robust health and who rarely if ever got sick, this had come as a great shock. He could not but avoid the conclusion that he was reaching the end of his life, followed by the dread of doing so with none of his family around him. Reluctantly, for he was not one to beg or complain about his troubles, he had instructed Ambrose Cranshaw to send a telegram to his sons, informing them of his illness. Then, he had set about waiting impatiently for their arrival.

Now, reclining in his armchair, with Francis and Jasper nearby, along with their wives and children, he felt the tightness in his chest ease and a sense of calm wash over him. Yes, the end was near; he could be in no doubt of that. But before he left this mortal coil, he would enjoy one last festive season with his family. He would also make plans as to how the vast Stanton patrimony would be portioned out after his death. Tomorrow, he would summon his lawyer from London for that very purpose.

The earl's eyes landed on Grace, who sat across from him at the other end of the room. Over the last decade, she had grown into a beautiful and spirited young woman. He was fond of all his grandchildren, but there was a special place in his heart for Grace, ever since that brave young girl had questioned him about the horses at Stanton Hall while showing no fear of him. He gestured to her now. "Come closer, child. Do you expect to converse with me from such a distance?"

Her lips quirked, but she resisted a smile as she stood and approached her grandfather. "Where do you wish for me to sit, sir?"

"Jasper, make way for your daughter," said the earl testily. "I have had enough discourse with you for now."

Jasper got to his feet, dropping an affectionate kiss on the top of Grace's head as she replaced him by the earl's side. "I see where I am not wanted," he said humorously. "I shall go entertain my dear wife instead."

As Grace settled herself on the chair by her grandfather's side, the earl observed her keenly. She had her mother's russet eyes and fair hair, but her nose, lips and jaw were all Stanton. Those distinctive features gave her face character and prevented her looks from being cloyingly pretty. "Tell me Grace," the earl wheezed, "what did you think of Mr Sedgwick's sermon at church today?"

Grace replied cautiously, "He seemed well versed in the scriptures, sir, and spoke at length, without being too lengthy." She hoped this answer would satisfy her grandfather, as in truth, she had paid little heed to the sermon. Used to the preacher back home who droned on interminably, she had drifted off into a reverie almost as soon as Mr Sedgwick began to speak. Her eyes had searched the congregation for any person of interest and found a gentleman sitting on the end of a pew a few rows ahead of her. He looked to be in his early to mid-thirties, and he sat alone, seemingly with no wife or children. Her attention was drawn to the sensuous line of his lips and the muscular build of his body in the well-cut coat he wore. She determined to find out who he was at the earliest opportunity. With such tantalising thoughts, it is little wonder that she missed most of Mr Sedgwick's sermon, praiseworthy though it might have been.

The earl grumbled, "Is that all? Please enlighten me further, as I am keen to know how well Mr Sedgwick is getting along as our new curate."

Here, her uncle who sat on the earl's other side, came to the rescue. "I was impressed with the sermon, father. As Grace said, he showed a thorough understanding of the scriptures and spoke with clarity and great humility about God's love, and the path to redemption we can all take by following Jesus's example. He reminded us of our duty to look out for and help our neighbours in this season of goodwill. Charlotte enjoyed listening to him as much as I did, didn't you my love?"

His wife smiled. "Yes indeed, it made a nice change from the fire and brimstone sermons we are subjected to back home. And Grace was right about the sermon being just the right length. It was long enough to expound on the subject without sending the congregation into a torpor."

"That is good to hear," responded the earl. "Young chap, you know — recently ordained. Only natural he should show some nerves his first few times at the pulpit."

"As to that," said the viscount, "let me put your mind at rest. Mr Sedgwick spoke with a quiet confidence and conviction that I found impressive. I do believe, father, that you made the right choice in appointing him."

The earl nodded his head, clearly pleased. The conversation drifted around him, with talk of what was planned for the morrow, including a shopping expedition to the neighbouring town of Witney. After a time, the earl felt a hand touch his arm gently. "Father," the viscount said in a low voice. "You are looking a little weary. Perhaps, I should ring the bell for Jenrick to assist you to your bedchamber."

The earl made a small gesture of acquiescence. Without another word, Charlotte rang the bell. A moment later, his long-serving valet, Jenrick, entered the room and without fuss, helped his master get to his bed.

CHAPTER 7

THE FOLLOWING MORNING, a group comprising Grace, her mother, her cousin Isabella and her aunt Charlotte climbed aboard the opulent Stanton carriage and began the short journey to Witney, a small market town just over three miles away. It was a cold, drizzly day, but this did not stop the girls from being eager to explore the town's shops and purchase new gowns to wear at the forthcoming Christmas ball. Charlotte, ever the bookworm, hoped to browse in the bookshop, and Ruth was happy to keep them company on these delightful errands.

They reached their destination in less than an hour and happily set about exploring. They soon lost Charlotte to the thrall of a bookshop, and the remaining three ladies continued on their way, browsing the vast array of shops on the High Street. They found a dress shop and spent a good long hour looking at fabrics and designs, getting measured up by the seamstress and finally making their choice of gowns. These they were promised would be ready to collect within a week, and so, their mission accomplished, they went to look for Charlotte—who was still happily ensconced in the bookshop.

Having reconvened, the ladies decided to stop for some refreshment before commencing the journey back to Stanton Hall. "I see a tavern just a few paces down this street," said Ruth. "Let us go there. Being as it is located on the High Street, I do not think it can be too uncouth an establishment."

With their assorted parcels in hand, the Stanton ladies made their way to the Angel Inn, as it was called, and stepped into its dimly lit interior. They were greeted by a jovial innkeeper who promised to bring them some draught ale and lemonade. Grace took her seat at the available table, looking around the room curiously and noting the various patrons. Her heart began to flutter excitedly when her eyes spied, sitting at a corner table and reading quietly, that same gentleman that had caught her eye at church the day before.

She nudged Isabella, who had sat down next to her, and whispered. "Look, Bella. That's him! The man from yesterday. Oh do be careful not to stare."

Isabella, who was a year older than Grace and of a serious disposition, studied the man surreptitiously under cover of rearranging the parcels at her feet. She then turned back to her cousin and said in a low voice, "He seems a trifle old, Grace."

"Fiddlesticks!" retorted Grace, using one of her father's favourite expressions. After her adventure with Mr Drummond on board the RMS Persia, Grace had started quite liking the idea of an older man, experienced in the ways of the world.

"What is it you two are whispering about?" enquired Charlotte.

"Nothing—"

"Grace is wondering about that man sitting alone in the corner," interrupted Isabella. "We saw him at church yesterday."

Just then, the innkeeper arrived bearing a tray with their drinks. As he served them, Charlotte and Ruth both took the opportunity to cast a quick look at the man in question. Once they were alone again, Ruth mused, "He is certainly a personable looking gentleman. Did you enquire who he was?"

"Not yet, but I mean to find out."

"Why don't you walk over and say hello?" encouraged Isabella.

"No," said Ruth, her voice adamant. "That would not be proper. You will simply have to wait until you are officially introduced. I am sure if he is a local gentleman, there will be many opportunities for us to make his acquaintance."

"He does not appear to be married, mama," said Grace, "for he sat alone at church, as he does now."

"That does not signify. There may be any number of reasons why he was sitting alone, and we should not jump to conclusions. Are you that taken with his looks, my love?"

Grace sighed happily. "I do like a man to be tall, dark and handsome."

Charlotte laughed. "Seeing as both our husbands fit that description, I would not disagree! But Ruth is right. We shall have to wait until there is an opportunity to make his acquaintance and ask as to his reputation."

The conversation flowed on to other matters, as the girls exclaimed over their purchases and discussed things to do in the days ahead. They would of course help out with the decoration of the tree and ensure the house looked as festive as possible for what could possibly be the earl's last Christmas on this earth. Every so often, Grace sneaked a glance over at the mysterious gentleman in the corner. The third time she did so, her eyes happened to meet his as he looked up from his book. He inclined his head with a sardonic, knowing smile. She blushed and looked away, but could not help stealing another glance not two minutes later. He really was a very good looking gentleman.

Her admiration of the mystery man was rudely interrupted by the tavern door opening and the entrance of two further people into the room. Grace recognised Mr Sedgwick at once. He was the new curate, whose sermon Grandpa had quizzed her about last night. With him was a lady who gazed at them curiously before her eyes caught sight of the gentleman in the corner. "Mr Templeton," she cried, going forward to greet him. "What a pleasant coincidence."

So that was his name! Mr Templeton. Grace had little time to digest this piece of information before Mr Sedgwick was upon them, standing a little uncertainly.

"Lady Stanton, Mrs Stanton, misses Stanton," he said formally. "How do you do?"

"We are well, thank you," replied Charlotte with a kind smile. "We came into town to do some shopping and are just taking some refreshments before we head back home."

"Oh," said Mr Sedgwick, "that is what we are here to do too." He glanced down at his shabby jacket then looked up again, saying with a slight flush. "Miss Cranshaw has convinced me that I need to update my wardrobe if I am to look respectable." He turned towards the lady that had come in with him, beckoning her. "You have not met Miss Cranshaw, I think," he stated. As the lady reached his side, he said, "Miss Cranshaw, may I make you known to Lady Stanton, Mrs Stanton, and their daughters."

Miss Cranshaw executed a quick curtsy. "How do you do?" she said, her voice correctly polite.

Charlotte rose to her feet. "Miss Cranshaw, I am so happy to make your acquaintance. I have heard many good things about the work your brother does for the earl."

Miss Cranshaw's expression became far more amiable. "I am glad to hear it. Please do not disturb yourselves on our account. We are only here a short time until Mr Phipps, who kindly drove us to Witney in his carriage, is finished with his business in town. I shall leave you to your refreshments in peace, but I do look forward to furthering my acquaintance with you in due course."

Grace saw her chance to inveigle an introduction to Mr Templeton and was quick to take it. "Miss Cranshaw," she said. "I see you know the gentleman sitting in the corner. Perhaps you could introduce him to us?"

Miss Cranshaw's lips tightened infinitesimally at this, but she responded cordially enough. "Of course." With a gesture of her hand, she bade Mr Templeton to join them. He was by their side in seconds, smiling affably. "Mr Templeton," began Miss Cranshaw. "May I make you known to Lady Stanton, Mrs Stanton and their daughters come to visit the earl from America."

Mr Templeton bowed and said smoothly, "A pleasure to make the acquaintance of such fine ladies."

The Stanton ladies murmured their polite responses, then Grace, wanting to make the most of this encounter with the delicious Mr Templeton, made a suggestion. "Now that we are all acquainted, let us ask the innkeeper to rearrange our tables so we can sit together."

Miss Cranshaw looked a bit doubtful. "I do not want to put him to the trouble," she began, but was overridden by Mr Templeton.

"No need to trouble the innkeeper. Mr Sedgwick and I can quite easily bring over the table." With this, he quickly strode to where he had been sitting, and with Mr Sedgwick's assistance, carried the table up close to the ladies. It was but short work to then rearrange the chairs so that everyone could sit together. To Grace's chagrin, in the ensuing melee, she found herself seated next to Mr Sedgwick, while Mr Templeton was placed between Miss Cranshaw and Isabella. What poor luck!

She watched in annoyance as he began to converse with his two companions, laughing gaily at something that Isabella said. In contrast, her end of the table was silent as her neighbour, Mr Sedgwick, sat seemingly with nothing to say. Observing her predicament, Ruth came to the rescue, enquiring of the young curate, "Mr Sedgwick, I hear you too are recently arrived in the locality. I do hope you have settled in well."

"Thank you, yes," replied Mr Sedgwick. "I am fortunate to have good friends here in Mr and Miss Cranshaw, whom I have known since early childhood."

"Oh, how nice! It makes such a difference to have good friends living close by, especially for a bachelor such as yourself. The earl tells me you are recently ordained, is that right?"

As her mother and aunt continued to converse with the young curate, Grace took a moment to examine him more closely. He was slim, with a wiry build quite unlike the broad burly men she was used to seeing work on the farm back home. He had gentle eyes and his face was kind, she saw, as he smiled at something her mother said. The longer he conversed with Charlotte and Ruth, the more at ease he became, speaking with thoughtful intelligence. Grace's eyes wandered over his shabby clothing, noticing a neatly darned tear in the elbow of his jacket. Poor man, she thought. What he needed was a good woman's love and care—Miss Cranshaw's perhaps?

Grace's attention strayed once again towards Mr Templeton. Now, that was one fine figure of a man. She could not make out the gist of his conversation from afar, but the deep tones of his voice sent a welcome tingle to the pit of her stomach. Oh yes, she would need to cultivate his acquaintance. Just then, Mr Templeton happened to look in her direction. This time, rather than flush and look away, Grace gazed back steadily, exchanging a little smile with him—nothing too coquettish, just a token show of interest. His eyes gleamed with speculation before his attention was once again commandeered by Miss Cranshaw.

Soon after, Mr Phipps arrived, and it was time for Mr Sedgwick and Miss Cranshaw to go. They stood, making their farewells. The Stanton ladies and Mr Templeton also stood, readying to leave. They all emerged into the drizzling November afternoon, bid each other goodbye and got into their waiting carriages.

CHAPTER 8

THE JOURNEY BACK to Stanton Hall was accomplished with much animated discussion among the Stanton ladies about their new acquaintance, Mr Templeton. All were agreed that he was a fine figure of a man with charming manners. It fell to Ruth to sound a word of caution, "Mr Templeton is undoubtedly handsome, but I perceived a certain dissimulation in his manner that makes me a trifle uneasy. Such a contrast with Mr Sedgwick's open, thoughtful demeanour which I found much more pleasing."

At this, Grace exclaimed, "Oh Ma! How can this be? Mr Sedgwick could not have been more awkward in his manner, with nary a word to say until you engaged him in conversation."

Ruth smiled at her daughter, "All I will say, Grace, is that with the wisdom of age, my eyes may look upon Mr Templeton and Mr Sedgwick differently to yours. In any case, I am sure we shall have the opportunity to further our acquaintance with the both of them over the coming weeks and to form more accurate judgements."

"I do hope we shall see Mr Templeton again soon," sighed Grace.

"I am sure we will," said Isabella, "and we are bound to see Mr Sedgwick too, for I hear that he is diligent in visiting the sick and has already called on Grandpa twice this last week."

"We must invite Mr Sedgwick to dine with us if he does call," mused Ruth.

"Yes indeed," concurred Charlotte. "I too noted his very pleasing manners and the great intelligence in his conversation. We are fortunate to have him as our curate."

"It seems I am outnumbered," said Grace with a humorous twist to her lips. "Very well, I shall take the opportunity to study these pleasing manners you speak so warmly of. But I also reserve the right, when all is said and done, to prefer Mr Templeton's charming wit over Mr Sedgwick's."

"That is your prerogative, my dear," said her mother with an indulgent smile.

No sooner was this said than the carriage came to a stop in the driveway of Stanton Hall, and the ladies disembarked in high spirits from their successful expedition into town.

AND WHAT OF the poor, awkward man who had sat beside Grace? Benedict Sedgwick had taken one look at the golden-haired beauty and become tongue-tied. His eyes had stared at a small scuff on the wooden table as he tried and failed to engage in the polite chit-chat required in such social situations. Fortunately then, Mrs Stanton had enquired about him, and he had been able to begin to converse with her and Lady Stanton. They had been cordial with him and posed intelligent questions, so that at length he had become a little more at ease. At no point though, did he lose awareness of the glorious female at his side. He had caught faint notes of Grace Stanton's scent—something seductively floral—and while he did not look directly at her, his eyes had noted the elegant line of her fingers as she lifted the tankard of ale to her lips.

So aware of her had he been, that he'd felt her stare across the table at Mr Templeton. He had caught the glint in that gentleman's eyes in return, the glint of a hunter studying its prey. "*So that is where the land lies,*" he'd thought. Of course, it made sense. Mr Templeton was both personable and highly eligible.

Now, as he sat in the carriage with Sarah and Mr Phipps, Benedict recalled this most recent encounter with the Stanton ladies. His body burned at the memory of Grace's presence by his side. He did not think he had ever reacted to a female like this before. A moment of interest perhaps, or a fleeting desire, but never anything so powerful as this. What was it about Grace Stanton that made her stand out so?

Undoubtedly, she was beautiful—with creamy skin that he longed to touch, eyes of a vivid coppery brown colour and plump pink lips that beckoned him temptingly for a kiss. But he could not ascribe her irresistible allure to any individual or combined features of her face. It was something more to do with her spirit. He sensed in her an untamed quality, an exuberant passion for life, a boldness—all qualities that he himself lacked. *"She completes me,"* he thought, then immediately berated himself. How could he even contemplate such a thought when it was clear that he stood no chance with Miss Grace Stanton, and even if he did, he would not have the first idea of what to do about it.

Throughout the journey home, he listened absentmindedly to Mr Phipps prattling on and Sarah's polite responses, while his mind and body churned. Eventually, the carriage stopped to let him off in the middle of the village. He bade the occupants farewell and stepped down. Walking down the lane towards the church where he kept a small office, he tried to shake off these turbulent feelings and to regain his equilibrium. The likes of Grace Stanton were not for him, and he would be well served to remember it.

CHAPTER 9

THE FOLLOWING TWO weeks passed quietly by. The earl's condition remained stable but did not improve. He was able some days to leave his bed and sit with the family for an hour or two before retiring to his room. On other days, members of the Stanton clan took it in turns to sit with the earl in his room, reading aloud to him, conversing, or simply keeping a quiet vigil.

A few days after the arrival of his family, the earl received a visit from his lawyer, a Mr Ridley. He stayed closeted with him for over two hours, but upon that gentleman's departure, remained close lipped about what had been discussed or decided, much to Jasper's amusement. "Oh the suspense!" the latter exclaimed with merriment in his eyes. "Who will it be to inherit this monolith of a fortune?" His brother was rather less amused, for Frank lived with the fear that, as the eldest son, the immense responsibility for the Stanton estate would fall onto his shoulders.

As requested, Mr Cranshaw saw to it that a large fir tree was conveyed to the house and placed in the grand hallway. A vast array of decorations—colourful baubles, paper snowflakes, gold painted stars and angels—were delivered shortly after, and the Stantons spent a cheery time putting them all on the tree. Once they were done, the earl was wheeled out of his room to see the decorated tree and pronounced himself satisfied with the result.

During this time, the family did not do much in the way of socialising. Widespread knowledge of the earl's ill health meant that few persons came to call at the house, and much to Grace's disappointment, Mr Templeton was not seen again except briefly at church service on Sundays. On such occasions, flirtatious glances were exchanged, but there was no opportunity for anything more. Grace's desire to find a new lover, however, had been tempered by the gravity of the earl's situation, which could not but weigh down on her with every day that his health failed to improve. It remained unsaid among members of the family that it was only a matter of time before the end came, but everyone knew it in their hearts.

In those two weeks, the sole visitors to the house were Ambrose Cranshaw, who came to discuss the business affairs of the estate, though this was now with the viscount rather than the earl, and Benedict Sedgwick, who, taking his parish duties seriously, visited the earl every few days to check on his physical and spiritual wellbeing. Charlotte or Ruth always insisted at the end of such visits that Benedict join them for the family meal.

At these dinners, Benedict took the opportunity to make a study of Grace, not just of her physical beauty—of which he was very much aware—but of her character too. He noted the teasing banter she exchanged with her father and the fond respect she showed for her mother. He heard the loving way she talked of the horses at Stanton Hall, especially of a young mare named Butterscotch, and of Willow, her horse back in America. He was amused by Grace's condescending manner towards her younger brother and sister, never letting them forget she was their senior, much to their irritation.

All this, Benedict learned about the Stantons during his visits to their home. His infatuation with Grace was such that he became avid in wanting to know everything he could about her. That he discovered flaws in her character did not, to his dismay, lessen his feelings for her. He realised just how ridiculous it was to harbour them, but he prided himself on being able to successfully conceal his hopeless passion.

Grace, for her part, was oblivious to all the feelings raging under his breast. If she took any notice of Benedict Sedgwick, it was either to feel pity for him or fleeting amusement at how easy it was to get him flustered, such as on this particular Monday evening. Grace happened to find herself sitting next to Benedict at dinner, with her mother on the other side of him. Ruth addressed the curate with a smile, "Mr Sedgwick, may I say how much I enjoyed listening to your sermon yesterday. Forgiveness is an important tenet of our faith, all too easily forgotten these days in our haste to take offence for even the most minor of slights."

"Yes indeed," he replied. "We talk of turning the other cheek, but few of us in fact do so."

"I applaud you, Mr Sedgwick, for raising the issue," said Charlotte. "I too found your sermon most enlightening."

"And so did a good many people in the congregation," added Grace mischievously. "Did you not notice Mrs Phipps and Mrs Stubbs vying for a front pew seat? You are gaining quite the following, Mr Sedgwick."

He mumbled, "You exaggerate surely."

"Not at all, Mr Sedgwick. In fact, I overheard Mrs Stubbs extol your virtues to all who would hear. 'What an uncommonly wise man Mr Sedgwick is,' she said."

Benedict looked down at his plate. "Now I know you must be ribbing me."

"And such excellent knowledge of the scriptures in one so young!" continued Grace, mimicking Mrs Stubbs.

Benedict felt his cheeks flush with embarrassment.

"Do stop," said Isabella sharply. "Can you not see you are putting Mr Sedgwick to the blush?"

Now Benedict wished the floor would swallow him up. Beside him, Grace merely chuckled and said, "My apologies, Mr Sedgwick, though I spoke only the truth."

Ruth thought it judicious here to change the subject. "The date for our Christmas ball fast approaches, and as the orchestral band is set to play a variety of dances, it may be a good idea for you girls and boys to put in some practice." She turned to Benedict, saying, "In rural Ohio, there are too few opportunities to dance, and we are all sadly out of practice. Do you dance Mr Sedgwick?"

Benedict had managed by this point to regain a modicum of composure. He smiled wryly. "As someone with five older sisters who oftentimes needed a dance partner, I could not avoid it."

"Well in that case, Mr Sedgwick," suggested Jasper, "perhaps you could help us out. Would you be able to drop by tomorrow morning or Wednesday to put our boys and girls through their paces?"

At this, Daniel and Benjamin made a face. "Must we really?" they asked in unison.

"Yes," said the viscount firmly, stepping into the fray. "If Mr Sedgwick does not mind, then it would be a very good idea for you to get a little practice in the fine art of dancing. After all, we would not want local society to label us as rustics."

"I-I do not mind, of course," Benedict stammered. "Tomorrow, I am promised to help out Mrs Stubbs decorate the village hall, but Wednesday perhaps?"

Grace laughed at this. "Mrs Stubbs has managed to monopolise your time, Mr Sedgwick? I rest my point from earlier."

"Grace, that is enough," said Ruth sternly to her unrepentant daughter.

It was agreed then that Benedict would come to practise dancing with them on Wednesday, and the meal resumed with no further embarrassments for the young curate.

In the day that followed, Grace spared little thought for Mr Sedgwick or for dancing, as something troublesome came to occupy her mind. In the morning while she bathed, it occurred to her suddenly that she had not yet had her monthly bleeding. Doing a quick calculation in her head, she realised that her menses were a week late. She told herself not to worry. The long overseas journey most likely had affected the normal functioning of her body. In another week or two, her menses would come and all would be right. She had been careful after all, hadn't she? It was highly unlikely that she could be with child.

Her mind, however, refused to do her bidding. At odd times during the day, the question flitted through her head. What if she were to have a child? If so, the father could only be Mr Drummond, for she had bled right before leaving for England. There was no possible way of communicating with him, and in any case, what could he do if he knew? He was already married. She was in a quandary. Without recourse to him, what alternatives were there? Her mind could not come up with any suitable answers.

By the time Benedict arrived the following morning, Grace's turbulent imaginings had reached a fever pitch. It was a welcome relief to her therefore, to have the distraction of dancing. She smiled brightly on seeing him. "Mr Sedgwick, I hope you have worn your most sturdy shoes, for undoubtedly today your feet are going to get trampled on."

Sensitive to her every mood, Benedict perceived at once that all was not well with her. The smile she gave him felt a little forced. Was she perhaps worrying about her grandfather? That seemed the most obvious possibility. He replied steadily, "Miss Stanton, I am wearing my usual shoes which are sturdy enough, but I do not foresee they will be trampled on."

She responded with a smile, "We shall see soon enough."

And so they began. The viscount had been recruited to play on the piano, seeing as he was the most proficient musician in the family. His wife, Charlotte, nominated herself as Mr Sedgwick's assistant. She soon began herding the younger Stantons into position. "Grace, pair up with Daniel, and Isabella with Benjamin," she said. "Beth and John can make the final pair. What dance shall we begin with, Mr Sedgwick?"

"The polka perhaps?" he suggested.

The viscount rustled among the sheet music until he found a polka and struck up the first notes. The three pairs of Stantons took up their positions and began to dance, only to have Charlotte clap her hands together a few moments later and call out, "Stop!"

The viscount paused his playing, and the dancers looked askance at her. "Remember, it is left foot forward, right foot forward, to the count of four," she explained. "Gentleman leads, Beth, not the other way around. For you ladies, the feet are reversed, so you should be doing right foot backwards, left foot backwards. Mr Sedgwick, perhaps you and I could demonstrate?"

"Of course." Benedict went to stand opposite Charlotte taking hold of her right hand and placing his other hand to the small of her back. For someone who got flustered easily around females, this was one situation where he could hold his own, and for this he had his sisters to thank.

The viscount resumed playing the piano at his wife's nod, and Benedict began twirling her around the room, demonstrating the steps of the polka. The other Stantons stood by, observing. *"Fancy that, the curate is quite graceful when he dances,"* thought Grace in some surprise. The others privately concurred. Benedict stood straight and tall, smiling at his partner as he flew across the room with quick, well-co-ordinated steps.

"Bravo!" praised Daniel when they finally came to a stop.

Charlotte flushed with pleasure. "I do so enjoy dancing," she said. Looking across at the viscount, she added, "I cannot wait to waltz with you again, my love."

The viscount rose and took hold of his wife, kissing her soundly to the horrified groans of his children. "And I too," he murmured, then took his place at the piano again.

The tutoring went on for some time longer until the young Stantons had mastered the steps of the polka, then it was the turn of the waltz. Once again, Benedict and Charlotte demonstrated, then allowed the other dancers a chance to practise. When they stopped to rest, Charlotte had this to say, "Well done everyone. Now I think we should all change partners. I will dance with you, Benjamin, and Daniel, you should partner Beth. Isabella, how about you dance with John, and Grace with Mr Sedgwick."

Benedict's heart took a leap at this, but he endeavoured not to show it. He went towards Grace and bowed politely. "Miss Stanton, may I have the pleasure of this dance?"

She curtsied graciously, "You may, sir."

Benedict slipped an arm around Grace, breathing in a feminine floral scent that sent his head spinning. With the opening strains of the waltz, he began to spin her around the room. It was fortunate that his feet knew the steps without his having to think about them, for his mind had momentarily deserted him. He smiled bashfully at Grace as they danced, and she smiled back with none of her usual mischief, for she was too busy enjoying the sensation of being led in a dance by a sure and confident partner.

They were at the corner of the room closest to the door when the dance came to an end, and Benedict let go of Grace, giving her a formal bow. As he did so, he heard someone call out in amusement. "Look where you are, Grace, right under the mistletoe! You know what that means." The voice belonged to her younger brother, John, who did not waste any opportunity to provoke her.

Benedict looked above him. They were indeed right under a sprig of mistletoe that had been hung from a sconce on the wall behind them. He felt a telltale blush warm his face. Did they expect him to—? Oh Lord! The decision was taken out of his hands as Grace shrugged carelessly and stepped forwards on her tiptoes to plant a quick kiss on his cheek.

Up close, Grace breathed his scent for the first time—a pleasant mix of lemon and cedar with something else subtly seductive. *"He really is rather nice,"* she thought, surprised by him for the second time that day. Then she stepped away, delighting in the bemused look on his face as the younger Stantons chortled their amusement. Even the viscount could not prevent a smile escaping his lips. It was droll to see the earnest curate so flustered.

It fell to Charlotte to rescue poor Benedict from his predicament. "Mr Sedgwick," she said, "thank you so much for helping us out today. May I offer you a glass of lemonade or something stronger as a refreshment?"

He cleared his throat. "Err, thank you, Lady Stanton, but I ought to be getting along now. However, I am glad to have been of help."

"We do appreciate it," said the viscount.

With a vague smile at the people in the room, Benedict murmured, "If you will excuse me, I really should be on my way." He bowed and made a hasty exit.

It was cold and blustery outside, but Benedict didn't mind. The chill was welcome on his heated cheeks as he made his way along the avenue that connected Stanton Hall to the main village. He was keenly aware of how foolish he had appeared just now and reflected on the dangers of spending any further time in Grace's company. He would be well advised to avoid that lady from here on end. Poor and socially inept he might be, but he still had his pride, and he had no wish to become the object of her entertainment. It was high time he nipped his infatuation for Miss Stanton in the bud and concentrated his attention on more serious matters. He would of course continue to make his calls on the earl, but he would not linger beyond what courtesy required. Taking a decisive breath in, he hurried his footsteps. There was work to do and parishioners to see to.

CHAPTER 10

IT WAS A relief for Grace and the rest of the family when the day of the Christmas ball finally dawned in the middle of December, for they hoped the festive spirit of the occasion would help dispel some of their worries about the ailing earl. The latter was adamant that he would leave his bed and play the gracious host to the local folk that had been invited. Privately, his sons doubted he would have the strength to do so for even an hour, but they did not stand in his way, agreeing between themselves to keep a sharp eye on him.

A week had passed since Grace had first suspected that she might be with child. Every day, she looked for signs of her menses, becoming hopeful when she spied some pale pink spotting of blood one morning. Nothing came of it though, and now by her calculations, she was over two weeks late. Even worse, just the previous day, she had felt a queasiness in her stomach after the evening meal. She knew enough about the symptoms of pregnancy to see this as yet another unwelcome sign that she was indeed with child.

Grace worried relentlessly, but there was no one to talk to about her troubles. All attention was fixed on the dying earl, and she could not face adding to her family's woes at a time such as this. Perhaps she should speak to Mr Sedgwick, in his capacity as curate. He had a kind face, and after all, was it not his duty to administer to the needs of his flock? But what if he judged her for being sinful in laying unwed with a man? She prevaricated. Best to wait a while longer before she approached him on the matter. She continued to hope and pray that her suspicions were wrong and that things would come about in the end.

Grace dressed now with care, allowing her maid to assist her into her new ballgown, a delightful confection of violet silk with delicate white blossoms embroidered into the bodice, full skirt and sleeves. Over it she wore a cream shawl to help stave off the cold. She glanced at herself in the mirror. She was a trifle pale, but there was nothing else to suggest her internal turmoil. With a smile of thanks at her maid, she made her way down the great staircase towards the ballroom. Guests would be arriving soon, and the viscount had made it clear that he expected all the Stantons to be there to greet them. There would be dancing first, followed by a lavish dinner and last of all, a fireworks display outside. In accordance with the earl's wishes, no expense had been spared for this occasion.

Jasper observed his daughter enter the ballroom with pride. Once she reached him, he kissed her cheek. "You look beautiful, Grace. I predict you'll be leaving a trail of broken hearts behind you tonight."

"I sincerely hope not!" said Ruth with some asperity beside him. Then she smiled, "But you look lovely tonight, my darling."

"Thank you, Ma and Pa."

Ruth looked over her daughter's shoulder. "Your grandpa is here," she murmured in a low voice.

The earl had just been wheeled in by his faithful servant, looking dapper in black evening dress, his thinning white hair neatly combed and pomaded. Despite the gauntness of his frame and the greying tinge to his skin, his eyes looked alert, lighting up at the sight of his sons, their wives and his grandchildren. He nodded in satisfaction. "Good evening all," he rasped.

"Good evening, sir," came the echoing response.

"Let the orchestra begin to play," instructed the earl, looking towards the raised platform at the end of the ballroom on which were assembled various musicians. The viscount raised his hand in signal to the orchestra leader, and soon they began to play a jaunty tune. Shortly thereafter, the first set of guests were announced—Mr Driscoll, the aging vicar, and his matronly wife. They were followed by an endless stream of arrivals, all dressed in their finest.

Grace lost track of the number of times she pasted on a smile and said, "How do you do?" Some faces were familiar from having seen them at church, but many others were strangers who gazed curiously at her. Halfway through the proceedings, a genuine smile came to her face as she greeted a tall, dark and handsome gentleman with a devilish gleam in his eyes. "Mr Templeton, how do you do?"

"I am very well, thank you, and all the better for setting eyes on your delightful countenance," he replied.

"I thank you, sir. Perhaps then you won't mind saving a dance for me tonight," she said with an arch look.

"Miss Stanton, for shame, you have deprived me of the privilege of asking you for one."

"It is a host's privilege, don't you know?" came the smart reply.

He laughed. "Of course. In that case, I would be honoured to save the waltz for you."

"It is the fourth dance in the set. Do not be tardy."

"I would not dare!"

His eyes twinkling, he moved along the line to say his hellos to the rest of the Stanton clan. Grace's heart beat with excitement at the prospect of a flirtation with Mr Templeton tonight, and perhaps something more? She desperately needed the distraction of a handsome man to chase away the worries pressing down on her mind. Absently, she greeted the next guests in the line, Ambrose and Sarah Cranshaw, followed by Benedict Sedgwick.

For Benedict, the brief encounter with Grace Stanton proved to be bittersweet. He had stayed true to his promise to avoid her company, politely declining a dinner invitation the last time he had paid a visit to the earl. He had hoped that this distance would go some way towards diminishing his infatuation for the blonde beauty. He saw now that all efforts to quash his feelings had been hopeless. The glorious sight of her made his pulse race and his loins tighten uncomfortably in his trousers. He stammered a greeting, hoping she did not notice how affected he was by her. Grace, however, was too busy following Mr Templeton with her eyes to cast more than a cursory glance at him. With an internal sigh of relief, he moved along the line and made his escape.

"Will you take pity on your poor brother and friend, Sarah, and save us each a dance?" asked Ambrose as they emerged into the busy ballroom where people were already taking their positions for a country dance.

"I suppose I shall have to, though only if one of you promises to come out and look at the sky with me tonight," replied Sarah. "You may have your doubts, but I have been painstaking in my calculations, and I am sure tonight we shall see a meteor shower."

Ambrose groaned, "Not that again! Remember when you made us stay out the whole night, freezing to the marrow of our bones, on the promise of seeing meteors? And tell me, what did we see?"

Sarah huffed in exasperation. "We saw only cloudy skies, but this is different. Firstly, the sky is clear tonight and secondly, I have come much further along in my scientific studies. I am certain my calculations are correct and we shall see something tonight."

Ambrose still looked doubtful, so it was Benedict that took pity on her. "I'll take you out to watch the sky," he said. "When do you propose to do it?"

"In another two hours?"

"Very well, I shall brave the cold with you then."

"Oh thank you, Benedict! Come on, let us quickly take our places for the dance," said Sarah, grinning broadly.

"Yes, of course," smiled Benedict and held out his arm to her.

THE BALL PROCEEDED apace with lavish entertainment and much merriment. The earl remained just long enough to see all this before retiring to his bed, content that the dignity of his family had been restored and that his plans for their future were properly set in motion.

Grace watched him leave, sadness clutching at her heart. He looked so frail. She was struck then with the portent that it would not be long before the end came. Without warning, emotions came to the fore, and it all became a little too much for her as she tried to blink away the tears. She was about to lose her beloved grandpa while also be exposed as a wanton hussy, just as soon as the news of her pregnancy came to light. There was no hope anymore of any benign outcome. All she had was tonight, her last chance to be carefree before the world collapsed at her feet.

A light touch to her arm made her turn. It was Mr Templeton, come to claim his second dance with her. Throughout the evening, they had exchanged suggestive banter and many a flirtatious glance. He stood before her now, tall, handsome and charmingly roguish. Who better to forget her woes with than Mr Templeton. With a shuddering smile, she put her hand on his arm and let him lead her onto the dance floor. To the lively strains of the music, her feet flew, exhilaration in her chest as she threw away her cares for one last time.

As the dance came to a close, guests were summoned to partake of the festive food laid out on a buffet table in the adjoining dining room. A line of people formed, and seeing this, Mr Templeton laid a hand on Grace's arm, murmuring, "Miss Stanton, unless you are very hungry, might I suggest we wait for the dinner crush to subside and enjoy a walk out in the gardens? It is dry and not too windy out tonight, and I believe a little fresh air will do us good after all our exertions."

Grace felt a pulsing of excitement. Could this be an overture to a seduction by Mr Templeton? If so, she would be a willing participant. There was too much water under the bridge now to worry about her virtue or her reputation. She would have one last hurrah of happiness tonight before the realities of her situation became too obvious to ignore. So she beamed at him. "I think that is a marvellous idea. Let me just get a woollen cloak to wear over my ballgown. Come with me."

She led him to a cloakroom set behind the grand staircase and took a long black cloak that was hanging from one of the hooks, finding another for Mr Templeton to wear. Once they were both suitably wrapped up, they exited the house through the main entrance, which was lit with several lamps, Grace nodding her head in acknowledgement to Siddons, Stanton Hall's butler, on her way out. Mr Templeton took her arm in his as they braved the chill night air and began to walk the path towards the ornamental gardens, the faint glimmer of the moon above them lighting their way.

"Now that we are alone, Miss Stanton," he said, "will you allow me to call you by your given name?"

"Only if you will let me call you by yours," she replied playfully.

"Then call me Philip and I shall call you Grace."

"Very well, Philip. Will you tell me something?"

He quirked a brow. "What would you like to know?"

With a wicked smile on her lips, she responded, "I would like to know what your real intentions were in suggesting we take a walk outside while all are occupied with serving themselves dinner."

"Ah, that."

"Yes, that."

He examined her face curiously. "Grace, you are young, yet I sense from you a certain level of experience in your dealings with the opposite sex. Am I right?"

"I can neither confirm nor deny," she said coyly.

He looked amused. "Very well, then let me put my cards on the table. Grace, I think you are ravishingly beautiful and dream of doing all sorts of scandalous things with you. Only, I do not ravish innocents, and I have to make clear that my intentions are entirely dishonourable. I am not the marrying kind, you see. Have I shocked you?"

Her laughter tinkled in the quiet night. "Far from it." They walked on a little further before she spoke again, in a more serious tone, "You may have some idea of the situation at the moment with regards to my grandfather. It is like a long drawn-out goodbye while we wait for the end to come. I do not wish to beg for sympathy, only understanding, when I say the past few weeks have been a trial for all of us."

He nodded, his face softening.

She continued in a rush, "All I wish to say is, I would welcome the distraction of being ravished, and I am no innocent."

Mr Templeton stopped. In a low growl, he said, "Come here."

Grace stepped into the shelter of his arms, and he drew her to him. He held her like this for a long minute, then pulled back so he could gaze into her shining eyes. Slowly, intentionally, he brought his lips to hers. His first kiss was gentle, experimental. He pulled back to gaze into her eyes again, assessing her reaction. What he read there must have reassured him, for he quirked his lips and came back for a second kiss. This one was not so gentle. His tongue came out to caress her lips and demand entry. She allowed him in, her own tongue seeking his, revelling in the masculine taste of him.

He held her tight as he plundered her mouth. When finally they came up for breath, he rained kisses along the line of her throat, the scratchiness of his whiskers making her squirm in delight. It wasn't long before his lips were back on hers, claiming yet another deep, hungry kiss, only to be interrupted by a loud gasp.

"Oh my God!"

They pulled apart instantly and saw who had just come upon them. Only a few feet away stood Mr Sedgwick and Miss Cranshaw. It was she who had gasped and called out. Her jaw tightened now as she stared at them, shock and disapproval evident in her gaze, together with the hint of something else — could it be hurt?

Mr Templeton recovered first, smiling sardonically at her. "I am very sorry, Miss Cranshaw, to have shocked you so. We had not expected anyone else to come out here and thought we were alone."

She hissed an outraged breath. "And does being alone excuse what you were doing?"

"I am not going to excuse our behaviour. However, I trust you will have a care for Miss Stanton's reputation and not speak of this to anyone."

Now it was Benedict Sedgwick that spoke, in a cold, stony voice. "It is a pity you did not have a care for her reputation yourself."

"Indeed," concurred Miss Cranshaw in a self-righteous tone. "Perhaps it would serve as a warning to all the local young ladies to learn of your depraved behaviour, and the consequences of such loose morals."

"You will do no such thing, Sarah," snapped Benedict. "*Judge not, that ye be not judged.* Or have you forgotten your scriptures? There will be no malicious gossip spread in this parish on my watch. If I do hear anything, Sarah, I shall know it came from you."

His companion cowered a little at the ferocious expression on his face. Even Grace was arrested by the sudden fierceness exhibited by the normally meek-looking curate. With eyes cast down, Sarah nodded and muttered, "Very well, I shall not speak of it."

Next, Benedict levelled his gaze at Mr Templeton. He had not let his eyes wander to Grace at all. "Now," he said grimly, "I think it best if you escort Miss Stanton back to the house before she is missed."

"That I will do, but I could ask what the two of you are also doing out here alone."

"You may ask, and I will gladly answer. We are out to gaze at the sky, for Miss Cranshaw expects a meteor shower tonight."

"Stargazing again Miss Cranshaw? Of course. Well, I shall leave you to enjoy it." Mr Templeton sketched a bow and turned to Grace. "Miss Stanton, shall we?"

Grace placed her arm in his and allowed him to lead her back to the house. All her earlier exhilaration was gone, replaced by a tight knot in the pit of her stomach. It seemed she was not to be allowed that final hurrah of happiness after all. And she had most definitely not liked to see that grim expression on Mr Sedgwick's face.

CHAPTER 11

GRACE LINGERED IN bed the following morning reliving the events of last night in her mind. After the debacle in the garden, Mr Templeton had escorted her back to the house, staying by her side while they helped themselves to some of the delicious food laid out on the buffet table. He had apologised to her during their short walk back inside.

"I am sorry, Grace, to have put you in a compromising position. At my age, I really should know better, but I'm afraid I got carried away."

"You did not do anything I did not myself permit."

"All the same, I should not have tried to seduce you in a public space as I did. I am usually a lot more circumspect in my affairs. If it is any comfort to you, I do believe the curate to be a man of his word, and Miss Cranshaw too, much as it galls her, will not speak a word of this. Your reputation is safe."

Grace had nodded, a voice in her head mocking her, "*Yes, but not for long with a baby on the way.*"

Later that evening, they had all trooped out to watch the fireworks display and been rewarded with another marvellous sight—a meteor shower—as if the gods of the sky had deemed their own man-made entertainment to be paltry and decided to put on a real show for them instead. In the midst of this spectacle, Grace had felt herself being observed and looking around, found Mr Sedgwick's gaze fixed on her. His expression had been solemn, lips pursed in a tight line. It ought not to have mattered to her that she had fallen in the young curate's estimation, but for some reason, it did. She had looked away then, troubled.

In the cold light of the morning, she chased that troubled feeling away and forced herself to dismiss Mr Sedgwick with a contemptuous huff. So what if the curate thought poorly of her? He was just an inconsequential individual after all. Grace stretched her arms out in a yawn and pulled the bell to summon her maid—oh how she had gotten used to the luxuries of life at Stanton Hall! It was not long before the maid came in bearing a basin of steaming hot water which she placed by the hearth. She then stoked a fresh fire with some kindling, while Grace roused herself from bed with an effort. She felt so tired these days.

After going to sit on the commode in the adjoining dressing room and relieving herself, she returned to her room to wash. By now, a brisk fire was roaring in the hearth, warming up the chilly room. Grace pulled her night rail over her head, throwing it carelessly over the bed. Standing naked, she went to the dressing table and took out some hairpins to tie her hair securely in a bun. Next, she took a clean washcloth and dipped it into the hot water, wringing the excess liquid before rubbing a little soap into it. Quickly and efficiently, she wiped the cloth across her face, the back of her neck and the rest of her body. Once she had scrubbed herself clean, she rinsed the cloth in the water and brought it back to her body, wiping off all traces of the soap, repeating the process several times until she was satisfied. The maid had left a fresh towel for her beside the water basin, which she now used to dry her body. Feeling clean and fresh, she hastened to dress.

Down the grand staircase she went, then made her way to the dining room in search of breakfast. There, she found her sister, Beth, and her mother lingering over the remains of theirs—both of them looking solemn. "Good morning," she called out with a cheerful smile.

"Good morning, darling," replied Ruth, pouring a cup of coffee for her.

Grace sat, helping herself to some toast and butter. She did not feel like she could eat anything more. She took a careful bite, chewing slowly, wondering if the queasy feeling from the other day would return. When it didn't, she began to eat with a little more gusto.

Ruth watched her daughters in silence, a sad smile on her face. Finally, she spoke, "I'm afraid your grandpa overexerted himself yesterday, much as we feared."

"Oh no," said Grace in dismay.

"Your father and uncle are with him now. I went to see him myself, just a half-hour ago, and he looked very frail indeed. My dears, I want you both to prepare yourselves for the worst."

Tears welled in Beth's eyes, but she said nothing, simply nodding. Grace spoke in a calm voice that belied her inner turmoil, "We have been expecting this, Ma. I shall go sit with him as soon as I am done here." She forced herself to finish her slice of toast, even though her appetite had all but disappeared.

"It is best we are not all in there at once," decided Ruth. "We can take it in turns. You go ahead and sit with him for an hour, then let someone else take your place."

"Yes, Ma."

Shortly after, Grace made her way up to the sick room, her heart heavy. She entered gingerly, not wanting to disturb her grandpa if he was sleeping. The room was dim, the curtains drawn. A lamp in one corner cast a low glow, and a fire crackled in the hearth. Her father and uncle sat quietly on each side of the bed. The earl was awake, his eyes following her trajectory across the room until she reached his bedside. He was too weak to speak and merely blinked twice to acknowledge her.

Jasper shifted his chair backwards to allow Grace to approach the bed. She knelt beside the earl and took his hand. "Grandpa," she murmured, and kissed the gnarled fingers. Nothing more was said for a long time. Eventually, Grace felt a hand on her shoulder.

"Come sit down, Gracie," her father said. He pointed to the chair he had vacated and went over to sit on another chair by the fireplace. Grace did as she was told. As she sat, she noted that the earl seemed to have drifted off to sleep.

Together, the three sat in silent vigil, the viscount reading from a bible, finding solace in the words he murmured under his breath. As promised, sometime later Ruth came in to relieve Grace, and as the day progressed, each member of the Stanton clan took it in turns to sit with the dying earl.

Mid-afternoon saw Grace sitting in the large library, composing a letter to her cousin, Clara Ellis, who lived on the neighbouring farm in Ohio. She had just dipped the nib of her pen in the inkwell when the door opened with a start and her cousin Daniel walked in, looking agitated.

"What is it?" asked Grace quickly, fearing the worst.

"Grandpa managed to speak a few words just now. He asked for Mr Sedgwick. I-I think it is so he can have the last rites administered. I must go now to fetch him."

Grace stood. "I will come with you. Let me just get my coat and bonnet."

She made her way quickly up to her room to fetch these items, tying them on, then hurried back down again. A footman had been dispatched to the stable for the carriage and horses to be made ready forthwith. A few minutes later, it drew up outside the front steps to the house where Daniel and Grace waited impatiently. "Take us to Mr Sedgwick's house in the village and make it quick," Daniel instructed the coachman, then held the carriage door open for Grace. They climbed aboard and were soon on their way.

The journey to the village took no more than ten minutes, but it felt like hours to Grace's heated brain. When finally they stopped in front of the modest terraced house that was home to Mr Sedgwick, Daniel was quick to open the carriage door and help Grace down. A moment later, he was rapping peremptorily on the wooden door. Grace looked around as they waited for it to open. The house was small. There could only feasibly be space for one room upstairs and one down. Grace had of course been aware that the curate was of modest means, but the difference in their stations was now brought sharply home to her.

Barely had these thoughts flitted through her mind than the door opened to reveal Mr Sedgwick. His appearance was different to what she had become accustomed to. The wire-rimmed glasses he usually wore were gone, revealing dark brown eyes that stared at her in surprise. He was not wearing his usual shabby coat, but was in shirtsleeves, the sleeves casually rolled to his elbow and the shirt unbuttoned at the collar. Her eyes took in sinewy forearms sprinkled with fine hair, a thick vein jutting down their side. All this she glimpsed in an instant, before she was brought back to the reason they were here. Mr Sedgwick too, had recovered enough from his surprise to work out why they were at his door.

"The earl?" he queried.

"He has asked for you," replied Daniel. "We do not have much time."

Mr Sedgwick nodded, pulling back the door to allow them in. "I won't be long. Please do sit down." He pointed to a small square table with two chairs. An opened letter lay discarded on top. Mr Sedgwick must have been reading it when they knocked at his door.

Grace went to sit down, but Daniel, ever the practical man, headed towards the fireplace. "I shall bank down the fire," he said.

Mr Sedgwick smiled. "Thank you. Please excuse me for just a moment."

He hurried up the stairs to get himself ready while Grace settled herself at the table to wait. In front of her was a steaming cup of tea and a half-eaten shortbread biscuit on the saucer. Without thinking, she took the biscuit and popped it into her mouth. She had always loved shortbread. She chewed on it, savouring the buttery sweetness. Then of course, she needed to wash it down with a sip of hot tea. She brought the cup to her lips and drank. The tea was just as she liked it. Nice and strong with a touch of creamy milk. She took another refreshing sip before putting the cup back down.

As she did so, she caught Daniel staring at her. "What is it?" she demanded.

"You've just eaten his biscuit and drunk his tea," said Daniel, mystified.

She shrugged. "Waste not, want not. That's what Ma always says."

"I suppose so, but that was a bit strange."

She ignored him, picking up the letter to peruse it quickly.

"Grace!"

"Oh stop it. I was just casting a quick look, that's all."

He shook his head in exasperation. "I shouldn't need to lecture you about this."

She put the letter down with a loud huff. She hadn't managed to read much except the bottom bit where it said "Christmas won't be the same without you. I will miss you so. Your loving, Emily."

She wondered idly whether Mr Sedgwick had a sweetheart back home, a girl he was promised to perhaps. For some reason, she did not quite like that idea. She did not have long to ponder the matter as the curate reappeared, wearing a jacket, his collar all buttoned up. He held a thick coat in his hands which he passed his arms through as he came down the stairs. He went to a sideboard and collected from it a stoppered glass jar filled with a honey-coloured liquid, which he placed in a small leather bag.

"What is that you put inside your bag?" asked Grace.

"It is holy oil for anointing."

"Oh, I see."

"I am ready. Shall we be on our way?"

As she stood, his eyes took in the empty cup and the saucer bereft of the biscuit. He said nothing though, striding to the door and holding it open for them to pass through, then closing it after them. A moment later, they were all in the carriage as it began its journey back to Stanton Hall.

NO SOONER HAD he arrived than Benedict was ushered into the earl's bedchamber. He nodded a quick greeting towards the viscount and Jasper, but his attention was on the dying man. The earl was awake, barely, his eyes gazing weakly at the curate.

Benedict smiled back at him reassuringly, then turned to address the viscount. "If you will excuse us, I need to be alone with the earl for the Preparation and Reconciliation. I will call you back when we are done so that we can pray together."

The viscount nodded his acquiescence. He pressed his father's hand, then stood to leave, Jasper following in his wake. Alone with the earl, Benedict sat at his bedside. He spoke gently, "In preparation for what is to come, sir, I will recite some psalms and say the Lord's Prayer. I can see you are weak and cannot speak, but perhaps you can repeat the words in your heart."

The earl made a gruff noise that sounded like, "Yes."

Benedict took hold of the earl's hand and bowed his head. Then he began. "The Lord is my light and my salvation; whom then shall I fear? To you, O Lord, I lift up my soul. Into your hands I commend my spirit; for you have redeemed me, O Lord God of truth." Then he intoned the Lord's Prayer in a firm, authoritative voice. As he finished the prayer, he glanced up at the dying man. The earl stared back, his eyes welling with a mix of emotions—fear, gratitude, regret.

Benedict was struck then by how differently people prepared to meet their death. The earl, once so proud and arrogant, was now reduced to this fearful, needy being. Mrs

Lawson, the poor cottager's wife who had died a few days ago, had radiated peaceful acceptance of her fate. *"What use our riches in this moment?"* he wondered. Before him was a man who he sensed was bowed with regrets for the life he had lived. He felt a profound pity for him, but also an urge to comfort him. Here was his mission in life, what some would call his vocation. He loved his eccentric pursuits, but it was this that gave him a sense of purpose—the ministering to the needs of the people around him.

With this purposeful fire burning in his soul, Benedict began administering the Sacrament of Reconciliation. "Lord Jesus Christ, Son of God, have mercy on me, a sinner." The earl's eyes flickered shut. His breaths evened. He lay quietly, not quite unconscious, not quite awake. Benedict continued reciting the words of reconciliation, then when he was done, he stood and went to the door. Outside it, the earl's family were assembled. He hesitated a fraction, unsure whether he was doing the right thing or not. If this were his own father facing death with a conscience full of regrets, then he would want to do what he could to relieve him of this burden.

With this thought in mind, he addressed the earl's two sons in a quiet voice. "I have completed the Reconciliation. I hope you do not think me forward in saying this, but I do believe it would ease the earl's mind to hear some words of forgiveness. I sense a deep regret in him about things he may have done in his life, perhaps thing to do with the both of you. It would comfort him in his last moments to be forgiven."

Jasper sighed. "I forgave him long ago."

"And I too," concurred the viscount.

"Let him hear the words," said Benedict gently.

They nodded and re-entered the room, followed by Grace and the rest of the family. The viscount and Jasper went to their father's side, each in turn whispering private words of forgiveness into his ear. The earl's eyes fluttered; his hand came out to grasp his eldest son's. Benedict heard the viscount murmur, "Lay down your worldly concerns and have peace, father. All who love you are here around you." The earl's eyes blinked, acknowledging those words. The viscount kissed his father's brow then sat back, his eyes on Benedict questioningly.

"Let us pray," said the young curate.

For the next hour, he led them in prayers, the others in the room joining him in supplicating the Lord to have mercy on the earl. Grace sat across from the bed, by the crackling fire in the hearth, her eyes on her grandpa. This was her first experience of seeing the death of someone close, and it felt all at once frightening and unreal. Was this really the end for her grandpa? Could it be that after this, he would be no more? Logically, she knew this was so, but her heart and mind still refused to believe in that loss. In these stormy seas, the soothing sounds of Benedict's voice felt like an anchor, tethering her to the shore. She watched the curate anoint her grandpa with the holy oil and suddenly felt contrite for the thoughts she had had of him that morning. He was far from inconsequential.

The family and Benedict continued with their vigil and their prayers, as the afternoon turned to night and the night became dawn. Occasionally, Grace fell into a light dose, lulled by the crackling warmth of the fire in the hearth, then she would jolt awake. One such time, she caught Benedict's gaze on her and stared back into his kind, compassionate eyes. He shook his head at her and mouthed, "Not long now."

She sat up straight, clutching her hands together. In the bed, the earl lay still. After a while, she watched as Mr Sedgwick felt the earl's wrist then a point at his throat. In a soft voice, the curate said, "He is gone." He stepped away from the bed and began to recite words of prayer. She heard a sob. It was John, her brother, sitting to her right. Grace placed a comforting hand on his. She watched her father, tears streaming down his face, kiss his own father's cold cheek, then turn to find solace in the arms of his wife. Throughout the next few minutes, or was it hours, she maintained a strange, unearthly calm as the Stantons said their goodbyes and wept and held each other. No tears left her eyes. She was too weary for that.

Eventually, she went back to her bedchamber and laid her head to rest, not bothering to disrobe completely. Sleep came in sharp fragments. One moment she was in slumber, the next her eyes were open, staring up at the opulent ceiling. She watched dispassionately as a maid knocked on the door and came in to stoke the fire in the hearth, but she did not move from her bed. The winter sunlight outside trickled into the room, dappling the white bedcovers with shadows. *"Strange,"* she thought. *"Outside, the world carries on as usual. Children are playing, farmers are tending to their animals, their wives putting a pot of stew to cook on the fire. Will this be what it is like when I am gone? While loved ones mourn me, others carry on with their day?"* She wondered at this strange disconnect between her world and the world beyond.

There was another knock on the door. This time, it was her mother. "Gracie," she said. "Did you manage some sleep?"

"A little."

Ruth came over to the bed and sat on the edge. "How about you wash and put on some fresh clothes, then come down to have something to eat? It is teatime, and you must be hungry."

Grace sat herself up, feeling hunger pangs at her mother's words. "Yes, I am."

Ruth smiled. "Good. I'll send Millie in with some hot water, and I've asked her to press your mourning dress for you to wear."

Grace nodded. Black would now be the colour of her dress, for weeks and months to come. Privately, she did not see the need to wear her grief for all to see, but she understood well enough the strictures of society.

Sometime later, she emerged from her room, washed and dressed in the black clothes of mourning. As she made her way down the staircase, she saw Mr Sedgwick in the hall about to depart. She called his name, hurrying down the last few steps.

He paused on hearing her voice and turned. He looked a little dishevelled, his brown hair mussed and the shadow of a beard on his jaw. She went over to him, holding out her hands. "Mr Sedgwick." Then again, "Mr Sedgwick."

He took her outstretched hands in his. She felt their reassuring warmth. "Miss Stanton."

"I-I wanted to say thank you, Mr Sedgwick, for everything you did. You were a great comfort to Grandpa and to us."

"It is what I do," he said, his tone wry.

"Nevertheless, I wanted you to know, Mr Sedgwick, how thankful I am."

"If it helped ease your burden, then it is I who is thankful."

She clutched at his hands, unaware she was doing so. "Mr Sedgwick, he is gone!"

"Yes, my dear, I'm afraid so."

"He is gone," she repeated, almost to herself. And then it happened. Her breath caught on a loud sob which wrenched out of her heaving chest, followed by another and another. Somehow, she found her face nestled into the top of Mr Sedgwick's waistcoat and strong arms around her, holding her to him.

"Oh Grace," he murmured above her ear. "It's alright. Let it all out. You needed to cry."

And cry she did, for how many minutes she did not know, as he held her, rubbing soothing hands along her back. When finally she became aware of what she was doing, she lifted her head and looked at him. His arms dropped to his sides immediately as she sniffed and hiccupped the last of her tears. He reached into the pocket of his jacket and took out a blue handkerchief. "Here," he said. "Take this."

She took it gratefully and wiped her eyes and nose. "Thank you. I am so sorry. I do not know what came over me."

"Do not be sorry, Grace. It is good to cry."

"And I have soiled your waistcoat."

"No matter," he said. Then he added, "I had best be going."

She nodded. "Goodbye, Mr Sedgwick, and thank you again."

He smiled, executed a quick bow, then took his leave.

In the Stanton carriage which took him home, Benedict laid his head back and closed his eyes. He was bone weary, yet all he could think of was Grace. She had felt good in his arms just now, like she belonged there. He snorted in disgust. What a fool he was! It was no good berating himself though. Foolish or not, he knew indubitably that his infatuation had transformed into hopeless, ever to be unrequited love.

CHAPTER 12

A LARGE GROUP of people sat expectantly in the great library of Stanton Hall. The new Earl of Stanton and his brother Jasper were there, together with their wives and children. Further to one side sat Ambrose Cranshaw and with him, Benedict Sedgwick. The old earl's valet, Jenrick, together with Siddons, the butler, and other household staff, made a group to the back of the room. All were gathered here this day to listen to Mr Ridley, the family lawyer, read out the late earl's will.

It was a rainy morning on 23rd December, and a day after the earl's funeral. The family had decided not to postpone the event until after Christmas, preferring a quiet interment without fuss or pomp. Now, they all gathered to listen to the earl's final bequests.

Mr Ridley cleared his throat. "As you may know, I came here only last month on the late Earl of Stanton's request to prepare a new draft of his will, which was duly witnessed and signed. I am sure you will agree that he was of sound mind at the time of the writing of this will, and that therefore the terms of this document are incontestable. The earl was very clear and particular in his wishes. I think it best now, without further ado, to read the will."

There was a murmur of approbation from those gathered. Mr Ridley cleared his throat again, then began. "I, Henry Laurence Stanton, of Stanton Hall in the county of Oxfordshire, being of sound mind, declare this to be my last will and testament, hereby revoking all prior wills and codicils made by me." The lawyer continued with the legal preambles until he reached the bequests, starting with the earl's legacies to the servants in his household, including an annuity of £50 to his faithful valet, Jenrick.

Mr Ridley took a sip of water before continuing with his reading. "To my estate manager, Ambrose Cranshaw, I bequeath a sum of £250, in appreciation of his loyal and excellent service. I also take this opportunity to express my desire that Mr Cranshaw be kept on as estate manager following my demise, though this must of course be at the discretion of the inheritors of my estate. To Benedict Sedgwick, I bequeath a sum of £80 in recognition of the excellent work he has done as curate of this parish in the short time he has been here. I also take the opportunity to enjoin the inheritors of my estate to grant him a permanent living once one becomes available, again at their discretion."

Grace glanced over at Mr Sedgwick and bit back a smile as she saw him look down at his feet, a delightful blush of happy surprise heating his face. Meanwhile her uncle Frank, the new Earl of Stanton, who sat in front of her, focused his attention on something else entirely. In a whisper to her father, she heard him say, "The lawyer said 'inheritors', in the plural. Could this mean the estate is to be divided?"

Jasper nodded. "I noticed that too. Let us hear the rest of it."

Mr Ridley read on, "To my grandsons, Benjamin and John Stanton, I bequeath each the sum of £2,000. To my granddaughters, I bequeath estates as follows. To Isabella Stanton I give Netherwick Hall, to Grace Stanton, I give Mulverley Grange and to Elizabeth Stanton, I give Gorston Manor. Finally, to Daniel, the new Viscount Stanton, I bequeath Stanton Hall and the townhouse in St James's Square, London."

There were murmurs of surprise from those assembled in the room as it became clear that the Stanton patrimony was to be divvied up rather than passed down as a whole. Mr Ridley paused as exclamations of shock were heard from those gathered. He looked across at the Stanton family members and addressed them directly. "I understand your surprise at the terms of this will, but I think it best if you let me complete the reading, as the late earl goes on to explain his reasons for dividing the estate in such a manner. Please, let me continue."

With another clear of his throat, he continued to read the will, "In the matter of the arable land pertaining to my estate, which exceeds 10,000 acres and yields an annual income of £30,000, I would like to bequeath 2,000 acres apiece to each of my granddaughters, the remaining acreage to go to Daniel, the new Viscount Stanton—the exact boundaries of these bequeathed lands to be determined by the executors of this will."

There were more murmurs to be heard as it became apparent that the late earl's two sons, Frank and Jasper, would not be inheriting any part of the estate. However, a severe look from Mr Ridley quieted them. He resumed his reading. "I was once told by someone I love that the massive Stanton fortune is a gilded trap which has brought me little in the way of happiness in my life. At first, I dismissed those words in my anger and disappointment at the circumstances in which they were said, but over the years, I have come to see the truth in that statement and to realise that I have no wish to pass on such a gilded trap to any member of my family. It became clear to me therefore that the Stanton estate had to be broken up into lesser but still substantial parts.

"I have thought long and deeply about how best this could be done. In so doing, I took into account these considerations. Firstly, that my beloved sons, Francis and Jasper, having built their own fortunes upon the land they have claimed in America, are not in need of the Stanton fortune, nor desirous of the responsibilities it entails. With this in mind, I thought it best to pass the estate on to my grandchildren, but here too, I had some further considerations. Should I divide the estate into six parts, one for each of my grandchildren? What then of the Stanton lands in America? Who would take these over once Francis and

Jasper eventually passed on? In the end, I came to the decision that it would be right and proper for John, being Jasper's only son, to inherit his father's house and lands in America. That is why, John, I did not bequeath any property to you and gave you a sum of money instead. It is in no way indicative of any lesser feelings I have for you.

"I then had to decide which of Francis's two sons should inherit a portion of the Stanton estate. Here, it seemed to me that it would be fitting for Daniel, as the next in line to be Earl of Stanton, to be given Stanton Hall, the ancestral home of our family, and sufficient land to generate a proportionate income for the upkeep of that great house. Benjamin, that leaves you to inherit your father's house and lands in America, as I hope you will do so. As in John's case, that is why I have not bequeathed any property to you, but a substantial sum of money for you to use as best you see fit. Please know that I have no less regard for you than any other of my grandchildren.

"In dividing the Stanton patrimony in this way, I am very aware that it will entail a split of the family into two branches, one in England and one in America. I cannot do anything to change this, but though I know it will be difficult for my sons and their wives to be separated from some of their children—who are now mostly grown into men and women—I hope that engineering innovations over the years will facilitate communication and travel between the two continents, thereby mitigating the separation.

"I would like to address a final word to my sons, Jasper and Francis. I want you both to know how proud I am of your achievements. Please also know that my not bequeathing any worldly goods to you is in no way a signal of my lack of affection, quite the contrary. Jasper, you once told me I was a disappointment to you as a parent. Francis, I know that my interference in your life was one of the causes that drove you away from me to seek your fortune in America. I have had time, over the years, to reflect on my actions and to have many a regret. I cannot change what is past, but I can humbly beg for your forgiveness and tell you that my actions, misguided as they may have been, were always driven by love. Goodbye, my dearest sons. May God shine a light upon you always. Goodbye, Charlotte and Ruth, my dearly loved daughters. My sons are most fortunate indeed to have you as their wives. Goodbye, Daniel, Benjamin, Isabella, Grace, John and Beth. May God bless you all and allow you to prosper in life. Your loving father and grandfather, Henry Laurence Stanton."

Having finished reading the will, Mr Ridley put the document down on the table in front of him. He brought his gaze down, maintaining a respectful silence. The new Earl of Stanton was doubled up, his shoulders shaking as he sobbed quietly into his hands. His wife, Charlotte, stroked his shoulders comfortingly. A few seats away, Jasper Stanton fared no better, for he too was sobbing into his wife's shoulder. In fact, there was not a dry eye amongst any of the Stanton family.

Even Benedict Sedgwick, an outsider, was surreptitiously wiping a tear from his eye. He could not help then, turning his gaze to Grace. As he watched her in concern, she pulled a blue handkerchief from her sleeve and sobbed into it. His heart pounded in his chest as he recognised the handkerchief. It was his, the one he had given her in the aftermath of the old earl's death. It meant nothing of course. It could not. All the same, he felt a warmth in his heart knowing that something of his was in her hands. It was as if an invisible cord were tying him to her.

She looked up then, intercepting his gaze. He smiled, and she smiled back through her tears. The moment was quickly gone. Ambrose Cranshaw stood to excuse himself, and Benedict knew that it was time for him to go as well. Later, as he walked alone down the avenue to the village, Benedict reflected on the ramifications of the earl's will. Grace was now a substantial heiress, further removed from his reach than ever. More importantly, she was now an heiress to a property here in Oxfordshire, less than a mile from his home.

Would she return to America with her parents and let Ambrose manage the property on her behalf? Or would she stay, perhaps under the protection of her cousin, the new Viscount Stanton? His heart quickened at the thought that she might stay, even though it would be sweet agony to see her from afar and yet know he could never have her.

CHAPTER 13

CHRISTMAS CAME AND went with little fanfare as the Stanton family grieved. They attended church service and exchanged gifts after a quiet family meal, but did little else to mark the festival. As executors of the old earl's estate, Jasper and Frank were kept busy ensuring the terms of the will were put into effect. They commissioned a land surveyor to come after the holiday and assist them in setting the boundaries for each of the newly created estates, which would then be put into title deeds for each of the four inheriting grandchildren of the earl.

It would take time and considerable legal work to disentangle the large Stanton patrimony and divide it into separate parts as requested in the will, but all in the family approved of the earl's decision to do so, most of all Frank and Jasper, neither of whom were in the least disappointed to have been passed over as inheritors. The promise of that vast wealth had once been used to constrain Frank into following the path his father had set out for him—a path that brought him little happiness and nearly cost him the woman he loved. Turning his back on that enormous fortune had at first seemed like an impossible feat for Frank, but he had finally broken free and left for America twenty-five years ago to be with Charlotte and forge his own path in life.

Both Frank and Jasper's lives were now firmly entrenched on the land they had claimed in Ohio and the homes they had built. As they busied themselves with their work as executors of the old earl's will, they also worried about their own properties in America and how they were being managed in their absence. Sooner rather than later, they would need to return home. The news trickling through from America about growing unrest between the states in the north and the south added to their worry and their impatience to be gone. Then of course, there was the question of who was to go and who was to remain in England. At the age of fourteen, Beth was too young still to be without the guidance of her parents, despite her new inheritance. There again, if the conflict conflagrated between the northern and southern states in America, would it not be safer for her to remain in England?

On Boxing Day, the family convened in the library to discuss these matters. As the most senior person in the Stanton clan, Frank chaired the proceedings. "We need to discuss how we move forwards from this point," he said, "and I want to hear from each of you. Jasper and I are agreed that we cannot delay our return to America beyond the middle of January. For this very reason, we are working hard to expedite the execution of father's will. This leaves us with the question of who is going to stay behind in England. We do not need to decide this right away, but it would be good to start the discussion. And before we do so, let me also say that I have worked with Mr Cranshaw long enough to ascertain that the estates would be in good hands under his stewardship were we to decide to all go back home—though this would only be a temporary measure. So, let us start with you, Daniel. As the new owner of Stanton Hall, do you wish to remain here or go back home with us in January?"

At twenty-four, Daniel was a handsome young man who greatly resembled his father in appearance, yet was more similar to his mother in disposition. That is, he had courage and cheerful optimism in equal measures. Back home, he had taken on duties alongside his father, as had been expected of him. He loved his home and his family, but he realised now that he had reached a crossroads in his life. "Ma, Pa," he said gently. "I am faced with a difficult choice."

Charlotte laid a hand on his arm in understanding. "I know, my love," she told him. "Speak your thoughts. We are listening."

"I cannot envisage being far from you all and from the place I have called home my entire life. Yet I also feel a pull towards this place. It has been the home of my family for generations and Grandpa entrusted it to me. I want to prove worthy of that trust."

Frank gazed at his son, pride warring with emotion. "So you mean to stay."

"Yes, sir."

Frank turned to his other son. "And you, Benjamin?"

"I go home with you," replied that young man quickly. "I can take on Daniel's duties and work with you, Pa."

"I know you can, son, but it is only fair that you are given a choice. England is your home too, and if you wanted to stay here and be close to your brother, there is my own small estate at Hartley Court that I could put in your name. With that and the money you inherited which you could invest, you would have the means to live well here, if that is what you wanted."

"Thank you, Pa. I own it will difficult to be parted from that rascal over there." Benjamin smirked at Daniel. "I will reflect upon it, but I do not think it will change my mind. I wish to go home with you."

Frank nodded, a lump in his throat. Then he turned to his only daughter. "And how about you, Isabella? What do you wish to do?"

As her serious nature dictated, Isabella had pondered this question carefully, weighing in her mind all the advantages and disadvantages. Therefore, she was ready with her answer. "I wish to stay here and take charge of my estate, with Mr Cranshaw's guidance."

Frank frowned. "You are young and cannot be living alone at Netherwick Hall."

"I am aware of that," replied Isabella. "However, I can live at Stanton Hall with Daniel until such time as I am old enough to live independently or until I marry. My estate is not ten miles from here, and it should be easy enough to make regular journeys there to visit tenants and ensure the property is well maintained. I mean to take an active role in its management, and I have no wish for anyone to remind me that I am a female. My brain is as good as that of any male in this family."

"We would not dare say such a thing," chuckled her father. "Are you sure of this Bella? It will pain me greatly to be parted from you."

She stood and went to her father, hugging him tightly. "It will pain me too, Pa, but I want to do this. I have long wanted something more for myself than to be just decorative and manage a household. Ma runs her school back home, and I want some useful work for myself too."

Frank kissed his daughter's brow. "If your mama agrees, then I will not stand in your way."

Charlotte joined them, stroking her daughter's hair tenderly. "If that is what you wish, then do it, Bella, but remember that you are not burning your bridges. If you are unhappy or change your mind about staying here, then come home to us."

"I will."

Frank levelled a look at his eldest son. "Daniel, I am trusting you to look after your sister well."

Daniel smiled lazily from where he was sitting. "Do not worry, Pa. I'll keep her in check."

"That is not what Pa asked of you!" spluttered Isabella angrily.

"Oh how easy she is to wind up," observed Benjamin. "I shall miss doing that."

"Well, I shall certainly not miss your annoying and interfering ways," countered his fuming sister.

"That's enough!" thundered Frank. "Daniel, Benjamin, is it too much to ask that you refrain from teasing your sister for just one day?"

"Sorry, Pa," mumbled Daniel. Then he added, "But you need not worry about Bella. I'll look out for her."

"Very well, let us move on to Jasper's children. John, what is it you wish to do?"

John straightened in his seat. "I am needed at home, so there is no question that I shall be returning with you."

Ruth reached over to her son and squeezed his shoulder. Frank now addressed Beth, who sat next to them. "What about you, Beth, now that you are heiress to Gorston Manor?"

In a hesitant voice, Beth spoke, "I think I shall go home with Ma and Pa. Mr Cranshaw can manage the property on my behalf, can't he?"

"Yes, of course he can," Jasper assured his daughter. "Perhaps you can rent it out and earn some extra income from it. You can visit again when you are older and decide then what you wish to do with the property."

Beth smiled happily. "Yes, that is what I shall do."

Lastly, Frank turned to his other niece. "And you, Grace?"

Grace had been sitting with her mind in disarray, for unknown to the others in the room, she had another, more pressing problem to consider. She would miss her family terribly if she stayed on in England, all the more so if she had to deal with a pregnancy without her ma to help and guide her. She was now nearly four weeks late, added to which these last few days, she had felt nauseous at nearly every meal. It was becoming less and less easy to dismiss the likelihood that she was with child. If so, what were her choices? Should she go home to America and confess all to her parents there? Or perhaps she should stay on, wait until after their departure and enlist her cousin Daniel for his help. Maybe he could take her abroad somewhere to have the child. And then what would she do? Would she give her child away? Instinctively, she put a protective hand to her belly. No, she could not do that.

All eyes were fixed on her as they waited for an answer. She did not know what to say, so she did what she had been doing a lot of lately. She burst into tears. "I-I don't know!" she wailed, pulling out Mr Sedgwick's handkerchief and burying her face in it. Even though she had rinsed it clean a few times, it still carried a hint of his comforting scent.

Grace sensed her cousin Isabella's thinly veiled impatience with her tears, but at this moment, she could not care less what her cousin thought. She was scared and did not know what to do. Her family, too, had noticed her increased propensity to cry of late, but they attributed it to her grief at the loss of her grandpa. That was partly true of course, but not the whole story.

Jasper enfolded his daughter in his arms. "It's alright, Gracie, no need to decide now."

"I think Grandpa would have wanted me here to take charge of my inheritance," she sniffed, "but I would hate to be parted from you all. And I miss Willow!" The tears flowed again as Grace thought of her beloved mare.

Jasper soothed his troubled daughter. "I know, sweetheart, I know. Think it over for a few days more. There is no rush to decide." And they left it at that.

AFTER LUNCH, OF which she had eaten very little, Grace felt too restless to settle inside with a book or some needlework. She decided to brave the cold and go for a walk. It was always easier for her to think when she walked, and she had much to think about. She got herself ready, putting on a thick coat, a bonnet and mittens, and made her way down. She passed her mother on the stairs.

"Grace, where are you going?" asked Ruth in surprise.

"Just for a walk to clear the cobwebs and think about things."

"Would you like some company?"

Grace shook her head. "If you don't mind, Ma, I would prefer to be alone."

"Very well, my love, but please do not be long. It will get dark in another hour or two."

"I won't."

Grace continued on her way, hurrying down the front steps of Stanton Hall. She considered which way to go. She could walk to the village, or she could head towards the lake and woodland inside the grounds of the house. A walk to the village, she decided.

She set a brisk pace, trying to keep warm. As she walked, she began to think about this baby. Was it a boy or a girl, she wondered. "Hello, you," she said, striking up a conversation with her unborn child. "It's me, your mama… I don't know what the future holds for us, little one. I am trying to find a solution to our dilemma. I haven't found any answers yet, but don't worry, I am going to make sure you are well taken care of, no matter what."

She walked on in silence, thinking, then spoke again to her baby, "I have money of my own now. Maybe with Daniel's help, I could go somewhere far from here to have you, then rent a small house there and hire a good nurse to care for you. I would visit as often as I could." Then she sighed. "I know, baby, it is not the best solution. I would miss you dreadfully. There must be a better way."

What better solutions were there though? Every time she considered telling her parents, something held her back. Poor Pa already had so much to contend with—his grief over losing his father, trying to get the terms of the will executed, worrying about what was happening in America. She could not add to these burdens. And she very much feared her pa's reaction. He would be disappointed in her, and angry. He would want to know who the father was. How could she tell them it was a married man she had met aboard the steamship they'd travelled on? It all sounded so tawdry, though at the time it had not felt so.

She came to the end of the avenue that led to the village and ventured forward, passing by the churchyard. Few people were about on this cold, drizzly day. She walked randomly and yet it seemed her feet knew where they were going. When she stopped in front of a small terraced house, she realised this was where she had been heading all along. She knocked on the door and waited.

It creaked and opened slowly, revealing Mr Sedgwick, jacketless and in shirtsleeves as before. "Miss Stanton," he said in surprise.

"Mr Sedgwick," she replied nervously. "I wonder if I could speak with you awhile. There is a matter troubling me."

Benedict hesitated, considering the propriety of inviting her into his home unaccompanied, then murmured, "Come inside." She followed him into the small parlour room and went to sit at the table. Without a word, he fetched a cup and saucer from the sideboard, and poured her some steaming tea from a large teapot. He added milk to it and stirred with a spoon, having observed her enough times to know just how she liked to drink it.

He busied himself with this activity, taking time to regain his composure. His face felt flushed, and he knew it was not just down to the fire crackling in the hearth, making the room comfortably warm, but to her presence in his home again. She would need something else with the tea, as he was sure the walk in the bracing December weather would have made her hungry. Reaching up to one of the shelves on the sideboard, he brought down a large glass jar and took a shortbread biscuit out of it, which he placed on the saucer. Then he brought the whole thing over to her.

"Thank you," she breathed.

He went and sat across from her and waited, taking a sip from his own cup. She opened her mouth to speak, but no words came out. What on earth could be the matter? He put down his cup and looked at her expectantly, giving her an encouraging smile. Still, she did not speak. Instead, she took a bite of the biscuit, then another until there was not a crumb left. Then she drank her tea. He waited patiently, not hurrying her, though his mind was racing to work out the reason for this visit.

Finally, with nothing left to drink or eat, she could put it off no longer. In a rush, she said, "You once reminded Miss Cranshaw of the scripture, '*Judge not, that ye be not judged*'. I am hoping, Mr Sedgwick, that you live by this principle."

"I try to, Miss Stanton."

She took a deep breath in and blurted, "I am with child."

He blinked and looked at his hands, trying to clamp down on the surge of emotion elicited by this statement. Then, he raised his eyes to hers. "I see," he said gently. "Is it Mr Templeton's?"

She laughed, with a touch of hysteria. "No, no. I have not been with him like that! It is someone else's."

"Someone back home in America?"

She shook her head, tapping her fingers on the edge of the saucer. "I met him aboard the RMS Persia, on our journey here."

"Is there a way to write to the gentleman in question and tell him of your situation?"

"No, that is not possible."

"How can you be so sure? This man should take responsibility for what he has done, or at least be given the opportunity to."

She shook her head violently. "No, it is not possible."

"Grace, whyever not? Do you wish me to find him for you and speak to him on your behalf?"

She stared. "You would do that for me?"

There was little he would not do for her, even if it pained him. Clearing his throat, which had suddenly become dry, he murmured, "I will do anything I can to help you."

"That is very kind of you, Mr Sedgwick," she said with a wistful smile, "but it won't do."

"Call me Benedict. Why won't it do?"

She looked away. "You will not judge?"

"I will try not to."

This next confession seemed to be more difficult for her than the first. She took another deep breath. "He is a married man."

"Oh, Grace," sighed Benedict.

"It was just one time, during a storm at sea when everyone else was laid up in bed. It just happened."

"Just happened? A man took your virtue and it just happened?"

She looked away. "He was not the one who took my virtue. I was already, er, experienced."

"I see," was all he could say, his voice flat.

"You are judging me!" she cried, pointing an accusing finger at him.

"I am trying not to," he replied heatedly. And indeed, he was trying his hardest to combat the strong emotions welling inside of him—anger at these other men, disappointment, hurt and a not inconsiderable sense of jealousy.

In a huff with him, she reached across and took the half-eaten biscuit on his saucer. Benedict narrowed his eyes at her. "It seems to be a regrettable habit of yours, Grace, to help yourself to what does not belong to you." His tone was curt, still stung from her recent round of revelations.

She munched on his biscuit and stared him down, undaunted. "I am not returning the handkerchief," she stated. "I find it far too useful, and besides, you gave it to me. As for the biscuit, well that is what happens to your things when you leave them lying around."

"I was not talking about either of those things, Grace."

"Oh."

"A man who has plighted his troth to another is not yours for the taking."

She lifted a haughty brow. "I did not take; he offered."

"Oh for the love of God!" spluttered Benedict in frustration. He could feel his blood boiling, so at odds with his usual calm nature.

"If you must know," she replied defiantly, "Mr Drummond's wife is very understanding of his long absences at sea and told him she does not mind if he seeks solace in the arms of another."

He stared at her aghast. "And you think that makes it right? Grace!" He stood and began to pace the room, trying to regain his temper. Finally, he sighed loudly, "In any case, what is done is done and cannot now be changed. The question is what to do about it."

She regarded him enquiringly. "That is why I am here. I have mulled this over and over in my mind, but cannot find a satisfactory solution." She placed a hand to her abdomen. "I cannot give this child away, Benedict."

The simple gesture pierced his heart, and so did the sound of his name on her lips. Perhaps that is why he said what he did next. "Then you must marry me."

"What? No!"

"I may not be wealthy, Grace, but I am the son of a gentleman and well-regarded in these parts. I am willing to give you my name and be a father to this child."

She reeled in shock. "No, no, we cannot marry. That is absurd."

His mouth thinned. "If you say so. The offer is there, should you change your mind. Short of marriage, Grace, I cannot advise you further except to encourage you to speak of this matter with your father and mother. They may know what is to be done." He crossed his arms, making it clear their conversation was over.

Grace stood, feeling much put out. She followed him to the door, which he held open for her, saying coldly, "Good day, Mr Sedgwick."

"Good day, Miss Stanton."

She marched off in the direction of Stanton Hall, feeling unreasonably indignant. Marriage to Mr Sedgwick? What a preposterous idea! She had no thought to marry, at least not just yet, and if ever she imagined who her husband might be, it was never someone like Mr Sedgwick! She imagined a man of the world, sophisticated, experienced, strong and authoritative—not a man who blushed in the presence of a female. No, this was simply too ridiculous.

She walked on, gradually letting her indignation subside. She couldn't marry Mr Sedgwick. She couldn't. Another voice in her head interjected, *"But he is kind, and smells so nice."* No, no, that was not reason enough to marry him. *"Well how about this?"* said the voice. *"He will allow you to keep your child and ensure he or she is born in wedlock."* Her steps slowed. Perhaps she had been a trifle hasty to refuse his offer. *"Beggars cannot be choosers,"* the voice continued, repeating another of her mother's pithy phrases. The sad truth was, she was in a pickle, and Mr Sedgwick was offering her a way out of it. She could marry him—a kind, sweet man whom she did not love—and keep her unborn child, or she could stay unwed but have to give it away. Viewed this way, her choices were stark.

She stopped and took in a deep calming breath, placing both hands to her still flat belly. "Baby," she whispered. "Your ma is not going to leave you." Then she turned around and retraced her steps. She knocked peremptorily on Benedict's door. When he opened it, she demanded, "Why do you wish to marry me? What is in it for you?"

He gaped at her in astonishment. "You ask me this? A beautiful, wealthy woman who would ordinarily be out of my reach. You wonder why I would want you for my wife?"

"So it is my money you want."

He corrected her, "It is *you* I want."

Her heart pounded in her chest. His pounded even faster. They stared into each other's eyes, neither looking away.

"Very well then," she breathed. "Let us get married."

CHAPTER 14

ONCE HE HAD recovered enough from his shock, Benedict snatched his jacket, coat and hat. "No time like the present," he explained, ushering her out and closing the door. "I will walk back to Stanton Hall with you and beg an audience with your father."

She placed her arm in his, and they began to walk briskly in the cold December rain. At first, they did not speak, taking care not to slip on the muddy road. Grace was still too stunned from what she had just agreed to. She was going to marry Mr Sedgwick—Benedict. What would her pa have to say about that?

For his part, Benedict too was in a state of excited turmoil. Could it be true that he had proposed to Grace? And had she really said yes? Then of course, he had to worry about the forthcoming interview with Jasper Stanton. With each muddy step, his eyes took in the sad state of his shoes and the spatters on his trousers. What kind of impression was he going to make arriving so late on a rainy, windblown afternoon, looking as unpresentable as this?

He spoke abruptly. "If you do not mind my asking this, Grace, how far are you along?"

"It happened seven weeks ago," she replied, "so that must be how old the baby is."

He made some quick calculations in his head. "That would mean it will be born around seven and a half months from now."

"Yes, I suppose so."

"Then there is no time to lose in our getting married. There is only one way I know of to get married quickly."

He lapsed into silence then, so she asked impatiently. "Well what is it?"

"Hmm? Oh, for that, we would need a special license granted by a bishop or archbishop. I am not sure how easy it would be for me to gain an audience at short notice with one such person and get them to agree."

"Perhaps Uncle Frank can help with that. He is an earl after all."

He cast her a quick glance. "That would mean telling your father and uncle about the child. It will not be possible to hide this from them."

She clutched his arm. "Will you be there with me when I tell them?"

"If you want me to."

"Yes, Benedict, please."

How could he refuse such a plea? He placed a hand over hers. "I shall be with you then. Try not to worry too much over it." But worry they both did, all the rest of the way to the house. On arrival there, Benedict spoke to Siddons, requesting an audience with both the Earl of Stanton and Mr Jasper Stanton. It was a highly irregular time to be calling, but nevertheless, he was shown into the drawing room to wait. Meantime, Grace went up to her room to freshen up her appearance. There, she too waited for the summons that would inevitably come.

It was a few minutes before the drawing room door opened and the Earl of Stanton walked in. Benedict rose to his feet.

"Mr Sedgwick," said the earl. "This is a surprise. What can I do for you?"

"My lord," began Benedict nervously. "I have an important request to make, but if you will forgive the impertinence, I would prefer to wait until Mr Stanton is also here with us."

"Yes, of course," the earl frowned. "He is on his way; I am sure he will not be long. I must confess to being curious as to what this matter might be."

"I will explain shortly," replied Benedict.

"Are you well, Mr Sedgwick?"

"Yes, quite well thank you." That was a matter of some debate, for his heart was pounding uncomfortably in his chest and a trickle of sweat was forming on his brow.

"And your family? I hope there is nothing amiss with any of them."

"They are all well, thank you, my lord."

"They are in Leicestershire I believe, is that not so?"

"Yes, my lord. All except for my sister, Emily, who is married to a solicitor in London."

"I see."

There ensued an uncomfortable pause. Benedict was about to launch into some innocuous conversation when the door opened and Jasper Stanton walked in. Benedict rose to his feet again.

"Mr Sedgwick," said Jasper. "How delightful to see you. Please, do take a seat."

As they all sat, the earl told his brother, "Mr Sedgwick has some rather mysterious request to make of us. I am intrigued to know what it is."

The two brothers turned their attention to poor Benedict, who was beginning to feel very ill at ease indeed. He took a deep breath. "Actually, my lord, it is a request I need to make of Mr Stanton, but I would be grateful if you could lend us your ear in this matter."

"Now I am more intrigued than ever. What is it?" demanded the earl.

With an effort, Benedict faced Jasper and looked straight at him. "Mr Stanton, I have come to most humbly request your permission to ask for your daughter, Grace's hand in marriage."

"Well I'll be damned," murmured Jasper in astonishment. Meanwhile his brother lounged in his seat, an amused expression on his face.

"This is unexpected, Mr Sedgwick," said Jasper finally.

"Yes, I imagine this has come as quite a surprise," agreed Benedict. He braced himself for the next request he had to make. "There is also something else," he said.

Jasper raised a brow in query. "Yes?"

"*Here it comes*," thought Benedict. Aloud, he said in a voice that shook, "I would also humbly request that you give us permission to marry quickly, within a week if possible. It is a matter of some urgency."

Now Jasper's jaw tightened in anger. "Explain!" he barked.

Benedict spewed the words out quickly before he could lose his nerve. "Grace is with child, and as the person responsible for this, I would like to remedy the situation as soon as possible and give our child my name."

Jasper got to his feet in fury. "Have you gone mad? How dare you slur my daughter with these lies?"

"It is no lie, sir. Grace is with child and I am the father."

"Why you—"

"Jasper, stop!" interrupted the earl sharply, laying restraining hands on his brother, who had caught hold of Benedict's shirt collar. With a strong tug, he pulled his brother away from the curate. "Stop at once and think!" he said again.

"You heard him!" rasped Jasper furiously, going for Benedict once more. The earl, however, was quicker, placing arms of steel around his brother and pulling him back.

"Enough I said!" Frank roared, then steered Jasper back to his chair, holding him down with firm hands. With an icy look at the curate, he went on, "Mr Sedgwick, you cannot expect us to believe that in the six short weeks we have been here, you have somehow managed to impregnate my niece. I had not thought you one for deceit, but deceiving us you must be. Now I think it is best to ask Grace to come here, so that we may get to the bottom of this." He took one hand away from the still maddened Jasper to ring the bell.

A moment later, Siddons appeared at the door. "My lord?"

"Siddons, please ask Miss Grace to come down here and to be quick."

"Yes, my lord."

Siddons retired to do the earl's bidding. Meanwhile, Jasper's mind was taking in his brother's previous statement. He looked at Benedict with accusing eyes. "My brother is right. You cannot be telling the truth, so I must surmise you are making this story up for some other reason." He scowled. "Could it be the fact my daughter is now a rich heiress and you would like to get your grasping hands on her fortune? Well you can rid yourself of that idea, for it is not happening, ever!"

Benedict clasped his hands together in consternation. "Sir, please believe me when I say I have only the most honourable intentions towards your daughter."

"And yet you make these unspeakable claims about her."

"I-I think it best we wait until she can come and speak for herself."

"I think we are all agreed on that," said the earl severely.

Thereupon they all sat in tense silence, waiting for Grace to appear. The following minutes were the longest in Benedict's life as he endured Jasper Stanton's malevolent stare. Finally, the door opened, and Grace stepped inside the room. She took one look at the angry faces of her father and uncle, and elected to go over to sit beside Benedict, sliding her arm in his. Then she faced her father. "I see Benedict has told you," she said, lifting her chin in determination.

"He has told us a story which frankly, we find unbelievable," gritted Jasper. "Perhaps you could elucidate on this matter, Grace."

She nodded. "Pa, I know this is a shock and disappointment to you, but I am going to have a child, and Benedict has kindly proposed marriage to me."

The earl's ears sharpened at this. "Mr Sedgwick claims the child is his, Grace. Is that the truth?"

She glanced at Benedict in surprise. Oh the sweet man was trying to protect her honour, whatever was left of it. But it was no good to lie. She would have to brave the truth. She turned her gaze back to her uncle. "It is very kind of him to do this, but no, he is not the father of this child. He is merely trying to help me, so please Uncle Frank and Pa, if you are to be angry at anybody, be angry at me, not him."

By now, Jasper had his face in his hands. His precious daughter. How could this be? So it was up to Frank to do the interrogating. "Then who is the father, Grace?"

"It happened on the RMS Persia," she said in a small voice.

"Who, Grace?"

With bowed head, she mumbled, "Mr Drummond."

"Hell and blazes!"

Now Jasper rose to his feet again. "That cur! Just let me get my hands on him—"

"You will do no such thing!" The earl glowered at his brother. "Jasper, sit down and try to think clearly for once in your life."

Jasper, however, began to pace about furiously. "A married man at least ten years her senior. He must have taken advantage. I cannot let that lie."

"We will deal with Mr Drummond in our own good time, but we have more pressing matters to contend with." The earl turned back to his niece. "Grace, if this happened as you say, then I am guessing you must be around seven weeks along in your pregnancy. Is that right?"

"Yes sir, I think so."

"And how does Mr Sedgwick come into all this? Explain yourself."

She burrowed a little closer to Benedict, trying to gain courage from his comforting presence. "I have been worrying about it these past two weeks, but with Grandpa and everything, I could not find a way to tell you. So today, I went to see Mr Sedgwick and confessed all to him. He asked me to marry him, and I accepted."

"That is a very generous thing for him to do. I would ask, Mr Sedgwick, why you would wish to take on responsibility for a child that is not yours."

"Isn't it obvious?" growled Jasper. "He's a fortune hunter, plain and simple."

"Yes," mused the earl. "It would seem so."

Benedict felt his face grow hot at the accusation. What could he say in rebuttal? Very little, it seemed. But Grace would have none of it. "No indeed Pa, he is not. He has offered marriage because he wants to help me, and because he wants me, not my money. Please stop being unkind to Benedict. I will not have it."

"I think, Grace, it is time for us to have a private word with Mr Sedgwick," said the earl. "You may go now."

She hesitated then squeezed Benedict's arm. "Do not let them browbeat you."

He gave her the sweetest of smiles. "There is no need to worry about me, Grace. Go now, and I will speak with them."

On impulse, she kissed his cheek, then quickly stood and left the room. He could not help but place his hand to the spot where her lips had been and feel a sense of wonderment. Across from him, both the earl and Jasper stared in bemusement at him. Then Jasper narrowed his gaze.

"Mr Sedgwick," he said coldly. "It seems you have acted honourably in this matter, but let me make something crystal clear. You will not ever be getting your hands on Grace's money, even should you marry her. Our lawyer can ensure that her inheritance is held in a trust which only she can touch, and I can guarantee it will be watertight. You will not enrich yourself at my daughter's expense."

"Mr Stanton, I would also like to make something crystal clear," replied Benedict, his earlier nervousness fading now that the difficult part of this interview was out of the way.

"Although it is true that living at Mulverley Grange will be far more luxurious than my current situation, I have no designs on Grace's fortune and will never lay a finger on it. It is entirely hers to do with as she pleases. I only hope that in the fullness of time, I may obtain a church living and be able to earn enough for my family's needs through my own toil."

"Fine words," Jasper said with a sneer, "but the proof of them is yet to be seen. You will forgive my natural scepticism when all I see is an impecunious gentleman taking advantage of my daughter's misfortune in order to get a leg up in this world."

Benedict sighed. "Yes, I know how it looks. Unfortunately, I do not have the ability to travel forward in time and show you how much I will cherish Grace. All I have to give you now is my word, and I would hope that my reputation is such that my word has some weight."

Jasper sat back in his chair and gazed contemplatively at Benedict. "Let us get to the crux of the matter, Mr Sedgwick. Tell me plainly and honestly why is it you wish to marry Grace."

"*Plainly and honestly, I love her,*" thought Benedict. However, even he was not brave enough to utter such words to her father. He settled for part of the truth. "From the moment I met Grace, sir, I was drawn to her, and not just to her beauty. I have observed her closely and seen just how distinctive she is from most other people. She is impetuous, forthright, thoughtless at times, but there beats within her chest a heart so generous and loyal that I would consider it the greatest privilege in the world to be the one to share a life with her. I have known, of course, that this could not happen. I dared not even hope. And then she came to me today in obvious distress at her situation. Sir, when she placed her hand protectively over her unborn child and told me she could not bear to give it away, I could not help myself. I had to ask her to marry me."

"And she said yes?"

Benedict laughed ruefully. "Actually, she told me it was an absurd idea and flounced away much put out."

Now Jasper looked amused. "That sounds like my Grace."

"I have said, have I not, that she is impetuous and forthright. I cannot be unaware of her faults when she trampled all over my feelings."

"I almost begin to feel sorry for you, Mr Sedgwick," drawled Jasper.

"Ah, but not a quarter hour later, she was back, pounding on my door and demanding to know why I wished to marry her, much as you have just asked me. So I told her, perhaps not as eloquently as just now, and she agreed to be my wife."

There was a pause. Having made his confession, Benedict felt curiously light-headed. There was a slight tremor to his hands, which he tried to mask by clasping them together between his knees. He had done all he could. If Grace's father said no, then that would put pay to his chances of ever marrying her.

The earl stretched his legs out before him and addressed his brother, "I do believe, Jasper, that Mr Sedgwick has fallen in love with Grace."

"Yes, I can see that," replied Jasper. "Think you he can put up with her? She is quite a handful and likely to play havoc with his feelings."

"Oh, she will lead him a merry dance. I almost wish I could be here to see it."

Jasper considered the matter. "Yes, but Grace should not be with someone who will dance to her every tune. She needs a husband who is strong, not meek."

The earl's glance fell on Benedict as he spoke. "He may look meek, Jasper, but it took courage to speak to us as he did today. I would not underestimate him."

"But is he worthy of her?"

"No man on earth will ever be worthy of our daughters, Jasper. You know it."

"She is still so young…"

A myriad of emotions converged in Benedict's chest as the two brothers spoke of him, ignoring his presence in the room. His mind drifted into a reverie about Grace and that kiss she had given him. What he would give for more of her kisses. He was brought back to the present abruptly at hearing Jasper Stanton address him. "Mr Sedgwick, I will need to discuss this matter further with Grace's mother before I can give you an answer. Will you wait here a while longer?"

"Yes, of course," mumbled Benedict.

Jasper stood, nodding briskly, then strode out of the room. His brother, the earl, lingered only to say, "Good luck, Mr Sedgwick. I believe you will need it." Then he too took his leave.

CHAPTER 15

BENEDICT WAS MADE to wait in the drawing room another hour while the Stantons deliberated the matter. During that time, Siddons took pity on him and sent in some refreshment in the form of a tray of tea with some freshly baked scones. The length of the wait had Benedict's emotions run the gamut between abject despair and faint hope. At least they had not dismissed his offer out of hand. That was a good sign surely. The longer they took, however, the more pessimistic his thoughts became.

Finally, the door opened and Jasper Stanton strolled back in. He sat himself opposite Benedict and looked him over for a good minute or two. When he spoke, his voice was cool and authoritative. "Mr Sedgwick, I give you permission to marry Grace. And as time is of the essence, my brother will be going to London first thing tomorrow morning to obtain a special license from the Archbishop of Canterbury. The earl will also visit our family lawyers to draw up the necessary documents that will protect Grace's fortune. If all goes to plan, you will be married in two days' time in the village church at Stanton Harcourt—Mr Driscoll will come out of his retirement to perform the ceremony."

At this speech, Benedict's face broke into a happy, relieved smile. "Thank you, sir. I promise you will not regret it," he babbled.

Jasper, however, was not yet finished. "Before you break into a jig, Mr Sedgwick, I have these further words for you." He leaned forwards and skewered Benedict with his stare. "I may live hundreds of miles away, but I will have eyes and ears on you, Mr Sedgwick, and they will report back to me. Take one step out of line with my daughter, and there will be consequences for you, I promise."

Benedict's smile grew even wider. "I would not expect anything less, sir. You have my word as a gentleman that I will do everything in my power to ensure Grace's happiness."

At this, Jasper's expression softened a fraction. "I will hold you to it, Mr Sedgwick." He stood, and Benedict too got to his feet. "Now, Benedict—for as a new member of our family, I can, I hope, address you by your first name. I suggest you go home and start preparing for your big day. I trust you have something suitable to wear for the occasion. If not, may I suggest an urgent trip to your tailor."

Benedict looked down at his shabby attire and said a little awkwardly, "I promise to look respectable for the occasion, sir." Then he bowed and made to leave, "Good day, Mr Stanton."

"Oh and Benedict. Do not forget the ring. I trust I can leave it to you to procure one?"

"Yes, of course sir."

"Nothing too ostentatious, but it has to be of good quality. I will not have my daughter plight her troth to a cheap trinket."

"I would not have it either," came the reply.

Jasper nodded in dismissal, and Benedict took his leave.

UNBEKNOWNST TO BENEDICT, the person who had tipped the balance in his favour was none other than Ruth Stanton. At first, Jasper had not been inclined to give the young curate the benefit of the doubt.

"I do not like it, Ruth," he had said to his wife. "The man may be enamoured of Grace, and who wouldn't be, but no doubt it is her money that is his prime attraction. In any case, there is no need for a hurried marriage. I am sure we can arrange for Grace to go abroad somewhere to have this child."

"And then what would happen to the child?" had queried Ruth.

Jasper had shrugged. "We could find some respectable childless couple and pay them to raise it. I am sure it can be done."

"Absolutely not!" Ruth had thundered, spots of colour forming on her pale cheeks.

Jasper had gazed at his usually placid wife in bemusement. "Ruthie?" he'd ventured, not knowing what else to say.

"Jasper, we are talking about our grandchild, the flesh of my flesh, and an innocent child who did not ask to be brought into this world as a guilty secret. I will not have him pay for the mistakes of his mother by being exiled from his family. This child is going to be born in wedlock and be brought up by Grace, not some stranger. I will not have it any other way."

Jasper had sighed then. "Think you that Mr Sedgwick will do right by her?"

His wife had laid a comforting hand on his arm. "I have had an opportunity to take the measure of the man these last few weeks. I believe him to be of good character, and I think perhaps he will be a steadying influence on Grace."

"That girl can be so wild and reckless," Jasper had said, with a shake of his head. "I do wonder sometimes where she gets such tendencies from."

Ruth had looked at her husband in amusement. "Really? You do know the saying, Jasper, about the apple not falling far from the tree."

With a quirk of his lips, Jasper had swept his wife into his arms and kissed her thoroughly. "You would not have me any other way, Ruthie," he'd murmured.

"No," she'd said with a smile, "I would not."

Now Ruth made her way to Grace's room to have a much needed talk with her errant daughter. She found Grace sitting on the bed, arms tucked around her bent legs.

On hearing the door, Grace looked up wearily at her ma. Was she here to castigate her? Ruth said nothing, simply coming to sit on the armchair beside the fireplace. Mother and daughter stared at each other wordlessly. It was Grace who broke first. Bringing her eyes down, she muttered, "I am sorry, Ma."

"I know you are."

"Will Pa agree to this marriage to Benedict?" Grace asked in a small voice.

"He has already spoken to Benedict to give his consent."

Grace sighed in relief, but Ruth was not done. "However, Grace, I have some concerns about this marriage."

Grace looked up at her mother in surprise. She knew that Ruth thought a great deal of the curate and had expected her approval of the match. "What concerns might these be?" she asked.

"Grace, with this marriage, you will have to leave childhood behind and show some maturity."

"I will, Ma."

Ruth regarded her sceptically. "It means, Grace, that you will have to leave your irresponsible ways behind. No more wild adventures once you are married and with a child."

"I can be responsible, Ma," protested Grace.

"I know you can be," Ruth said sternly. "But you must pledge to me now that you will honour your vows to Benedict, or else I cannot with good conscience sanction this marriage." She eyed her daughter keenly. "I am well aware, Grace, that Mr Drummond cannot have been your first. I think even he would have stopped short at deflowering a virgin."

Grace hugged her knees tighter as a tense silence ensued.

Ruth had one question. "Who was it?" When Grace didn't answer, Ruth murmured, as if thinking to herself, "Jimmy."

Grace looked up in agitation. "Please, Ma, do not get him into trouble."

Ruth held up a hand. "I have no intention to. If something happened between the two of you, then I am sure you were both equally at fault. The important thing here is to understand that these adventures must now stop. I saw your interest in Mr Templeton and the way you flirted with him at the ball. You cannot be doing this anymore once you are married to Benedict."

Grace envisioned her future bereft of illicit escapades and in that instant, felt like the door of a cage was being slammed upon her. She thought wistfully of her delicious flirtation with Mr Templeton and what might have been. Then she put a hand to her belly and realised that all this, she would willingly give up for this child, who she loved already. "I won't," she said, very quietly.

"I know, my love, that Benedict Sedgwick is not the person you thought to marry, but I want you to make the best of this marriage, even if circumstances have forced it on you. I believe Benedict cares for you, and there is every chance that you can find happiness together."

Grace sighed, playing with the ribbon on the sleeve of her dress. "I had hoped to find a love match like you and Pa, but it is not to be."

"The Lord knows, it might yet turn out to be. I was not much impressed by your father when I first met him, and it took him a long time to win me over. Keep your faith strong, Grace, and your heart open."

"I will try," Grace promised.

"Good." Ruth came over and embraced her daughter.

"Oh Ma," cried Grace, throwing her arms around Ruth. "I am going to miss you so!"

"And I you. But you are strong, Grace. You will endure and thrive, I am sure of it." She stroked her daughter's hair gently then stood to go.

THAT EVENING, THE Stantons gathered for their dinner, as usual. However, unlike the last few evening meals that had taken place in mournful solemnity since the old earl's demise, tonight there was intrigue and excitement in the air as rumours of Grace's upcoming nuptials had spread through the household. The younger Stantons were raring to find out more.

Daniel looked across at his cousin and started the ball rolling. "So, I guess that means you'll be staying in England, Gracie," he remarked.

"It certainly looks that way," she responded demurely.

"Mr Sedgwick! Who would have thought that you would marry him?" wondered Isabella.

"Indeed Grace," interjected Benjamin. "Do enlighten us as to how this came about, for none of us noticed you showing him any partiality. If anything, it was Mr Templeton who seemed to have your attention. When did you switch your affections?"

"And why the rush in getting married?" added Isabella.

Grace was about to respond, but she was stopped by her uncle, who gestured with his eyes towards the servants waiting upon them. She understood at once. Gossip about her unborn child should not be allowed to spread. Instead, she shrugged nonchalantly and replied, "I think it was when he came to teach us how to dance. He was so light on his feet and elegant. Then of course, he was such a comfort to me throughout the final days and hours of dear Grandpa's life. My feelings and estimation for him grew, and so here we are."

Her cousins regarded her doubtfully, none of them convinced. Isabella tried to get to the bottom of this mystery once more. "Yes, but why get married at such short notice?"

The Earl of Stanton frowned at his daughter. "Isabella, your question is verging on the impertinent. For the avoidance of doubt, let me clarify the situation to each and every one of you. We are all in mourning and most of us will shortly be returning to America. When then, would you suggest would be a good time for Grace to get married? Her father needs to be here for the ceremony to give his consent and blessing. Once we are in America, however, it may be a very long time before we are able to return. You would not be so cruel, I hope, as to suggest we make Grace and Benedict wait years before they may marry?"

Chastened, Isabella mumbled, "No, Pa, what you say makes sense."

Looking across at all the younger Stantons, the earl spoke curtly, "If anyone asks or speaks in your presence about the haste of this marriage, you know now what to say. I am making myself clear, I hope."

"Yes, sir," came the muttered replies.

The table was quiet after that, until Beth asked eagerly, "What will you wear for your wedding, Gracie?"

"I am not sure. I have not thought of it yet."

"Well, you must as the wedding is only two days away."

"And for this reason," said Ruth smoothly, "there will be no time to fashion a new gown. We must not forget also that we are in mourning. I think, Grace, that we could embellish your pale grey satin gown, perhaps by embroidering some delicate pink lace rosebuds to the bodice."

"Yes," smiled Grace, "that would do very nicely."

"I have just the thing for your gown," said Isabella, trying to make amends. "I purchased some blush pink rosebuds for my Christmas ballgown, but in the end did not make use of them. I am sure they would look lovely with your grey satin."

"Thank you, Bella."

"We'll get to work on it first thing tomorrow," pronounced Ruth.

"Where will you live after you are wed, Gracie?" wanted to know Beth.

"I suppose we shall live at Mulverley Grange. I have not had a chance yet to visit it, so I do not know whether it is in a fit state for us to move in, or whether it will require refurbishment."

"As far as I know," replied the earl, "it has been well maintained since the last tenants moved out a few months ago.

Jasper, perhaps you can speak to Mr Cranshaw about it in the morning and ask him to make sure the house is made ready for occupation."

"I will speak to him and go over there myself to make sure the place is fit for Gracie, as well as see what servants we may need to hire." He looked fondly across at his daughter. "Before we leave for America, I want to see you comfortably settled in your new home, my love."

"Isn't it exciting Gracie? You will be mistress of your own home," cried Beth.

"I suppose so," responded Grace, and promptly burst into tears. She tried not to. Indeed she was very irate with herself at this constant need to cry. It was no good though. The thought of living in a strange home, far from the family she loved, and then to have a child without her mother to turn to for help, set Grace into a spiral of fear and worry. She reached for the large blue handkerchief tucked into her sleeve and wiped the tears.

"She is always crying," complained John. "It is getting tiresome."

"Hush, John," rebuked his mother.

"Why does your handkerchief have the initials B.G.S embroidered on it?" wondered Isabella.

Grace sniffed. "That is none of your business, Bella."

"It must belong to Mr Sedgwick," guessed Benjamin. "Although I do not know what the G stands for."

"If you must know, his full name is Benedict George Sedgwick." Grace had made it her business to find out not long after the handkerchief had come into her possession and she had traced the delicately embroidered initials with the tip of her finger.

"How came you to have it?" insisted Isabella.

"Benedict gave it to me the day Grandpa died," replied Grace, directing her gaze to the blue square of linen in her hands and wondering why she was so attached to it. Perhaps it was a reminder of Benedict's comforting presence.

"So it is true what you said before about how you came to be engaged," marvelled Benjamin. "Forgive me for doubting you, Gracie, but I had thought the whole story far-fetched."

"Me too!" agreed Daniel.

"Well that goes to show how little you young men know or understand about the inner workings of the heart," said Charlotte, stepping into the fray. "Now, I think it best we leave Grace alone and move our discussion on to other subjects." And the subject was effectively closed.

CHAPTER 16

ON THE GREY, drizzly morning of 29th December, 1860, Benedict Sedgwick and Grace Stanton were quietly married in the church at Stanton Harcourt. The gathering was small, consisting of the bride and her family, the groom, Mr and Miss Cranshaw, as well as the vicar's wife, Mrs Driscoll.

The ceremony was presided over by Mr Driscoll. Both the bride and groom repeated their vows in clear, confident voices. The marriage was blessed, the register signed and the wedding party conveyed back to Stanton Hall to partake of the wedding breakfast.

Grace had not seen Benedict at all since that day he had proposed. She had woken the morning of her wedding feeling resigned to her fate though not a little anxious. It seemed like such an immense step to pledge herself to another for life—a man she barely knew. The night before, she had traced and re-traced the initials B.G.S on the handkerchief he had given her. Soon, she had mused, she would be Grace Stanton no more, but Grace Sedgwick. How strange that name sounded to her.

She had dressed with care, her mother on hand to help. Sensing her nerves, Ruth had held her and murmured, "It will be fine, my love. Keep your faith strong." Grace had nodded in reply, her fears only slightly allayed.

Then not a half hour ago, she had walked into the church on her father's arms, a bouquet of colourful sprigs in one hand, and caught her first glimpse of her soon-to-be husband. As she paused before him, Benedict had given her that peculiarly sweet smile of his. His brown eyes had been suffused with warmth. It was then that she had felt her fears recede as she smiled back at him.

And now, they were husband and wife. They sat beside each other at the dining table, listening to various members of their family congratulate them. Festive food was passed around, of which she ate little, and bottles of the finest champagne were uncorked, of which she also drank little. She smiled and made polite responses, but felt removed from the proceedings, as if they were happening to her in a dream.

It was around halfway through the wedding breakfast that she felt Benedict's hand enfold one of her own under the tablecloth. She turned her hand in his, clasping the warm palm. All at once, she was brought back to her surroundings, intensely aware of that palm against hers. For the remainder of the meal, her hand remained clasped in his. "*My husband,*" she thought in bemusement. "*Can it really be true?*"

Benedict's thoughts were of a remarkably similar nature. "*My wife. Mine to cherish and protect.*" He was flooded with the powerful sensations of love, but on the back of these sensations, came a worry. "*Will she ever grow to care for me?*" He held her small, delicate hand in his and felt the intensity of their connection. He wished they could be away from the crowd of people around them, just the two of them.

Soon enough, the meal came to an end, and they rose to their feet. A carriage awaited them by the grand front steps of Stanton Hall. It was time for goodbyes—temporary ones, for of course they would be visiting over the coming days and receiving visitors in their new home—but for their wedding night and the day that followed, they would be alone.

Jasper Stanton held his daughter in his arms, unable to stop the welling of emotional tears. "My Gracie," he murmured. "You may be all grown up, but you will always be my sweet, beautiful girl. Have a care for yourself."

"I will, Pa."

As Grace went to embrace her mother, Jasper turned to face Benedict, giving him a firm handshake and speaking in a low voice, "Remember what I said, Benedict. My eyes and ears will be on you if ever you take one step out of line with my daughter."

"I will cherish her for the rest of my days, sir, I promise."

Jasper nodded. "See that you do."

And then it was time to go. Benedict took Grace's hand and led her to the carriage, helping her to climb aboard. In a moment, he was beside her. The carriage door shut and they were away to their new home at Mulverley Grange.

In the carriage, they sat, hand in hand. No words came at first, then Benedict said softly, "You look beautiful, Grace. I am the luckiest man on earth to have you for my wife."

"Thank you, Benedict. And I am fortunate to have the kindest, sweetest man for my husband."

He took the hand clasped in his and brought it to his lips. They were silent, watching the green fields pass them by. After a time, she asked, "Will we be happy, do you think?"

"I shall make it my life's mission to ensure you are, Grace. It may take a while for us to adjust to our new life together and to get to know each other's habits. If ever I do something that displeases or discomforts you, tell me so immediately so that I may remedy it."

She leaned her chin on his shoulder. "The same goes for you, Benedict. You must tell me if ever I do or say something that bothers you."

"Very well. Tell me now though, how are you feeling? I have heard the first few weeks of pregnancy can be quite a trial, and I did not see you eat much at our wedding breakfast."

She played with a stray lock of his hair. "I have developed an aversion to some foods, that is true, but regardless of my pregnancy, I do not think I could have eaten very much today. I am sure I shall feel famished once I have recovered from the excitement of the day."

He smiled tenderly. "That won't be a problem. I know Ambrose has had the house well stocked with every conceivable thing we shall need."

"Have you been to it?" she asked curiously.

"No, I have only seen it from afar. It looks to be a large rambling stone house full of character, but I do not know what it is like on the inside. Ambrose assures me it is very pleasant and comfortable, but we shall see."

"And the good thing is it is not far at all from Stanton Harcourt, less than a mile away, so you will not have to travel far for your work."

He took her hand and placed it on his cheek. "It also means you will be close to your family, should you wish to see them."

She enjoyed the smooth feel of his freshly shaved skin beneath her palm. Without conscious thought, she leaned in closer to breathe him in. She closed her eyes as she was flooded with his delicious scent of cedarwood, lemon and something uniquely him. Continuing the train of the conversation, she murmured, "You will need a horse to get about though, as you will not be able to do it on foot as you do now. Do you ride, Benedict?"

"Hmm?" He was too entranced by her proximity to think clearly. "Oh, yes I do. Perhaps not as well as you, but I get by."

She breathed in deeply, then on the exhale said, "I shall have to pick a horse for you from the Stanton stable, and bring it over together with Butterscotch."

"If your family will allow me the use of one of their horses, then I shall be very grateful."

She nuzzled his cheek with the tip of her nose. "It is your family now too, husband."

He smiled. "Yes, wife."

She laughed and sat up straight as the carriage came to a stop. "We are arrived," she said, looking out of the window curiously. He leaned over to open the carriage door, then jumped down to assist her. She stepped out cautiously and looked about. They were in front of a substantial rectangular stone house of indeterminate age. The carriage was stopped on a wide, circular drive, from which a large flight of steps gave access to the house. Its front door now opened, and several people came out to stand on the steps in welcome.

With her hand tucked into his arm, Benedict walked towards the first person, who looked to be the butler. "Mr and Mrs Sedgwick," said he, "may I congratulate you on your marriage and welcome you to Mulverley Grange. I am Winford, at your service sir, madam."

"Good day to you, Winford," said Benedict. "I understand you are related to Siddons."

"Yes, sir, I am his nephew."

Grace smiled at him. "I am pleased to make your acquaintance, Mr Winford. Please, make the rest of these good people known to us."

Winford bowed. "Yes, madam. This is Mrs Hawkins, the housekeeper."

Mrs Hawkins bobbed a pleased curtsy. "Mr and Mrs Sedgwick," she said, "may I congratulate you both on your nuptials. And please do not hesitate to ring the bell for me should you wish for anything."

"Thank you, Mrs Hawkins," smiled Grace.

They moved along the line and were introduced to the cook, the two housemaids, Betty and Hester, and the groundsman, Willis. *"What a lot of people to care for just the two of us,"* thought Benedict, unused to the extravagance of so many servants.

Grace's thoughts too, were uncannily similar. *"What a lot of people I shall need to be mistress of. I do hope I shall be up to the task."*

The introductions complete, they were shown into the house. The entrance hall was a large rectangular shaped space dominated by a wide oak staircase that bifurcated into two sets of stairs on either side. They followed Mrs Hawkins as she gave them a tour of the house. On the ground floor were two large drawing rooms, a study, dining parlour and a sun room towards the back of the house, as well as the kitchen. Upstairs, they were led to their two bedchambers, connected by an internal door. They were assured that all their belongings had arrived and been unpacked. Grace wondered which of the two bedchambers they would sleep in, for she was used to her parents sharing one room at night. Hers was decorated in unfussy shades of lemon, beige and hints of pink, while Benedict's had striped burgundy and cream wallpaper.

However, she did not have time to ponder the matter further as they were led to inspect three further bedrooms and a washroom with a large claw-footed tub. The final room they saw was currently set up as a private parlour, though Mrs Hawkins told them it had once been the schoolroom, when there had been children living in the house. Benedict and Grace looked at each other then, each telegraphing the same thought. Someday, this could be their children's schoolroom.

Once the tour of the house was over, Mrs Hawkins suggested they take some refreshment in the sun room before they went to inspect the grounds outside. Accordingly, they made themselves comfortable on the armchairs there. Freshly baked iced buns were brought in shortly after with a pot of tea. "You better eat yours quick, Benedict," teased Grace, "else I cannot answer for whether I will restrain myself from taking a bite out of yours."

He grinned at her. "What is mine is yours, my dear wife."

"Careful now, husband," she parried back, "or I shall take you at your word." With dexterous hands, Grace poured them each a cup of tea and added a splash of milk, just as they both liked. Then she served them each an iced bun on a plate. They ate them contentedly, though Benedict was careful to leave half of his on the plate, in case his famished wife wished to have it.

She finished her bun and drank her tea, putting down the cup with a happy sigh. "What think you of the house?" she asked.

"It is by far the grandest home I have ever lived in," said Benedict with a wry smile.

"Our house in Ohio is of a similar size, if a little larger, though we do not have quite the same number of house servants there as we seem to have here. And also, the house back home feels a lot more homey and less grand, for Ma has little time for fripperies."

"Do you think you can make this place feel like a home to you, Grace?"

She mulled over the question. "In time, I suppose it will. We shall have to render it a little less grand and a little more lived in."

He smiled. "Children will do that to a home. I remember my poor mother complaining that she could not maintain a well ordered house when there were so many children to misplace things."

"Yes, we shall have to fill this place with many children." She looked directly at him as she said this and delighted in his blush. Then her eyes alighted on his half-eaten bun, and quick as a flash, she helped herself to it. He watched her with a mild expression as she gobbled it down.

"Better?" he enquired.

"Yes, thank you. Much better."

"Well then, shall we avail ourselves of this tour of the grounds?"

"If you will give me a few minutes to get myself ready, I shall meet you in the main hall."

"Of course, take all the time you need." He stood as she got to her feet. With a little wave, she skipped out of the room. He watched her go, happiness and longing etched on his face.

LATER THAT AFTERNOON, after they had been shown the extensive grounds, which included some delightful parkland, a small trout-fishing lake with a cosy lake house, an apple orchard, a walled vegetable garden and even a glasshouse, they returned to the house. Grace stifled a yawn, feeling decidedly weary.

"How about making use of that private parlour upstairs, Grace?" suggested Benedict. "I saw it had comfortable armchairs and a chaise longue you can rest on while I do some reading."

"Yes, I like that idea."

Benedict informed Mrs Hawkins that they would spend the rest of the afternoon in the upstairs parlour, and asked her to bring up a warm blanket for his wife. Then, he held out his hand to Grace and walked with her up to that room. It was a cheerful space, perhaps one of the least formal rooms of the house, with windows overlooking the parkland behind. At one end of the parlour was a pretty tiled fireplace and along the wall to its side stood a wide recessed bookcase, overflowing with various tomes which Benedict was eager to explore. Arranged around the room was the chaise longue he had noticed before and two sets of armchairs with matching footstools. A rustic looking side table completed the furniture.

The floor was laid with a colourful rug, on which sat a circular brown pouffe or ottoman as these were often called. Benedict picked it up and placed it at the foot of the chaise longue. "Come and lie here, Grace, and I will sit on this ottoman to rub your feet, if you will allow me. That is what father often did for my mother at the end of a long wearisome day."

"Mmm, yes please, Benedict." She sat sideways on the chaise longue and began to take off her shoes. "Your father sounds like a very nice man. Do you take after him?"

"I believe I do. He instilled in me many of the values I live by. Now that he is widowed, he lives a quiet life and does not go out much. It has been three years since mother passed, but he still misses her greatly."

"Have you written and told him of our marriage?"

"Yes, I have. Unfortunately, it was too short notice for him to make it here for the wedding, but I received from him a letter saying he would like to visit us in the new year."

Grace went to lie down on the chaise longue but grimaced. "The hoops of my crinoline are making me uncomfortable. Would you mind very much if I took it off?"

Benedict felt his face flush. "No, of course not. Please do whatever is most comfortable for you. This is your home."

She stood, and without a care, lifted the skirt of her dress to her waist, exposing the crinoline and slim legs beneath, encased in pale cream stockings. With quick fingers, she untied the strings and removed the offending garment, handing it to a befuddled Benedict. He took it from her and placed it carefully on one of the armchairs. The skirt dropped back to the floor, and Grace settled herself once more on the chaise longue. "That is much better," she said. "Now how about this offer you made earlier?"

Had he really said he would rub her feet? What must have he been thinking? Feeling bashful, he straddled the leather pouffe at the end of the chaise longue. She lifted her skirt a few inches and wiggled her feet at him. With a fast beating heart, he took hold of one foot with careful hands. She squirmed. "Oh, that tickles!"

He threw her a brief, apologetic glance. "Sorry." He took hold of her foot again, this time more firmly, and began to press the sole with his thumb, the way he had seen his father do.

She sighed. "That feels heavenly. Please do not stop."

"I won't." He concentrated on his task, feeling pleased each time he heard a little murmur of pleasure from her.

She relaxed back on the chaise longue and shut her eyes. "Benedict?"

"Yes?"

"Tell me more about your family."

"Well, as you may know, there are seven of us and I am the youngest."

She giggled. "The baby of the family."

"Yes," he smiled. "I did not rule the roost like you do, being the eldest."

"I feel for you, Benedict," she murmured.

"Ah well, it had its benefits as well as the disadvantages."

"Tell me about your brothers and sisters—oh, that was good. Do that again!"

He obliged, pressing his thumb in a circular motion to the ball of her foot, right in the middle. "My brother, Gideon, runs the estate. It is modest, compared to yours, only six hundred acres, but it is fertile land with good yields of wheat, barley and corn. At forty, Gideon is the eldest. He is married to Anne, and they have three children, two boys and a girl…"

He continued telling her about each member of his family, all the while pressing his fingers to her soft, dainty feet. Several minutes into this monologue, he heard her heavy breathing, followed by an elegant little snore. He smiled to himself and stood, taking hold of the blanket that Mrs Hawkins had brought in a few minutes ago. A maid had also come in to light the fire, which was crackling merrily in the hearth. Carefully, Benedict placed the blanket over Grace, tucking it in at her sides. She made a small murmur in her sleep, but did not wake. Then, he went over to the bookcase to browse through the books, choosing one for himself. He settled into the armchair across from her and began to read, every so often raising his eyes to drink in the sight of her.

As the evening fast approached, he began to wonder about the night ahead. He was assailed by doubt. Did Grace expect him to consummate the marriage on their wedding night? If so, was he up to the task? He had a vague understanding of the mechanics of sexual intercourse, but no experience of the act at all. Now, he wished he had taken the time to inform himself a little more on the matter.

How could he be sure, though, that Grace wished such intimacies with him? He was deeply aware that the only reason she had agreed to marry him was for the child she was carrying in her womb. They had not courted. There was no illusion of love. This was purely, for her, a marriage of convenience. In terms of the legalities, her soon to be growing belly would be proof enough to the world that this marriage had been consummated. True, she had talked earlier about having many children, but that could be something for the future, once she had grown to care for him. He could not assume anything.

After much deliberation, he concluded that until she gave him an indication that she wished to be intimate with him, he had best keep his distance from the marriage bed. That would also give him time to investigate the matter more fully so he could acquit himself well when he was called upon to do his marital duty.

CHAPTER 17

EARLY EVENING AT seven o'clock, they dined just the two of them in the large dining room. Grace had awoken from her nap feeling much invigorated. She had stretched her arms above her head, praised the excellence of her husband's foot rub, then taken herself off to her room to change for dinner. Benedict too, had changed into evening attire, which had been purchased just yesterday from the tailor in Witney at what for him was an exorbitant price. He was glad of it now though, when he saw his wife come down to dinner in a severe black mourning gown which only served to accentuate her beauty.

They conversed as they ate, discussing their plans for the following day. "I have letters I need to write," said Benedict. "Perhaps I can do so after breakfast, and then we may walk up to the village together to post them. That will give us a chance to explore the surrounding area and introduce ourselves to people."

"Yes, that is a good plan. I, too, have letters to write, so we can post them together." She ate some more of the delicious potage, a thick and creamy vegetable soup that Cook had prepared for them. Grace's appetite had returned in full force, with little of the nausea that had begun to plague her. She suspected this was a temporary respite and was determined to make the most of it.

Benedict observed her eat, a pleased expression on his face. "How do you plan to fill your days, Grace, in the weeks ahead?" he enquired.

She put her spoon down. "I suppose you mean me to be the perfect clergyman's wife and make visits to the poor and needy in the parish."

"If that is what you wish to do, then of course I would applaud it, but you are free to decide. I will not impose upon you to do anything you do not wish to do."

"Well, I know Ma believes it important that we care for our community. She would want me to get to know the families and provide help where it is needed."

Benedict reached across to touch her hand. "If it helps, I can come with you on these first visits, and we can introduce ourselves to the local families together."

She breathed a sigh. "Yes, that would help, thank you, Benedict. You may find it hard to believe, but I am not a very sociable person, especially when it comes to meeting people I do not know."

"Then I shall be there with you," he smiled reassuringly. "Visiting people is part and parcel of my work, and I am an old hand at it. But tell me, Grace, what else would you want to do with your time?"

She reflected on the matter and hesitated. He saw this and ordered, "Out with it. Tell me."

"Well, I have often thought I would like to work with horses and the breeding of them. I was wondering if we could begin some such thing here. The stable building is spacious enough and can house several horses. Perhaps we could get one of the stallions at Stanton Hall to come and breed with Butterscotch. She is such a fine mare with strong hindquarters and a wonderful temperament, and at the right age to breed. What do you think?"

"With your passion for horses, I think it a splendid idea, but best perhaps to start small, with just a few horses, and build it up slowly. You will need to employ a groom to help you."

"I am sure I can ask the head groom at Stanton Hall to recommend someone reliable."

Benedict beamed. "An excellent plan!"

They finished their meal in high spirits, each excited about what the future might hold for them. Having eaten, they withdrew to the drawing room and sat next to each other on the settee, close to the warm fireplace. Lamps had been lit by the servants, casting an orange-yellow glow over the room. It was still early, barely eight o'clock, but Grace was already thinking of the night ahead. It had been a good seven weeks since she had made love to Mr Drummond aboard the ship. The unhappy events of the past few weeks had stifled her natural urges, but now, she felt her body re-awakening to those needs.

She wanted to make love again, and her thoughts of Benedict had begun to take a decidedly carnal turn. She remembered his sinewy forearms, sprinkled with fine dark hair, and the thick vein running down their side. She felt an urge to stroke her fingers down the length of his arm, tracing the trajectory of that vein. She had found herself at odd moments today leaning in towards him to inhale his scent. She had also noticed his mouth, the soft pink texture of it, the charming cupid's bow, the bottom lip slightly fuller than the top. What would it feel like to put her lips to his? How would he taste? Last night, thinking about Benedict, she had stroked herself to blissful completion, but it was not enough. She wanted him in her bed, and his cock deep inside her. How soon would it be appropriate to retire for the night?

Benedict was also thinking of the night ahead, but not quite in the same light. His earlier reflections on the question of their wedding night kept running through his mind. He was not sure how best to proceed. None of his life experience so far had prepared him for this. He felt woefully inadequate.

To distract himself from these troubling thoughts, he cleared his throat and enquired of his wife, "How do you usually spend the evening, Grace? Would you like to play a game of cards or do you prefer to read? Perhaps we could read aloud to each other."

"I had other plans," came her immediate thought. Aloud, Grace said, "I read sometimes, and enjoy listening to Pa read to us. I also like to do some cross-stitching or sketching. Which reminds me, I would like to draw you, Benedict."

He smiled diffidently. "I am sure you have other, far more interesting subjects to draw."

"No, I do not. Why do you talk so of yourself?"

He shrugged. "I suppose because I am a realist, and I am fully aware of how ordinary I look."

She studied his face. "At first sight, you appear so, but actually you are not. I would like to make a sketch of you, and perhaps also paint you."

He bowed his head, his face turning rosy. "I am at your disposal, Grace."

"Then I shall go get my sketching book and some pencils. You may read your book while I sketch you."

"Very well," he smiled.

She stood and hurriedly made her way upstairs to her room. If she had to while away the time until they could retire for the night, she might as well do something interesting. In her dressing room, she rummaged around for her sketching book and pencils, then carried them back down to the drawing room. "Go and sit on that armchair opposite me, so I have a good vantage point of you. Take your book too."

With a smile, he did as he was bid and settled himself down on the chair. "Is there any position you would like me to assume?" he asked.

"None," she said tartly. "Pretend I am not here and be totally at your ease."

He frowned. "That is easier said than done."

"Just pick up your book and start reading. Once you are immersed in the story, you will almost forget I am here."

His lips quirked. "I think it unlikely, Grace, but I shall do as you ask." He picked up the book, stretched his legs out in front of him, and began to read.

Grace studied his face intently for a few minutes, noting the pinkening of his cheeks. Then, she picked up her sketchbook and pencil, and began to sketch. Every so often, she paused to look at him, then resumed her work. He did not look up from his book, though she could tell from his stance that he was very much aware of her. Eventually though, he became more at ease, his attention caught by whatever he was reading. Now Grace got into her stride, making quick strokes of her pencil on the paper to try to capture his likeness. She was unhappy with her first attempt and turned the page to start anew. Somehow in that first sketch, she had not managed to capture the sweetness of his expression. It was subtle. A warmth in his eyes, a crease to his lips.

On and on she sketched, unaware of the passing of time, until finally, she put down her pencil. He raised his eyes to hers. "All done?"

"Yes, for now. You are a very difficult person to sketch, Benedict."

"Am I? Why so?"

"Your features are regular enough, but I have struggled to capture your expression."

He put the book down on the side table. "Will you show me?"

In answer, she passed him the sketch book. He skimmed the pages, examining her sketches until he came to the final two pages which were of him. He studied them for a minute, then said, "You are gifted."

"It is just a hobby."

"A hobby you excel at," he said, handing back the sketchbook.

"That is kind of you to say. I am not bad, but there is room for improvement."

He laughed. "Isn't there always?" Glancing at the clock on the mantelpiece, he added, "It is getting late. Are you ready to retire for the night, or would you like to stay up a bit longer?"

"I am ready for bed," she assured him quickly.

He smiled and stood. "Then shall we?"

She stood too, her heartbeat accelerating, and put her arm through his. Together, they walked out of the drawing room. Benedict paused to pull the bell for Winford, as he had been instructed to do. The butler emerged from below stairs a moment later. "Good evening, Winford," said Benedict.

"Good evening, sir, madam," replied the butler, then went into the drawing room to bank the fire and extinguish the lamps.

They continued on their way up the stairs, then down the corridor towards Grace's bedroom door. There, Benedict faced her. "Goodnight, my dear." He bent forward to kiss her brow, then turned and walked on to his own room shutting the door after himself with a quiet click.

Grace stood frozen for an instant before entering her own room. What was the meaning of this? Was she to spend her wedding night alone? Or perhaps he was giving her privacy to change into her night clothes before he paid her a visit. Yes, that must be it.

Quickly, Grace went into her dressing room and discarded her dress, crinoline and corset, then the rest of her undergarments. She relieved herself on the commode and poured some water from the nearby jug into the basin on the dressing table. Using a linen washcloth, she quickly cleaned herself, making sure to pour a drop or two of lavender oil into the water to freshen her scent. She dipped her toothbrush into the jar of tooth powder and gave her teeth a quick scrub, rinsing out the charcoal and chalk mix with several gargles of water. When she was done, she put on her cream silk night rail and took the pins out of her hair, brushing it until it gleamed. She stood and examined herself in the mirror. Satisfied that she looked her best, she returned to her room, pulled back the bedcovers and climbed into bed.

The remnants of the fire in the grate cast a faint red glow across the room. The lamp above the mantelpiece provided further illumination. Grace lay in her bed and waited. The minutes passed, but there was no knock on her door. It gradually began to dawn on Grace that her husband was not coming to spend the wedding night with her. Slowly, anger grew in her breast. How dare he shun her so? This was not right. No newly married woman should expect to spend the night alone. Her indignation was so great that she could not settle down to sleep. With a loud huff, she threw off the bedcovers and got out of the bed. Tiptoeing on bare feet across the cold floor, she rapped on the interconnecting door. She had never understood why the heroines in the romances she had read were so put off by a closed door. Not waiting for an answer, she turned the handle and opened it.

In the dim light of the dying fire, she saw Benedict stare back at her in astonishment from where he lay on the bed. "What is the meaning of this, Benedict?" she exclaimed, gesticulating angrily with her hands.

"Th-the meaning of what?" he asked in nervous puzzlement.

"Why do you shun me on our wedding night? Do I have the plague? Is it because I am used goods and no longer a maiden? Have you such a disgust of me?"

Benedict sat up in his bed abruptly. "No, no. Of course not."

"Then why do you leave me alone?" she cried, on the verge of tears.

"I-I thought that was what you wanted. I did not wish to impose."

"Impose? How could you think that?"

By now, Benedict was out of his bed and standing before her in his nightshirt. Hurriedly, he said, "Grace, I am not unaware that this is a marriage of convenience for you. I thought perhaps you would wish to wait until you had developed sufficient affection for me. I am sorry if I was mistaken."

She bit out the words. "Even though circumstance has pushed us into this marriage, it is a real one, Benedict. I have pledged myself to you for life. You made a vow to me in church—*with my body I thee worship*. Well, what are you waiting for? Do as you vowed!"

Her chest heaved as she stood before him, and his eyes could not help but stray to the tantalising outline of her breasts through the thin silk of her night rail. So softly she had to strain to hear him, he whispered, "I do worship thee with every part of my body, Grace."

"Then show me," she breathed.

He touched gentle fingers to her cheek, stroking along her jaw and down her neck to her collar bone. "I am unschooled in the art of lovemaking," he murmured. "I have never done this before and do not know how to go about pleasing you."

She took his hand in hers. "Then come with me, and I will show you." She led him into her room, which was still lit by the lamp above the mantelpiece. There, she faced him. "Kiss me." His deep brown eyes stared into hers as he slowly bent his head. His lips hovered an inch from hers, so close that their breaths mingled. She parted her lips and brought them a fraction closer. He closed the distance until finally, they touched. That touch seemed to ignite something in him. Suddenly, his hands were buried in her hair, drawing her close as he kissed her over and over with an unrelenting hunger. She sensed his need, and that he did not know how to assuage it. So, she showed him.

Her parted lips met his next kiss with a light flick of her tongue. He startled at the wet contact, pulling back a fraction then coming back for another feel of it. She flicked her tongue at him again, bringing it to the seam of his lips, asking to be let in. He understood and parted his own lips. She did not hesitate, plunging her tongue into his mouth, seeking contact with his. He made a guttural sound in his throat as he felt her explore his mouth. For a novice, he was a fast learner. Soon he had taken over the kiss, holding the back of her head firmly with both hands as he explored hers in return, taking as much as giving. She had wondered what he would taste like. Now she knew. He tasted so heavenly she would never get enough.

They lost track of time as they held each other in a tight embrace, mouth to mouth, in a communion of their body and soul. They came apart finally, perhaps to draw a breath, and stared into each other's eyes. "With my body I thee worship," he whispered raggedly.

"Show me your body," she whispered back. "Let nothing hide you from me."

Slowly, his eyes never leaving hers, he lifted the nightshirt over his head and threw it to the floor. She drank in the sight of him. He was beautiful. Lean, but strong, his chest carved to perfection. His skin was fair, covered with a smattering of dark hair that trailed in a line from his belly button down to—oh my! Standing proud to attention was the finest cock she had ever seen, thick and long, with smooth satiny skin. Her eyes completed their inventory, taking in the muscular thighs dusted with dark hair and his well-shaped limbs. Back up her eyes went, to stare into his again. It was her turn now. Slowly, she took hold of the delicate silk of her night rail and pulled the garment over her head, revealing her body to him, inch by inch. She threw the silky garment to the floor and stood, awaiting his inspection.

Face flushed with desire, he took her in from top to toe. His eyes lingered on the curve of her pert breasts, tipped by taut nipples. He wondered how they would feel to the touch. With his eyes, he worshipped the unblemished smooth skin that covered her shapely body, the dimple of her belly button, the fair nest of hair at her mound.

She took a step closer to him until less than the span of his hand separated them. "You are allowed to touch," she breathed. He lifted a hand and brought it down gently to her neck, delighting in the softness of her skin. Slowly, he trailed his fingers down the centre of her chest, placing his entire palm flat along her breast bone. She covered his hand with hers and guided it to one breast. He took hold of it and squeezed the soft flesh in wonderment. His other hand flew up to cup the second breast. He hissed out a breath. "Beautiful, simply beautiful." Then his eyes, hard with possessive desire, blazed into hers. "And mine. All mine."

Suddenly, she was in his arms again. Benedict wasn't sure if it was her or him that had made the first move. All he knew was that her soft silken body was wrapped tight in his arms, and he never wanted to let her go. He kissed her hungrily, craving her like a parched man in the desert craves water. His shaft was hard and throbbing with need. She must have felt it pushing into her, because a soft hand snaked down his body to wrap around its girth. He gasped. The pleasure of her touch on him was such that he was sure he would spurt his secretions any moment. "Ah Grace," he groaned.

She seemed to understand. "Come to bed," she murmured. He let her go long enough to follow her to the bed, and to crawl in beside her. He lay on his side, head supported on one elbow, as his eyes, then his fingers, stroked down her body. When he got to one breast, he paused to rub the pad of his finger back and forth on the pebbled tip, marvelling at the texture. "*One day*," he thought, "*our babe will be suckling on this breast.*" He gazed at it longingly, a wicked idea forming in his mind.

"Touch me with your lips," she begged, almost as if she could read his thoughts.

He bent his head and kissed the tip of one breast. She gave a sharp intake of breath, rising off the bed to meet his mouth. Encouraged, he kissed her there again, this time snaking his tongue over the puckered flesh.

"Ah," she moaned.

He raised his eyes to hers. "You like that?"

"Yes, Benedict. Please."

He did not need to be asked twice. Lowering his head again, he took the dusky bud into his mouth, stroking it with his tongue, then with a rush of boldness, beginning to suckle it. He heard her moans, and they were all the encouragement he needed. He sucked and tugged and pulled at the pebbled teat, wondering absently how something designed for the essential function of reproduction could also provide such pleasure. His mouth released the darkened, swollen teat and moved across to lavish attention on the other. Beneath him, Grace's breathing grew strained as she moaned over and over again.

"I need you," she panted.

"I need you too," he responded huskily.

Frustration clouded her eyes momentarily as she rasped, "Benedict! I need you inside me."

"Oh, yes. I see." He hesitated, not quite sure how to proceed. He supposed he should position himself above her so his male organ could enter her aperture. He had not glimpsed it, but he vaguely recalled it was situated at the apex of her legs. Carefully, he shifted his body above hers, pushing back on his elbows so as not to crush her with his weight. His straining, throbbing shaft pressed against her belly. Awkwardly, he began rooting around, trying to find the entrance to her body. He felt his face flush with the effort and embarrassment as he kept knocking against bone and flesh, without finding any place to slip himself into. Oh God! Why had he not researched this more thoroughly before the wedding night? What must she think of him?

"Here," she said, and with a hand guided him to the correct location. "That is it, there. Now push inside slowly."

He did as she asked, feeling the tip of his shaft burrow into a tight, wet, heated passage—so tight, surely he would not fit? Gritting his teeth with the effort to go slow and not simply ram himself into her, he pushed in a little further.

"Yes! Deeper! Keep going."

He pushed in more, feeling the grip of her around him, suctioning him in. Oh great Lord! Never in his life had he felt such intense pleasure. Unable to stop himself, he plunged the rest of the way in until his whole shaft was buried in her blissful heat. A million thoughts and sensations assailed him in one instant. A divine feeling of ecstasy. The powerful, instinctive need to rut inside her. The wonder at their two bodies being joined so intimately. He was inside her, in her very core. Oh what bliss! What privilege! Was this what he had missed all these years? Had he but known it would feel like this, perhaps he would not have been so resolute in his abstinence. Did she feel this too? If it was as good for her, then it was little wonder she had indulged in this divinely sinful activity outside the sanctity of marriage. Who could blame her?

He stared down at her in desperate need. "Grace," he croaked.

She closed her eyes as she moaned, "Ah, keep moving."

He gave in to that powerful instinct and began to move, plunging in and out, feeling that unbearably wonderful friction with each thrust of his shaft into her welcoming heat. He wanted this feeling to last for ever. Each heavenly thrust was accompanied by a blissful moan from her. He must be doing something right. But try as he might to make the feeling last, he could not. All too soon, he felt that thickening of his shaft that heralded the moment of completion. He increased the speed of his thrusts, rutting into her desperately, needing to reach that pinnacle. And then he was there. With a loud groan, he spurted his seed deep inside her, his pleasure intense. The lids of his eyes shut as he lost himself in ecstasy.

When he was done, he flopped down over her in exhaustion. He was not sure he could ever move again. He buried his face in her neck, breathing in her sweet scent. Her voice roused him from his stupor.

"Benedict, you are heavy on me."

"Oh." He lifted himself off her, and as he did, his shaft pulled out of the warm sheath it had been resting in. He felt the loss of that heat intensely, wishing he could bury himself inside her again and never leave. However, he obliged her and rolled over to his back. As consciousness returned, he turned his head to her, frowning. She looked… cross. "Are you alright, Grace? Was I too rough?"

She gave him a smile that did not quite reach her eyes. "I'm fine," she said.

"Was it good for you?"

She nodded. "Hmm."

He stared at the ceiling, mystified. If she had enjoyed it, then why did he get the distinct feeling she was annoyed with him? Sometimes, he wished the inner workings of the female mind could be less of a mystery to him. He considered. Perhaps, she simply wished him to leave so she could have privacy to clean herself up. Lovemaking was a messy business, he realised. It was best he not overstay his welcome. With a cheerful smile, he kissed her brow and said, "Thank you, Grace. I will bid you goodnight."

Carefully, he edged out of the bed, bent down to pick up his discarded nightshirt, then went into his room, closing the connecting door behind him.

CHAPTER 18

GRACE LAY IN bed, stewing in frustrated anger. She had been so close. His thick cock had filled her beautifully. Each thrust had brought her closer and closer to her climax. And then it had been over, much too soon. Could he not have waited a little longer? Men! Only thinking of their own pleasure. And then, he had had the gall to leave her, yet again. What was the matter with her that he was so hasty to quit her presence? Did she smell noxious to him?

In high dudgeon, she got out of bed and went into her dressing room to clean herself up. Once she was fresh again, she put her night rail back on, put out the lamp and got into bed. But sleep was elusive as she stewed some more. So, was this to be her married life? Furtive visits to her bedchamber before he decamped back to his? This was not how it was with her ma and pa. She knew they slept only in one bed each night. As a child, she had slipped into their room in the mornings and seen them lying close in each other's arms as they slept. That was what married people did in her world. Was she to accept this abandonment each night? Absolutely not!

With another huff, she got out of bed once more and marched to the connecting door. She did not bother to knock this time, but simply turned the handle and walked in like she had every right. Which she did. In the shadowy darkness, she discerned his form on the right side of the bed, so she went over to the other side, lifted the covers and climbed in.

"Grace?" he murmured.

"Please shift over a little more; you are taking all the space."

He did as he was bid. She tucked the covers around her neck, settled herself comfortably and mumbled, "Goodnight."

"Goodnight," came the quiet reply.

Her leg crept out to the side until it met his. She rubbed her foot along his calf, warming herself up on him. Then her hand reached between them to rest on his hip. *"That's much better,"* she thought. Feeling more mellow, she closed her eyes and was soon drifting off to sleep.

Slumber was not quite so easy for Benedict. He was acutely conscious of her leg tangling with his and her hand on his hip. He could hear each breath she took in and out. When she had walked into his room, he had thought at first she had come to berate him about the thing that had caused her to be upset with him just now, but she had simply gotten into the bed. As the realisation came that she meant to sleep with him, a happy feeling formed in his chest. He had not dared expect that they would bed together each night as his parents had. He was aware that in the upper echelons of society, husbands and wives slept in separate rooms. So Grace's decision to come here tonight warmed his heart.

But still, it was hard to sleep when every fibre of his being was marvelling at her presence in his bed. He took in a deep breath, inhaling her subtle sweet fragrance. His right hand came to rest gently on the hand she had on his hip, feeling the softness of her skin. He spoke to her in his head. *"You feel so right here with me, my love."* With a concerted effort, he closed his eyes and willed himself to sleep. It took a long time to come.

In the morning, he was first to wake. As he surfaced into consciousness, he became aware of a warm body draped along his side. Grace. His eyes flew open. She was burrowed against him, one leg draped over his thigh, her face nestled into his shoulder, an arm splayed over his chest. He dared not move in case he disturbed her. For endless minutes, he lay motionless, listening to the sound of her breaths, feeling his heart pulse under the hand on his chest. Eventually though, nature's call compelled him to move. He shifted gently away until he reached the edge of the bed. He heard her moan of protest, but she did not wake. Quietly, he stood and went to the adjoining dressing room to relieve himself and wash. Then he pulled out a fresh set of clothes from the wardrobe and got dressed. On his return to the bedroom, she stirred awake.

He went to sit on the edge of the bed. "Good morning, Grace," he said.

She yawned and sat herself up. "Morning," she croaked.

"Did you sleep well?"

"Hmm," came the indistinct reply.

"I shall leave you to wake in your own time, my dear. Come down to breakfast when you are ready."

"Mmm," she grunted.

He hid a smile as he left the room. His Grace, it seemed, was not a morning person. Downstairs, he was greeted by Winford. "Good morning, sir."

"Morning, Winford."

"Breakfast has been laid out for you in the dining room, sir. There are freshly baked rolls and slices of cold meat, and Cook is happy to prepare some eggs and sausages if you should so wish."

Mindful of his previous conversation with Grace about her newfound aversion to some foods, he decided it best to avoid the sausages—their pungent smell might not be what she wanted first thing in the morning. "Just eggs, please," he replied. "Fried or scrambled, I do not mind."

"Yes, sir."

Benedict settled himself at the dining table and helped himself to some delicious smelling bread rolls, buttering them generously. Winford came back into the dining room and offered him fragrant coffee, which he accepted with a smile. There were definite advantages to this new life of his at Mulverley Grange. Back at his small terraced house, he would have made himself a fresh brew of tea in the morning and cut some thick slices of bread for his breakfast, which he would have eaten with some butter and a wedge of cheese. This meal, and all the others he had had since his marriage, was a step up from what he was used to. He did not want to feel like he was leaching off his wealthy wife, and he was determined not to do so, but it would seem churlish not to be grateful for the good food he was being served.

Winford had just brought in a plate of eggs when Grace slid into the seat opposite him. She was dressed in yet another black mourning gown which accentuated the paleness of her creamy skin and the vivid russet of her eyes. In the cold light of day, memories of what they had done last night came rushing to him, causing him to stutter as he said, "I-it looks to be a fine day for walking to the village."

She glanced out of the window and replied stiltedly, "Yes, the bright sky makes a change from the drizzle we have had the past few days."

Why were they being so awkward with one another? It continued this way the rest of the meal, their conversation trivial, interspersed with uncomfortable pauses. It occurred to Benedict that he was not the only one feeling this discomfiture. Grace, too, looked ill at ease. He studied her covertly. She played with the food on her plate, and as she took in a bite of eggs, there came on her face a brief look of disgust. As Benedict could not fault Cook's prowess in the kitchen, he surmised that this was yet another instance of her pregnancy-induced aversion to some foods. He watched her carefully. She forced down another bite, then stopped suddenly. An expression of horror came to her face as she clutched a hand to her chest. Instantly, he understood. There was not a moment to be lost. He cast around desperately for a suitable receptacle. From the table, he picked up the silver cloche that had been used to cover the plate of eggs. Its dome shape would, when turned upside down, give the appearance of a deep bowl.

"Here," he said hurriedly, holding it out to her. It was not a moment too soon. She took the silver container and began to retch into it. He went to stand behind her, rubbing her back soothingly. "It's alright, dearest. Let it out," he crooned. She took a gulping breath, then retched again. When finally she was done, he wet the edge of his napkin with some water and used it to wipe her mouth. Then he brought a glass of water to her lips. "Drink this, my dear."

Obediently, she drank. He looked at her in concern. "How do you feel now? Better?"

She nodded, then looked down in dismay at the upended cloche in her hands and its displeasing contents.

"Let me take this from you," he said.

"What will the servants think?" she worried, as he took it from her hands.

"Do not concern yourself with this, my dear. Winford will handle it, and I will make sure he understands discretion is of the essence." Benedict stood, holding the cloche carefully in his hands, and pressed the bell. In a few moments, Winford appeared. The butler took one look at the scene before him and quickly came over to take the sullied receptacle from him. As he did so, Benedict spoke in his most authoritative voice, "Winford, Mrs Sedgwick was unfortunately taken sick. However, she does not want any fuss to be made about her condition and no loose gossip to be spread about it either. I trust I can leave this matter in your capable hands?"

"Of course, sir."

"Good."

Once Winford had left the room, Benedict went back to Grace's side. "Would you like to go rest in your bedchamber?" he asked of her.

"No, thank you, Benedict," she said in a low voice. "Could we perhaps go sit in the upstairs parlour, while you write your letters? I shall be fine in a little while, and then we can go out for our walk."

"Are you sure you are up to going out?"

"Oh yes, the fresh air will invigorate me."

"Very well, let us go upstairs." He held out his arm and she slipped hers into it, feeling oddly comforted. Together, they went upstairs and into the parlour. As Grace sat on the end of the chaise longue and took her shoes off, Benedict considered her thoughtfully. "Perhaps you should take off any undergarments that are causing you discomfort," he said.

She nodded and stood, raising her skirt. "Will you do it for me, Benedict?"

"Of course." He came over to her and looked closely at the crinoline. "How does this unhook?" he asked, unsure.

"There are hooks at the top."

"Ah, right, I see them." With gentle hands, he undid the hooks and pulled the hooped garment down her body, allowing her to step out of it. He discarded it quickly on a nearby armchair. "How about this?" he asked, pointing to her corset. "It does look to be tight around your waist."

"Perhaps we could loosen it a little?"

"Turn around; let me do it."

She turned, and he lifted her skirt up and over her shoulder as he examined the laces that held together the corset she wore. With deft fingers, he unlaced the garment, allowing Grace to breathe a little easier. "You will need to dispense with this altogether as your belly grows," he said consideringly.

"Yes, but for now, I think I may continue with it, tied more loosely." She let the skirt drop back to the floor then turned to face him again. Instinctively, she put her arms around him for a hug. "Thank you," she murmured into his neck.

He held her to him, savouring her closeness. All too soon, the embrace was over. With a smile, she settled herself on the chaise longue and said, "Now I will rest a short time while you write those letters. Who are you writing to?"

He took hold of a nearby blanket and draped it over her. "There are several. First to my father, to give him the news of our marriage and an invitation to come stay with us—that is if you do not mind?"

"No, of course not. I would dearly love to meet your father."

"I'm glad," he smiled. "Then, I need also send letters to my brother and sisters. And lastly, I am writing to Hatchards bookshop in London to see if they have a particular book I am looking for."

"Oh? What book would that be?"

He looked uncomfortable. "It is a newly published work entitled 'The science and art of midwifery', written by an eminent American doctor called William Lusk."

"Why would you want to read a book about midwifery?" asked Grace, confused.

He paused and glanced meaningfully at her belly. "You are doing this for me?" she wondered, even more bewildered.

"I want to know as much as possible about your physical condition, Grace, as you progress through this pregnancy and labour to give birth to our child."

"Oh." She seemed to ponder this. "I see. Well, do not let me keep you from your letters. I shall close my eyes and rest for a while."

He started for the door, saying, "Let me get some writing materials, and I shall be right back."

Once outside, he made his way down to the study, and found some paper, pen and ink in the desk there. Before returning to the parlour, he made sure to ask Mrs Hawkins to send up a pot of tea and a plate of biscuits, hoping Grace would be able to swallow some food down. Back upstairs, he settled himself in one of the available armchairs, drew the side table towards him, and began to write. When Mrs Hawkins came in with the tea tray some time later, Grace roused herself from her light slumber.

She smiled. "How kind, Mrs Hawkins. Thank you."

"You may thank Mr Sedgwick, madam, as this was entirely his own suggestion."

Grace's eyes flew to Benedict, who had paused his writing. "He is such a thoughtful husband," she mused.

Mrs Hawkins chuckled. "That he is."

Benedict felt his cheeks heat, so found it expedient to resume his letter writing. The door clicked shut quietly following Mrs Hawkins's departure from the room. He heard the clink of cutlery as Grace poured the tea into individual cups and placed a biscuit on each saucer. She stood and brought his cup over to him. "Thank you," he smiled gratefully.

"No, it is I should be thanking you." She leaned over and kissed his cheek. Just like her hug previously, this was a carelessly affectionate gesture on her part. He should not read anything more into it for he knew, from having observed her, that she was generous in her affection with the people close to her. Still, he treasured every touch she bestowed on him.

She settled herself in the opposite armchair, moving the discarded crinoline aside, and ate her biscuit with the tea. They sat in contented silence for a while longer, until Benedict looked up from his letter-writing and said, "I won't be much longer with the letters, just a few minutes more. Then we can go for our walk."

"In that case, let me go and get myself ready." With this, she swooped her crinoline and shoes in her hands and flew out of the room.

As before, they met in the main hall and proceeded to go outside. The air was chilly, but it was made worthwhile by the wintry sunshine which cast a gilded glow over the surrounding parkland. Benedict offered Grace his arm, and they began their walk towards the village of Standlake, which was situated half a mile from the house. As they walked, he was glad to see the earlier awkwardness between them dissipate. They spoke easily, she of her plans for the stable at Mulverley Grange and he offering occasional advice, but mostly listening. It was clear to him that this project was close to her heart, and he was determined to help her in any way he could to make it a success, though he himself knew little of the breeding of horses. Perhaps he should look into ordering some books on the matter. His character was such that he liked to read as much as he could about any subject that took his interest. He made a note to himself to also search through the vast library at Stanton Hall for an appropriate tract on horse breeding.

It was not long before they reached the village. Their first stop was the post office, where the letters were duly dispatched. The post master, a florid man by the name of Brigham, was cheerful and friendly as he took the letters and stamped them. "I'm right glad the Grange is occupied by its owners again," he said. "It's been let out here and there over the last few years, but nobody stayed long enough for us to get to know them proper like. It is nice to see a newly married couple such as yourselves, Mr and Mrs Sedgwick, settle hereabouts."

"Thank you, Mr Brigham," replied Benedict smoothly. "We do look forward to getting to know our new neighbours. As you may be aware, I am curate of the next parish in Stanton Harcourt, and shall naturally be travelling back and forth there most days, but I do hope to also get involved with the affairs of the local parish, if you will allow me."

"That we would indeed!" cried Mr Brigham. "Let me but tell the missus of your visit today, and I am sure she will regret having missed it, for she would I'm sure want to join me in inviting your good selves to our annual wassailing—though I hope you are not one of those newfangled clergymen that frown upon such practices as being pagan?"

Benedict smiled, highly amused. "Doubtless it is a pagan practice, but there is no harm in it."

Grace looked puzzled. "If you will pardon my ignorance, what is wassailing?"

"Ah," said Benedict. "Wassailing did not, I see, make its way over to America as a custom."

"No, indeed not. Please enlighten me as to what it is."

Now it was Mr Brigham that explained, "Mrs Sedgwick, it is a festival held on the feast of Epiphany in the apple orchards way yonder to the north of the village. There is singing, dancing and much merrymaking to call to the spirits of the orchard for a good harvest next season. There will be plenty of spiced cider to drink too. I do hope you will join us for it."

"That does sound rather pagan," said Grace, looking intrigued, "but I should be most interested to see it." She glanced over at her husband, a look of enquiry on her face.

"If it pleases you to go, Grace, then we shall," he said in answer to her look.

"Ah, that is splendid!" boomed Mr Brigham. "We hope to see you then, six o'clock on Twelfth Night at the Templeton orchard."

"The Templeton orchard?" queried Grace.

"Yes, the orchard to the north of the village belongs to Mr Templeton. You have perhaps chanced to make his acquaintance?"

"Yes," smiled Grace. "We do know Mr Templeton. I had not realised that his lands were so close to ours."

"They border with Mulverley Grange," explained Mr Brigham, "so he would be your most immediate neighbour."

"Mr Templeton, our neighbour? How delightful!"

Benedict was not quite so delighted, though he tried not to show it. He did not like having this uncharitable reaction, but he could not find it in himself to be happy that the man, whom he had last seen kissing Grace with passionate abandon, was to be their neighbour.

Their business in the post office complete, Benedict and Grace said their farewells and headed out again. Over the next half hour, they walked about the village, visiting the general store and making a few sundry purchases while getting acquainted with Mr and Mrs Philips, the owners of the shop. They took a walk along the churchyard and had a look at the church building, some parts of which dated back to medieval times, Benedict taking particular interest in the stained glass lancet windows in the north transept. Grace was not much captivated by the sight of some windows in an old building, but she waited as patiently as she could while Benedict inspected them admiringly. Eventually, he noticed her ennui and suggested they begin their walk back to the house.

They were quiet on the return journey, each mulling over the latest events. Benedict could not help his mind from wandering to the issue of Mr Templeton. He was well aware that Grace was attracted to the handsome landowner, but did this mean she would continue her flirtation with him after their marriage, or even go further than that? He could not know for sure. He found that he could not view such a thing with any degree of equanimity.

Grace, too, was thinking of Mr Templeton, mindful of the conversation she had had with her mother a few days ago. Much as she was delighted to learn he was to be their neighbour, she knew that it was much too late to pursue any relationship with the charming, handsome rogue. She took a moment to regret what could have been, then put him firmly from her mind. She was married to Benedict now and to him she would be true.

CHAPTER 19

THAT EVENING, THE newly married couple retired to bed at around nine o'clock. After last night's misunderstanding, there was an unstated agreement between them that they would be having conjugal relations tonight and that they would end the night in one bed. As they reached Grace's bedroom door, they stopped and faced each other, as they had the night before. However, this time, Benedict did not bid her goodnight. Instead, he looked down at his shoes and mumbled, "I will leave you to undress, my dear. Will you join me when you are ready?"

"Yes, I will."

He nodded, turned abruptly and entered his own room. Grace went into her own bedchamber and quickly set about getting herself ready for bed. In her thin night rail, shivering slightly, she knocked on the connecting door and entered. She found Benedict in bed, a book in his hand. At her entrance, he put the book away and lifted the bed covers in invitation with a shy smile. She climbed in beside him and brought the covers back up. Shivering again, for the night was chilly, she murmured plaintively, "Warm me up, Benedict; I am cold."

He turned on his side and enfolded her in his embrace. He felt so wonderfully warm that for several minutes, she snuggled up to him, burying her cold feet between his legs and rubbing her hands into the warm crook of his neck. "Ah, that feels better," she purred happily. "You are like my own personal furnace, Benedict."

She felt the rumble of his chest as he laughed. "I am glad to be of use."

"You are very useful at warming your wife," she said, "but let us also see what other uses you may have." She looked at him with a gleam in her eyes. She was keen to make love again and to see whether he would improve as a lover second time around.

"What might you have in mind?" he asked with feigned innocence.

She inched a little closer until the tips of their noses touched. "Oh, I don't know. Perhaps you may wish to sing me a lullaby or preach me a sermon, seeing as you are a man of the cloth."

He rubbed his nose to hers. "But my voice is unequal to the task of singing, and I am very much afraid that my preaching is set aside for when I am in church."

"Hmm, so that leaves us with only one more useful thing you could do, husband."

"And what is that?" he asked in a low, husky voice.

She pressed her mouth to his ear and whispered, "You could make love to me."

His breath hitched at her words. "That," he said huskily, "I am happy to do." Next moment, his lips were on hers, last night's hesitance gone as he plundered her mouth, hungry for her taste. She gave herself to him, wrapping tight arms around him as she welcomed his invasion of her mouth with his tongue. Her legs tangled with his as he pressed his body to hers, letting her feel the hard jut of his cock. Her core throbbed and slickened with the juices of her own arousal. She needed him inside her.

When next their lips parted, she breathed, "Now, Benedict. I need you now." She sat herself up and with impatient hands, drew her night rail over her head. Following her example, Benedict also threw off his nightshirt. They came together again, this time skin on naked skin. His mouth found hers for another ravenous kiss.

As he pressed his body to hers, she felt the hot swell of his cock burrowing against her. She could not resist snaking her hand down to touch it, running a finger along its velvety skin. He groaned, "Ah, Grace." Taking hold of his thick length, she guided it to her slick passage. Unhesitatingly, he pushed inside her with another ecstatic groan. Then, he was fully sheathed in her wet heat, stretching her deliciously. "You feel so good," he said thickly.

"You too," she breathed.

He began to move inside her, plunging in and out in a rhythm as old as time. His thrusts were deep, creating exquisite friction. Her hands clutched at his buttocks, urging him into her with his every thrust. Oh that felt heavenly. She could sense the wave of a glorious climax begin to build. Oh God. Oh yes. His thrusts quickened. She felt him thicken inside her then give a rough cry as he pulsed into her frantically. And then, he stilled.

Disappointment blanketed her again. Why could he not wait a little longer for her to reach her own climax? He lay heavily upon her for several beats before lifting himself on his elbows, a wondrous smile on his face. "That was spectacular!" he marvelled. "Thank you, dearest Grace. Did you find it as pleasing as I did?"

She did not have the heart to tell him the truth, so she stretched it a little by saying, "It was very pleasing indeed." Which was not in itself a lie. She had enjoyed it greatly, as far as it went. He gave her that singularly sweet smile of his and kissed her lips. Then, very gently, he pulled out. As he did so, a warm gush of his spend flowed out of her and onto the bedsheets.

He saw it and got to his feet quickly. "Let me get a cloth." In two strides, he was at his dressing room door and walking in. Through the open door, she saw him dip a cloth in the basin of water and use it to wipe himself clean. Then he dipped the cloth again and wrung it, coming back to her. "Here, my dearest. Use this."

She gazed at him lazily. "You clean me."

"Will you let me?"

"Of course."

With another sweet smile, he set about this task, bringing the cloth to her wet cunt. She obliged him by spreading her legs wide. She saw his eyes gape as he took in the sight of her damp, swollen folds. It was clear he had never before seen this intimate part of a woman. He stared in fascination as he cleaned her gently with the cloth. She basked in his gaze. "Do you like what you see?"

He nodded. "The wonders of God's creation will never cease. You are perfection, Grace." He passed the cloth one more time over her, making sure to mop up any stray emissions. His eyes, though, stayed glued to the glistening pink flesh.

"You are allowed to touch, Benedict. With your fingers."

He took a heavy breath, then discarded the cloth on the night table. Gentle fingers wove through the silky blond hair on her mound, before sliding down towards the pink folds of her sex. He touched her in wonder. "Such soft skin," he crooned, "and so pretty." As his finger slid over a little protrusion at the top of her cunt, she gave a gasp.

He looked up quickly. "Did I hurt you?"

"No, quite the contrary. That felt good."

Hesitantly, he touched her there again. "Mmm," she moaned.

His fingers traced down lower, while his eyes came up to study her reaction. "Is it just up there that it feels pleasing?"

"It feels pleasing all over, but that place you touched before is particularly sensitive."

He brought his fingers back to that pink nub of flesh. She moaned again, "Ah, yes." He studied her in fascination, the thought coming to him that perhaps this little protruding nub brought her the same kind of sensation as his own male shaft did to him. But how could this be? His male shaft was designed to go inside her body for the purpose of procreation. What could be the purpose of this little nub? Reluctantly, he stood, picked up the cloth and took it back to the dressing room.

As he walked away, he surreptitiously held his fingers to his nose and inhaled the scent of her cunt. It was… heady. In the darkness of his dressing room, he could not resist another sniff. A minute later, he came back and picked up his nightshirt, shrugging it on. He reached over to the other side of the bed and gave her the night rail she had discarded so impatiently earlier in the night. She slipped it over her head, then lay back next to him on the bed as he brought the covers over them. He sat up long enough to extinguish the lamp, then drew her to him under the blanket. "Goodnight, dearest Grace."

"Goodnight, husband mine."

In the dim light of the darkened room, they found each other's lips and shared a sweet kiss. Then they both settled for sleep, drifting into deep and restful slumber.

Grace awoke the following morning to the feel of his body pressed all along her back, his arm wrapped possessively around her waist—and his hardened cock rubbing along the plump cheeks of her bottom. She shifted, pressing back against him. She felt his breath in the curve of her neck. "Good morning," he whispered.

"Mmm," she moaned, unable to articulate words so early in the day.

"Grace," he whispered again.

"Mmm?"

"I have need of you."

She rubbed her bottom against the hardness of his cock as if in confirmation.

"Will you let me—let me make love to you?"

"Mmm."

"Is that a yes?"

It was still too early for speech, so in answer, she let her hand roam backwards, under his nightshirt, until she gripped his throbbing appendage. Her night rail had ridden up during the night, exposing her backside, so she was able to guide him to her entrance without hindrance. "Can we do it like this, from behind?" he wondered.

Shifting her stance a little to accommodate him, bending her knees and lifting her bottom towards him, she moaned an affirmative "Mmm".

"Oh, yes, I see how this could be," murmured Benedict. With care, he positioned himself at her entrance and pushed forward until he was in. With another, more powerful surge, he drove deeper, all the way to the hilt. They moaned in unison at the wonder of their union. For a moment, he stilled deep inside her, then he began to move in slow rhythmic thrusts. With eyes closed, she reposed on her pillow, enjoying the sensation of being filled while still half asleep. It was really rather pleasant.

He too seemed content to take his time, holding her close from behind. In her ear, he crooned words of praise. "You feel so good… Oh that's good… Oh Grace, oh my dear, dear Grace… Oh… Aghh!" That last exclamation was on a grunt, as he began to plunge into her in quick, sharp succession until at last, he reached his climax with a gruff cry.

His movements stilled, but he remained inside her. "I am the luckiest man alive," he murmured, then his breathing deepened as he fell back to sleep, and she with him. They slept an hour longer, still intimately joined. She awoke again to the feel of his member thickening inside her as they enjoyed a second round of lovemaking in this position. "Grace, I do not think I will ever get enough of this," stated Benedict after he had reached another climax. "You have become my new addiction."

She smiled. Even though she had not enjoyed a climax as he had done, it had been pleasant to be so thoroughly filled—and she gloried in the thought of having brought him such intense bliss. She pushed aside any disappointment she might have felt for herself. Benedict was a comfort to her, and she knew he would be a good father to her child. It would have to be enough. She took his hand and kissed it. "Good," she breathed.

Eventually, they roused themselves enough to get out of bed, wash and dress. It was New Year's Eve, and they had promised to spend it at Stanton Hall. After a leisurely breakfast, in which Grace was careful only to eat some slices of toast, they got themselves ready for their overnight trip, bid Mrs Hawkins and Winford farewell, and boarded their carriage.

CHAPTER 20

THE STANTONS CELEBRATED the coming of the new year quietly and without fuss. Two weeks had passed since the old earl's demise, and the family was still in the throes of acute grief, especially Frank and Jasper. Their father had been a colossal presence in their lives, even after they had emigrated to America. Over the past week, they had kept themselves busy with their work as executors of the will, trying to ensure all was in order before their departure back home. Now, as the year drew to an end, they paused in their travails, only to feel a profound melancholy.

Jasper and Ruth had been pleased to welcome their daughter back after her brief honeymoon. Both parents observed her keenly for any sign that the marriage was anything less than harmonious. On this, they were able to set their minds at rest. Grace looked at ease with her new husband, treating him with her usual brand of careless affection. She looked content, and though a trifle nauseous at supper, in good health. As for Benedict, it was clear to all that the young curate was devoted to his new wife. Even Benjamin remarked on it in an aside to his brother, saying, "That poor man is head over heels for Grace. Mark my words, she is going to lead him a merry dance and have him firmly under her thumb." Daniel could only but concur with this assessment.

The only person unaware of the depth of Benedict's feelings was Grace herself. She knew of course that he cared for her, much as she cared for him. That his feelings went beyond this though, was not immediately obvious to her. On a few occasions, she had detected a certain warmth in his gaze that had given her hope that there could be something more between them than simple affection. But the warm look was quickly gone, making her wonder if she had imagined it.

The truth of the matter was that Benedict had too much pride and sense of self-preservation to openly display his feelings. He was affectionate and thoughtful, as ever, but he made sure to mask the intensity of the feelings that lay beneath the surface. Whenever she was turned away from him, however, he could not help but follow her with besotted eyes. It was still unbelievable to him that this wonderful creature, so surely out of his reach, was his wife.

After their meal, the family gathered in the drawing room, playing card games and engaging in desultory conversation. The older Stantons did not wait up to see the new year, retiring to their beds not long after ten o'clock. Beth too, could not keep awake and decided to head for bed. The rest of the family stayed on, wanting to wait until midnight before going to their beds. Bottles of wine were procured to see them through the coming hours and to toast the new year with.

Before going up to her bed, Ruth drew Grace aside. "Darling," she said. "Please have a care not to drink wine excessively in your condition. I fear it may induce more of that nausea you have been struggling with and may also prove harmful to the child you bear."

"Yes, Ma. I do not think I will be able to take more than a few sips of the wine, but in any case, I shall be careful not to drink to excess."

"Good," smiled Ruth, kissing her daughter goodnight.

Therefore, as the evening progressed and the wine flowed, Grace found herself the only sober person in the room as all around her, including Benedict, became very merry indeed. It was amusing to see her husband inebriated. He was a happy drunk, displaying the same cheerful disposition as usual, but with a little more gaiety of spirit and just a hint of salacious humour. Towards the last half hour before midnight, Benjamin proposed a game of Questions and Commands, much to everyone's delight.

"I will start," he said. "This question goes to everyone in the room. If you do not answer it truthfully, then I will have to command you to perform a forfeit."

"What forfeit will it be?" queried John.

"Hmm," considered Benjamin. A gleam came into his eyes. "It must be a sizeable forfeit to discourage any of you from withholding the truth. I know! Anyone who does not answer the question truthfully will need to bare their bottom to receive a spanking with this fireplace iron," he said, brandishing the brass object for all to see.

"Ouch," retorted John. "It hurts just to think of it."

"A suitable deterrent then. All you must do, is answer truthfully," rejoined Benjamin. "Are we all in?" There were murmurs of assent from all around. "Very well," continued Benjamin. "Here is my question, and we can start with John. Who have you kissed in your life so far? And I don't mean the familial sort of kisses but the sexual, locking of lips variety. John?"

John's face went beet red, but he answered valiantly, "I have kissed Dorothea Browning twice."

"Ooh!" was the communal response to this confession. "Where and when?" Benjamin wanted to know.

"Both times it was in the vestry at church, when we were putting away the sacristy at the end of the service."

Daniel laughed, "I didn't think you had it in you, John, to be so sacrilegious. Watch out, for we have a man of the cloth among us."

"I have heard of far worse goings on for this to shock me," replied Benedict, drunkenly amused.

Benjamin turned to his brother. "Now it is your turn, Daniel. Who have you kissed in your life so far?"

Daniel pondered the question for a few moments. "There have been eight girls. First kiss was Daphne Carter, then, in no particular order, I kissed Roberta Flynn, Rosie Hatton, Jenny Maitland, Olivia Breane, and Mary, Rachel and Chastity Hewitt."

"Three sisters!" exclaimed Benjamin.

"Well, not at once but in turn, yes, I experienced the delights of kissing all three Hewitt sisters."

"I always knew they were hussies," said Isabella in disgust.

"Now, now," Benjamin replied. "We will not shame anybody with our confessions. And it goes without saying that whatever is discussed here tonight goes no further but stays between us. Are we clear?"

The assembled all responded with a "yes".

"So, who shall answer next?" continued Benjamin.

"I am not yet finished," said Daniel quickly. "You did ask who I had kissed so far. I have only answered for the girls. There is one more person I have kissed and that was Ezra Matthews."

"You kissed a boy?" cried Isabella, horrified.

Daniel shrugged. "I did, just to try it. And if I am being honest, it was the best kiss of the lot."

"Do you meant to say, Daniel, that you are a—a sodomite?" asked his stricken sister.

He chuckled at her dismay. "Rest easy, Bella. I like girls well enough, but truth be told, I wouldn't say no to indulging in more tomfoolery with a man if the fancy took me."

"But is that not wicked sinfulness?" wondered his perturbed sister.

Daniel looked to Benedict. "Perhaps we should ask the only person here qualified to answer this question."

"That kind of thing was commonplace when I was at Oxford," remarked Benedict flippantly. "It was mostly harmless, except on a few occasions when the two men fell violently in love with one another. Unable to have that love sanctified by marriage and in some cases, forced by their families into marrying someone else, these dalliances resulted in heartbreak for the poor fellows."

"But that does not answer the question of whether it is a sin," pointed out Isabella.

Benedict sighed, making an effort to arrange his jumbled brain into order so he could answer the question. "Canonically speaking," he said, slurring only slightly, "only relations between a man and a woman can be sanctified by the Church, but I would not go as far as to say that men engaging in sexual acts are committing a sin. My observation is that it is in their nature to be attracted to the same sex, and anything that is inherent in nature is something created by the Lord and part of God's plan. It is infinitely beyond my capabilities to rationalise these mysteries, and I would be loath to pronounce judgement on those that have such inclinations. Love in all its forms is love, and that is all I will say on the matter." He sat back, pleased to have finished his speech without impediment, though a little startled with himself for having been so forthright. Had he been sober, he would have been more circumspect, he was sure, but there was no harm in it. He was in the presence of family.

Grace looked at her husband in surprise. She had never properly considered the matter of men falling in love with each other, but she was sure that such things were frowned upon by the Church. She had not expected Benedict to express views that were dissonant with established doctrine. That he could make his own judgements, counter to what convention dictated, pleased her enormously, tickling the rebellious part of her nature.

Daniel too regarded the young curate approvingly. "Well I must say, Benedict, that you are proving to have many hidden depths."

Benedict laughed. "I thought it was the depth of my erudition that got me the position here of curate in the first place."

"Yes, but there is the erudition based on dogma, and then there is the erudition based on intelligent thought. Yours is the latter."

Benedict made a mock bow. "Well in that case, I thank you for the compliment."

Grace came to stand behind her husband, resting her chin fondly on his shoulder. "Benedict is a very wise and kind man," she stated.

Daniel held out his glass to him. "I see that. Cheers, Benedict," and took a swig of his wine.

Benjamin turned his attention to his cousin. "And now we come to you, Grace. Answer us truthfully. Who have you kissed?"

She felt Benedict stiffen under her. Oh dear, this was a tricky one, but she was not going to have her bottom paddled in front of everyone, so she placed her arms around her seated husband and answered, "I have kissed four men. Jimmy, Mr Drummond, Mr Templeton and Benedict." On that last word, she tilted Benedict's head towards her and planted a kiss on his lips before continuing, "And by far the best kisser was Benedict." She had meant this last statement as a palliative for her husband's pride, but realised, in a rush of sudden surprise, that it was indeed true.

Emboldened by the alcohol swishing in his veins, Benedict drew her to him for another kiss, this one long and deep. Around them, they heard cheers and hoots of laughter. When at last they separated, Benjamin called out, "That was a fine show, but Grace, explain to us Mr Drummond. How on earth did that happen?"

She glanced at him disdainfully. "It was when you were all wallowing in seasickness. I was bored, and the opportunity presented itself. I will say no more."

"And what about Mr Templeton?" Isabella wanted to know.

Grace shrugged. "It was just a little fling at the Christmas ball, before I realised that Benedict was the one for me." She pressed his shoulder reassuringly. His hand came on top of hers, holding her to him.

Benjamin raised his glass to her. "Very well. And now it is your turn, Bella. Do tell us who you have kissed."

Isabella looked down to her hands clasped in her lap and muttered, "I have not yet kissed anyone."

Benjamin chortled at this. "Oh poor Bella, always missing out on the fun."

But Daniel, perhaps wearing his eldest brother hat, remarked severely, "Quite right, Bella. Do not let any forward young man take advantage of you."

"You are not alone in being inexperienced in the matter of kissing," said Benedict consolingly. "Until I married Grace, I too had never kissed anyone."

Grace ran affectionate fingers through his hair. "All the more remarkable then, that you have proved to be so adept at it." She was rewarded with one of his blushes, the sight of which made something tug at her heart.

Benjamin took hold of the wine bottle and went around refilling everyone's glasses. "Let us raise a toast to indulging in some very good kisses in 1861."

The assembled company raised their glasses, murmuring, "Hear, hear."

A look at the clock in the far corner of the room told them that the midnight hour was fast approaching. Daniel took it upon himself to stand and make another toast. "Here's to 1861 being a year of joy, health and success for all of us. Happy New Year everyone." As the clock struck midnight they all raised their glass and cried, "Happy New Year!" Then it was time for hugs and kisses all round.

Even Benjamin, so often at odds with his sister, held her to him and kissed her cheek. "I shall miss you, Bella," he murmured.

She hugged him back. "I shall miss you too, annoying as you are."

Grace stifled a yawn. "I do believe, now that we have welcomed in the new year, that I should get to my bed."

Benedict rose at once and held out his arm to her. "Yes, let us do so." They bid their family goodnight and walked up the stairs together to the room which they were to share tonight.

"Did you have fun?" enquired Benedict.

"I did, especially seeing you, dear husband, getting quite inebriated."

"I am not so inebriated as to be unable to do this," he said, and swooped her into his arms.

She cried in alarmed surprise, then placed her arms around his neck for balance. "Ooh! Carrying me to my bedchamber. How dashing, Benedict."

He walked quickly to their room, for in truth the hoops and long skirt of her dress were making this process very awkward indeed. She obliged by turning the handle of the door, then they were in and he was dropping her on to the bed. With his courage spiked by wine and the revelations of the evening, he barked, "Undress wife, and make it quick!" As he spoke the words, he shrugged out of his dinner jacket and began to untie his neckcloth.

Grace tumbled out of bed and began to divest herself of her many layers of clothing while her husband watched her hungrily. When she pulled the chemise over her head, baring her beautiful breasts to his gaze, he paused in removing his drawers and simply stared. "Oh Grace, you are exquisite," he murmured huskily.

She smiled saucily, throwing the chemise to the floor and bending to remove her drawers. Soon, they were both naked. They stood awhile, caressing each other with their eyes. Then Benedict grunted, "Come here."

She ran to him, throwing her arms around his neck. With another show of manly strength, he lifted her once more, supporting her weight with two hands under her bottom as she wrapped her legs around him. He strode with her in his arms to the edge of the bed, depositing her on to her back. The height of the mattress was perfect for his needs, coming to just below the top of his thighs. "Spread your legs, Grace, and let me inside you," he growled.

She followed his instruction with alacrity, revelling in her husband's newfound dominance. He took hold of his engorged cock and rubbed it along her glistening slit. "Look at you, Grace. So perfect and ready for me." He tapped the tip of his cock to that little nub that gave her so much pleasure.

She reared up in desperate need. "Please, Benedict."

"Please what?" he grunted.

"Make love to me!" she cried.

"With pleasure." In one thrust, he plunged all the way until he was fully sheathed inside her. She gasped at the delightful intrusion. He drove in again. Tonight, he was not gentle; his need was too great. Grunting with the exertion, he plunged into her repeatedly until he groaned, "Oh Lord!" and collapsed on the bed above her.

It took a minute, maybe two, for the both of them to regain their breath. Grace held him tight to her, not wanting to let him go. As before, she had not derived the same enjoyment as he did from the act, but the feel of their two bodies joined was infinitely precious, and she was loath to have him withdraw. Seeing Benedict's unbridled passion just now had been a revelation. He had been so firm, so dominant, so authoritative. She shivered at the memory and closed her eyes, inhaling his scent.

Eventually, Benedict bethought to raise himself back to standing and withdraw from her silky depths. A stream of his ejaculate oozed out of her cunt, and he watched it in fascination for a moment before he bestirred himself to get a cloth. With the gentlest of hands, he cleaned her up. As he finished, something made him bend his head and reverently kiss her perfect cunt. She quivered at the touch of his lips. Then, throwing the cloth to the floor, he climbed on to the bed and reached under him for the covers, tucking them around himself and Grace. With one last effort, he extinguished the lamp on the bedside table and drew his wife to him. They slept, bodies entwined, not bothering to put their nightclothes on.

BENEDICT AWOKE THE next morning with a pounding head. Oh the perils of overindulging in alcohol! As gently as he could, he dislodged himself from Grace's embrace and made his way to the jug of water, pouring some into a nearby glass and taking a long, parched drink. Seeing that Grace slept on soundly, he went to the adjoining dressing room where he made use of the commode, washed and dressed in fresh clothes. Then, very quietly, he stole out of the room and left his wife to her slumber.

Down in the dining room, he met up with the older Stantons and some of their offspring, looking decidedly the worse for wear. Jasper observed him critically upon entering. "And we have another one," he remarked sardonically. "You had best pour him some of your reviving herbal tea, my dear," he said to his wife who sat beside him.

Ruth did so, handing Benedict the tea with the admonition, "Drink this. It will help with your headache."

He took it with a grateful smile. "Thank you, Mrs Stanton. I have not imbibed quite so much wine since my university days. I thought I had learned my lesson then on the harmful ill-effects of overindulgence, but it seems not."

"It is our corrupting influence on you, Benedict," remarked Daniel cynically.

"Perhaps, but I shall not assign blame on anyone but myself."

"Where is Grace?" enquired Jasper.

"She was sleeping so soundly I did not have the heart to wake her," responded Benedict.

Ruth stood. "Seeing as I am done with breakfast, I will go to her."

Benedict recalled the state of the room he had just left, with their clothes strewn all over the floor from last night and Grace naked under the bedcovers. For a moment, he felt compelled to stop Ruth, but could think of no decent excuse to waylay her. Then, he shrugged internally, saying to himself, *In for a penny, in for a pound.* He drank the herbal tea, which tasted vile but did help to revive him enough that he enjoyed a good breakfast of sausages, eggs and toast.

During a lull in the general conversation, it occurred to him to broach the subject of Grace's horse breeding ambitions to her father and uncle. He cleared his throat. "Mr Stanton—"

"Oh, do call me Jasper, Benedict. No need to stand on ceremony."

"Jasper," said Benedict, "I have been meaning to discuss with you a matter concerning something Grace wishes to do at Mulverley Grange." Benedict went on to explain that Grace wished to breed horses, starting with a pairing between Butterscotch and one of the stallions from the Stanton Hall stable.

After a moment's consideration, Jasper responded, "This will require expert help to make it a viable proposition."

"Yes," agreed Benedict. "That is what I thought too. Perhaps you could help find a suitable groom and horse trainer to work at Mulverley Grange."

"I am sure we can," smiled Frank. "I will speak to the head groom today about it."

"It is a good idea," continued Jasper, "and there is suitable horseflesh here to consider a breeding programme." He frowned then, "However, I do not want Grace to be doing any riding while in her condition, so she will need to promise to be sensible about it before I endorse any project of this sort."

Daniel glanced up quickly. "In her condition? What do you mean?"

Frank spoke sternly to his son, "He does not mean anything by it, so let us move on. Jasper, you speak to Grace and I will look into finding a suitable person to work at the Mulverley Grange stable."

Daniel's eyes narrowed at this, but he said nothing more. Meanwhile, Ruth had made her way to her daughter's room, knocking on the door before entering. In one glance, she took in the discarded clothes all over the floor. Grace, who had just awoken, sat up in bed, pulling the covers to her chin. "Morning, Ma," she croaked.

"Good morning, my love." Ruth stooped to pick up the black gown and crinoline from the floor and place it on a chair. She bent again, this time retrieving a set of male drawers, looking at them critically before placing these, too, on the chair.

Grace coloured. "It was late when we came up last night, and Benedict was quite tipsy," she said by way of an excuse.

Ruth laughed. "You do not need to explain yourself to me! I well remember the early days of my marriage." She went to sit on the edge of the bed, eyeing her daughter. "How do you feel this morning?"

Grace yawned. "A little tired, but fine otherwise. I took your advice, Ma, and did not indulge in too much wine."

"I am glad to hear that you do take my advice sometimes!" responded Ruth with a little asperity. "And how are you getting on with your new husband? Is all well between the two of you?"

Grace nodded. "Benedict is so kind and thoughtful, but…" She paused, a little unsure of herself.

"What is it, Gracie? Speak."

Grace examined her coverlet with undue fascination. "I have grown to care for him, Ma, more than I thought I would."

"That is no bad thing, surely?"

"I suppose not, but what if he does not feel the same way?"

"Oh Grace," said Ruth in a rush of sympathy. "I am a firm believer in the old adage that love begets love. Do not be afraid to open your heart to a husband as good and kind as Benedict. I think he already cares greatly for you, and that affection can only deepen with time."

Grace nodded, then raised her chin to look at her mother with a hint of defiance. "That is not to say that I am in love with him."

Ruth smiled in understanding. "Of course not."

Grace sniffed. "Caring for someone is very far from love, the kind that would have a man build a house to win his woman."

Ruth laughed quietly and drew her daughter to her for an embrace. "It is not the same thing," she agreed, "but it is the first step towards it. In any case, give it time, as it is best not to force such a thing. Let it occur naturally."

CHAPTER 21

GRACE AND BENEDICT returned to Mulverley Grange later that afternoon, with a promise from her uncle Frank that a suitable groom would be sent over in the next few days together with the horses that were to be Grace's inheritance. Over the next few days, they settled into their new life together as man and wife, coming together each night to make love.

For Grace, the experience was bittersweet. Her inability to reach a climax during their lovemaking was a disappointment, and she missed the heady thrill she had experienced with her previous lovers. She was self-aware enough to realise it was the very illicit aspect of her trysts that had made them exciting. Being with Benedict was comforting and the very furthest thing from illicit.

That is not to say that making love with her husband was unpleasant or a chore. She enjoyed the feel and scent of him, and the intimacy of their joining. More so, she took great joy in making him happy, as was evident from his delighted expression at the end of their coupling. It was unlike her to be quite so selfless, but seeing the look of bliss on his face as he reached his climax had become one of her favourite things to behold. If she touched herself surreptitiously afterwards and quietly spent into her hand, then there was no harm in it surely.

As for Benedict, newly inducted into the pleasures of the flesh, their lovemaking was as satisfying to him as he dared to imagine. He delighted in seeing and touching his naked wife, and in joining their bodies together for that sacred conjugal act. He noticed once or twice that she did not seem to be as enraptured as him on conclusion of matters, but when he enquired, "Was that pleasing for you, my dear?" she always hastened to assure him that it was.

On further reflection, he ascribed her lesser enthusiasm to the delicate condition she was in. She still suffered from bouts of nausea at mealtimes and showed increased fatigue. It was only natural, therefore, that she would not obtain as much delight from the act of lovemaking as he did. The book he had ordered on midwifery had arrived in the post, and he read it with great interest. The good doctor that authored it suggested that married couples should refrain from excessive sexual relations during pregnancy. Perhaps he should not impose himself on Grace quite so often? However, when one night he suggested that he leave her to rest, she acted quite horrified and insisted he make love to her. So, Benedict was reassured that indeed she enjoyed the act, if not quite as much as he did. Nevertheless, he took care to be gentle with her at all times and not to re-enact the ungentlemanly roughness he had shown on New Year's Eve.

In the mornings, Benedict left Grace alone to fulfil his duties as curate. A fine stallion called Midnight had arrived at Mulverley Grange along with Butterscotch and two other carriage horses. On Midnight, Benedict rode each day to visit his parishioners in Stanton Harcourt. Grace occupied herself in his absence, spending time with the horses, reading and sketching. On the first Sunday after their marriage, they rode in the carriage together to church where Benedict was to lead the service. All eyes were on the new bride, with whispers everywhere about the haste of their marriage. Those whispers, however, were quickly shut down by the Earl of Stanton, who made it his business to tell all that Jasper had wanted to see his daughter settled with her husband in their new home before leaving for America.

It was at church that Grace came face to face with Mr Templeton for the first time since her marriage. He bowed over her hand and looked at her closely as he said, "I am surprised, Mrs Sedgwick, at the suddenness of your marriage, but do offer my heartiest congratulations."

Grace felt her cheeks heat a little at the subtle question in his tone. "Thank you, sir," she mumbled.

His eyes gleamed in his handsome face as he added, "And I also hear you are now settled in Mulverley Grange. I have the double pleasure, then, in welcoming you as my new neighbour. I am, of course, delighted, and look forward to furthering my acquaintance with you and your good husband in due course."

"Indeed," smiled Grace, recovering her composure. "I too was delighted to discover that our new neighbour was none other than yourself, Mr Templeton. We shall see you again sooner than you think, for Benedict and I plan to join the wassailing celebration in your orchards."

He laughed. "I am glad to see the good curate is broad-minded enough to take part in such pagan festivities."

"My husband is very wise," avowed Grace proudly.

Mr Templeton's eyes sharpened at this. "Yes, I quite see that. I look forward then, to seeing the both of you on the feast of Epiphany. Good day, Mrs Sedgwick."

"Good day."

From across the crowded church, Benedict witnessed this tête-à-tête with a frown. He could not tell what was being said, but he saw Templeton bend his head close to Grace and flash his flirtatious smile. He felt a mad urge to cut through the many people separating him from his wife and pull her away from that devastatingly handsome smile. But hemmed in by parishioners, many of them wanting to congratulate him on his marriage, he could not. All he could do was ball his fists in frustration and vow to himself that he would not let that man drive his wife astray.

Thus were the affairs set between Benedict and Grace when the day of the feast of Epiphany came upon them. As was proper, Benedict—and Grace with him—celebrated this feast with a special service in church. On their return home, they rested and had a light repast before getting ready to go out again to join in the wassailing. Benedict felt duty bound to try to dissuade his wife from going and encountering Mr Templeton.

"Are you sure you still want to go out tonight, my dear?" he asked solicitously. "You do look a trifle worn out."

But she would have none of it. "I am fine," she said with a smile, "and looking forward to seeing this pagan celebration."

Accordingly, at a quarter to six in the evening, Benedict and Grace set out, wrapped warmly in their coats, hats and scarves, to the Templeton orchard. They headed over to the boundary between their property and Mr Templeton's, then walked down the short avenue towards the main house, from whence was a forked path that led to the apple orchard. Before even reaching the orchard, they saw from afar the sparkle of a large bonfire, which helped guide them to their destination.

On arrival there, they were greeted by a cheery Mr Brigham, his round-faced wife beaming by his side. "Well good evening, Mr and Mrs Sedgwick," he called out, "and welcome to our wassailing feast. I can tell you, the village folk are most eager to make your acquaintance, including Mrs Brigham here."

"Indeed," smiled Mrs Brigham. "I am very glad to meet you."

"How do you do?" murmured Grace politely, feeling shy and out of her element. Benedict was a little more easy in his greeting.

"Now," said Mrs Brigham, "before you go around introducing yourselves to everyone here, you must have a drink of the wassail. There is a large pot of it keeping warm over the fire. See over there where Mr Templeton is standing? Do please have yourselves a steaming brew—it is made to a recipe that dates back to Anglo-Saxon times."

"Thank you, Mrs Brigham," said Benedict. "We will be sure to try it out."

They walked as directed towards the bonfire, smiling at various people and saying their hellos upon the way. On catching sight of them, Mr Templeton hurried over. "Mr and Mrs Sedgwick, how good to see you! Will you have a drink of the wassail?"

"What is in it?" asked Grace curiously.

"Well, I don't know the exact contents, for it is a closely guarded secret of Mrs Brigham's, but it is chiefly composed of cider, sugar, spices and apples. Do try it. You will find it warming on this cold night."

"Thank you, I will," said Grace, "but do only give me a little."

"How about you, Mr Sedgwick?" asked Mr Templeton.

"I shall have some too, if I may."

"Of course you may!" Mr Templeton procured two large tankards and poured a measure of the steaming drink into each, then handed them over to Benedict and Grace. He then held out his own tankard to them and said, "To your good health!"

They toasted him with their tankards in return, then Grace took a careful sip of her drink. It was indeed very warming, especially the quantities of ginger which she detected in the drink, but not at all nausea-inducing. Over the next half-hour, she and Benedict were introduced to countless people that she lost sight of their names. There was the doctor, a Mr Benson, then a minor squire called Mr Johnson, and his shrewish looking wife. They greeted the village baker, who promised to send them a fresh batch of hot-cross buns on the morrow, and a whole host of other locals.

Their socialising was cut short by a loud clang. "Aha," said Mr Templeton. "It is time to make a hullaballoo. After all, the purpose of this festival is to ward off the evil spirits and rouse the good spirits of the fruit trees to supplicate them for a good harvest next season. Do help yourselves to some pots and pans from the table over there, and walk along the trees, clanging them together." He grinned. "Be as loud as you can!"

Benedict took Grace's arm. "Shall we, my dear?"

"Oh yes, let us do so."

They went and armed themselves each with a small pot and a shallow pan. All around them was noise, as the assembled folk began their hullaballoo. With a merry laugh, Benedict and Grace joined in the procession around the trees of the orchard, clanging along, and then stopping to sing some carols. It was all very jolly and fun. Grace was glad to have made the effort to come. After the carol singing was over, there was another round of drinking from the wassail cup and more friendly chit-chat. Somehow, she got separated from Benedict as various people monopolised his attention. She stood apart from him, sipping from her drink, and nodding politely to those around her.

"Ah, here you are." It was Mr Templeton. She welcomed his arrival, for she was finding it difficult to maintain a conversation with these good people whom she had only just met. "Come along, Mrs Sedgwick, and let us have a little gossip you and I." He winked at Mrs Johnson and whisked Grace away from those gathered around her. She took his proffered arm and walked with him a little way.

"Well, Grace, and how did you enjoy the wassailing?" asked Mr Templeton.

"It was rather jolly I thought."

"Yes, it is that." He paused. "Now that I have you to myself, let us make use of the time to talk freely. Tell me, Grace, what is the real story behind your rushed marriage. I hope it is not due to anything I did on the night of the Christmas ball."

"No, rest assured it is nothing to do with that." She did not know whether it was wise to confide the truth to him.

"So why the hasty marriage?" he prompted.

She hesitated. "I should not be telling you this, Mr Templeton."

"Have we not established that in private, you should call me Philip? And I assure you, I can be discreet. Tell me, what is it?"

"Philip, I-I found I am with child."

"Ah… The father?"

"It is not Benedict, but someone I met on the ship coming here from America."

"I see. And Mr Sedgwick gallantly stepped in to save the day, is that it?"

Grace nodded, looking down at the ground. "Yes, he has been absolutely tremendous."

Philip Templeton laughed sarcastically. "And got himself a wealthy wife in the bargain, lucky fellow."

Grace looked up then, fire in her eyes. "Do not, I beg, speak ill of Benedict. I will not allow it, for I do believe he would have married me with or without my wealth. He is the very best of men, and it is I should count myself the lucky one!"

A little taken aback, Philip said in a rueful voice, "I would not dare when he has such an able defender of his virtue as you, Grace. I see you are already well disposed towards your husband, and I wish you well in your marriage."

"Thank you."

He scrutinised her curiously. "It never occurred to you to come to me for help?"

"No, I fear not. If you will pardon my saying so, Philip, you made it clear you were only interested in a fun romp and that your intentions were entirely dishonourable."

"That I did," he laughed, despite himself. "I am sorry you did not feel you could talk to me about your troubles, but perhaps you are right. I am a confirmed bachelor, and I do not think I could have done what Mr Sedgwick did and offered you marriage."

"You might have had an easier time of it, for with your own wealth, you could not have been accused of being a fortune hunter. Poor Benedict had quite a difficult time facing the inquisition from my father."

"I can well imagine," chuckled Philip.

"And yet he was so brave. He even tried to save my shame—for the father of this child is a married man—by claiming the child was his. Such a sweet gesture it was."

"Indeed." Philip smiled indulgently. "In any case, it seems to have all worked out well. Please know though, Grace, that you have a friend in me whenever you need one."

"Thank you, Philip. That is good to know." She looked up at him gratefully as he lowered his head to kiss her brow.

"Grace!" A hard, cold voice had them jumping apart. Benedict stood a few feet from them, a forbidding expression on his face. "It is time for us to get back home," he said in a clipped voice. "Please make your farewells."

Heart sinking at her husband's demeanour, she quickly murmured, "Good evening, Mr Templeton."

He bowed. "Good evening, Mrs Sedgwick, Mr Sedgwick."

Benedict nodded curtly and offered Grace his arm. Together, they walked stiffly away, saying the necessary farewells before they could make their escape. Once alone, traversing the parkland that led to their home, Grace finally spoke. "Benedict, it is not what you think. Truly."

"And what is it I think, Grace?" His voice dripped ice.

"You think perhaps I was having some kind of flirtation with Mr Templeton. And I suppose, given what you saw on the night of the Christmas ball, you might have probable cause for your suspicions. But I do assure you it was nothing of the sort, merely a conversation between friends."

"And for this conversation between friends, he needed to draw you apart from everyone else and to kiss you?"

"He wanted to ask about our marriage, for he was curious. And of course for us to speak freely, we needed privacy. As for the kiss, it was nothing but a friendly peck, nothing like the one we shared at the ball."

"Do not remind me of it!" exclaimed Benedict sharply.

"I only wished to compare it with the simple innocent kiss he gave me tonight. Truly, Benedict, it was nothing."

His voice was still frigid as he said, "You will oblige me, madam, by refraining from such kisses in future, platonic or otherwise, and by ensuring you are never alone in that gentleman's company."

Now it was Grace's turn to get angry. "Why, Benedict? Do you not trust your wife? Is it that you think I would be so lacking in honour as to be unfaithful?"

"Only you can answer that question, Grace."

She stopped and faced him with stormy eyes. "Well I am telling you now, categorically and without doubt, that I am a person of my word. I made a vow to you, and I mean to keep it. Do you think, just because I had relations with men before you that I am somehow unworthy of your trust? Do you?"

He stared at her for a long moment, then sighed. "No, Grace, I do not. I am sorry to have doubted you."

"And so you should be!" Grace was not ready yet to let go of her anger.

"See it from my point of view. What was I to think when I saw the both of you walk alone to a sheltered spot behind the trees? And then as I approached, I saw him smile tenderly at you and kiss you. And all this after I had on a previous occasion caught the two of you in an embrace. Do you not realise how that would look to me?"

Grace took a step closer to him and placed her hands flat on his chest. "I suppose so," she said grumpily, "but you should know me by now, Benedict, know the person I am."

"I do," he replied huskily. "Forgive my moment of doubt, please."

"If you will forgive my carelessness tonight."

He placed his arms around her waist and drew her to him. "Done." He paused a moment, then said, "Do you know, Grace, that when I asked your father for your hand in marriage, he demanded to know why I wished to marry you, and I told him there beats within you a heart so generous and loyal that I would consider it the greatest privilege to be the one to share a life with you. You are loyal to your very backbone, Grace. I should have known better than to doubt you."

She trembled in his embrace, shaken by this admission. Benedict did not see her simply as a beautiful, wild vixen. He saw beyond the surface appearances to what she was truly at her core. It made her heart catch painfully in her chest. Looking up into his meltingly kind brown eyes, she asked, "Had I been truly doing what you suspected, would it have mattered so much to you?"

"Of course it would have."

"Because of your pride, or something else?" she wanted to know.

"Do I have to spell it out for you, Grace?"

"I think perhaps you do."

He let out a long breath. "Grace, you have my heart. Please, do not trample on it."

"Never!" she vowed and brought her lips to his. He tightened his embrace and deepened the kiss, urging her to part her lips and let him in. With a soft moan, she did, feeling the rough possession of his tongue as he kissed her over and over with a hunger only matched by her own.

"Grace!" he chanted in between kisses. "Oh Grace."

She ran her fingers in the soft strands of his hair, pulling him closer, wanting more. When next they broke apart to catch their breath, she gazed at him pleadingly. "Benedict!"

He understood, for his need was as great. "I cannot wait until we are back home," he gritted. "I need you now, Grace."

She looked beyond him to a clump of tall oak trees. He followed her look. "Yes," he breathed. He led her quickly to the shelter of the trees. With hands that shook, he pulled off his coat and draped it on the mossy ground. She followed suit, dropping her coat next to his. Then he undid his trousers and let them drop, taking his swollen cock out of his drawers. Quickly, with equally shaky hands, she undid the crinoline and discarded the inconvenient hooped garment. She pulled down her own undergarments and lifted her skirt, offering herself to him.

"Lie down on top of the coats," he ordered thickly.

She arranged herself on the ground and drew her legs as far apart as the undergarments down her ankle would let her. He threw himself on top of her and guided his cock into the moist recesses of her cunt. They both moaned as he slid all the way home. "Oh Grace," he cried.

"Give it to me hard," she panted in response. "Do not be gentle!"

"I do not think I can be," he grunted as he speared her with his thrust. Leaning on elbows to either side of her, he began to pound into her body as if his life depended on it. Each plunge of his hard cock sent quivers of voluptuous sensation deep in her centre. She dug her fingers into the firmness of his buttocks, pressing him to her, urging him on.

"Grace!" Benedict cried again, devoid of reason, stripped back to his most elemental self, a man possessed with the need to impale his woman. He drove into her again and again, his eyes fixed on hers. He saw the moment they fluttered closed, followed by an expression of bliss on her face. In that same instant, he felt her tighten around his cock in a pulsing motion, and that was all it took for him to go over the edge. With a roar, he thrust repeatedly into her, emptying his seed deep into her womb. Then, exhausted, he collapsed atop her.

They stayed like this, intimately joined, for endless seconds until finally, he raised himself on his elbows to look apologetically down at her. "Oh, Grace. See what you do to me?"

"I like it. Did you not feel my pleasure just now?"

He smiled wonderingly. "I saw it on your face, and I think I also felt it down below." He frowned then as something occurred to him. "Does that mean that ordinarily when we make love, you do not get to experience such joy?"

"No," she said softly. "It is very pleasant, but it does not send me into ecstasy. And often, Benedict, you finish before I have the chance to get to that state."

He withdrew from her slowly and used his handkerchief to clean her up as best he could. As he did so, he murmured, "Why did you not tell me?"

"I did not wish to hurt your feelings."

He looked into her eyes then, pained. "It hurts me infinitely more to know you have kept this from me." He stood, pulling his undergarments and trousers back up. Grace too got to her feet and began to get her clothes back in order. Benedict picked up her coat and wiped it as clean as he could before handing it to her. "I am sorry, Grace," he said finally. "Quite clearly, I have not paid enough care as to your feelings when we make love. My only defence is that I have little in the way of experience. It is only natural that it will take time for me to learn how to do it well. But I can only do so if you to tell me when I do things that are not quite right."

She tucked the coat closely around her, for now that the throes of their passion was over, she could feel the biting cold. "I am sorry, too," she said, lips trembling. "I wish now that I had. It is just that, you seemed so happy with our lovemaking that I found it difficult to tell you that it was not so much the case for me."

Seeing her shiver, he drew her to him, rubbing his hands along her back. "I will try to get better at it if you will be patient with me," he said earnestly.

She tucked her face into the warmth of his neck and murmured, "I believe you already are, judging by your performance just now."

He pulled back a little to look into her eyes. "You like it when I am rough with you?"

"Well, I would not want it so rough as to hurt, but I like it when I see you stripped of your control. It makes me feel infinitely desirable."

He stroked her cheek gently. "You are, Gracie. There are no words to describe how much I desire you." He dropped a kiss on her lips. "Come, let us be getting back."

She slipped her arm in his, and they resumed their walk home. Benedict became lost in thought as they walked, his shortcomings as a lover at the forefront of his mind. How could he remedy the situation? There were no books, so far as he knew, that could instruct him in the matter. He could not think of a single person he could speak to about this. Ambrose perhaps? He discarded the idea. Certainly he could not approach Grace's father or uncle about this. He would have to muddle along somehow, paying more attention to Grace as they made love and trying to learn the ways to please her.

On arriving at Mulverley Grange, they retired to their bedchambers, undressing and washing in their separate dressing rooms, Grace availing herself of the bidet to rinse her nether regions clean before donning her nightclothes. By mutual consent, they were spending all their nights in Benedict's room, so she joined him there shortly thereafter, climbing into the bed and wrapping herself around his body for warmth. "I do not know how I managed all these years in bed all by myself," she whispered. "I am quite sure I could not go back to sleeping alone now that I have you to keep me warm at night, Benedict."

He laughed softly, holding her close. His feet rubbed against her cold ones. Dropping a kiss on the top of her head, he murmured, "I am quite sure I could not go back to sleeping alone either. I love the soft feel of your body, and the scent of you makes me believe I have died and gone to heaven."

She giggled. "It is the expensive Eau de Cologne my father got me for my eighteenth birthday."

"That and more, a scent that is elusively you. It makes me very happy."

She kissed his chest through the thin material of his nightshirt. "You make me happy too, Benedict. I am glad I married you."

His hold on her tightened. "Even though I do not please you in our lovemaking?"

She rubbed little circles with her fingers along his hard chest. "You have pleased me—tonight in the woods—only at other times, you leave me wanting more. I like it when you are inside me, and I feel as if I am about to reach a very pleasurable place, but somehow, I do not get there. And then it is all over."

He mulled this new information, then came to a decision. "Gracie, I am going to make it my mission to ensure you do get there. Give me time, and I will learn all the ways to please you."

She smiled teasingly. "Will you read books about it as you have for my pregnancy?"

He sighed. "If only there were books to inform husbands and wives of such matters. If there are any, I will be sure to read them, but I suspect I shall have to be a little more creative in my research. Never fear though. I promise to be the most assiduous of students when it comes to learning about pleasing my wife."

She yawned. "I have every faith in you, husband mine." Already half asleep, she slurred. "G'night."

"Goodnight, darling." He kissed the top of her head. Soon, she drifted off to sleep while Benedict lay beside her, thinking. He knew there was very little he would not do to ensure Grace's happiness. He loved her that much. And the longer he thought, the more obvious his next course of action became. He did not want to do it of course, but for her, he would.

CHAPTER 22

WHEN GRACE AWOKE the next morning, she was alone in the bed, the indented space on the pillow beside hers cold to the touch. Benedict must have gotten up quite some time ago. She rose from the bed, made her ablutions and dressed, then went down to the dining room for breakfast. En route there, she encountered Winford.

"Good morning, madam," he said in his correct voice.

"Good morning, Winford. Have you seen Mr Sedgwick?"

"Yes, madam," replied the butler. "He breakfasted early and went on his parish duties."

"Oh." A sense of disappointment filled her. This meant she might not see Benedict until late in the afternoon. The nature of his work made it unpredictable. She knew he liked to make his visits to parishioners in the morning, then spend time going over administrative duties in the church, where he had a small office. If there was someone sick or dying, however, he could be called out again and be late returning. She smiled at Winford. "Well, I suppose I shall have my breakfast alone."

"Will it be tea and toast, madam, or shall you be requiring something more?" asked Winford.

"Tea and toast will be fine thank you, Winford."

Grace went to sit at the table. On the salver, she saw a letter addressed to her in her mother's writing. She opened it and read.

Dear Grace,

I hope this finds you well. The news from here is that we have now fixed our date of departure, which will be on the 10th January, five days from now. Your uncle and father are greatly worried about what is happening in America, with the tensions running high after the secession of South Carolina from the union. They are keen, therefore, to return to our property as soon as it is possible. As you may imagine, they are working busily to finalise arrangements both for our travel and for matters relating to your grandfather's affairs. However, I know your father will wish to come visit you in your new home before we leave, as do I. We hope to come dine with you at Mulverley Grange the day after tomorrow, and I also hope you will come stay at Stanton Hall on the eve of the 10th to see us off the following day. I dread the thought of leaving you, dear child, but we must endure and be strong.

Your loving mama,

Ruth Stanton

Grace put the letter down, her heart sinking. She had known of course that this day was coming, but she had not thought it would come so soon. How was she to go on without her ma, pa, brother and sister? Never before had she been separated from them. She tried to console herself with the thought she would not be alone. She had Benedict and her cousins that remained at Stanton Hall. It would have to be enough.

She placed a hand to her still flat belly. When this baby came, her ma would not be on hand to celebrate the birth and guide her through the early days of motherhood. She would have to rely upon herself. All of a sudden, her eighteen years felt very young indeed. The glimmer of tears shone in her eyes, but with a concerted effort, she held them back. She would not cry.

After finishing her breakfast, she went to see Mrs Hawkins to discuss the forthcoming visit of her family. The housekeeper suggested a menu of artichoke soup and poached salmon to start with, followed by roast pheasant with vegetables, and to finish, a steamed ginger pudding with a vanilla custard, all of which Grace agreed to. Then, to assuage her bout of loneliness, she put on her coat and boots, and went to visit the horses in the stable. She greeted the new groom, John Saunders, then went over to see Butterscotch. "How is my sweet darling?" she crooned. From her pocket, she took out a carrot, which she offered to her mare. Butterscotch took the offering with a soft neigh.

John Saunders spoke from behind her. He was a sturdy young man in his mid-twenties, who had come highly recommended from Stanton Hall's stable. "She's a bit frisky, madam—doesn't like it when Midnight goes out with the master. Acts like she's missing her mate, like."

Grace stroked Butterscotch's silky coat, feeling empathy with her horse. *I too am missing my mate,* she thought wistfully. She missed Benedict terribly when he was gone during the day and was always glad to see him when he came home. However, she wouldn't read too much into it. It could simply be due to her loneliness in that great big house, accustomed as she was to having family around her. Then she thought back to what he had said last night. *You have my heart.* The confession had made her own heart clench. Again though, it was much too soon to surmise anything from this other than that she did care for her husband greatly.

Aloud, she said, "That's good, although I do feel sorry for poor Butterscotch being left behind. But it must mean they are likely to breed if we put them together. When do you think we can try?"

"Butterscotch is not yet in heat, but I will keep a look out for signs that she is. In the meantime, I am increasing the grain in Midnight's feed to build him up for this. Perhaps in a few weeks, we can be ready to give it a try."

Grace nodded. "Good."

With a doff of his cap, John went to resume his chores. Grace leaned closer to Butterscotch and whispered into her ear, "Then we can both have our babies, you and I. What do you think, sweetie? A sweet little foal for you and a lusty little boy for me." Butterscotch snuffled as if in agreement. With a smile, Grace patted her a few more times, then left to return to the house.

While Grace was visiting her horse, Benedict was also making a visit, though a much less enjoyable one. He sat in Mr Templeton's main parlour after having been shown in by the butler, and awaited that gentleman's arrival. He had been here for a good twenty minutes; Mr Templeton obviously in no rush to grant this audience. Now, the parlour door opened, and that gentleman strode in.

"Mr Sedgwick." Mr Templeton stopped a few paces from him and eyed him coolly. "Need I get my sword or boxing gloves for this visit of yours today?" he enquired caustically.

Benedict frowned. "I am not a man of violence, Mr Templeton, and I take my ten commandments seriously."

"Well, that is a relief." Mr Templeton strolled to the chair opposite Benedict and sat, stretching out his legs in a comfortable pose. "So," he said, "seeing you are a man of the cloth, are you here then to preach me a sermon?"

"I do not think it would do much good if I did."

Mr Templeton chuckled. "I think you may be right. So perhaps you are here to warn me off from an indiscretion with your wife."

"Do I need to do so?" parried Benedict.

Philip Templeton regarded him in amusement. "I should make you aware, Mr Sedgwick, that I do not involve myself with married women—that is unless they and their husband are in full agreement to the liaison. I have too much respect for my wellbeing to ever want to run the gauntlet of a jealous husband."

Benedict smiled wryly. "I see your point, Mr Templeton, but I am not here for that. I have trust in my wife and do not need to warn off anyone, unless they present a danger to her person."

"Now I am curious. What could possibly be your objective in coming to see me today?"

Reminded of the purpose of his visit, Benedict felt a flurry of nerves overcome him. This conversation was not going to be an easy one for him. He looked down at his joined hands, wondering if he had made a mistake coming here today. Perhaps he could make his excuses and go—but that would leave him with his problem unresolved. With an effort, he raised his gaze to the gentleman sitting across from him. "I have come here today, Mr Templeton, to seek your advice."

"My advice? On what matter would that be?"

"Mr Templeton, you are a man of the world, I think, with a vast experience of relations with the fair sex."

Philip Templeton straightened in his chair and stared at him in puzzlement. "I suppose I am," he said.

"And I—well it will not come as any surprise for you to know that I am not."

Mr Templeton smiled faintly. "You have every demeanour of a virtuous man of the cloth, Mr Sedgwick."

There was a pause as Benedict gathered the courage to say his next words. He took in a deep breath and launched into speech, "So it is with regards to this disparity in our worldly experience that I come seeking your advice. Grace and I have had a difficulty which I am hoping you may help me resolve."

"You have my full attention, Mr Sedgwick. Speak freely what is on your mind."

Benedict blinked but did not look away. Instead, he continued on bravely, "It is to do with intimate matters in the bedroom. I came to this marriage with no prior knowledge of such matters, and I see now what an impediment this has proved to be."

Mr Templeton's eyes shone with humour. "I am in full agreement with you there, Mr Sedgwick, for I am a great believer in the advantages of such experience in the bedroom. But do enlighten me as to the nature of your difficulty. If you do not mind my asking, have you consummated the act of marriage?"

Benedict let out a long breath. "Yes, I have. That is not the issue."

"Well, that is a relief!" Mr Templeton put a hand to his chin and stared at him intently. "Tell me then about your problem."

"It has come to my attention," said Benedict with a touch of uncertainty, "that is Grace and I have spoken on this matter, and it seems she does not derive sufficient enjoyment from the act to… to reach that pinnacle of pleasure."

"Ah."

Another pregnant pause. Then, "I was hoping, Mr Templeton, that you could furnish me with advice on how I could help Grace to achieve this enjoyment." There, it was all out in the open, and Benedict sat back in his chair feeling the relief of a Greek athlete having just completed a marathon.

"Mr Sedgwick, I would of course be delighted to assist you, but I am not sure how to go about this." Mr Templeton thought a moment, then added, "There are so many reasons as to why a lady might not be achieving an orgasm, for that is the word you seek to describe that pinnacle of pleasure."

"What are the most common of these reasons?" asked Benedict, eager for any crumb of information.

"One problem, I'm afraid to say, is to do with the size of the man's sexual organ. If it is too small, then the man will fail to achieve the right depth of penetration to stimulate the woman sufficiently."

Benedict felt himself colour at this. "I do not believe this to be an issue for me. I-I am aware that my organ is of larger than average size."

"My, my but you intrigue me, Mr Sedgwick," said Philip Templeton on a purr.

Benedict thought of something else. "I should also add that on one occasion, Grace did achieve what you call an orgasm, but that time was due to a particular event."

"Now you have my curiosity piqued, Mr Sedgwick. Do tell."

"It was last night…" Benedict stopped, not sure he should go on.

"Oh do continue. What happened last night?"

Benedict could not look at Mr Templeton for this, so he fixed his gaze on the mantlepiece behind him. "I was displeased with Grace for slipping away from the crowd to have a private word with you. On our walk back home, we had words, call it our first argument. And the culmination of this was a kiss that excited us both so greatly that we sought the shelter of some trees and made love out in the open."

Mr Templeton burst out laughing. "Oh Mr Sedgwick, what a delight you are turning out to be! You had outdoor sexual congress? It does not seem as if you need any tutoring from me in the art of love."

"Well, but this was an exception. All other times, I have not managed to give Grace the enjoyment she deserves, and I most particularly want to."

"Ah," smiled Mr Templeton. "One must always remember that the act of lovemaking is not purely physical. It is also in the mind and the emotions. For example your little tryst in the woods yesterday. I am sure the risk of getting caught in flagrante, though small, must have acted as a stimulant to your senses, and of course the heightened emotions engendered from your jealous fight with your wife must have added to the stimulation."

"Yes, I see that," frowned Benedict, "but surely there must be a way for us to achieve this pleasure without having to fight constantly or make love in the outdoors."

"Of course there is," laughed Mr Templeton.

"Will you not tell me how?"

"I would not know where to start." Mr Templeton contemplated the matter in his head for several moments then stood. "Come with me, Mr Sedgwick. I have an idea."

"Where are we going?"

"I believe what you need is instruction from a lady rather than from myself, for only she can tell you about a woman's wants and desires. I am taking you to a particular acquaintance of mine with whom I have regular intimate relations—I do not like the term mistress, for that is not what she is."

Benedict stopped short. "Oh, I do not think this would be appropriate."

"On the contrary, it is the very thing you need, and I guarantee the lady's discretion. Come!"

A little uncertainly, Benedict followed in Mr Templeton's wake. In a few minutes, they were both astride their horses and riding down the avenue that led from his house to the village of Standlake. Just before they reached the village, they took a detour down a lane and stopped at a charming stone cottage with a thatched roof. As they dismounted, Benedict looked at it in even more confusion. "But that is the doctor's house," he said.

Mr Templeton smiled. "Indeed it is. We are come to visit Mrs Benson."

Benedict turned to face him in growing suspicion. "I thought you said, Mr Templeton, that you did not dally with married women."

"You forget that I added the caveat, unless the lady and her husband are in full agreement."

"Do you mean to say that Dr Benson knows about this and approves?" asked a very bewildered Benedict.

Mr Templeton grinned. "Not only does he approve, but he sometimes takes part in our playful encounters."

Benedict shuddered. "Mr Templeton, I cannot think what iniquity you are leading me into, but I must tell you now how uneasy it is making me. Do not forget I am a man of the cloth and that I try my utmost to follow the teachings of my faith."

"I have no plans to lead you astray," retorted Mr Templeton. "I am fully aware that the way I choose to conduct my own life is not in keeping with your moral standards, Mr Sedgwick. However, all I ask from yourself is an open mind and a willingness to learn from a lady who knows infinitely more about the pleasures of the flesh than I do. Remember, you are doing this for Grace, and I think in time, she will thank you for it."

The two men walked their horses to a nearby outbuilding and tethered them. As they did so, Benedict said uncertainly. "Very well, Mr Templeton. I am, reluctantly, putting my trust in you."

That gentleman smiled. "It is not misplaced, I promise."

Together, they made their way up the front path to the cottage, and Mr Templeton rang the bell. A few moments later, a young scullery maid opened it and let them in, promising to fetch Mrs Benson. They made themselves comfortable in a pleasingly furnished parlour decorated in a pale shade of green. The good lady did not keep them waiting long. To the rustling sound of her skirt swishing, she entered the room, a polite smile on her face. "Mr Templeton, Mr Sedgwick, good day. What may I do for you?"

"Rest easy, Amy, we are not here on official business, but as friends."

She regarded him doubtfully but with ingrained courtesy, invited them to sit and ordered some refreshments to be brought in. Once they were settled comfortably, she gazed at them with a look of enquiry.

Mr Templeton launched into an explanation. "Firstly, Amy, I want to assure you of Mr Sedgwick's complete discretion. He may be a clergyman, but he is not one to spread gossip. I know that for a fact, so please be at ease. The reason I have brought Mr Sedgwick here, is that he is newly married and encountering some difficulties in the marriage bed. He came to me for advice and it occurred to me that you would be better placed to mentor him in the arts of pleasing a woman."

"I see." Mrs Benson remained on her guard.

"It seems Mrs Sedgwick is not achieving her pleasure during lovemaking, and her husband is very keen to remedy the situation. I would add, at the risk of embarrassing him further, that until his marriage, he had no experience of the act itself, so he is very much in need of instruction."

Throughout this speech, Benedict's eyes stayed rooted to the floor. He could not think of any other situation in his life that was as acutely mortifying as this. Only the thought of Grace kept him from bolting for the door. Observing him now, Mrs Benson's stance relaxed as she enquired. "Is that true, Mr Sedgwick?"

Benedict had to perforce look up. "Yes," he replied. "I am afraid it is, and I am sorry to intrude on you in such a fashion. You may imagine my mortification at having to do this."

Mrs Benson's expression softened. "There is no need to feel any shame, Mr Sedgwick. On the contrary, I applaud you for taking the steps necessary to ensure your wife's felicity in the marriage bed."

Benedict looked at her imploringly. "I do so wish to know where I am going wrong. Grace says she finds it pleasant, but she does not reach that point of rapture that I do, and I can sense her disappointment."

Mr Templeton interjected, "And before you ask, Amy, Mr Sedgwick is sexually well endowed, so his size is not the problem."

Benedict felt his cheeks flush. Could this day get any more mortifying?

Mrs Benson thought about the matter, her brow furrowed in concentration. She was a woman past the age of thirty but not yet forty, still in the prime of life, with a full figure and fresh, rosy complexion. At last, she said, "There are any number of reasons why a lady does not achieve orgasm. Unlike the male, a female cannot easily achieve her pleasure through the act of penetration itself, though of course it is possible to do so if she is stimulated enough and the man penetrates her at a certain angle. But mostly, her pleasure will be derived from stimulation of a little nub at the apex of her sex called the clitoris."

Benedict nodded vigorously. "I have found this nub, and Grace enjoys when I stroke it with my fingers."

Mrs Benson smiled approvingly. "Well, then you are well on your way to success in the bedroom if you know your way to the clitoris. There are many things you can do to increase your wife's pleasure by stimulating that little nub. Of course, one great act of intimacy is for you to stimulate it with your tongue in a quick, fluttering motion."

She sat back and watched Benedict's reaction to this, a smile playing at the edges of her mouth. Benedict stared at her, mouth agape. It had never occurred to him to lick that nub or any part of the downstairs anatomy, though he remembered suddenly that time he had placed a kiss there, and how Grace had quivered in reaction. At the time, he had thought it was due to embarrassment, but could it be she had enjoyed his mouth there?

"I can see the wheels turning in your head," said Mr Templeton, sounding amused. "Yes, it is quite common for men to worship a woman's cunt with their mouth. The flavour of a lady down there is incomparable."

"It is one of Dr Benson's favourite things to do," affirmed his wife. "You may wish to lick and suck her there until she reaches her orgasm before the act of penetration takes place. Be prepared to take your time, so find yourself a comfortable position to do it. Place a pillow under her to lift her hips to a more manageable level. You may also increase her pleasure by inserting a finger into her cunt while you lick her."

Benedict was beginning to lose his embarrassment in the midst of all this fascinating new knowledge, which he was imprinting to his memory. "I see," he said.

"Perhaps," suggested Mr Templeton, "we should give Mr Sedgwick a little demonstration. What do you think, Amy?"

Her eyes glittered as she stared at her lover consideringly. She cast a glance at Benedict and nodded. "I think it may be the very thing." She stood then, and without a hint of shame, lifted her skirt to untie her crinoline hoop. Next, she slipped off her shoes and drawers, keeping her gaze on Mr Templeton. Once she was free of these garments, she strutted over to an armchair and settled herself on there, her skirt bunched up at the waist.

Benedict was speechless. He did not know where to look. Surely this was wrong! In embarrassment, he trailed his gaze to stare at a decorative moulding on the wall opposite.

"If you are to learn anything, you must look," barked Mr Templeton with a laugh.

Hesitatingly, Benedict brought his eyes to the spectacle before him. Mrs Benson had her legs open wide, showing a cunt that was surprisingly devoid of any hair. Benedict peered at it, perplexed. Mr Templeton, who had dropped to his knees on the floor, intercepted this look.

"Amy, I do believe Mr Sedgwick is wondering at the bareness of your cunt," he drawled in amusement.

"It is not a requirement," the lady replied, "only a personal preference of Mr Benson's. He finds it more pleasant to minister to me when there is no hair to get in his way."

"I—I see," stammered Benedict.

Having placed a cushion under his knees for extra comfort, Mr Templeton now said, "Watch and learn, Mr Sedgwick." With that, he bent his head and began to lick Mrs Benson.

Benedict could not believe what he was seeing. It was so extraordinary that he could not look away, despite the wrongness of it. To add to his discomfort, he felt a swelling in his groin. He could not help being aroused by the sight before him and the thought of doing this to Grace. So, he watched in fascination as Mr Templeton licked and sucked, as he fluttered his tongue over that nub—the clitoris—and as Mrs Benson writhed beneath him in obvious enjoyment.

After a time, Mr Templeton pulled away, only to stick a finger inside the lady's cunt. "See what I am doing?" he asked conversationally. "With my finger pointing upwards, I am searching for an area that feels spongy to the touch." Mrs Benson gasped. "And there, I have found it," Mr Templeton said in satisfaction. "Now I will resume my licking while at the same time stimulating this pleasure point inside Mrs Benson." He bent his head and demonstrated.

Mrs Benson's moans grew louder and louder. Benedict watched her fingers clutch at Mr Templeton's head, urging him on. "Oh yes there, darling!" she cried. A moment later, she gave a long, drawn-out moan and fell back on the armchair, eyes closed, chest heaving.

Mr Templeton slowly withdrew his finger and lifted his face, which was smeared with Mrs Benson's pleasure juices. He wiped them away with the back of his hand. "And there you have it, Mr Sedgwick. A lesson in how to bring your lady to orgasm with your tongue."

He looked across at Benedict and noticed the tenting in his trousers with a knowing smirk. He rose to his feet, his own arousal also in evidence. "Of course," continued Mr Templeton, "a female can return the favour by licking and sucking a man's cock. Mrs Benson is particularly gifted at this, are you not, my love?"

The lady, still resting languidly on the armchair, protested feebly. "Oh Philip, do stop."

"Well, but we must not neglect Mr Sedgwick's education." Mr Templeton turned to Benedict with a gleam in his eye. "There is one position which the French, bless them, call the 'soixante-neuf'—if you draw the number 69, you will get a sense for it—in which the male and female mutually lick each other's sexual parts by lying in opposition to each other. It is most enjoyable, and I heartily recommend it."

Benedict felt overwhelmed with all this new knowledge coming his way. He almost felt he should be sitting at a desk, with a pencil and paper, jotting it all down as if he were back in school—though a unique kind of school.

Now Mrs Benson sat up, drawing her skirt back down, and continued with her instruction. "Another important thing to take into consideration is your position while in the act of penetration. I gather when you make love to your wife, you do so by lying on top of her?"

"Yes, of course," responded Benedict.

"There is no of course about it. Think about changing your position so that she can derive greater pleasure. For example, let her sit astride you, or take her from behind while she is on her hands and knees. That position is useful for it allows you to reach her clitoris with your hand and stimulate it while you penetrate her." She sighed then. "There are so many different positions that I could not begin to describe them all to you today. Be creative, Mr Sedgwick, and try different ways to do the deed—perhaps also vary the location. A bed is not the only place for sexual congress. A chair can be equally useful, or the back of a door! Experiment all you like, but never let it become a chore. It should be an enjoyable activity for the both of you." She came to the end of her speech then, and it was clear the time for instruction was over.

Benedict stood. "Mrs Benson, I cannot begin to thank you for the advice you have given me."

She too, got to her feet. "You are most welcome, Mr Sedgwick, and I wish you and your wife luck in your endeavours." She paused, as if thinking of something new. "Oh, and one last thing, Mr Sedgwick. In the privacy of the bedroom, normal rules of social comportment can be discarded. Think of it as playing a role, like a villain in a dramatic play. Put on a show of dominant masculinity, be commanding as you never would in your ordinary life, and use crude, vulgar language. It will give a thrill to your lady to see you like this and can be very arousing. You may also find it liberating to shed that veneer of social respectability and become a more elemental version of yourself." She smiled knowingly.

Benedict nodded. "Thank you again, Mrs Benson. I shall bid you good day."

"Good day, Mr Sedgwick." She turned to Mr Templeton, a look of enquiry on her face. He understood at once and said, "Go on up, Amy, and I shall join you shortly. Let me just see Mr Sedgwick out."

With an inclination of her head, she left the room. Benedict frowned, regaining his senses after that shocking and unbearably arousing show he had witnessed. "I will have you know, Mr Templeton, that I am not at all comfortable with the ethics of what I saw you do just now and what you are about to engage in. What of Dr Benson?"

"And as I have told you, Dr Benson does not mind at all. He and his wife have an understanding in their marriage where they consort with others, both together and apart, as long as it is done discreetly. Our relationship is long-standing, although it has been many weeks since I paid Amy a visit. The arrangement works well for us, however, I know it does not accord with your moral viewpoint."

"No, indeed it does not, but I make it a point never to judge others if I can help it."

Mr Templeton nodded. "And for this, Mr Sedgwick, you have my wholehearted admiration."

Benedict started for the door. "Mr Templeton, despite my moral concerns, I thank you for your kindness today. I have learned much from you."

"Not at all. It is oddly pleasing to be inducting someone new into the pleasures of the flesh. I wish you the best of luck with Grace."

"Thank you. Good day, sir."

"Good day to you."

Benedict took his leave, as Mr Templeton hurried up the stairs to continue his tryst with the delightful Mrs Benson. With brisk strides, Benedict went to fetch his horse. He mounted it and began his ride to Stanton Harcourt, where he had several parishioners to visit. Throughout the journey, his mind played over and over again what he had seen today. It had been shocking and depraved, but instructional too. He did not regret going to seek Mr Templeton's advice, for in doing so, he had come far in accomplishing his mission—to learn how to please Grace. As he reached his destination and dismounted his horse, he determined one thing. He would put this new knowledge to the test with Grace at the earliest opportunity.

CHAPTER 23

WHEN BENEDICT RETURNED home later that afternoon, it was to find Grace cast into despondency at the news of her parents' forthcoming departure. There was no opportunity, therefore, to put his newly acquired knowledge into practice. That night, for the first time in their marriage, they did not make love. Instead, Grace nestled into his arms and he held her close to him as she drifted off to sleep.

Jasper and Ruth Stanton, accompanied by John and Beth, came to dine at Mulverley Grange the following evening, observing him keenly with their daughter. He understood their need to be assured of Grace's wellbeing before they left on their long journey, and he hoped that he was able to allay some of their fears. The meal served was excellent, and much praise was heaped on Grace, who demurred and insisted that it was really Mrs Hawkins and Cook who deserved the plaudits. Nevertheless, Grace was clearly proud to have acquitted herself well as a hostess in her own home for the first time. By extension, Benedict was proud too.

Their guests stayed overnight, as it was deemed too treacherous to ride back on the icy roads in the dark. Having other people sleeping on the same floor postponed yet again any plans Benedict may have had to re-enact what he had seen Mr Templeton do to Mrs Benson. When he finally got to worship Grace's cunt with his mouth, he planned to drive her to such ecstasy that she cried out loud. It would not do, therefore, to have the presence of others nearby, and particularly not her parents.

That night, he contented himself with something else which he hoped would still bring them both satisfaction. Once Grace joined him in bed, he wrapped his body around hers from behind, kissing the nape of her neck. "Darling wife," he whispered into her ear. "I am going to make love to you, but you need to be a good girl and promise to be quiet. After all, we do not want to disturb our guests."

"I promise," she hastened to reply.

"Good." He then began a long and leisurely exploration of her body with his hand, stroking all the dips and contours of her smooth skin until his fingers reached the soft curls at the apex of her legs. He wondered briefly what it would be like for this part of her body to be shorn of hair, then decided he liked it just as it was. Further down, his fingers went, touching the moist folds hidden beneath, searching for that special little nub. He knew he had found it when he felt her involuntary jolt. "You like it when I touch you there, don't you?" he asked softly.

"Yes," she breathed.

"How would you like it if I stroked you there while I fucked you with my cock?" Benedict felt very wicked speaking in such a coarse manner, but he saw the immediate effect his words had on Grace.

She trembled in his arms and breathed, "I think—I would like that very much."

With his fingers, he searched for her opening, then notched his cock to it. With infinite care, he slid himself inside. Once he was fully sheathed in her heat, he remained still, savouring the sensation of their joining. "Do you feel, dear wife, how we are one?"

"Yes."

"You are mine, Grace. Say it!"

Her breath caught at the vehemence of his words. "I am yours," she murmured obediently.

"Good girl." He brought his fingers back to her clitoris and began to caress that little nub.

"Oh Benedict, that feels good. Do not stop."

"I won't." He pulled his thick length back and plunged deep inside her again, all the while letting his fingers continue their work.

"Ah," she moaned.

"Shh, remember your promise to be quiet."

"Sorry." She turned her face into the pillow to muffle any more sounds.

Benedict now began to drive his cock into her in deep, slow strokes. He was determined to give her all the time she needed to reach her orgasm before he spent his seed inside her. He felt her thrash against the fingers working furiously at her core, and the surge of slick fluid that came from her the more aroused she became. Soon, his fingers were coated in her sticky juices. He longed to lick those fingers and get his first taste of her essence, but he dared not stop what he was doing. Instead, he whispered words of praise into her ear, telling her of his desire.

She whimpered, the walls of her cunt tightening around his shaft. He knew instinctively that she was close to her climax, and his thrusts picked up speed, his fingers on her nub becoming more urgent in their strokes. "That's it, Gracie," he coaxed. "You can do this. Oh darling, you take me so well."

And then he felt it—a pulsing on his shaft and on his fingers, followed by a long, muffled moan. All his self-control was at an end. In a frenzy, he pounded into her, seeking his own crescendo. With a barely repressed groan, he emptied himself into her, lost to sensation and to the powerful satisfaction of having pleasured his wife so thoroughly. Finally, he stilled inside her, nuzzling her neck. "Oh my Gracie," he whispered. "You were magnificent."

"And you, Benedict," she sighed happily.

Gently, he withdrew, feeling his spend ooze out of her. "Let me clean you up." He went quickly to fetch a cloth and soon had them both cleaned up. Then he gathered Grace to him and tucked the covers around them. "Goodnight, darling," he murmured.

"Goodnight, dear Benedict. I knew you would excel at your studies, as you always do."

"That is only the beginning. I promise there is more to come."

She yawned. "Good. I'm glad. Sweet dreams, dear."

Soon, he heard her deepened breaths, indicating she had fallen asleep. He took a moment to savour his little victory tonight before he too drifted off to sleep.

TWO DAYS LATER saw Benedict and Grace leave once again for an overnight stay at Stanton Hall. This time, the journey was melancholic, as they were on their way to bid goodbye to the Stantons that would be departing for America the following day. They left early, straight after breakfast, so as to allow Grace time to spend the day with her family. Benedict did not linger after the initial greetings, but set off to undertake his parish business. He would re-join them later in the day.

Due to Ruth's efficiency and organisation, there was not much left to do on this last day in the way of preparation for the forthcoming journey, so mother and daughter were able to spend valuable time together. As the day was dry and bright, they opted to go for a gentle promenade in the parkland surrounding the house. Slipping an arm through her daughter's, Ruth walked contentedly with her, not talking much at first but simply enjoying her presence.

At last, Ruth spoke, "It is going to be a wrench tomorrow, saying our goodbyes. Gracie darling, it seems almost like yesterday that I was holding you in my arms for the first time. How the years have flown." She sighed, then went on, "And now here you are, fully grown and married, and about to have a child of your own."

"There are times, Ma, where I do not feel at all grown up," said Grace, holding on to her mother's arm a little more tightly.

"I know, dear. It all feels a little overwhelming, but you are stronger than you think. Of course you will be tested, as we all are in life. Do not walk in fear though. I want you to keep your faith strong in the days ahead, and to ask for help from the people around you when you need it, for you are not alone. Benedict, I am sure, will be a tower of strength. I have observed him closely. Despite his diffident demeanour, that man has backbone and strong morals, but more than anything, a kindly heart. He cares for you greatly, Grace."

"Yes, Ma, I know. And I have come to care for him too." She was not yet ready to admit quite how much. Grace was quiet a moment, thinking about her husband, remembering how he was on their first meeting—flustered and shy. "It is odd, is it not?" she went on. "He is not at all the kind of man I ever expected to marry. I always thought I would be courted by a debonair man of the world."

Ruth chuckled. "Someone, perhaps, like Mr Templeton?"

"Yes, like him. You do know, Ma, that he is now our closest neighbour?"

"Well, that does not signify, for you are now married to Benedict." Ruth gave her daughter a stern look. "I hope you will not look to that gentleman and compare your husband unfavourably with him. You know the saying about the harvest always being richer in another man's field."

"Yes, Ma, I do know," Grace quirked her lips humorously and could not resist teasing a little, "One cannot deny though that he is very handsome and charming."

"I have found, on greater acquaintance, that Benedict is just as handsome in his own way," retorted Ruth. "And he has many charming qualities of his own."

Grace laughed. "Ma, you do not have to convince me of them. I assure you that I do appreciate my husband."

"See that you do and that your eyes are not turned by a handsome rogue that lives next door."

"Ma! Of course not." Grace knit her brows in annoyance. "I do wish people did not think of me as flighty."

"I do not think you flighty, only impetuous—and sometimes unable to see the wood for the trees. While you may have dreamed of a debonair man of the world, my dream for you was always that you find a good man who would truly love you."

Grace dropped a kiss to her mother's cheek. "I believe I have found such a man, Ma."

"I believe so too. Treasure him, Grace."

"I will."

Mother and daughter continued their walk, the conversation moving onto other matters. Upon their return to the house, they learned that Mr Ridley, the family lawyer, had but arrived in the previous hour and was closeted in the library with the earl and Jasper, having brought with him documents for them to approve and sign before their departure. Grace settled onto a comfortable settee in the drawing room with her mother and Beth for company, where they availed themselves of a tray of tea and biscuits. The brisk walk had tired Grace, and without realising it, she drifted off to sleep, her head nodding onto her mother's shoulder.

She was woken by John's entrance in the room and his call of her name. "Gracie, Pa wishes to speak with you. He is up in the library still with Mr Ridley."

Grace sat up straight and stifled a yawn. "I shall be up shortly," she said.

A few minutes later, she was knocking on the library door and entering. In the room were Mr Ridley, her uncle Frank, Daniel and her papa. Jasper smiled warmly at his daughter. "Gracie, do come and sit."

She went over to his side and settled herself down.

"So, Gracie," said Jasper taking her hand in his and raising it to his lips. "All the documents have been drawn up. Here are the new deeds to Mulverley Grange and to your lands. As you can see, they have been put into a special trust that is administered by myself and Mr Ridley. Should anything happen to me, Daniel will take over my position as trustee."

At these words, Grace threw her arms around her father. "Oh Pa, please do not talk of such things. I cannot bear to even think of it."

Jasper hugged his daughter, then pulled back and said, "It is just a precaution, Gracie, for I have no intention to snuff this world quite yet. Let me explain to you how this trust will work. All the income generated from your land will be paid into an account that we will administer on your behalf. Mr Ridley will ensure the servants and household expenses are paid from this account every month, and Mr Cranshaw will continue to oversee the management of the tenants on the estate, so there is nothing you need worry about. I have also arranged for you to be a paid a generous allowance of £5 a month for any personal expenditures you may have. If for any reason you require more than this, you may write to Mr Ridley or myself explaining your reasons, and we will disburse the funds. I hope you know we have done all this to protect you, Gracie. Much as I have come to like Benedict, I want to ensure that your money stays yours and that he does not touch a penny of it."

"Oh Pa, I do not think Benedict has any interest in taking my money."

"Nevertheless, I want to make sure all the legalities are watertight. If I am to live so far from you, then I need to have peace of mind about you and know that whatever happens, you will never lack for funds."

Grace kissed her father's cheek. "I know, Pa, and I am grateful for all you have done."

Jasper held out a finger. "One more thing, Gracie. I want your promise, here in front of these witnesses, that if ever you are in trouble, or in any way needing help, you will come straight here to Daniel. Consider Stanton Hall your second home, and in my absence, Daniel is here to look out for you. He has promised to keep me apprised of any matter that comes up concerning your wellbeing, though of course, it may take time for communications to reach me. Will you promise me this, please?"

"Oh Pa, you worry too much. You must know that I am in good hands with Benedict."

Jasper frowned. "I know nothing of the sort. People can show you one face today and another tomorrow. I hope my worries are for naught, but in the event of anything going wrong, I need your promise."

Grace heaved a long breath. "I promise, Pa, though truly, it is not necessary." She thought of something and laughed suddenly. "Ma spent most of our walk this morning telling me what a good man Benedict is and how much I should treasure him. And here you are telling me to be on my guard with him. I never expected to receive two such opposing pieces of advice from my parents!"

Daniel laughed out loud. "I think it is safe to say Uncle Jasper is being a trifle overprotective."

"Just so you know, Gracie," interjected Jasper, "I have no reason to believe Benedict is anything other than honourable, else I would not have sanctioned your marriage to him. Nevertheless, I do not want to leave any stone unturned when it comes to ensuring your protection."

"I know." Grace buried her face into her father's lapel, feeling her emotions rising to the surface. She was going to miss her pa.

Over her shoulder, she heard Daniel speak again. "In any case, Grace, I am here for you should you ever need my help. You have my word on this."

She looked up at him with glistening eyes and simply nodded. After a while, she composed herself enough to stand and smile. "Well, and now that is over with, perhaps we can adjourn for lunch."

Frank spoke then, "There are still one or two more things for us to discuss with Mr Ridley. Give us another half-hour, Gracie, and we shall come down for lunch. Would you let Siddons know?"

"Yes, of course. If you will excuse me." Grace left the men to their business and returned to the drawing room where the Stanton ladies were assembled.

It was there, that not ten minutes later, Benedict found her, having completed his parish visits. On sight of him, Grace felt her heart beat a little faster. Of late, she had been getting such a reaction when seeing him after he absented himself for the day. What this meant, she was not ready to think about just yet.

Benedict's eyes searched the room and brightened when they landed on her. He greeted everyone with his customary courtesy, but then came straight to her side. Taking a seat beside her on the settee, he enquired gently, "How goes it with you, my dear?"

A warmth suffused Grace's body, akin to the feeling of drinking a cup of hot chocolate on a cold day. She found his hand, lying on his lap, and upon her touch, he turned it palm up to enfold hers. Comforted, she sighed happily, "All goes well." Then, remembering the conversations of the day, she told him laughingly, "I have been adjured by Ma to appreciate your good qualities and by Pa to be on my guard and make sure you do not touch a penny of my wealth. Such conflicting advice! I am sure I do not know what to make of it."

Benedict smiled in amusement. "Follow both, I say. Do make sure you keep appreciating your husband, and do all you must to keep my greedy paws from your money."

She turned the hand in her grasp so it lay palm down and admired its lean perfection. Two pulsing veins ran down the smooth skin on the back of it, leading to long-tapered fingers, the nails neatly trimmed. Idly, she traced the path of each vein with her fingers. Leaning towards him, she whispered into his ear, "What if I want these greedy paws on something other than my money?" With secret delight, she saw a flush paint his face.

Their little tête-à-tête was interrupted by Beth, who sat on a chair opposite to them. In an earnest voice, she said, "Do not mind Pa, Benedict. He only wishes to protect Grace, as he does all of us."

Benedict replied cheerfully, "I do not mind at all, for if it were my daughter, I would probably do the same. I have never before, I must say, been cast in the role of a dangerous brigand, so I am enjoying my notoriety."

Ruth laughed. "Hardly that, Benedict. Jasper is simply falling prey to his protective fatherly instincts, but you must know we all hold you in high regard."

Benedict beamed his sweet smile. "I am glad, for I hold you all in equal regard."

A happy, fluttery feeling lodged itself inside Grace's breast, compounding that warmth she had felt earlier upon seeing Benedict. She had little time to reflect on it before Beth remarked, "It is strange, is it not, that even though we have known you not two months, you already feel like one of the family."

"Perhaps," agreed Benedict, "but I am glad you feel this way."

Grace considered this. "I think it is because Benedict was with us during those unhappy days leading to Grandpa's passing. He shared our time of grief, and that must have been instrumental in creating a familial bond."

Charlotte, who had been sitting reading quietly up to this moment, now chimed in, "You may be right, Grace. But I think it must also have been when he came to teach us to dance that we accepted him into the fold."

"You mean, when he saw what terrible dancers we were?" asked Isabella.

"Well, it made us seem less high and mighty, did it not?" replied her mother. "And I think we all saw Benedict in a new light when he proved to be such a graceful dancer."

"Yes," said Grace, tucking her chin into his shoulder. "I think that must have been the moment I began to take notice of you."

His eyes found hers, blazing with heat, but he spoke mildly enough, "Then I am forever indebted to my sisters who insisted I partner them in every dance."

In truth, Grace had noticed Benedict well before then. In a fit of honest self-reflection, she recalled their first meeting in the tavern, when she had looked into his kind face and seen his threadbare jacket, and concluded he needed a good woman's love and care—only of course, she had not realised then that she was the one destined for that role. But she had noticed him, and continued to do so. Why else was it that she had enjoyed teasing blushes out of him every time he came over for dinner? And why else had he been the first person she had sought help from in the matter of her pregnancy?

The conversation turned to other matters, but she paid it no heed, lost in her own reverie. As if sensing her inner cogitations, Benedict brought her hand to his lips for a kiss, then enfolded it in both of his. There it stayed until the Stanton males came down with Mr Ridley, their business concluded, and they all headed to the dining room for lunch.

The remainder of the day passed quickly, too quickly for Grace who tried to savour every last moment with her family. That night, she tossed and turned in bed, fretting about the morrow, until Benedict took her in his arms and made tender love to her. He cleaned her then carefully and held her close until finally, she slept.

And then came the time for goodbyes. The trunks were loaded onto carriages that would take the Stantons to Oxford, from where they would catch a train to London and then to Liverpool. The family assembled in the grand hallway for the final embraces. Grace hugged her mother tight, determined not to cry, but it was of no use. All faces present, even Benedict's, held the shimmer of tears. Eventually, needing to put an end to the protracted and emotional goodbyes, Frank signalled to Jasper that it was time to go. Without a word, Jasper nodded and helped herd the departing Stantons to their carriages. With a final wave, they were off.

Grace watched them depart, a tight knot forming in her chest. She felt Benedict come behind her and wrap his arms over her shoulders, letting her lean back against his body. He offered quiet comfort without pointless platitudes, for what could he say in this moment to ease her mind and heart? Beside her, Isabella sobbed into Daniel's arms. They were all having to face the difficult reality that their tightly-knit family was now split asunder.

CHAPTER 24

THE DAYS IMMEDIATELY following her family's return to America were very hard on Grace. Despite Benedict's solicitous care and the presence of her cousins not a mile away, Grace could not shake a profound sense of loss. It did not help matters that her nausea was at its worst, making it difficult to keep down most foods. In these wretched times, she wanted her ma to soothe and assure her that all would be right.

Succour arrived from an unexpected quarter in the form of Walter Sedgwick. Benedict's father came to stay with them one misty grey day towards the end of January. Grace was in the upstairs parlour when she heard the clatter of a carriage on the cobbled drive outside. She knew who it must be, for Benedict had left with the carriage not two hours ago to collect his father from Oxford train station.

Quickly, she stood, then regretted her haste as she felt a roll of queasiness in her stomach. She took several deep, steadying breaths. She would not retch. After a few moments, she was able to continue on her way downstairs. There, she followed the sound of voices to the sun room, where she found Benedict and an elderly gentleman sitting in animated conversation. Both stood on hearing her enter and Benedict made the introductions. "Father, this is Grace, my wife."

Grace held out her hands to Walter, her usual reserve with strangers overridden by her eagerness to get to know her father-in-law. "Mr Sedgwick, welcome. I am so glad to meet you."

Walter Sedgwick was taller than his son and slightly stooped, with snowy white hair and ruddy cheeks. He took her proffered hands in his and regarded her with kindly brown eyes that were very reminiscent of Benedict's. "You must call me Walter, and I too am so very glad to meet you and to welcome another daughter into the family. You cannot know how happy I was to hear that Benedict had married, though I would have wished to have been in attendance." That last remark was thrown at Benedict, who had the grace to look a little sheepish. "However, now that I see with my own eyes how lovely you are, I am sure I can understand Benedict's haste in wanting to marry."

"I am sorry you could not be there," apologised Grace, "but there was so very little time as my father wished to see me settled before the family returned to America."

He patted her hand in sympathy. "Of course, I do understand."

They sat once more and Grace enquired, "I am sure you must be in need of some refreshment after your long journey, Walter. I do hope it was not too arduous."

"Not at all. Benedict wrote to me with very clear instructions on which trains to take and where to connect. The whole journey, I am glad to say, took less than four hours to complete and was extremely comfortable. When I think how back in the days of my youth such a distance would have taken a full day's ride in a crowded stagecoach, I am full of wonder and thankful to have lived long enough to witness this progress."

"That does mean too, father," said Benedict, "that you will be able to visit us often, I hope. By the way, Gracie, I spoke to Winford on our way in and asked for a pot of tea and some light refreshment."

No sooner had Benedict spoken than the door opened and Winford stepped forward, bearing a tray which he placed on a table in front of Grace. He then bowed and made a discreet exit from the room.

Walter followed him with his eyes. "I must congratulate you both on your beautiful home and the excellence of your servants. I have only been here a few minutes and already feel well pampered."

"It is certainly the most luxury I have ever known," concurred Benedict, "though Grace and I both agree that the house is a little too grand and formal. We shall have to make it feel more home-like."

"Once it fills with children, I am sure it will," observed Walter. "By the by, Benedict told me the happy news on the way here. Congratulations, my dear."

Grace coloured, not yet used to her pregnancy being openly acknowledged—she had only been married a mere month after all. "Thank you," she murmured as she passed her husband and his father their tea, then handed out iced buns on a plate. They had been freshly baked by Cook upon Grace's request this morning. She was slowly learning the art of being mistress of her new home, and had conferred with Mrs Hawkins about a suitable menu for her father-in-law's first dinner with them, then thought to stop by and ask Cook to have the buns ready for the afternoon, when their guest was due to arrive.

She watched now, full of pride, as Walter took a first bite of his bun, a pleased expression on his face. "These are extremely good," he praised. "Please do pass on my felicitations to your excellent cook."

"Thank you, I will." Grace now served herself. The buns smelled delicious, and she was hungry. However, she had barely eaten half of her bun before the dreaded nausea assailed her again. She put her plate down hurriedly and took several deep long breaths to try to quell it.

"Gracie?" Benedict was by her side immediately, rubbing gentle circles along her back. He also took hold of the bowl, which he had instructed the servants to leave in each room for Grace, in case it was needed. "Here, darling," he said, placing it before her.

She smiled faintly. "I am alright, but I think perhaps I shall refrain from eating any more of this bun, delicious though it is."

He kissed the top of her head, then took the bowl away and placed it back on the side table.

Walter gazed at her with compassion. "I am sorry to see you indisposed, my dear. Have you tried drinking a ginger infusion? I know Anna, my late wife, found it very helpful in her pregnancies."

"No, I haven't," replied Grace. "Perhaps I should give it a try."

"I will make sure we have a good supply of ginger from here on," promised Benedict.

"You might also want to have a supply of wafer biscuits to hand," added his father. "They are light and easy on the digestion, and useful to nibble on throughout the day."

Benedict gave a self-derisive laugh. "In all my efforts to inform myself about women's pregnancy, I failed to remember to ask you about it, father, and now I see what a fount of knowledge you are."

"Well, I do know a thing or two, having fathered seven children. Ask away, and I shall be happy to help in any way I can."

"Benedict has been so keen to learn," said Grace with a touch of pride. "He has been reading all kinds of books about it."

Walter chuckled. "How very like Benedict."

CHAPTER 25

BY EARLY THE next morning, Benedict had ensured that a good supply of dried ginger had been procured, which had necessitated a ride to the village shop at first light. It had still not opened when Benedict arrived, though a few bangs on the knocker had brought down Mr Philips, the owner, who fortunately lived above the shop. After a few grumbles, Mr Philips had been persuaded to open up and serve Benedict the ginger he desired.

As soon as he returned to Mulverley Grange, Benedict had asked Cook to prepare it in a hot infusion. Now, he took it up to Grace himself and placed it by her bed. She woke on hearing the clink of the tray as he placed it on her bedside table. She sat up slowly, blinking awake.

"Good morning, darling," said Benedict. "I have brought you this freshly made ginger infusion. I hope it can help settle your stomach."

Grace made an indistinct sound in the back of her throat. Benedict was accustomed by now to his wife's incoherence first thing in the morning, so he only smiled encouragingly and held the drink out to her. She took it and sipped on it cautiously. After a while, she put the cup back on the saucer and smiled, "Thank you."

Benedict leaned over to place a gentle kiss on her lips. "I hope it helps. I shall go down now and leave you to dress in peace."

When Grace joined him and Walter for breakfast some minutes later, she was relieved to feel a slight lessening of her usual nausea and was even able to eat a respectable meal. "You do not know how grateful I am to the both of you," she said, as she put her cutlery down on her empty plate. "I feel much better this morning than I have in many a day."

"I am so glad it has helped," said Walter.

"Good," said Benedict as he came to stand behind her chair. He leaned down to kiss her cheek. "I had best be off now. You will have father to keep you company while I am gone, and I shall try not to be late coming back in any case."

Walter gave her a warm smile, "I hope to keep you reasonably entertained with stories of Benedict's past misdemeanours."

"Misdemeanours?" repeated Grace, intrigued.

"I am sure you will find out how I nearly set the house on fire doing an experiment with a magnifying glass when I was twelve," said Benedict.

"And there was also that time when you tried to make fulminating powder and caused an explosion that shattered your bedroom window," reminded his father.

"Ah yes, that," said Benedict with a nostalgic smile.

"You sound like you were a menace," mused Grace, "and here I thought I was the wild one."

"It was all to do with a book that I gifted him one Christmas," said Walter. "It was called 'The Young Man's Book of Amusement Containing the Most Interesting and Instructive Experiments', though in hindsight, I would change the title to the most destructive experiments."

"I became so calamitous that poor mama begged father to take the book away and have it burned," chuckled Benedict.

"And did you?" asked Grace.

"Well, I did confiscate it," replied Walter, "but I could not find it in me to burn any book, so it remains hidden away somewhere in the attic at home."

"And on that note, I had best be gone," smiled Benedict, and took his leave.

Grace spent a pleasant day and many more in Walter's company. He did indeed regale her with more incidents from Benedict's childhood, but he proved to be as great a listener as he was a storyteller. Through gentle prompting, he learned about her ma and pa, how they had met and emigrated to America, and the life they had built in Ohio.

"Your parents sound like very courageous people," remarked Walter.

"That they are. I do miss them so." They were out walking through the grounds of the house, taking advantage of a rare sunny and dry day, despite the temperature being near to freezing. Wrapped up in their woollens, they headed towards the lake, where they planned to rest in the small lake house before starting the journey back.

Walter gave Grace's arm a light squeeze. "It is quite understandable that you should miss them, but it will get easier in time. Also, do not forget that even though you may have a family lost to you through the distance of a vast ocean, you do still have your cousins here and a whole new family to get to know. I hope you will come visit my home in Leicestershire and meet Benedict's brother and sisters. They are all very eager to know you. You could also go for a visit to London, see all the marvellous sights and meet Emily. She is my youngest daughter and closest in age to Benedict."

"Do you know I was once quite jealous of Emily," said Grace with a smile.

"How so?" asked Walter in surprise.

"It was when Daniel and I went to fetch Benedict for Grandpa's last rites. There was a letter from her which was lying on the table. As Benedict went upstairs to get himself ready, I could not help but snoop and have a little read until Daniel put a stop to it. She'd written that she missed him and signed it 'Your loving, Emily'. It made me think Benedict had a sweetheart back home. I did not like that idea at all."

They had by now arrived at the lake house. It was a white semi-circular stone structure built in the neo-classical style with Ionic columns and large glass-paned arches that overlooked the picturesque lake. Withdrawing a key from her reticule, Grace unlocked the door. Inside consisted of one large space furnished simply with two pairs of comfortable chairs, each with their footstool, a low wooden table and a small sideboard along the back wall. Grace went to it and opened a drawer, from which she withdrew two blankets to help ward off the chill. She returned to Walter, who had settled himself on a chair, and placed one of the blankets over him.

"Thank you, my dear," he smiled.

Sitting on the sideboard was a glass jar filled with wafer biscuits, placed conveniently there at Benedict's instructions. She brought it over and deposited it on the table beside Walter, then got comfortable on the adjacent chair. They sat quietly for a while, admiring the view before them.

"This lake house is utterly delightful," murmured Walter. "I can imagine how pleasant it will be here in the spring and summer."

"Yes," agreed Grace. "I think I shall come here often later in the year when it is warm. With all the light coming through the windows, it will be a perfect place to sketch and paint."

"Indeed." Walter paused, then returned to their original conversation. "I must say, Grace, that your being jealous of Emily puts my mind somewhat at rest."

She turned to him, perplexed.

His eyes were warm with amusement. "It is not that I want you to be jealous of Emily, for she is a lovely girl and I think you will get along well with her. It is simply that I want to make sure of your feelings for Benedict. I need to know that you care about him as much as he cares for you. I have worried, you see, about this hasty marriage of yours."

"Oh, but I explained—"

"Grace," interrupted Walter, "I am well aware that your unborn child is the reason for the haste of your marriage."

Grace went quiet for a moment, then decided to brazen it out. "I do not know quite what you mean by that, Walter."

"Oh my dear," chided her father-in-law, "please do not take me for a fool. I am quite capable of doing the maths. Had this child been conceived after your marriage, then it would be four weeks old at most, but the nausea you are experiencing usually does not make itself felt until six or eight weeks into the pregnancy. At first, I told myself that could not be so, for I know my son and he is not the kind to get a girl into trouble that way. The only other possibility then, was that Benedict married you to give his name to another man's child. Is that not the truth?"

Grace stared at him in horror. Finally, she stammered, "W-Walter, you are mistaken."

"Am I? I do not believe so. You conceived this child with another man, and then Benedict gallantly stepped into the breach to save the day when that man, for whatever reason, did not do right by you."

Grace was struck dumb. She could no longer deny the truth, yet she was unable to contemplate the consequences to Walter knowing her secret.

Walter continued gently, "Benedict married you because he has quite obviously fallen in love with you, but you married him out of convenience, to give your unborn child a father."

Grace bowed her head. "It started off that way, but..." She looked up at him defiantly. "I did care for him! And my feelings have grown ever so much."

"I see."

"You are angry with me. You must be."

Walter sighed. "No, my dear, I am not. Your actions are quite understandable. However, I have worried about Benedict and what it will mean for him to be in a marriage with someone who does not reciprocate his feelings. He deserves so much more than that."

"Please set your worries at rest," Grace said in a low, nearly indistinct voice. "His feelings are reciprocated."

"Yes, I see that now." Walter reached across to the jar on the table and lifted the lid. "Have a wafer biscuit, Grace." He offered it to her as he spoke.

She took one and nibbled the edge. He helped himself to another then replaced the lid back on the jar. They ate their food in silence.

After a while, Grace could not help but ask, "How will you feel about this child when it is born? Will you want to know him or her?"

"But of course! Grace, look at me." When she turned to face him, she saw his expression was stern. In a steely voice, he stated, "The moment Benedict put a ring on your finger, this child became his, and I, by extension, became its grandfather. Of course I shall love my grandchild, regardless of the circumstances of its conception."

She heaved a long breath of relief. "And what about me, Walter? Can you care for me knowing as you do about my past?"

He reached out his hand to hers. "Oh, dear child, I already care for you a great deal." She placed her hand in his and he clasped it reassuringly. "You are not alone, Grace," he said softly. "You are surrounded by people who care for you."

She nodded, eyes brimming with tears. "Then I am fortunate indeed."

"Come, let us make our way back." He stood, and so did she. They took some time to tidy up the lake house before heading out and locking the door behind them.

They spoke little on the return journey to the house, each deep in thought. As they neared their destination, however, Walter ventured to say, "Grace, I generally propound complete honesty between husbands and wives, but I do not believe it is in Benedict's interest to know of our conversation today. It would only sting his pride and cause him to worry. As far as I am concerned, the matter is settled. You are family now, and the child you bear is my grandchild—and let no one say otherwise."

"Perhaps that might be best," said Grace uncertainly. They walked to the side entrance of the house and let themselves in, divesting themselves of their coats and hats in the boot room. As she placed her coat on the peg, Grace saw Benedict's coat hanging on another peg and realised her husband was home. Suddenly, she could not wait a moment longer to see him. Mumbling her excuses to Walter, she rushed inside to find him. In the hall, she encountered Winford and asked him the whereabouts of her husband.

"Mr Sedgwick requested hot water be brought up to the washroom, madam."

"Thank you, Winford."

She flew up the stairs and down the corridor to the washroom, opening the door without ceremony. Benedict looked up in surprise. He was just about to remove his robe and enter the steaming tub. In quick strides, she reached him and fell into his arms.

He held her tight, murmuring, "My, my, that is quite the welcome."

All at once, she knew she could not keep a secret from him, no matter how benign. She had to tell Benedict right away. So, she told him. "Benedict, your father knows about the baby, about it not being yours. But do not worry, he and I had a talk and he is fine about it now."

Benedict furrowed his brows. "What? How?"

Quickly, she explained. "The nausea in pregnancy usually sets in at six weeks, and we are married but four. He worked out the truth, but he is not angry about it."

"Are you sure?" Benedict looked doubtful. "I had best speak to him the first chance I get."

"Speak to him if you must, but be assured that all is fine, truly. In fact, he suggested I refrain from telling you because it would cause you to worry unnecessarily. However, I could not keep anything from you."

He smiled faintly. "I'm glad. There should not be any secrets between us. Perhaps it is my turn now to make a confession, about Mr Templeton."

She looked into his eyes curiously. "Now that, I want to know, but do not let this steaming bath get cold. Tell me as you bathe."

"Yes, I shall." Benedict shrugged out of his robe, setting it on the chair. The bright sunlight streaming in through the window threw his lean, strong body into sharp relief, reminding her of a painting she had once seen of Michelangelo's David. Grace's eyes flared as she took in every sculpted inch of his chest and sinewy arms, leading down to his male appendage which was pointing straight at her.

"Oh my," she breathed. "You are quite beautiful, Benedict."

He smiled bashfully as he stepped into the tub and lowered himself into the hot water with a happy sigh.

"Let me wash you, as you confess to me about Mr Templeton," said Grace. She dipped a washcloth in the water then rubbed it with a bar of soap that had been sitting in the dish nearby. Once it was nice and frothy, she began to stroke the cloth along his back. "So, Benedict. Speak."

He bent forward to give her better access to his back. "The day after that fight we had about him, I went to see him."

"You did?" She paused in surprise before continuing with her ministrations. "Did you go to warn him off?"

He laughed good naturedly. "No, Grace, nothing of the sort. I know you, my darling, and there is no need to do any such thing."

"Well, I am glad that you trust me. So why did you go see him?"

A flush crept up his neck. "It was a most difficult thing to do, but I went to ask his advice for how best to…"

"Oh please, do not stop now. Do tell me."

He hesitated a moment more, then blurted, "I wanted to find out how best to pleasure you during lovemaking."

She stared at him, dumbfounded. "You mean, you actually asked him about lovemaking? Benedict!"

"Did I not say it was a most difficult thing to do? But I could think of no one else I knew who would have the knowledge I needed, and I so badly wanted to make things right for you."

Emotion welled in her eyes. "Oh, Benedict. I do believe that is the sweetest thing you have ever done for me, on top of a long list of sweet things you have done." She ran the washcloth down his arm, then under his armpit, making him squirm. Then she went around the other side of the tub to minister to his other arm. After a while, curiosity got the better of her. "And what instruction did Mr Templeton give you?" she wondered out loud.

So, Benedict recounted the events of that day, culminating in their visit to Mrs Benson and the nature of her instruction. Grace listened in varying degrees of astonishment while she washed the rest of his body and hair, interrupting his speech every so often with exclamations of "No!" and "Surely not!" and then, "How interesting!"

When he came to the end of his tale, she regarded him proudly. "You were so brave to go to Mr Templeton and seek his advice. Benedict, we must try that out—what you saw him do to Mrs Benson."

Benedict stepped out of the tub and into the towel Grace held out to him. "I have every intention to," he said as she dried his body briskly.

"Nobody has ever kissed me down there except you, that time on New Year's Eve." Her gaze turned to the lone chair by the tub. She took the robe draped there and handed it to Benedict. "There is no time like the present. On that chair perhaps. What do you think?"

Benedict's eyes gleamed as he finished tying the robe's belt around his waist. "I think, darling, now that you know, it won't be possible for me to wait any longer. Get your undergarments off, then sit on that chair for me."

He had not finished speaking before she started taking off these garments and throwing them across the room. Flushed with success, she lifted her skirt to her waist and sat on the velvet padded chair, offering herself to him. Benedict observed her calmly, the only hint of his excitement given away by the rapid rise and fall of his chest. "Lift your left leg and place it over the tub," he said thickly.

She splayed herself out, as instructed.

With intent in every move, he took the towel, folded it and placed it on the floor by the chair. Then he dropped to his knees, situating himself as comfortably as he could on the towel. He looked his fill at the wondrous sight of his wife's beautiful cunt which was level with his eyes. Then, he could wait no longer. He dove in for his first taste.

Grace saw his face dive between her legs and an instant later, felt the touch of his tongue. She nearly jolted out of her seat at the novel sensation and could not help letting out a little screech. "Oh!"

Benedict looked up at her with molten brown eyes. "You taste incredible," he said simply, then brought his face down for another taste.

Second time around, she was more ready for it, but still, this intimate touch took her breath away. She panted as she looked down at his dark head licking her—there. Her hips arched towards him, as if begging for more, until he placed his hands firmly on her thighs, keeping her in place. She could only sit back then and accept this most singular and wonderful of caresses. When his tongue fluttered over her sensitive spot, she cried out, "Benedict!"

He looked up. "Shall I stop?" he asked.

"Don't you dare!"

"Good. I was not planning to." And he went back to work.

She sank her head back on the chair and closed her eyes, unable to focus on anything but the sweet sensation of Benedict's tongue as it licked and laved in quick, sensual strokes. Little moans escaped from her as she lost herself to all reason. Soon, she felt something enter her channel and realised it was his finger circling inside her. Now there was heady pleasure both from within and without. It was too much. She groaned.

In response, Benedict switched from licking to sucking. She cried out, uncaring who heard her. Without volition, her hands flew to his head, pulling on his hair in desperation as she thrashed beneath him. This was the sweetest agony. She could not take much more. She was right on the edge of a cliff and about to fall. One more suck of his hungry mouth and she was over the edge. She cried out loud as she fell and was swept up by a massive wave of pulsing sensation. On and on she pulsed, crying out incoherently as she experienced a pleasure never known to her before.

She was not sure how long it was before she finally stilled. She lay back breathlessly, still in a daze. She felt the finger withdraw from her channel and Benedict's mouth lift from her cunt. Reluctantly, she opened her eyes and looked at him. He stared at her, a look of triumph on his face and a wildness in his eyes. His mouth was wet with her arousal.

All at once, he was on his feet and ripping his robe open to reveal his glistening, hard cock. "I need to fuck you now," he ground out. He looked into her eyes for a response, and she nodded her consent, unable still to articulate any words. Quickly, he straddled her on the chair where she lay with one leg splayed over the edge of the tub, allowing him to wedge his right leg under hers. He guided his cock to her opening, then pressed in as far as he could go.

For a moment, they sat facing each other on the chair in this bizarre embrace. Benedict took Grace's face between his hands, staring searchingly into her eyes before he brought his mouth to hers. She parted her lips and met his probing tongue, tasting the tangy essence of herself on him. He grasped her to him and deepened the kiss. As he did so, she felt his cock begin a pulsing rhythm inside her.

She lost track of time, locked in his embrace, devouring his mouth as he pressed his groin to her, his cock wedged deep in her centre. She was still achingly sensitive from her recent climax, and each little plunge of his cock caused exquisite friction along the inner and outer walls of her cunt. She could feel the beginnings of another orgasm build inside her.

His kisses did not let up, nor the gentle pulse of his cock inside her. It was as if they had all the time in the world. They simply existed on this plane where their bodies were joined as one, where all that mattered was the continued breath they shared. All the while, the blood vessels in her core throbbed and thickened, readying themselves for another climax. Her nerve endings tingled with the strength of her arousal. Her channel tightened, strangling his cock wedged deep inside.

Now his pulsing became a more vigorous set of thrusts, his kisses turning furiously ravenous. She felt his grunt, deep in his throat, as he punched his groin into hers. And without warning, she lost herself in another climax, convulsing around him and milking his own sweet release. They rested against each other, forehead to forehead, until at long last, Benedict pulled out of her and got to his feet. He reached over to the tub and took the washcloth, wringing it dry before using it to wipe the both of them clean. Gently, he helped her to her feet, fetching her undergarments and helping her dress.

As he adjusted his own robe, which was in sad disarray, she finally found her voice, "I think we can say with some certainty, Benedict, that your studies in how to please a woman have been successful."

He grinned. "And yet, this is just the beginning, Grace. Things can only get better from here on end."

She smiled, suddenly filled with emotion, "Thank you," she said. She hugged him tightly and repeated, "Thank you."

CHAPTER 26

WALTER'S VISIT TO Mulverley Grange lasted a full week in which time he and Grace became firm friends, much to Benedict's delight. Father and son also found the time for a long and honest conversation, which went some way to putting each of their minds at rest. All that remained was for Walter to attend church service on Sunday and see his son at the pulpit for the very first time.

"We shall have to arrive early to reserve seats at the front," Grace told Walter, "for there is a veritable competition between Mrs Phipps and Mrs Stubbs for who can get there first and occupy a position as close as possible to their hero."

"I did not realise Benedict had such a following," replied Walter, a little disconcerted.

"I used to tease him about it, though I must say I do not find the matter quite as entertaining as I used to."

Just then, Benedict came down the stairs, ready to depart for church. They descended the front steps of the house and climbed into the waiting carriage. Soon, they were on their way, Walter looking about interestedly at the local landscape. They arrived twenty minutes before the service was due to start and saw that there were already people about, finding their seats. Benedict kissed Grace's forehead, murmuring, "I shall see you later, my dear."

Off he went to the vestry to get himself ready, while Grace and Walter made their way to the front pews. To her dismay, Grace saw Mrs Stubbs sitting in pride of place at the front, her voluminous gown taking up enough space for two people. Not a minute later, Mrs Phipps strolled in, her husband and sons at her side. Shooting daggers at Mrs Stubbs for taking the spot she had wanted, she contented herself with sitting along the other side of the front pew.

Grace turned to Walter. "I'm afraid we shall have to sit behind them, but you will still get a good view of Benedict delivering his sermon."

"That's quite alright," he said.

They slid into the second row, sitting themselves behind Mrs Stubbs, whose elaborate bonnet obscured Grace's view, much to her annoyance. That lady turned around in her seat to acknowledge them, looking enquiringly at Walter, and perforce, Grace had to make the introductions.

"Mrs Stubbs, this is Walter Sedgwick, Benedict's father, come to visit."

Her face wreathed in smiles, Mrs Stubbs welcomed Walter. "What an honour to make your acquaintance, Mr Sedgwick. May I say just how impressed we all are in this parish with your son's wonderful sermons. And may I also say, just how conscientiously he goes about his duties. Everyone is full of the most fulsome praise for him."

Looking a little bemused, Walter mumbled, "Well that is good to hear." He was saved from further conversing with the lady by the timely arrival of Daniel and Isabella Stanton. Grace waved at her cousins, and in moments, they had joined them. Introductions were duly made and Walter, with pleasing easy manners, began to converse with them. Soon, it was time for the service to begin, and they all got to their feet. Benedict walked up to the pulpit, watched proudly by his father and wife, who listened attentively to his sermon—for now that she was his wife, there was no more daydreaming about other men for Grace, though she could be forgiven perhaps, for the occasional lapse into a reverie about recent events in a bathroom.

At the end of the service, Benedict came out to greet his parishioners as was his wont. Mrs Stubbs rushed up to him and gushed, as per usual, about the excellence of his sermon, looking at Benedict with hero worship in her eyes. Watching her, Walter frowned. "I would have a care for this lady," he whispered to Grace. "I do not like the forwardness of her manner, and in my experience, that is always a sign of some sort of nefarious goings on."

"She is harmless," responded Grace. "Just a poor widow, craving a little attention."

"Perhaps. But be on your guard, dear."

"I will."

After church, they all convened at Stanton Hall for a family lunch, much in the tradition of the lunches they used to have in Ohio. They were joined at this lunch by the Cranshaws, who were included by dint of their close friendship with Benedict and by the growing rapport between Ambrose and Daniel as they worked together on managing the vast Stanton estate.

Ambrose and Sarah were delighted to see Walter, and he to see them again after several years' absence. All in all, it made for a very convivial gathering, filling a hole in Grace's soul that had been left there by the departure of her family. She recalled Walter's words. *You are not alone, Grace. You are surrounded by people who care for you.* Looking around now at the people gathered at the table, Grace realised how true those words were. She took a moment to be grateful for what she had been given. As she did so, she felt Benedict's hand clasp hers under the tablecloth, as if he sensed the thoughts going through her head.

And then there was Benedict, another cause for her to be grateful. Never did she think, when she had accepted his offer of marriage, that he would become so important to her happiness. But somehow, this mild mannered, earnest man had inveigled his way into her affections. Soon, very soon, she would finally have to come to terms with how she felt about him.

Her wandering thoughts were interrupted by Isabella asking, "What are your plans tomorrow, Grace? Will you join me for a shopping expedition to Witney?"

"I would love to join you, but can we make it Tuesday instead? Tomorrow will be Walter's last day with us."

Isabella smiled, "Of course."

"We can ride in the carriage together on Tuesday morning," said Benedict, "and you can drop me off in the village before you continue on your way to Isabella."

She nuzzled his cheek briefly and said, "Very well."

Monday came and went, and with it a sad farewell to a departing Walter. The sadness of the goodbyes were alleviated by his promise to start a regular correspondence and to return for another visit soon.

And then it was Tuesday. As planned, Benedict rode with her in the carriage to the village, where he went to visit his parishioners on foot while Grace continued to Stanton Hall to collect Isabella before heading off to Witney.

The two young cousins spent an enjoyable time browsing the shops. Isabella, now cognizant of Grace's pregnancy, was eager to help Grace shop for baby things of all kinds—clothes, linens and even lingered a while admiring a wooden rocking horse.

Their purchases complete, they returned to their carriage. Grace wished she were already home and able to have a restful nap, but perhaps the next best thing would be to use Isabella's shoulder as pillow on the ride back from Witney. This she did, waking with a start when the carriage stopped in the drive of Stanton Hall.

Isabella gathered her belongings and prepared to step out of the carriage. "Thank you for keeping me company today," she said. "We must do this more often. Perhaps next time, we can go further afield and explore the shops in Oxford."

Grace reached over to embrace her cousin. "It was fun, and yes, we shall."

Once Isabella was safely deposited home, the carriage continued on its way to the church, where Benedict would be at this time, as he liked to attend to administrative tasks and hold meetings with his parishioners in the small office he had over there. It took but a few minutes to reach this destination. Grace alighted from the carriage and entered the church, walking to a side door beside the altar which led to Benedict's office. As she neared the door, it opened and a lady walked out of it. It was Mrs Stubbs, Benedict's ardent admirer.

That lady stopped in surprise upon seeing Grace. "Mrs Sedgwick, how do you do?"

"I am well, thank you," replied Grace in glacial tones. "And yourself?"

"Yes, thank you, I am well."

"Were you visiting Mr Sedgwick?" Grace enquired coolly.

"No, that is yes, but only to bring over some of my fruit cake, for I heard Mr Sedgwick had a partiality for it."

"Indeed?" Grace skewered the lady with her glance, then forced a smile. "That is most kind of you, Mrs Stubbs. I am sure Mr Sedgwick will appreciate such a thoughtful gesture, but I must not keep you. Good day."

"Good day," echoed Mrs Stubbs, and continued on her way.

Grace watched her leave the church, a frown furrowing her brow, then turned to march towards her husband's office. She knocked on the door briskly before walking in. Benedict looked up from where he sat at his desk, his face transforming into a smile as he saw his wife. Setting down his spectacles on the desk, he stood quickly and came towards her. "Darling," he murmured, taking her into his arms and planting a kiss on her lips.

She kissed him back, before saying smartly, "I hear you are most partial to fruit cake."

He looked surprised at the statement. "Well, I suppose I am. You know me, I am partial to most cakes. Would you like a slice? Mrs Stubbs has just kindly brought one."

"Yes, I saw her as I arrived. Does she make a habit of bringing you cakes?"

He ran a hand through his hair, a little perplexed. "Well, not cakes no. Last week, it was shortbread she very kindly brought. So you see, I am never without something sweet to munch on while I work."

Grace's face took on a mutinous expression. "If you need something sweet to snack on, Benedict, I shall ensure Cook prepares cakes and biscuits for you every day from now on. There is no need to impose on the generosity of Mrs Stubbs."

"Oh." Benedict's face fell. "I had no thought that I had been imposing. Perhaps she heard me remark about my liking for sweet things and thought I expected something of the sort. Oh dear! Now I feel rotten about accepting all those offerings."

"Benedict!" Grace said sharply. "Surely you must know that she thought no such thing. Quite clearly, she was doing this to butter you up, and I must tell you that I will not have it happen anymore."

Benedict stared at his wife in astonishment. "What on earth would she want to butter me up for?" Then, seeing Grace's angry expression, he finally understood. "Oh. I had no idea. You must know, darling, that this kind of attention is foreign to me."

Grace's face softened as she placed both hands to his cheeks. "I am beginning to suspect, husband dearest, that you have had far more of it than you realise, only you have been oblivious." She kissed him gently. "You are sweet, handsome and so very wise. However, it has been remiss of me not to take steps to protect you from this kind of attention. I see now I shall have to do something about it."

Benedict regarded her in some amusement. "By all means, do so. What do you propose to do?"

"Hmm, never you mind, dear. Just know that I will do what is necessary to protect what is mine. Now, are you nearly finished with your work for today?"

He drew her back towards him. "Well, I very nearly am, but there is a problem."

"What would that be?" she asked, giving him a quizzical look.

"All this talk of protecting my honour has awakened this." He took her hand and placed it over his hardened cock, straining under the confines of his trousers. She pressed it between her fingers, and he groaned.

"Well, Benedict, we cannot have it suffer so."

He hissed in a breath, then growled softly, "Take off that dratted crinoline while I lock the door." With that, he let her go to stride towards the old wooden door and turn the key in the lock. Whipping around, he faced her again and watched as she lifted her skirt and undid the inconvenient hooped garment he decried so much. He prowled towards her until he stood a hair's breath away. With a sudden sweep of his arm, he sent the books and papers on his desk tumbling to the floor. The unfortunate fruit cake joined them too, still in its tin. His eyes gleamed a molten brown as he picked her up in his arms and set her atop the cleared desk. Gently, he pushed her backwards until she lay on the flat, wooden surface.

She watched him raptly from her prone position, her breaths coming in sharp pants. His eyes bore into hers. He rasped, "I think first, I shall need a taste of your nectar, dear wife."

"Yes," she murmured breathlessly. "I think perhaps you should."

Intent on his task, he raised the skirt of her dress to her hips, then gave a sharp tug on her drawers to bring them all the way down and off her legs, baring her mound. He gazed at the pretty picture she made, all mussed, her gown and petticoats spread on the desk, and the soft blond curls of her sex exposed to his sight. He parted her legs to display the glistening folds hidden below those curls. "So pretty," he crooned. Then his mouth was on her, desperate to taste, as he licked the soft, sensitive flesh.

Grace cried at the first touch of his lips to her. They had done this twice now, but she still marvelled at the wonder of him tasting her there, in such an intimate place. She closed her eyes and sighed as her husband licked her as if she were the tastiest dish in a buffet. His tongue fluttered tantalisingly over her, making her squirm. He held her down firmly with two hands. "Be still," he said sternly, before returning to his task.

Perforce she had to lay still as he ravished her with his tongue, bringing about the most exquisite sensations. Her eyes fluttered open, taking in her surroundings. They were in his office, inside the church. Across from her, the window looked out on to the deserted graveyard. Anyone passing by would see them. And yet here was her husband, without a seeming care for proprieties, making a feast out of her. The thought excited her senses. Of course, she did not want them to be discovered, but the possibility of it was infinitely arousing. Her core swelled and throbbed under his ardent touch. It felt so impossibly good. She closed her eyes again and gave in to the sensation. Pleasure spiralled within her, building and building with each flutter of Benedict's tongue, until she could take it no more and cried out, pulsing helplessly under his touch.

He continued his ministrations until he felt her still beneath him. Then he straightened, the lower part of his face glistening from her juices. With rough hands, he freed his raging erection from his trousers and pants. Pulling her to the edge of the desk, he brought her legs up to his shoulders, positioning his cock at her entrance. Expression fierce, he grunted, "I cannot promise to be gentle, wife."

"Don't be!"

In one slick move, her entered her as far as he could go. She gasped. He pulled back and thrust again. Then he began a punishing rhythm, plunging in and out repeatedly, his face set in a grimace and flushed with exertion, making grunts of sweet agony as he buried himself in her tight heat. Her core, still throbbing from her earlier orgasm, felt each thrust of his thick length into her. A second orgasm began to build on the previous one, this one deeper, more powerful. His eyes burned into hers as if he could sense her impending release.

"Do it!" he rapped sharply. "Let me feel your pleasure."

"Benedict!" she cried.

"Do it, Gracie!"

And then she came apart, feeling as if she were bursting into flames. She cried out loud, and he joined her, groaning his ecstasy as he emptied his seed into her. When finally he came back to his senses, he withdrew gently and brought her legs down from his shoulders, kissing each dainty ankle before he deposited them on the desk. Quickly, he tucked himself back into his trousers. He pulled out a handkerchief from his pocket and cleaned her up the best he could, then he fished around of the floor for her undergarments, helping her to get dressed. With steely strength, he lifted her off the desk and back to standing.

She stared at him in wonder. "That was…"

"Incredible." He grinned and kissed her, then looked around at the mess they had made. "We should not make a habit of having such public trysts," he said ruefully, "but like that time in the woods, the excitement was intoxicating."

"Yes," was all she could say in return.

He led her to the chair and sat her down. "Wait here while I tidy this up."

She watched him as he picked up all the books and papers strewn on the floor, rescuing his spectacles in the process and putting them back on. "I love you, Benedict," she blurted. She had not thought to make this confession at quite such a moment, but the words escaped her mouth before she could stop them.

He paused and looked back at her, giving her that sweet smile she loved so much. "And I love you, my darling Grace." He came and kneeled before her, taking her hands in his. "I fell for you from the moment we first met." He smiled wryly, "Do you remember how tongue-tied I was?"

"As a matter of fact, I do."

"Well, it was because I was lovestruck by you."

"While I was making eyes at Mr Templeton."

He let out a breath. "Yes, I was very aware of that."

"I am sorry, Benedict. I have been such a fool."

He brought her hands to his lips. "Not so foolish, my darling, when you agreed to marry me. You are mine now, and that is what matters."

"Yes, and you are all mine."

"Forever and always."

He stood then, and resumed his work. Within minutes, the office was tidy again. He took his coat from a peg by the door and pulled it on, saying, "I do not think I am capable of doing any more work today. Let us go home."

She got to her feet and let him lead her out, remembering at the last minute to take the fruit cake with her, which she handed over to the coachman as they reached their carriage. "This is for you, Stanley," she said.

The coachman took it in surprise. "Thank you, madam," he said gruffly.

Benedict laughed, helping his wife into the carriage then coming to sit beside her. "I see I have been banned from such collations," he teased.

"I will let Cook bake you a fruit cake to Ma's recipe, which I assure you will be infinitely better."

He took her hand and kissed it. "I am sure it will be."

CHAPTER 27

THE FOLLOWING DAY, Benedict set out for his parish visits after breakfast, as usual. Grace waved him off with a smile then went to see Mrs Hawkins. She spoke with newfound confidence, explaining what she wanted. The housekeeper listened attentively and responded, "Yes, madam. I will see it gets done."

"Thank you, Mrs Hawkins."

With that done, Grace decided to go visit Butterscotch in the stable. A week ago, John Saunders had informed her that Butterscotch was in heat, and they had put her in the breeding stall with Midnight. It was too soon to tell yet whether or not the mare had bred, but Grace wanted to check on her in any case. She walked over to the stall, proffering a gift from her pocket, which Butterscotch munched on happily. Grace stroked her horse's mane and crooned, "Hello beautiful. How are you today?"

Butterscotch neighed softly.

"Good," replied Grace, as if they were having a real conversation. "I think perhaps you should let Saunders take you out for some gentle exercise today, what do you think?"

Butterscotch shook her mane.

"I know dear, you want me to ride you, but I'm afraid that's out of the question until after baby comes along, so you will have to make do with someone else for now."

The mare snuffled. Grace spoke to her a little more, then bid her goodbye. On her way out, she looked for Saunders and found him sweeping out an empty stall. "Morning, Saunders," she said.

He stopped and doffed his cap. "Morning, madam."

"Saunders, I shall be needing the carriage within the half-hour. Could you inform Stanley and have it ready? We shall be going to the church to visit Mr Sedgwick."

"Yes, madam."

With a nod, she left the stable and returned to the house, stopping in the kitchen to have a word with Cook. "Is the basket packed and ready?" she asked.

"Yes, madam," came the response. "It is right here. I have packed it with the fruit cake, some ginger biscuits, a few apples and pears, and a bottle of lemonade, just as you asked."

"Perfect, thank you. Please could you have it loaded in the carriage as soon as it is ready."

"Yes, madam."

A half-hour later, Grace set off in the carriage. With her was Hester, her maid, for she needed an extra pair of hands for what she meant to do. They arrived at the church shortly after ten o'clock and entered, encountering the churchwarden in the vestry as they made their way towards Benedict's office.

"Good morning, Mr Hopkins," said Grace airily.

"Mrs Sedgwick, good morning. I'm afraid Mr Sedgwick is not yet come from his parish visits."

She beamed. "Yes, and that is why I am here. I wish to surprise my husband."

"Indeed?" he frowned.

"I notice there is a small anteroom to the side of Mr Sedgwick's office, which will work excellently for my purposes."

"Your purposes?" enquired a bewildered Mr Hopkins.

"I have decided that my husband requires an assistant, someone who can ensure that he is allowed to work in peace and is not disturbed, someone who can speak to visitors and enquire as to their purpose in seeking out Mr Sedgwick, and to write appointments in his diary."

"A secretary of sorts, do you mean?"

She smiled. "That is exactly what I mean, and I shall volunteer of my time to do this for a few hours each morning while Mr Sedgwick is here. Of course, I shall need somewhere to set myself up, and as I said, that small anteroom is perfect for my purposes. There is a table and a chair. All it needs is a sweep and a bit of a tidy up to be ready."

He continued to stare, a frown knitting his brow. "This is highly irregular," he said at last.

"What could be more fitting than a clergyman's wife assisting him in the performance of his duties?" cajoled Grace.

"Well, I suppose, there is no harm in it. Will you require any assistance, Mrs Sedgwick?"

"None at all. I have my maid here to help me, and we had best get started as time is of the essence."

He nodded. "Of course. Please do call on me should you require any help." With this, he turned to walk away.

Grace called out to her maid. "Quick, Hester, let us get started."

An hour later, Benedict entered the church building, having visited his frail and sick parishioners. Something felt a little odd. He paused and looked around. A light shone from the small anteroom to the side of his office. He hurried his footsteps towards it. In there, at a small desk, sat Grace. The room had been cleared of much of the boxes of odds and ends that had been there before. On the desk sat a large leather bound ledger and an inkwell with a pen.

Grace put down the book she was reading and stood, coming around to him with a smile. "Darling, let me take your coat. You look frozen, poor thing."

Without thinking, Benedict undid the fastenings of his coat and handed it to her. She took it and placed it on a peg by the door. As he watched her, enough of his wits returned for him to ask, "Grace, what are you doing here?"

She pointed to her desk. "As you can see, I have set up a space for myself here." She came towards him then and put her hands on his shoulders. He drew her to him, meeting her lips for a kiss.

He drew back a little and quirked his brow. "Yes, but why?"

She cocked her head to one side. "It has become clear to me, Benedict, that you are in need of an assistant while you work in your office, and someone who can act as a gatekeeper of sorts. Who better than your wife to do this?"

His eyes sparkled. "This has nothing to do with your stated ambition to protect me from unwanted advances?"

"On the contrary, it has everything to do with it. Sitting out here, I can ensure nobody disturbs you in your work or demands your attention for frivolous purposes—your work is far too important for that. I can take appointments for you and write down messages in that ledger. In fact, I already have an appointment written in for the baptism of Mr and Mrs Trent's baby girl next Wednesday at eleven. Oh and Mr Hopkins said to remind you that the parish meeting has been moved from two to three o'clock tomorrow afternoon. Of course, I shall attend too, so that I can make a note of what is discussed in the meeting."

Benedict was grinning from ear to ear. "Grace darling, I am impressed with your initiative. That is the sweetest thing to do, but surely you will get bored sitting out here?"

"Not at all. It is only for a few hours each day, and I have both my sketching book and something to read with me."

He nudged her nose gently with his. "And what if your presence proves to be too distracting? I may never get any work done knowing you are so close."

She touched her lips to his in a light kiss. "Well, I do not know about you, Benedict, but I find thoughts of you very distracting to me throughout the day when I am at home alone.

This way at least, we can do something about it, and then get back to work."

He took her bottom lip between his teeth and nipped it gently. "You make a good point, Mrs Sedgwick."

There was a loud clearing of a throat behind them. They sprang apart to see a young man and woman standing together, watching them with inquisitive eyes. "Mr Sedgwick?" said the young man.

Benedict recovered himself quickly and smiled. "Mr Hobbs, what can I do for you?"

Mr Hobbs turned to the young woman beside him. "Miss Perkins has done me the honour of accepting my proposal of marriage, sir, and we are here to register for the banns."

"Mr Hobbs, Miss Perkins, you have my heartiest congratulations. May I make you known to my wife?" Turning to Grace, he added, "Darling, Mr Hobbs is the village baker, and his betrothed works in the millinery shop, is that not so, Miss Perkins?"

The lady bobbed her head. "Yes sir, that is quite right. Mrs Sedgwick, a pleasure."

Grace smiled graciously. "I am pleased to make both of your acquaintance. Please do come inside."

Benedict led them into his office while Grace returned to her sentinel position at the desk and resumed reading her book. A quarter of an hour later, the door opened and the young couple were led out, beaming happily. Benedict cast her a playful glance before returning to work at his desk. Grace picked up her book again and began to read. Not five minutes later, the sound of footsteps made her look up. Mrs Stubbs was walking towards Benedict's office door. Grace stood quickly and went to waylay her.

"Mrs Stubbs, good morning. What can I do for you?"

That lady startled, looking at Grace in dismay. "Mrs Sedgwick, this is a surprise."

"Indeed, Mrs Stubbs, I am as surprised as you. Is there anything I can do for you?" Grace stood guard in front of Benedict's door, not letting the audacious widow come any closer.

"I had come to ask after Mr Sedgwick and see how well he liked the fruit cake," replied Mrs Stubbs.

"How generous of you to give up your time to enquire after my husband, Mrs Stubbs. However, as you will understand, Mr Sedgwick is busy on parish business and cannot be disturbed."

But Mrs Stubbs was not to be thwarted so easily. She made as if to sidestep Grace, saying, "Oh, I shall only be a moment."

Here, she had underestimated Grace's tenacity, for Grace now stepped sideways to block her passage and spoke firmly, "I am afraid I must insist, Mrs Stubbs. Now, if there is nothing else, I shall bid you good day."

At an impasse, Mrs Stubbs conceded defeat. With an annoyed look, she murmured, "Good day, Mrs Sedgwick," and took her leave.

Grace watched her depart, breast heaving. Behind her, the door opened with a quiet click. She felt Benedict's hands on her shoulders as he drew her gently to his chest. "Be still, my beating heart," he murmured into her ear. She turned in his arms and held him tight.

"You are mine now, Benedict, and I do not share what is mine," she whispered back.

He kissed the top of her head. "The feeling is mutual." They held each other close for endless seconds. Finally, Benedict said softly, "I do believe I am going to like having you here with me every day, Gracie."

She pulled back a little. "Good," she said with satisfaction. "And now, my love, how about I bring you a bite to eat with a glass of lemonade?"

He laughed. "You spoil me, Grace. What have you got for me?"

She smiled saucily. "You shall see. Go sit at your desk and I will bring it to you."

And thus began Grace's new career as her husband's faithful assistant. The next day, she accompanied him to the parish meeting, which was held every week in the village hall. There, she saw an array of faces familiar to her from church. These included Mr Hopkins, Mr and Mrs Phipps, a local tenant farmer called Mr Johnson, and of course, Mrs Stubbs. There were various other people there whose names she could not quite remember. The meeting was presided over by Benedict, who took a seat at the rectangular table placed at the front of the hall, and invited her to sit beside him.

As she took her place by her husband, she spied the astonished glances thrown her way, for this was the first time she had been present at such a gathering. She pasted a smile on her face and tried to act nonchalant as she placed a leather bound book before her and took out a sharpened pencil. She would scribe the proceedings with it on a blank sheet of paper, then copy out her notes neatly in ink the following day. She had been surprised to learn that nobody took an official note of the meeting's proceedings, for she knew this was something her aunt Charlotte did back in Ohio, keeping a careful record of all village business discussed at the weekly meetings held over there. It was another reason why she felt her decision to become her husband's assistant was a timely one.

The meeting began with the airing of a dispute between two neighbours regarding the clearing of rubbish thrown onto the street. Benedict questioned the warring neighbours calmly, setting out the facts, before issuing a fair judgement on the matter, which was accepted by both parties. Grace scribbled away on her sheet of paper, summarising the main points as best she could. As she did so, she could not help a feeling of pride at Benedict's obvious aptitude for his work.

Next to be discussed were concerns about the state of Cogges Lane, which was riddled with potholes. Here, there were many irate voices to be heard. It was clear the road was in dire need of repair. Benedict confirmed that he had contacted a surveyor to come inspect the road and set out the costs of the required improvements. "In the meantime though," he suggested, "perhaps we can have the worst of the potholes plugged with some gravel. If someone could volunteer a barrowful of gravel, I would be happy to assist in spreading it over the most offending of the holes."

Mr Johnson replied gruffly, "That I can do, Mr Sedgwick. I'll have a cart filled with gravel brought to you by noon tomorrow."

Benedict beamed. "That is most generous, thank you. And now, on to our final order of business. This year, for Shrove Tuesday, we have discussed the idea of holding a pancake feast here in the village hall, as a way to celebrate together and to feed the hungry in our community. We shall need to start another collection for this, which reminds me, Mrs Stubbs, how did you fare with our Christmas collection? Have all the funds been distributed as agreed?"

Mrs Stubbs straightened in her seat self-importantly and flashed a smug smile. "The parish community was most generous, Mr Sedgwick, in raising £6 and twelve shillings. I am happy to say these funds were used to distribute necessities for our poorest families, such as blankets and warm clothes for the children, as well as food parcels that included oats, sugar and flour." She held out a stack of receipts kept together with a red ribbon, and a sheet of official looking paper. "Here are the receipts and the accounts recorded on this sheet. If you will kindly sign off for them here, Mr Sedgwick." She passed him the document, together with a pen and inkwell.

Grace frowned as she saw Benedict take the proffered pen, dip it in the ink and sign his name on the bottom of the page. A lesson that had been drummed into her by her father was that one should never sign any document without first reading it. How could Benedict be so trusting? She watched as he placed the signed sheet and stack of receipts in his leather bag, and then blithely continued with the meeting.

Grace noted down all the proceedings, but her mind was taken up by that document that Benedict had just signed. If there were any discrepancies in the accounts, then it would be Benedict held responsible, having signed off on them. She recalled Walter's warning about Mrs Stubbs and his suspicions of nefarious goings on. *Be on your guard.* She decided she would study those receipts meticulously the soonest chance she got.

The meeting over, she stood with her husband and waited patiently as he bade everyone goodbye. Once they were settled in the carriage and on their way home, he turned to her with a smile. "How did you enjoy your first parish meeting?"

"I found it quite informative," she replied.

He stroked a hand down her cheek. "I saw you write down all the main points most diligently—impressive work, Mrs Sedgwick! I can't think why nobody has done it before as it is very useful to keep a record of things."

She tucked her chin on his shoulder. "All the more reason why you need me."

"That I do," he said, kissing the top of her head.

"Benedict," she began.

"Yes, dear?"

"How long has Mrs Stubbs been in charge of the collection for the poor?

"I'm not sure. When I arrived here, she made herself known to me, telling me she and Mrs Wentworth had been charged with managing the collections, but that since Mrs Wentworth's sad passing last year, she had taken it onto herself to continue with that work alone."

"I see." Grace stroked her fingers along the top of Benedict's hands that lay palm down on his thigh "And do you ever check the work she does or assist her with it?"

When she looked up at his face, she saw he was flushed. "Grace, it is a shameful thing to admit, but from the first, I have not felt easy in that lady's presence. You know how I am, shy and awkward, and on my first meeting with Mrs Stubbs, she was so fulsome in her compliments that I did not know quite what to do. I found it easiest to smile vaguely and nod in acquiescence to whatever she said, then make my hurried escape. You think perhaps I should have made more effort to assist in the distribution of the alms?"

She considered the matter. "No, I think you were right to keep your distance from this female. However, I do not like that you signed her document of the accounts without once checking their accuracy. Do you always do that?"

"Yes, I suppose so. Is that wrong?"

She kissed his cheek. "Let us just say that from now on, those documents should be passed to me first before you sign them. Do you still have the receipts and documents of previous accounts?"

"Yes, they are in my desk drawer."

"Then tomorrow, I shall go through them all and check the amounts against each receipt."

He gazed at her uncertainly. "You think there will be discrepancies? I have not thought of Mrs Stubbs as being dishonest."

"I am sure she is not, but I would prefer to check any document to which you have put your signature, just to be on the safe side."

He smiled and drew her to him. "Oh Grace, I do not know what I would do without you."

"No," she mused, "I do not know how you managed before I came into the picture."

He laughed. "Very poorly, I think."

CHAPTER 28

NEXT DAY, AS promised, Grace sat with the stack of receipts and checked them one by one against the statement of account presented by Mrs Stubbs. The total value of the receipts was £4 and twelve shillings, yet according to the statement of account, it should have been £6 and twelve shillings. One of the receipts noted down in the accounts was missing. Grace looked for it again in the stack of receipts, but it was not there. In that stack, there should have been a receipt to the value of £2 for the purchase of blankets. It was not there. Could it be because that money had never been spent on blankets but been taken fraudulently?

Her brow creased in concern, she stood and went to Benedict's office. He had been called out earlier to minister to an ailing parishioner, but before he left, he had shown her the drawer where all the previous accounts and receipts were stored away. She opened the drawer and took out the sheaf of papers, taking them back to her desk. Over the next half hour, she painstakingly went over all the accounts that had been signed off by Benedict since he took over as curate three months ago. There were two further statements of accounts, one dated in November and one in December, and in each one, she found the same amount missing. Each account included a receipt for £2 that was nowhere to be found. All in all, this meant that Mrs Stubbs had defrauded the church by £6.

What was she to do with this evidence? Should she go and confront Mrs Stubbs? What if the dreadful female deflected the blame on Benedict? It was his signature after all on all these statements of account. On paper, it would look like he was the culprit. She could not have that. There was no possible way that she would allow Benedict's reputation to be tarnished. But then, how was she to proceed?

She rustled up all the papers into a neat pile and tied them with a ribbon, then she stood and put on her coat. With the stack of papers in hand, she marched out of the church and out to her waiting carriage. "Stanley, please take me to Stanton Hall," she instructed the coachman.

"Yes, madam," he said, as he opened the carriage door and assisted her inside.

Soon, they were on their way. Pa had made her promise, hadn't he, that if she ever needed help, she was to go to Daniel. Well, that was what she was doing. She hoped Mr Cranshaw would be there too, as he would know what to do.

Once the carriage had stopped in the main drive of her ancestral home, she rushed out and flew up the stairs to pull the bell. Moments later, Siddons drew back the door.

"Good day, madam."

"Good day, Siddons," she said, striding into the main hall. "Where may I find the viscount? I have urgent need to speak to him."

Siddons took the coat she had unfastened and replied, "He is upstairs in the library with Mr Cranshaw."

"Perfect, thank you, Siddons, I will show myself in."

With that, she ran up the stairs, lifting the hem of her skirt while holding on to the sheaf of papers in her hand. At the top of the stairs, she veered right, walking hurriedly down a long, carpeted corridor until she reached the library door. With a quick knock, she opened it and entered.

Daniel looked up at her in surprise. He was in his shirtsleeves, feet stretched comfortably in front of him, nursing an amber coloured drink in one hand and perusing a document with the other. Ambrose Cranshaw sat across from him at the desk, busily writing. He put the pen down upon her entrance and stood. "Mrs Sedgwick," he said.

"Oh, do call me Grace, please."

"Gracie," said Daniel, sitting up. "What is it?"

"I need your help, Daniel." She looked across at Ambrose. "And yours too, Mr Cranshaw."

He smiled. "If I am to call you Grace, then you must forfeit formality with me too and call me Ambrose."

"Very well."

"Come over and sit, Gracie, and tell us all about it." Daniel pointed to the chair beside him.

Grace went to settle herself down next to him, holding the papers in her lap.

"Is the problem something to do with these papers you are clutching?" asked her cousin.

"Yes, they are receipts and statements of account for the collection made in church each month for the poor. I was at the parish meeting yesterday with Benedict, and Mrs Stubbs handed him this statement of account, asking him to sign it, and Benedict did, without first checking that the receipts matched what was on the accounts."

"I see," said Daniel. "And now you have had a chance to check the receipts, you have found some discrepancy?"

Grace nodded. "There is a receipt missing to the value of £2. But that is not all. I then went and checked the previous accounts going back to when Benedict took over as curate in November, and there is £2 unaccounted for in each of those statements. And they have all been signed off by Benedict."

"Benedict is far too trusting for his own good," bemoaned Ambrose. "He always has been. It is just not in his nature to suspect anyone of wrongdoing."

"I know, but what are we to do? I thought of going to confront Mrs Stubbs, but I fear she may turn the tables on us and accuse Benedict of fraud just to cover her own back."

"Oh, we are going to confront Mrs Stubbs, of that have no doubt," said Daniel, his mouth drawn in a thin line.

Just then, the library door opened and in strolled Isabella. "I heard you were here, Grace." She went over to her cousin and dropped a kiss on her cheek, then paused, looking at her closely. "Is anything the matter?"

Daniel quickly summed up the situation for his sister. Isabella listened, an outraged expression forming on her face. "That dreadful hypocrite! Praising Benedict to the skies then stealing from him behind his back. What are we to do about her?"

"That is just what we were about to discuss," responded Daniel. He turned to his land manager. "Ambrose, do you know by any chance who owns the house Mrs Stubbs lives in?"

Ambrose's eyes gleamed. "I see you are thinking along the same lines as me. You are her landlord, Daniel, and the contract for her tenancy is in a box of papers somewhere on that shelf behind you."

"And what are the terms in the contract for ending the tenancy?"

Ambrose stood and went to fetch the box, which was labelled "Village Tenancies". He rummaged through it until he found the document in question. He brought it over to where everyone else was sitting, leafing through it until he got to the relevant section. "Ah, here it is. You are entitled to end the tenancy without prior notice if the tenant acts in a way that shows bad character or brings them ill repute."

"Perfect," smiled Daniel. "I should think defrauding the Church of money is a clear example of bad character, don't you?"

"But what if she says it's Benedict that did the defrauding, not her?" cried Grace.

"You were there in the meeting when she presented the accounts to him," retorted Isabella. "And so was half the village. Everyone witnessed her handing out the receipts to Benedict. If a receipt is missing, then the fraud points clearly to her. Let her but try to accuse Benedict in a court of law, she would not get very far."

"Well, but I do not want word of this to get out," said Grace urgently. "You know how people gossip, and I do not want Benedict's reputation compromised."

"I agree," said Ambrose. "No word of this must get out, but we can and should compel her to leave this village."

"She will need somewhere to go," said Grace. "I know Benedict, and he will not want it on his conscience to render a lone widow homeless, no matter how wicked she is."

"Bramble Cottage," pronounced Isabella, exchanging a glance with Ambrose.

He grinned. "The very thing."

Grace was confused. "Explain, Isabella."

"It's quite simple really," replied her cousin. "Bramble Cottage is part of the Netherwick Hall estate. It is quite small, but perfectly liveable, and has been vacant since the previous tenant passed away two months ago. It's ten miles from here, so it will get the dreaded widow out of our hair, and the rent is very reasonable, which should allow her to save enough each month to pay back what she owes."

"About the money," said Grace. "It would ease my mind if the missing funds could be repaid as soon as possible. I do not want anyone to ever point the finger of blame at Benedict."

"That won't be a problem. I can disburse the money from my funds right now," said Daniel, "and Ambrose can make sure to collect it back from Mrs Stubbs in instalments each month."

"That's very kind Daniel, but I can pay for this," protested Grace.

"You would have to write to Mr Ridley asking for the funds, and he'll want to know why. Before you know it, news of this will have reached your father's ears and you can bet he won't take kindly to it."

"No, you are right."

"So, let me do it," said Daniel gently. "It is easy enough for me to do, and I will make sure I'm paid back every penny by that disagreeable woman."

"Very well then," sighed Grace. "When shall we do this?"

"I say we do it now," decided Daniel. "There is no time like the present."

"Give me a few minutes to write a letter of notice to present to Mrs Stubbs," said Ambrose.

Accordingly, said letter was composed and the four of them trooped down to Grace's carriage, which still waited in the drive. Stanley was instructed to drive to the address in the village where Mrs Stubbs resided. Soon, they were on their way. Grace's heart beat rapidly as she contemplated the meeting ahead. She was glad Ambrose and her cousins were there, giving her courage for what was to come.

In a few minutes, they had arrived. The gentlemen helped the ladies alight from the coach, then Daniel strode forward and knocked imperiously at the door. A timid maid opened the door and was bade to fetch her mistress. In another moment, Mrs Stubbs was there, in a loud rustle of her silk skirt. She gazed at them with a puzzled frown. "Viscount Stanton," she said smoothly. "Mrs Sedgwick, Miss Stanton, Mr Cranshaw. Do come in."

They followed her into a small, fussily furnished parlour. "Please, do sit down. May I offer you some refreshment?"

"That won't be necessary," said Daniel coldly. "Mrs Stubbs, I am here to hand this letter of notice to you. As you will see, it states that you have a notice of two days in which to vacate this cottage." He placed the document into her hands and sat back.

She broke the seal and read through it quickly, her face frowning in concentration. Looking up, she exclaimed, "Viscount Stanton, I do not understand. What is meant by this accusation of showing bad character? I can assure you that I am a pillar of this community."

This was the opening that Grace had been waiting for. She spoke now, in a curt tone, "And I can assure you that you are a thief who has defrauded the Church of funds that were collected to help the poor. I have checked the accounts you presented at the meeting yesterday, and the previous ones you submitted. There are missing receipts up to the value of £6. I would think that was evidence enough of bad character."

"Mrs Sedgwick," spluttered the widow. "You accuse me unfairly. I assure you I have no idea what you are talking about. Everything I have done is above board and documented in the statement of account which was ratified by your husband's signature."

"Whether or not my husband signed these documents is immaterial. Countless people witnessed you, Mrs Stubbs, handing over the receipts—receipts that do not add up to the amounts in your statement of account. That, I think, is evidence enough, so please do not bother with the denials."

"Oh, but Mrs Sedg—"

"Enough!" cried Grace sharply. "Now listen, Mrs Stubbs, and do not speak another word. I am not so heartless as to leave a widow destitute without a home. If you will leave quietly and without fuss in the time allocated, you will be given tenancy of Bramble Cottage, on the Netherwick Estate. It is smaller than your current home, but in good condition and perfectly liveable. You will also agree with Mr Cranshaw a suitable schedule to pay back the money you owe, which he will collect from you each month. If, however, you do not comply with all these stipulations, then I am afraid the offer of the cottage will be withdrawn and formal charges of theft lodged against you with the authorities."

Mrs Stubbs had gone pale, her hands shaking. A great silence ensued, then the widow said quietly, "Very well."

"And one more thing. You will leave and never show your face in this village or Standlake ever again. You will not utter a single bad word, now or in the future, about my husband. If I hear any rumours, any untoward gossip, then my cousin Isabella, whose tenant you will be, shall end your tenancy at Bramble Cottage forthwith. Do I make myself clear, Mrs Stubbs? A nod will do."

Mrs Stubbs nodded.

Daniel stood. "Very well, then. Our business here is done. Good day, Mrs Stubbs."

One by one, they filed out of the house and made their way back to the carriage. Once the door had closed, it started on its journey back to Stanton Hall. Grace sat back in the plush seat, trembling in the aftermath of that encounter.

"Well done, Gracie," praised Isabella. "You were terrifying, just like a tigress. I loved the way you interrupted her and asked her not to speak a word."

"You were marvellous," agreed Daniel. "I had no need to step in and assist, as I thought I might. You did it all by yourself."

"I had to be, for Benedict," breathed Grace. "Do you think his reputation is safe now?"

"I think so," replied Ambrose, "but in any case, I shall keep my ear to the ground. And may I add my own words of praise, Grace. You were awe-inspiring just then. Benedict is a lucky man."

Grace smiled. "Thank you, all of you. I could not have done this without your help." Her smile fell as she thought of something else. "How am I to tell Benedict of all this? I know it will upset him."

"Yes, it will upset him to learn he was defrauded by Mrs Stubbs, but also that his wife had to ride to the rescue." Ambrose looked at her sympathetically. "He will be hurt and his pride stung, but there is nothing for it."

"If anyone can soothe the hurt, then it will be you, Gracie," stated Isabella with confidence.

"I shall try my best."

The carriage stopped in front of Stanton Hall. Daniel turned to his cousin. "Come down with us and have a celebratory drink," he urged.

Grace placed a hand to her still flat belly. "In my condition, it is best not to. In any case, I am eager to get back home and wait for Benedict to arrive."

"Good luck." Daniel leaned forward and kissed her cheek, then jumped down from the carriage.

Ambrose pressed her hand. "Good day, Grace. I will call to see Benedict tomorrow."

She nodded her thanks, and he too climbed out of the carriage, leaving Isabella, who asked, "Will you be alright?"

Grace nodded. "Yes, I just hate to see Benedict hurt, and I know he will be when he finds out."

"Hugs and kisses go a long way towards soothing the hurt, or so I hear."

Grace smiled. "He'll get plenty of those."

"You really have fallen in love with him, haven't you?"

"Yes," replied Grace, her throat thick with unshed tears, "utterly and madly in love."

GRACE WAS READING in the upstairs parlour when Benedict returned home a few hours later. He came straight up to find her. She sat up on the chaise longue as he entered the room, and got to her feet. He hugged her then pulled back with a smile. "I am in great need of a bath after the day I have had, first filling potholes with gravel, then spending hours in the sick room. I have asked Winford for hot water to be brought up for a bath."

"Good idea. Let me come with you while you change."

She slipped her arm through his and accompanied him to his room. There, he began to undress and so did she.

"Grace?" he asked, uncertain.

"I am going to share the bath with you, if you do not mind."

"I do not mind at all," he murmured.

She was down to her chemise and drawers. He stopped what he was doing and simply stared. Very slowly, she pushed the drawers down her hips and over her feet. Then the chemise came off, to be thrown carelessly over a chair. She stood naked before him, only a slight swell of her belly hinting at her pregnancy. "Your turn," she challenged.

Never taking his eyes off her, he finished undressing until he too was bare. "Have I told you lately how beautiful you are?" he asked softly.

"Not half as beautiful as you, Benedict. Will you let me sketch you one day, without your clothes?"

Colour rose to his cheeks. "If that is what you want, then how can I say no?" Turning brisk, he added, "Now let us get into our robes and bathe without further ado."

They both fetched their robes and tied them on, then hand in hand walked to the bathroom. As they reached it, the door opened and the two housemaids, Betty and Hester, emerged carrying empty buckets which they had just used to pour water into the tub. They bobbed a curtsy. "The bath is ready, sir," said Hester. Then her eyes came to rest on Grace. "Did madam wish for a bath afterwards? If so, I can heat some more water in the kitchen."

Grace laughed. "No, that is quite alright. I shall share my bathwater with Mr Sedgwick. Do leave us now, and I will ring the bell if we require any more hot water."

The two maids quickly withdrew, and Grace followed Benedict into the bathroom, locking the door behind her. He undid the tie of his robe and placed the garment on the chair, then stepped carefully into the steaming bath. "Oh, this feels good," he purred.

Grace followed suit, divesting herself of her robe, then stepping in front of Benedict in the tub. "Mmm, it's a tight fit, but if I bend my legs like so, we can manage." She lay back against his chest and sighed happily. "This feels nice."

Benedict reached for the washcloth and rubbed some soap into it. Gently, he began to run the washcloth over Grace's body. "Oh, I do like this, Benedict," she breathed.

"Me too. We must do this more often. And really, it is much more economical to share the bathwater, is it not?"

"Oh, absolutely."

They enjoyed their bath for a few moments longer in silence, gently stroking, kissing, fondling. Eventually, Grace spoke, "Benedict."

"Yes, dear?"

"There is something I must tell you."

He paused momentarily in his ministrations, then began gently to wash her hair. "What is it? Tell me."

Hesitantly at first, she told her story, starting with her discovery of the discrepancy in the accounts and ending with the visit to Mrs Stubbs's house. Benedict heard her out without interruption. When she was done, he said nothing, but started to rinse the soap from her hair.

"Benedict, speak to me."

"It seems I have much to thank you for, Gracie," he sighed. "I'm sorry. It is all my fault, I'm afraid. I should have overcome my shyness and engaged with Mrs Stubbs enough to ask questions about how the money had been used. I meant to, but each time I backed down. And so I got myself into this mess."

"Do not be too hard upon yourself, Benedict. The fault was hers, not yours. She it was that did wrong. And yes, you are too trusting, but that is because you are all good and find it hard to envisage the bad in people. But don't worry, I'm here now to look out for you." She trapped his hand to her heart. "This marriage is not just about you taking care of me. It is also about me caring for you. We complete each other, don't you see?"

He laughed quietly. "That was what I thought, the very first time I met you. I remember on the carriage ride back home listing all the qualities you had which I lacked, and thinking 'She completes me.'"

"I love you, Benedict," breathed Grace.

"I love you, too."

They lazed in the bath a moment more. Finally, Benedict said, "I will visit Daniel tomorrow to thank him for his help and to pay him back the £6 that is owed. If anyone should pay for this mistake, it should be me."

"Ambrose will be collecting the debt from Mrs Stubbs, never fear."

"And we can add that to the church fund when it comes in. Next time around, I want to make sure the money reaches the people it was destined for."

"We can work on this together, the two of us," suggested Grace.

"Yes, we can."

CHAPTER 29

GRACE'S PREGNANCY PROGRESSED apace. By the middle of February, the nausea that had plagued her receded, and so too did the excessive tiredness. She bloomed, waking each day with renewed vigour.

The only cloud on her horizon was the absence of her parents and the continued lack of communication. She waited for news of them to reach her, knowing it would take at least a month after their departure before any letter from them could arrive. When finally a missive did come through the post, it was with news that the Stantons had arrived safely back home in Ohio and that all was well there. Tensions were rising ever more between the states that remained in the union and those that had seceded, but business continued as usual on their home farm. Everyone was in good health and sent their love.

Grace read the letter with relief as well as nostalgia for the home she had left behind and the family she missed. She wrote back, telling Ma all about her adventures at the church and with the news that Butterscotch was breeding. Despite the moments of intense grief for her family, there was much for Grace to be thankful for, chief of which was the tower of strength that was Benedict. His love, attention and care made her loss so much more bearable. And there was the baby to look forward to.

In the middle of February, when she was fifteen weeks into her pregnancy, Dr Benson paid them a visit at Mulverley Grange. Grace worried that it would be an awkward encounter, given the knowledge she had of Dr and Mrs Benson's extra-marital affairs, but she need not have done so. The doctor was kind, cheerful and thorough in his examination. He pronounced Grace and the baby to be in good health, and calculated that the birth would be due at the start of August. He prescribed regular gentle exercise and a moderate diet. He also advised Grace to discontinue the wearing of a corset and crinoline. Benedict was present at this visit, taking in every word that the doctor said.

So it was, the following morning, that when Grace went to dress in a corset as usual, he placed gentle hands on her shoulders and said, "Darling, you know it is time to stop wearing this garment."

"I won't have the laces very tight, I promise," she cajoled.

"Grace!" Benedict's voice was sterner than she was used to hearing it.

"I shall look fat without it," she complained.

He drew her to him. "Oh Grace, your belly is going to swell with this baby, there are no two ways about it."

"But it has not yet done so, or at least very little. Can I not carry on as before for a bit longer?"

Benedict sighed. "You heard the doctor, Grace. It is not good for you or the baby to have the corset press so on your abdomen. And you will not look fat, I promise. The buttons of your dress will cinch it to your waist and still give you a very pretty shape." His voice turned husky as he kissed her and said, "You must know, darling, that you will always look beautiful to me."

Only slightly mollified, she kissed him back. "But you are partial, Benedict. What about the rest of the people I will encounter in the village or at church?"

Benedict chuckled. "Gracie, are you fishing for yet more compliments? If so, I will oblige. Darling girl, no one within miles of this village can hold a candle to your beauty, even when you are big with child. And Gracie, what matter their opinion? Is it not more important to have concern for the health of our child?"

She stroked her palms over his chest, which was still shirtless. "You are right, of course," she said, looking chastened. "I had not thought vanity to be one of my sins, but it seems I am not immune to it."

He trapped her hands to his chest. "It is a human frailty we all suffer from to some extent—and I include myself in this. Do you know, Grace, ever since you spoke of drawing me in the nude, I have not been able to stop wondering how I would look, depicted by you on paper. Now is that not vanity?"

She laughed. "Is it because I called you beautiful?"

His lips quirked. "Perhaps. I have not been used to such epithets in my life. So you see, it awakened my own vanity." He looked down at her hands on his chest. "Every time I feel the touch of your hands on me, I want to bask in your admiration."

She tucked her head into the crook of his neck. "It is the same for me too," she murmured, raining soft kisses on his smooth skin. Looking up into his eyes, she added, "Perhaps then, Benedict, I can begin to sketch you tonight. We can lock the upstairs parlour door while I do so."

His cheeks turned a little rosy at the thought, but he nodded. "Very well."

They finished dressing, she without the corset or crinoline, but with the addition of an extra layer of petticoats to give her skirt more body. "I suppose," she remarked, "that I shall have to go to the dressmaker in Witney to have some new dresses made that will accommodate my belly once it grows, and some suitable undergarments to replace the corset."

He looked up from the chair where he sat, pulling on his boots. "We can go into town later this week, if you wish. I have an errand to do there too—some items to collect from the chemist that I have put on order."

Benedict had continued with his investigations into pregnancy and childbirth, which were as thorough as his studies of lovemaking had been, if not more so, for the matter concerned Grace's safety and that of their unborn child. He had read numerous books and pamphlets, but still he felt ill-prepared for what was ahead.

As a clergyman, he was familiar with the part of the church service dedicated to pregnant women, in which prayers were made for their safe deliverance and preservation from the great dangers of childbirth. Now, however, each time he said the words of those prayers during Sunday church service, he thought of Grace and worried. What if something terrible were to happen to her and to the baby? He could not conceive of a worse fate. As his worry grew, so too did his determination to learn as much as possible about childbirth and to investigate how best to avert such a disastrous possibility. He pestered Dr Benson with endless questions and borrowed his copies of the Lancet to peruse them at length for any articles of interest.

Soon, he learned that the two major causes of maternal death were haemorrhage and the dreaded childbed fever which could attack and kill women days after delivering their child. These were the two evils which at all costs would need to be avoided for Grace, but how? More investigations followed. He read of instances where excessive bleeding was controlled by the ingestion of an infusion made with ergot powder, and determined to arm himself with a supply of this substance. On the matter of childbed fever, however, he was less successful in finding answers until a chance conversation with Sarah one evening when she and Ambrose came over for dinner at Mulverley Grange.

It had begun with a mention by Grace that just this morning, she had had to spit out her tea because the milk in it had spoiled. To this, Sarah had responded, "Well, if you do not heat your milk until it very nearly boils, then it is no wonder that it spoils."

"What do you mean?" had asked Grace with a frown.

"Surely you must know that it is the tiny living organisms in milk that multiply and cause it to spoil?"

Grace had laughed. "There are no living organisms in my milk, I do assure you!"

"But of course there are. These organisms, or germs as they are called, are everywhere. In the air, on the surface of your hands and in the milk you drink each day."

Grace had held up her hand and examined it closely. "I do not see any organisms here," she said a little mockingly.

"Of course you will not see them," Sarah had huffed. "They are so small as to be invisible to our eyes, but exist they do. It has been proven."

Ambrose had raised his gaze to his sister. "Proven? Now that is a bold claim, Sarah."

"Bold but true. It is in a paper I read just this week by Louis Pasteur, a French scientist. He conducted experiments which show that putrefaction is caused by living organisms that are present all around us, so small that we cannot see them with our bare eyes. I will not bore you with the details, but he has gone on to surmise that the spread of infectious diseases is due to these germs that we cannot see but which can multiply and cause putrefaction."

Now this had Benedict's full attention. "Will you send me this paper? I should very much like to read it."

"Of course," had answered Sarah. Turning to Grace, she added, "In the meantime, you would be well advised to heat your milk as soon as it comes from the dairy, and leave it covered with a clean lid. You will see then that your milk will no longer spoil."

Grace was sceptical, yet curious at the same time. "I will instruct Cook to do so," she promised.

In the weeks that followed, Grace discovered, to her slight annoyance, that Sarah was indeed right. The milk that was heated and kept covered seemed to last a very long time without spoiling. Could this mean that there were indeed tiny organisms everywhere that she could not see? In bed, one night, as they conversed before Benedict put out the light, she spoke of this to him. "You know, much as it galls me, Sarah was right about heating the milk. It no longer spoils, even when left for days on end. Do you think she is also right about there being tiny organisms that spread illness?"

Benedict ran a finger through Grace's long blond tresses, enjoying the silky feel of them. "I have read the paper she sent me with great interest," he said softly, "and I am beginning to think there might be some truth in it."

"Perhaps in some way, we have already known this. Ma always asked us to wash our hands thoroughly with soap before coming to the dinner table. She said people who did not wash were more likely to get sick."

"Your mother is very wise," smiled Benedict. "It would make sense that washing with soap and keeping surfaces clean would reduce the transmission of these micro-organisms, if they do exist. You know, it also makes me wonder if it is not the doctors themselves, going from patient to patient, that help sometimes to spread these diseases."

Grace shuddered. "Now you are going to give me an eternal disgust of Dr Benson. How am I to shake his hand if all I can think is that it is contaminated with disease-inducing organisms?"

Benedict chuckled and tipped Grace's face to his for a kiss. "Have you noticed, Gracie, that our minds seem to follow a similar trajectory? I too have been thinking the very same thing. In fact, I am minded to ask him to wash his hands before he next examines you." He also had another thought, which he kept to himself. Could it be the doctors and midwives who were the chief cause of childbed fever? If they were inserting unclean hands and instruments inside a labouring woman, might they not inadvertently be infecting her? He resolved to speak with Dr Benson about this at the earliest opportunity.

It was around a week later that this opportunity presented itself. Benedict had been called to the bedside of a sick farmer who lived on the outskirts of their village. There, he saw that the patient was being attended to by none other than Dr Benson. Afterwards, as they both made to leave, Benedict engaged the doctor in conversation. "Dr Benson, I have been meaning to ask for your thoughts on germ theory," he said.

"Germ theory?" Dr Benson wrinkled his forehead in perplexity.

"Yes, it is the theory that infection of diseases is transmitted by live micro-organisms that are too small for the eye to see. Have you heard of it?"

"Ah, I think I know what you mean," replied the doctor cheerfully. "There is a surgeon in Glasgow going by the name of Lister who insists on using carbolic acid to cleanse his instruments and hands before doing surgery. Claims it has reduced deaths in his hospital ward by a significant amount."

Benedict's eyes sharpened with interest. "So, you think this theory has merit?"

Dr Benson shrugged. "The theory runs counter to the established view that disease is caused by spontaneous generation of putrefying matter. I am not one to question orthodoxy unless I am presented with incontrovertible proof. Therefore, I cannot say that tiny live organisms are a cause for the spread of infections. It is a possibility though, I do admit."

"As it is a possibility," Benedict said in an urgent tone, "I think it would be best if we were to follow this surgeon's example when it comes to Grace's confinement. I do not want her to succumb to childbed fever."

Dr Benson laughed. "Mr Sedgwick, I fear you worry too much. Let me put your mind at rest. I have delivered hundreds of babies safely without recourse to cleansing in carbolic acid."

"But there have been cases where the mothers have died of this fever?"

"Sometimes, it is unavoidable" said the doctor gently. "However, you are a man of faith, Mr Sedgwick, and so I am sure you will put your trust in God."

Benedict felt a dash of irritation with the good doctor. Of course he would put his trust in God, but that did not mean he should be lax in his efforts to ensure Grace's safety. He tried to quash this irritation and smooth the frown that was forming on his face. With a bland look at Dr Benson, he remarked, "Nevertheless, I believe it is best to err on the side of caution. I will order some of this carbolic acid from the chemist in Witney and have it to hand for Grace's confinement."

Dr Benson smiled agreeably. "There is no harm in it and if it puts your mind at rest, then wash with carbolic is what we shall do."

So it was that Benedict and Grace made a trip to Witney shortly after she dispensed with wearing a corset—Grace to visit the dressmaker and Benedict to collect the items he had ordered from the chemist, including a supply of carbolic acid.

CHAPTER 30

THE SEDGWICKS SETTLED into their life as a married couple, Grace spending time with her horses first thing in the morning, then continuing on to the church to fulfil her self-imposed duties as Benedict's secretary. There were the occasional frolics to be had behind closed doors when thoughts of each other proved too much of a distraction, but Benedict maintained that having her there with him was highly beneficial to his work.

Spring turned to summer, and Grace's belly grew larger. Apart from minor discomforts that were inherent to her condition, she was fit and healthy. Dr Benson pronounced himself well satisfied with the progress of her pregnancy upon his visit to Mulverley Grange in mid-July. Glancing at Benedict, who hovered attentively by her side, he added, "I see your husband's many efforts to inform himself about your condition have borne fruit, for I have never seen a patient better cared for than yourself, Mrs Sedgwick."

Grace laid her hand on Benedict's. "I consider myself the luckiest of women for having the good fortune to be married to this wonderfully kind gentleman." As she had hoped, his cheeks turned pink at the compliment. One day, she needed to capture in paint that dear face in the throes of a blush.

The only thing to mar those happy months was the worrisome news arriving from America. In April, the first military hostilities had broken out in a war between the states in the union and those that had seceded. Letters, which already took far too long to reach their destination, now became more infrequent. Grace fretted about her family, even though

Benedict tried to reassure her that the Stanton farm in Ohio was far from the theatre of war. When at last, a missive arrived in late July, it brought with it mixed news. The family was well and keeping busy trying to manage the higher demand for grain precipitated by the war. However, a recruiting officer for the union army had passed by their nearest town and persuaded Benjamin to sign up, much against Uncle Frank's advice. Benjamin had left in early July, leaving Frank and Charlotte heartbroken and desperately praying for his safe return.

Ma wrote that John had also made noises about wanting to join the war effort, but a stern talking to had convinced him for now to wait until he was of age. She hoped and prayed that this war would be over by the time John turned eighteen. She and Jasper sent their love, expressing the hope that Grace was in good health and spirits.

It would be fair to say that upon the reading of this letter, Grace was in the opposite of good spirits. She set it down on the breakfast table and began to weep. Benedict, who had been observing her in concern throughout the reading, came to her side in an instant, placing comforting arms around her. "Grace, what is it?" he asked.

In answer, she handed him the letter while the tears continued to stream down her face. She mopped them with her napkin as Benedict read Ma's letter. Once he was done, he placed it back on the table and bent his head to kiss the top of her head. "Oh Gracie, I am sorry to hear of Benjamin's departure. Let us keep him in our prayers."

She nodded into the napkin, croaking, "And what of John?"

"I believe good sense will prevail," Benedict replied. "He is your mother's son after all and some of her wise nature must have rubbed off on all her children. He must surely know he is too young to enlist and that he is needed on the farm more than ever now that Benjamin is gone."

Grace took hold of his hand and brought it to her damp cheek. "I wish they were not so far away," she said with a catch in her voice.

"I know," murmured Benedict, and kissed her again.

Later that afternoon, while Grace napped on the chaise longue, Benedict composed a letter to his father, inviting him to visit them again, and to have a more extended stay this time. Perhaps his father could help bolster Grace's spirits, like he had the last time. Besides, he wanted him there for the birth of his grandchild.

A few days later, a response from Walter Sedgwick arrived, announcing that he would be able to join them the following Saturday. Benedict looked up at Grace with a pleased smile. "I have good news for you, Gracie," he said.

She stifled a yawn and smiled wanly in return. With the hot summer heat and her swollen belly, she had found it difficult to sleep last night. "What is it?" she asked.

"Father is coming to stay with us and should arrive on Saturday."

Now Grace's smile widened. "Oh good, I am glad."

On Saturday, right on schedule, Walter Sedgwick arrived at Mulverley Grange. Winford showed him in and led him to the paved terrace at the back of the house, where Grace and Benedict were lounging on this warm and sticky August afternoon. Grace reclined on a chaise longue under an awning to provide shade from the sun while Benedict stretched out comfortably in an armchair beside her, his feet resting on the pouffe they had brought down from the upstairs parlour.

While Grace napped, Benedict read quietly from yet another pamphlet about birthing that had just recently arrived in the post. For the past several weeks, he had been keeping up a regular correspondence with a Dr Edmunds, an expert on midwifery who had a medical practice in Bethnal Green. Dr Edmunds had come to Benedict's attention after he read a notice in the paper about a successful Caesarean operation performed by this gentleman. Intensely curious about this, Benedict had written to the doctor, wanting to find out more, and there had ensued a protracted correspondence between the two.

Now, on seeing his father being escorted in, Benedict put down his pamphlet and got to his feet quickly. Father and son exchanged a warm embrace, then Walter turned to gaze at Grace, who had been awakened by the sound of their voices. He put a hand on her shoulder, saying, "No dear, do not get up on my account. You look so comfortable there, I would hate to disturb you."

"You are not disturbing me at all, Walter. Just give me a moment."

She sat up and slid her feet into the slippers she had tucked under the chaise longue, then with a mighty heft—and some assistance from Benedict—stood. An instant later, she had thrown her arms around Walter. "Oh, it is so good to see you!"

Walter beamed, touched by the warm welcome. Gazing fondly at his daughter-in-law, he replied, "No happier than I am to see you, my dear. Tell me, how have you been?"

"I am well, though have been suffering dreadfully from this heat. I do so wish it would cool even a little bit so I could get a good night's sleep."

Walter settled himself on an armchair that Winford had brought out for him as everyone else also resumed their seats. "It is dreadfully hot, I agree," he said, "though it is very pleasant out here, I must say."

"Yes, it is very nice," responded Grace, "until evening comes and the midges start gathering. Then I'm afraid, we shall have to retire back to the house."

Just then, Winford returned bearing a tray of cold barley water and some hulled strawberries, freshly picked from the vegetable garden. These refreshments were placed on a small side table.

"We like it so much out here that we are dining al fresco these days," added Benedict. "I hope you do not mind, father." He handed a glass of the cold, sweet drink to his father, then one to Grace.

"Not at all," said Walter cheerfully. "In fact, it reminds me of that time long ago when I took your mother on honeymoon to Italy. The villa we stayed at had a terrace just like this where we ate most of our meals. I shall fancy myself on an exotic holiday rather than in the home country."

"Oh, I do so want to go to Italy someday," said Grace. "I hear the food is exceedingly good and that beautiful language is so musical to the ear."

Benedict leaned over to kiss her brow. "I am sure that can be arranged, though we may have to wait a little while longer to have a belated honeymoon of our own," he said, glancing meaningfully at her belly.

She stroked a hand over it and sighed. "I know. I do so wish this little one would hurry and make his appearance. The doctor says it could be any day now."

"Have you picked out any names yet?" asked Walter.

"If it is a boy, then we shall call him Henry, after my grandpa, and if it is a girl..." Grace's voice trailed as she exchanged a glance with Benedict.

"We would like to name her Anna, after mother," he said, completing her sentence.

There was a long silence. Finally, Walter spoke, a slight thickness in his voice betraying his emotion, "I am sure she would be very proud to have a grandchild named after her."

A WEEK PASSED, and then another. Grace's patience was almost at an end. When was this child going to make an appearance? It seemed like she was forever going to be lugging around this great big weight in her belly. She became irritable and snapped at Benedict, then immediately regretted her sharp words. He bore with it good naturedly. He could quite imagine how uncomfortable she was all the time. The one silver lining in the cloud was that the weather had finally cooled, with just a hint of an autumnal breeze in the air.

On the morning of 15th August, Grace woke a little later than usual, having finally had a long, restful night. A feel of the pillow beside hers confirmed that Benedict was already up and gone. With an effort, she came upright and got out of bed to wash and dress. Feeling decidedly hungry, she made her way down to the dining room, where she found Benedict and Walter, their breakfast finished, lingering over a cup of coffee.

"Good morning all," she called out in a cheerful voice.

Benedict blessed her with his beautiful smile as he stood and pulled the chair back for her to sit, pressing a gentle kiss to her cheek. "Good morning, darling. You look well rested."

"I am, and famished too!" replied Grace, helping herself to some eggs and cold beef. She took the slice of toast that Benedict had buttered for her with a smile of thanks. Winford came in, bearing a steaming pot of freshly brewed tea.

"Thank you, Winford," she said, beaming up at him.

Walter observed her in amusement. "You are looking remarkably cheerful today, Grace."

"I am feeling very cheerful. It must be the effect of having a good night's sleep." Turning to her husband, she added, "Darling, could we walk down to the village today? I do believe the exercise will do me good, and besides, I would like to stop by at the haberdasher's. This cooling weather reminds me I should get a little fleece blanket for baby. I remember seeing some such a while back in the shop."

"Are you sure you want to walk the half mile there? We could take the carriage."

Grace waved her hand airily. "No carriage please. I am fully up to walking. I have such a bounce in my step that I could walk twice the distance I am sure."

At this, Benedict exchanged a puzzled glance with his father who smiled knowingly back at him. Returning his gaze to Grace, he replied, "Of course, darling, but I think I will ask Stanley to follow us in the carriage, in case you tire and need it for the journey home."

"I won't," she smiled, "but let the carriage come along by all means."

A half-hour later, Benedict and Grace set off, Walter electing to stay at home and read. They walked at a brisk pace, enjoying the cool, pleasant breeze on their cheeks. Grace felt a wave of pure, unadulterated happiness. Life was good. She had the best of the best of husbands. And soon, they would have a baby to love and cherish, the first of several she dreamed of having. She could picture her home a few years from now, filled with the happy sounds of children,

Benedict too, was filled with a sense of joy. Seeing Grace happy inevitably lifted his mood, but there was also a pleasant sensation engendered from walking on such a fine day with the woman he loved on his arm. They traversed the bucolic parkland of Mulverley Grange, enjoying the sight of rolling green hills and feeling a sense of profound tranquillity. It was the sense that nothing bad could touch them. In the space they existed, there was only good.

In such high spirits, they reached the village and made their way to the haberdashery shop. Grace exclaimed over the fine white fleece blanket, feeling its softness with her fingers and vowing it was just the thing for baby. The shopkeeper, wreathed in smiles, went to pack their purchase while they waited at the counter. As Grace went to lean a hand on it, she suddenly felt a sharp pain and gave a little cry.

"What is it, Grace?" asked Benedict.

She put a hand to her belly where the pain had been. "It was a moment of pain, but now it has gone." She smiled, "I am fine."

Benedict took out his pocket watch and noted the time. "Let me know if it happens again. Have you been experiencing any other pain or fluttering in your belly?"

"Well, ever since breakfast, baby has been rather restless. But it's only been a minor discomfort, nothing I would call pain."

Benedict's face was creased in concern. "From what I have read, it does not start as very painful, but I believe your labour pains have begun, Gracie. We need to get you home as soon as possible."

The shopkeeper came back with their wrapped parcel. "Here you go, Mrs Sedgwick," she said.

Grace reached across for the parcel, and as she did so, felt another sharp pain. "Ah!" she gasped.

Benedict's arm came around her. "Come sit over here, darling," he said, leading her to a nearby chair. "Another pain?" he asked once she had sat down.

"Yes." She raised frightened eyes to him.

"Oh dear, Mrs Sedgwick," flapped the shopkeeper. "Are you quite alright?"

Benedict threw her an impatient glance. "My wife is fine, but I need to get her home. Our carriage is waiting outside. I wonder if you could carry the parcel and give it to our coachman, as my hands will be full helping my wife."

"Of course, of course."

Benedict kneeled in front of Grace, looking into her eyes. "Darling, nothing to worry about. Your labour pains have begun, so we are going straight home and to bed. I'll send for the doctor as soon as I have you settled. Do you think you can stand if I give you my arm to lean on?"

"Yes," she murmured.

He got to his feet and held out his hand to help her up. Slowly, with great care, he led her to the waiting carriage outside, which he was profoundly relieved he had had the foresight to bring. Once seated, Benedict rapped on the roof to signal that they were ready to go. They set off at a trot, just as

Grace doubled over under the pain of another set of contractions. "Oh," she breathed, after they had passed. "This one hurt a bit more."

Glancing at the time on his watch, Benedict said with a frown. "They are only a few minutes apart."

"Is that a bad thing?"

Benedict gathered her to him. "No darling. It simply means baby is in a hurry to come out."

She giggled. "I am in a hurry to see him. Or her."

He smiled. "So am I."

They remained silent while the carriage continued its clattering journey home. Another contraction ripped through her belly before they made it back to Mulverley Grange. Benedict held her, rubbing her back soothingly until it passed.

She raised anxious eyes to him. "Benedict, will it hurt a lot?"

He stroked a loose strand of hair back from her face. "We spoke of this, remember? There will be pain, but you can get through it. Remember what we read about taking deep breaths in and out to help with the pain. And if it gets to be too much, there is the option of taking some chloroform, just like Queen Victoria did. I have a bottle of it up in our room."

She nodded, reassured. "Will you stay with me, Benedict? I know husbands are not supposed to watch their children being delivered, but I would like you there with me."

"If that is your wish, then nothing will keep me from being with you."

Once home, he led her up to her room, calling out to Winford to send for Dr Benson. Upstairs, he helped her out of her dress and into a loose night gown, then settled her into bed. In anticipation of this day, he had already set out all the things they would need in one corner— clean sheets that had been washed in very hot water and folded in readiness for use, a set of medical instruments that had also been washed repeatedly in boiling water and placed in a sterile metal tin, the vials of chloroform and carbolic acid, a large sachet of ergot powder, some clean cloths, two jugs of water that had been boiled and cooled, then covered in clean gauze to stop contamination, a clean basin for washing hands.

He sat at her side, stroking a hand down her arm. "Do you need any more pillows, darling?"

She fidgeted in the bed, trying to find a comfortable semi-reclining position. "Perhaps one or two more?"

"I will get them from the next room." He went through the connecting door to his room and brought back two fluffy pillows which he placed behind her. "How is that?"

"Much better," she smiled, then gasped as another wave of contractions assailed her.

He stroked her back soothingly. "That's right. You're doing so well, brave girl."

Grace closed her eyes and let her head fall back on the pillow. She was not so sure she was being brave. She wanted her ma. With a sigh, she said, "I wish Ma were here."

"I know, darling, I know. Would you like me to send for Isabella?"

She nodded. He rang the bell by her bedside, and a minute later, there came a knock on the door. Hester, one the house maids, tiptoed in timidly. "Hester," said Benedict. "Could you speak to Winford, please, and ask him to send word to Stanton Hall that Mrs Sedgwick has started her labour pains?"

She bobbed a curtsy. "Yes, sir," and went out again.

Grace rested her head on the pillow. "Benedict."

"Yes, darling?"

"I have been meaning to ask you this for some time."

"What have you wanted to ask me?"

She took a deep breath and let it out. "Will you love this baby, Benedict, truly as if he were your own?" she asked, touching a hand to her belly.

He covered her hand with his. "The baby is mine, Gracie, in every way that matters. I am its father. Have no doubt about the depth of my love for him, or her if it is a girl."

She closed her eyes. "Good. I am glad."

There was peaceful silence for a minute or two, then, "Benedict."

"Yes, dear?"

"If you love this child as your own, you will do everything you can to protect it, won't you?"

"Of course."

"I mean, if things get bad during my labour and I become out of it for a bit, you will make sure everything possible is done to protect our child, won't you? I want you to be his champion when I am too weak to be."

Benedict's voice was thick with emotion. "I will." He laid his forehead against hers. "What would your mother say if she were here right now?"

"She would say to keep my faith strong."

"Then let me say it in her stead. Keep your faith strong, Gracie."

"I will." She gasped as another set of contractions hit her, clasping Benedict's hand tightly until it was over. Shortly after, there came a knock on the door.

"Enter!" called Benedict.

It was his father. "May I come in?" he asked from the door.

"Yes of course," called out Grace.

Walter stepped inside and came to sit on the edge of the bed. "How are doing, my dear?"

"Fine, I suppose. I was telling Benedict that I miss my ma."

Walter nodded. "That is understandable. You are in my prayers, dear Grace. May you have a speedy and healthy delivery." He leaned over to kiss her brow, then turned to Benedict. "I shall be in the parlour next door, should you need me." He squeezed his son's shoulder, then stood and left the room.

For the next hour, Benedict sat with Grace, occasionally walking her around the room, and soothing her as best he could through each set of contractions, each one more painful than the last. He was helped in this by Isabella, who had arrived soon after the message had been sent to Stanton Hall.

In the course of the second hour, Dr Benson arrived. Under instruction from Benedict, he first washed his hands in a solution of carbolic acid and water, before beginning his examination. With a jovial smile, he approached the bed. "Have no fear, Mrs Sedgwick. Everything seems to be progressing as it should. If you will pull back your gown, I will examine your abdomen."

Isabella helped lift the gown over Grace's belly, placing a sheet over her mound to cover her modesty. The doctor spent some time palpating her abdomen. Finally, he lifted the sheet to examine her below. "Good, good," he remarked. "Your cervix is dilated to just under an inch. That is what we want to see." He replaced the sheet and looked up. "Now for the news that is a little less welcome. It seems your baby is in the breech position. That is to say, its head is facing up rather than down. However, there is still time for the baby to turn. Let us try to encourage it to move as much as possible."

"How so?" asked Grace.

"Try to get into positions that will help it to turn. This will mean getting out of bed and bending your body forward so as to tilt your belly upside down. While you do so, your husband or cousin may massage your abdomen with some oil and try to coax the little one to turn. Stay active by moving around the room as much as you can. If you tire, of course, you may return to bed." He stood then, readying to go. "I will return in a few hours to check on your progress, Mrs Sedgwick." As he headed for the door, he made a sign to Benedict that he wished to speak with him outside in private.

Benedict kissed Grace's brow. "I shall return shortly, darling." Quietly, he stood and followed the doctor out of the room. They walked together a few paces down the hall, towards the parlour door that was open. Walter looked up from the book he was reading and seeing them, rose quickly to his feet.

Benedict looked worriedly at the doctor. "Please tell me what it is, doctor, and do not withhold any part of the truth."

Dr Benson sighed. "We must pin our hopes on the baby changing its position over the next few hours. If it remains in the breech position, then we may have a prolonged labour and further complications."

"I have read about this. It is possible for a baby to be delivered feet first."

"Possible, yes, but also highly dangerous for both mother and child, if, as it is likely, the baby's head becomes stuck in the birth canal. We may then need to use forceps to ease the baby out, but this can often result in damage to its cranium. Fatal damage." He paused. "Our very best hope is to get that baby to turn. Get your wife out of the bed and bending forward to tilt her abdomen, and if that does not work try putting pressure on the abdomen to help the baby move. I do not want to sound the alarm too soon, but being as this child is overdue, it is large and does not have much space to move within the abdominal cavity. But one must have hope." He patted Benedict's arm, then turned to leave.

Benedict followed him with his eyes, too shocked and distressed to do anything but stand stock still. Once the doctor was out of sight, Walter placed a hand on his son's shoulder. Turning to his father, Benedict said hoarsely, "I cannot lose her. I cannot."

"I know," said Walter quietly.

"We must do all we can to get the baby to turn."

"We must."

Benedict took a shallow breath. "And what if it does not work? What then?"

"Then all actions will be taken to preserve the life of the mother."

Benedict wiped a tear that had escaped his eye. "I have read about it, father, and it does not bear thinking about. A procedure they call craniotomy. More like savage barbarity. I will not let that happen to my child."

"Even if it means saving Grace's life?"

Now Benedict's expression turned agonised. "I-I cannot let her die. But if she learns that her life was saved by means of sacrificing her baby, then I fear she may never recover her sanity. I will not let that happen."

Walter sighed. "What is the alternative, son?"

Benedict's face took on a mutinous look. "There is one alternative—the Caesarean operation."

Walter hissed a shocked breath. "Surely you are not suggesting Dr Benson carry out such an operation?"

Implacably, Benedict replied, "No. If it comes to it, I will carry out the operation myself."

"Oh, Benedict."

"Let me be, father. Now, I must return to my wife."

Without another word, he strode down the corridor towards the bedroom.

CHAPTER 31

FOR THE NEXT eighteen hours, Grace laboured. In vain did they try to turn the baby from its breech position. It stubbornly would not move. With each hour that passed, Grace grew weaker as her pain increased. During one agonising set of contractions, Benedict could stand it no more and gave her a light dose of chloroform, which allowed her to rest for a little while.

Dr Benson came back on three occasions, each time shaking his head in dismay. On this last visit, he took Benedict aside to confer once more. "Mr Sedgwick, the time has come for a difficult decision. I fear your wife cannot last much longer in this condition. Her cervix is fully dilated, and I propose deliver this child, come what may. I will have to guide its feet out first and then gently pull it out, but in the likelihood its head gets stuck, then I am very much afraid I will have to use the forceps on its skull to help get it out. I know it is never easy to consign your child to such a fate, but we must now at all costs concentrate on saving your wife."

Benedict stared coldly at him. "No," he said.

"Mr Sedgwick, I am afraid there is no other alternative."

"There is. We can perform the Caesarean section operation to save both their lives."

Dr Benson gaped at him in astonishment. "You cannot be serious, sir."

"I have never been more serious, Dr Benson."

The doctor shook his head. "If we were in London, we could call on Dr Edmunds of Bethnal Green to assist, for he has successful experience of such a difficult operation. But here and now, such a procedure would be an impossibility. I could not in good conscience advocate it."

"Yet you would advocate the killing of my child."

Dr Benson spluttered, "Mr Sedgwick, that is an ungenerous thing to say."

"It is but the truth."

"The truth is, that in all probability, your child cannot be saved. It is your wife that must now have the highest priority."

"I always have my wife as the highest of priorities!" Benedict's tone was sharp. "And it is for this reason that I propose such a course of action. She would want me to protect her child at all costs."

Dr Benson shook his head in disbelief. "By sacrificing her own life? This is madness!"

"From a purely selfish perspective, I too would put Grace's life above any other. The temptation to go with your wishes, doctor, is strong, so very strong." Benedict's voice broke, and he had to take a moment to regroup before he could continue. "And yet, I know that to do so will irrevocably break her precious trust in me. I know with a deep certainty that Grace would want me to do everything in my power to save our child, even at the risk to her life. So, it is her choice I am making, more so than mine. She has entrusted me with the protection of our child."

Still, the doctor shook his head, so Benedict set out his argument further. "I do not propose to sacrifice any lives, doctor, but to save them both. I have read extensively about this procedure. I know where to make the incision and I have silver wire for the sutures. The two main risks it entails are uncontrolled haemorrhage and infection leading to a subsequent fever. With regards to infection, I am well prepared and will ensure that transmission of dangerous micro-organisms is minimised. As for the bleeding, I have ergot extract to help contract the uterus and can use pressure to stem the bleed. I know this is not without risk, but we are at the stage now where it is the lesser evil. Now, Dr Benson, will you assist me in this or not?"

The doctor was silent for a good minute. "If I do, I will not take any responsibility for your wife's life should she not make it through the procedure."

"I take full responsibility for this decision." Benedict's voice was firm and decisive.

Dr Benson hesitated, then abruptly nodded his head. In silence, they both walked back into the room. Benedict went to sit at Grace's bedside where she lay, weak and barely conscious. "Gracie," he whispered.

Her eyes fluttered open.

"Do you trust me?"

She nodded imperceptibly.

"We need to operate to save the baby. Make an incision in your belly and get it out. I think I can do it, but it is not without risk to you. However, if we do not do this, then we may not be able to save our baby."

With all her remaining strength, she clutched his hand. In a feeble voice that strained to be heard, she breathed, "Save baby. Promise!"

He squeezed her hand gently. "I promise." He looked up at Isabella, who was sitting on the other side of the bed. She stared at him for a long time, then nodded. Briskly, he got to his feet and went to the corner table with all his supplies. With unnatural calm, as if in a trance, he mixed a strong infusion of ergot powder with water into a small cup, then went to Grace's side again. "Gracie, you need to drink this." Gently, he lifted her head and aided her to drink the remedy. Then he stood again and faced the doctor. "We need to wash our hands in carbolic solution, then place this sterile sheet under Grace."

The doctor nodded and proceeded to do as instructed. Once Grace was positioned over the clean sheet, Benedict spoke again. "I am going to give Grace a stronger dose of chloroform to sedate her. Then, I will cleanse her abdomen with a carbolic and water solution. While I do so, please prepare the knife for incision, the wire and needle. They all need to be cleaned with carbolic acid."

Again, the doctor nodded in acquiescence. Benedict took a clean cloth and poured two drops of chloroform on it. He took it to Grace. Sensing his presence, her eyelids fluttered open. "Gracie, once I put this over your nose, it will send you to sleep. You will wake after the operation is finished. Will you let me do this?"

"Yes," she mouthed.

He kissed her then. "I love you," he whispered. A moment later, the drugged cloth was at her nose, and she fell unconscious. With a deep breath, Benedict stood. He looked at Isabella, who remained mute in her seat by the bed. "Keep a close eye on her, Bella. Should she wake, you will need to restrain her."

"Very well," she said.

Benedict went to his work table and took a fresh cloth which he doused in carbolic solution. He took it to Grace, cleaning her abdomen thoroughly. Once that was done, he held his hand up for the knife, which was handed to him. Speaking softly, he said, "I will make a transverse incision of around six inches just above the pubis." He held the knife in his hand and looked down at Grace's swollen belly. Could he do this? He had never cut through human flesh in his life. The prospect was daunting, if he thought about it too much. *"I must not let my hand shake,"* he thought. With a last prayer to God for Grace's safe deliverance, he brought the knife down and positioned it where the incision needed to be. Then, before he could let himself waver, he cut through the flesh in one slow, careful motion.

Blood oozed from the wound. "Give me a cloth soaked in carbolic solution and wrung dry," he instructed Dr Benson. The cloth was duly rendered sterile and given into his hand. Carefully, Benedict eased the cut flesh open. With a gentle hand, he probed inside. With a rapidly beating heart, he used the knife again to make a shallow incision to the uterus. Using the sterile cloth he had been given, he staunched the blood, then probed again. "I can feel the baby's leg," he said with a slight quaver to his voice. He probed further, pulling the muscular walls apart to get a better grip on the baby, then ever so gently, began to pull it out. Slowly, the legs, then the torso, then the head of the baby were brought out of Grace's belly. With bloodied hands, he held his child for the first time. The baby scrunched its face in displeasure, then let out a faint cry. "It's a girl; a wondrous, beautiful girl," Benedict murmured. Dr Benson stepped forward with a clean sheet and took the child, enveloping her securely.

By now, Benedict was intent on stopping the haemorrhage of blood that was streaming out of the open wound. "Isabella, take the baby from Dr Benson, but do not go far as we have not yet cut the cord. Dr Benson, I need you to exert pressure on this side of the abdomen."

While Isabella and the doctor followed his instructions, Benedict pressed down with the carbolic infused cloth on the wound, trying to staunch the blood. "There is the placenta," said Dr Benson, pressing down on one side of the abdomen. Carefully, Benedict eased the placenta out and placed it on the side of the sheet, soaking it with blood.

"Has the uterus contracted enough for us to close the incision?" asked Benedict, a hint of panic in his voice.

"Very nearly," soothed Dr Benson. "Keep pressing down gently." A minute later. "I think we can start the suturing now. Hold on while I get the silver wire and needle. Let me take over and do this, Benedict."

"Have they been soaked in carbolic?" rasped Benedict.

"They have."

It seemed an age before the doctor was back, holding the needle and wire, together with a fresh cloth doused in carbolic solution. Taking the cloth first, Benedict wiped the excess blood.

Then the doctor, needle and silver wire in hand, began to suture the wound closed. When he was done, a third cloth, soaked in the carbolic solution, was placed over the wound, cleaning it thoroughly. Only then did Benedict take out the sterile bandages he had prepared earlier, and with the doctor's help, wrapped them around the sutured wound, securing them with a knot. Finally he took a deep breath and looked at the doctor. "Please check Grace's pulse, doctor."

The doctor went to do so. He looked back at Benedict with a smile of relief. "She is breathing."

Benedict's heart threatened to explode, so fast was it pumping. He looked to Isabella, who still held the baby. "Time to clamp the cord." With hands that shook only slightly, the cord was duly clamped and Isabella was free to step away from the bedside with the baby. She took it to the basin, which the doctor had filled with water, and very gently, proceeded to wash the baby, then wrap her in a fresh set of sheets.

"Such a pretty thing you are," she crooned.

"Her name is Anna," said Benedict with pride.

Isabella brought Anna to him, and he took his daughter into his arms. He had managed to keep his emotions in check throughout the operation, but now, holding this precious bundle, a sob broke out of him. He held Anna close and choked out, "Get father, please."

Isabella nodded and went outside to fetch Walter Sedgwick. In moments, the older gentleman was in the room, taking in the sight of Grace sleeping and a bloodied Benedict holding the baby in his arms.

"Father, meet Anna," croaked Benedict, before succumbing to loud, uncontrolled sobs.

Walter took the baby from him and gazed at her in wonder. "She is beautiful."

"Just like her mother," cried Benedict, trying to regain control of his tears.

Isabella gave him a handkerchief, which he accepted gratefully and wiped his face with. Then with a deep, shuddering breath, he went to Grace and settled himself at her side. Stroking the hair from her face, he whispered urgently, "Gracie, wake up." At first, she did not respond, so he tried again. "Gracie!" And a third time.

Her eyelids fluttered, then opened. She was too weak to move or speak, yet her eyes held a question. "Gracie," Benedict said again. "Meet Anna."

Walter brought the baby over and placed her into her father's arms. "Look at our beautiful daughter, Gracie."

Grace stretched out a weak hand to touch Anna's soft cheek as tears flowed from her eyes. With utmost care, Benedict placed the bundled baby on the pillow beside her mother. Grace studied her wordlessly, then said very softly, "She's perfect." Looking up then at her husband, eyes brimming, she whispered, "Thank you."

EPILOGUE

BENEDICT

Three years later, Venice

IT HAS TAKEN three years, but finally here we are on our long-overdue honeymoon. We could have made the trip sooner, I suppose. Grace has been talking about Italy for years, dropping hints about her wish to make this journey.

At first, it was simply not possible with her pregnancy and subsequent long recovery from giving birth to Anna. Mercifully, Grace was spared the dreaded childbed fever, but the labour weakened her, and it took some weeks to regain her strength. Every day, I checked on her healing wound, anxious for any sign of putrefaction. I made sure it was cleaned and applied fresh, sterile bandages each time. Thankfully with these efforts and with God's grace, we were able to stave off infection.

Then came the time to remove the sutures. As I carefully cut the silver wire with scissors and then pulled it out, I could not help remembering that dreadful day when I had to put my beloved Grace to the knife. I sometimes have dreams about it, but in my dreams, something always goes awry at the moment of incision—a cut that goes too deep, a fatal haemorrhage, an artery accidentally severed. Always then, I awake shivering, my body bathed in sweat.

I do not know if I will ever truly recover from the anguish of that day. It was the most terrifying and difficult decision I have ever had to make in my life and one I hope never to face again.

For the doctor, it was simple—a childless mother is preferable to a motherless child, and the established view is to always prioritise the mother's life. But for me, the choice was far from straightforward. And now, watching sweet Anna grow from a babe to a merry young child, it is nigh on impossible to imagine the fate that would have awaited her had I not insisted on a Caesarean operation.

Grace has made a full recovery apart from the faint pink scar on her abdomen, which I make a point to kiss every single day, along with other parts of her delicious body. It still amazes me, even after all this time, that this beautiful, spirited woman is mine. Gracie. Her name is a melody on my tongue; her scent, a promise of paradise. There is very little I would not do for love of her—even wield a surgeon's knife in my nerveless hands to cut into her belly. So why have I held off on this trip to Italy until now?

Very simply put, it is pride, for though my wife is wealthy, the salary of a curate could not afford the cost of a journey of this kind. I thought perhaps to put funds aside each month so as to in time, accumulate enough to pay for the trip. I made a promise that I would never touch a penny of Grace's money, and I have kept to it. It is enough that I live in great comfort under the roof that is hers and that I ride her magnificent horse each day. I could not contemplate making any further incursions into her wealth.

And then a year ago, our aged vicar, Mr Driscoll, passed away after a long, debilitating illness. Daniel, Viscount Stanton, very kindly gave me the newly vacant living, which has raised my income from £60 to £600 a year. As the new vicar, with a tenfold increase in my earnings, I have finally been able to put together the funds for a journey to Italy. All that remained was to find a suitable person to take over my duties for the three months in which we would be absent. After extensive enquiries, I engaged the services of Mr Lowe as temporary curate of the parish. He arrived in the beginning of August and moved into my former lodgings in the village. I spent a week in his company—an amiable and dedicated man—handing my duties over to him. And then we set off on our adventure, much to Grace's and Anna's excitement.

Our first stop was London, where we spent a most enjoyable few days, staying at Daniel's opulent townhouse on St James's Square. We spent our days there engaged in sightseeing and went out one memorable evening to see a performance of the opera at Covent Garden. Anna, of course, stayed behind with her nurse, who has accompanied us on this trip. From London, we travelled to Dover and crossed the Channel to Calais. Using my copy of Bradshaw's Continental Guide, I mapped a route for ourselves along the railways of continental Europe, and that is how we have made our way to Italy.

We have ridden on many trains and stayed at different towns and cities along our route. I believe Anna's enthusiasm for the trains is nearly as great as mine. On the platform, her small hand held securely in mine, she waits for the train's arrival with great anticipation, whooping in delight when she hears it chugging into the station. Once on board, she ensconces herself on my lap and glues her nose to the window, watching the landscape pass by in fascination and listening to the chuff of the steam locomotive as if it were a musical symphony. Grace likes to call Anna my shadow, for my girl loves nothing more than to follow her papa in his eccentric pursuits. My precious, precious girl.

Our first destination in Italy is Venice, the city of waterways. Today, I have organised a special ride on a gondola, a Venetian type of canoe that conveys people from one place to another in this waterlogged city. The gondolier even promises to serenade us with a song or two along our journey. We arrive in good time in the freshness of the morning, for the heat becomes oppressive later in the day, and I give Grace my hand to help her aboard. She chuckles as the boat rocks under her feet, but soon settles herself on the seat. I follow suit and drop into the seat beside her. We watch in interest as the gondolier steers the gondola away from the dock using a long, pole-like oar. Slowly, we weave our way along the canal, leaving St Mark's Square behind us and heading left onto the Rio Del Palazzo, then towards the Bridge of Sighs.

Taking Grace's hand in mine, I raise it to my lips. "How do you like it so far, darling?" I ask, studying her lovely face.

She beams a radiant smile. "Oh, this is fun, and so romantic. Tell me why this bridge is called The Bridge of Sighs. Should I heave a great sigh as we travel beneath it?"

"Not unless you feel like doing so," I say with a smile. "This bridge connected the Old Doge's Palace to the prison—see the metal bars on all the windows up there—and new prisoners would walk along it on their way to being incarcerated. It is said that they would sigh as they looked through the bridge's window and saw their final view of beautiful Venice."

"Oh, how sad. I suppose it would make one want to sigh."

She looks up at the enclosed white limestone bridge with ornate windows as we approach and then pass beneath it. As we do, she lets out a deep sigh, then twinkles her eyes at me. "There, I have imagined myself a prisoner and sighed. What next for us to see?"

As we continue our leisurely journey, I talk her through the various sights we pass. As befits my way of doing things, I have read extensively all travel guides and histories of Venice that I could find before we embarked on this voyage, and studied maps of the city very carefully so that I should know where we are at all times. I point out interesting features of palazzos and basilicas as our gondola passes alongside them, trying not to bore her with too much detail, for I know my Gracie and she does not quite share my interest in architecture.

It is odd how we often think alike and yet diverge in our interests. It has happened so many times that I no longer wonder at it. Grace will voice a thought just as it passes through my head, as if she has a window into my mind. Perhaps she does. But when it comes to trains, astronomy and my love of old buildings, she does not muster as much enthusiasm as she does on talk of horses. That is just the way it is, and I have long lost my fear that we might be incompatible in our marriage. We complement each other in our differences, and in the things that matter, we are one.

Later in the evening, after we have consumed yet another delicious meal—containing pasta of course, for Grace has developed quite a love for this Italian delicacy—we get into bed for the night. I notice that Grace is wearing her flimsy peach night rail. It is her seduction gown, though in all honesty, she is seductive in anything she wears. But I know it is my signal that her menses are over and that she would like to be ravished. I, of course, am happy to oblige. As she settles herself beside me, I run a possessive hand over her left breast, cupping it gently then playing with that enticing nipple that peeks at me through the thin fabric.

I drop kisses along her collarbone and the soft skin of her neck, making her tremble in anticipation. "What does my sweet Gracie want from her husband tonight?" I ask softly. My hand travels down over the soft swell of her belly and on to her mound, cupping her cunt which is already slick with her arousal.

"You know what I want," she murmurs breathlessly.

"Tell me!"

"Benedict, I want you to fuck me."

That is all the encouragement I require. In an instant, I have her atop me and rasp commandingly, "Sit on my cock, vixen."

She does as I ask, straddling me on her knees as she lowers herself slowly onto my shaft, sighing in pleasure as I fill her. With lust-filled eyes, she gazes back at me, knowing that she needs to wait for my next instruction. It is a game we like to play, where I am the one to direct her and she to obey. I am nothing like this in my everyday life, but in the bedroom, I have come to relish this dominant side of me. "Fuck yourself on my great cock," I growl, "and while you do, I want to see you play with your gorgeous titties."

She begins to rock back and forth on my cock, riding me as if I were one of her beloved horses. Her hands are on her breasts, raising them in offering to me, plumping them up for my delectation, then toying with her hardened nipples. I see the look of abandon on her face as she chases her own pleasure, finding the rhythm that most pleases her and the angle of penetration that stimulates her. Soon, the sight is not enough. I want her bare. "Take off your gown," I grit through my teeth. She lifts it above her head and reveals the most beautiful breasts known to man—just the right size to fit into my hands, rounded and pert, with sweetly puckered nipples I long to suck. "Hands off your titties, vixen, and let me see them bounce… Oh yes, just like that… so beautiful," I purr in delight.

I do not forget though, that my Gracie needs to reach her orgasm. She finds great enjoyment in exhibiting herself to me shamelessly, but she will need more stimulation to reach that peak. So, I give her my next instruction. "Put your hand down on your clitoris, vixen, and touch yourself." She slides two silken fingers to the little nub at the apex of her legs and begins to rub herself, emitting moans of pleasure as she climbs towards that peak. And that is when I spring into action, having so far lain prone and allowed her to dictate the pace. Planting two firm feet on the mattress, I begin to thrust up into her cunt in quick, powerful strokes. "Do not stop touching yourself," I rasp, as I drive my length into her tight, wet heat.

Sweat beads on my forehead as I work to give Gracie her pleasure and strive not to come myself from the delicious agony of being inside her. I sense she is close. Her walls close around my shaft punishingly tight. "Come for me, Gracie!" I cry, giving another sharp thrust into her. She obeys my breathless command, pulsing around my aching cock and making sounds of pleasure loud enough to awaken the occupants of the room next door, but I do not care at this moment, for all I want is to see her soar. On and on, she pulses, her cunt gripping my cock like a vice, until finally she can do no more than collapse against my chest. I hold her to me, still buried inside her but not letting myself climax—I have trained myself over the years not to do so. I whisper into her ear, "I love you, Gracie."

She kisses my chest, near to where my heart beats for her, and whispers back, "I love you too, Benedict." We lay there in glorious contentment until she murmurs, "Darling."

"Yes, my love?"

"I want you to come inside of me. It is time Anna had a brother or sister."

I do not reply at once. I cannot view the prospect of another pregnancy and labour with anything other than anxiety and fear, but I have known that in time I would have to face this demon again. Softly, I say, "Yes, it is time. But first, I want you to climax once more." I shift my body and pull out of her, then crawl to the end of the bed, bringing her with me so her bottom sits on the edge. Dropping to my knees on the floor, which is thankfully covered in a thick rug, I open her up to my hungry gaze. Her soft folds glisten like the petals of a flower sprinkled with morning dew. "You are so beautiful," I croon, breathing in her musky female scent, mixed with a hint of mine. It brings out in me an unreconstructed caveman-like reaction. This woman is mine. All mine.

I bring my mouth to her and take my first taste of the wonderful essence that has become my addiction. Soon, I am busy licking what I am sure is the most perfect cunt in the world. She is still sensitive from her earlier peak and quivers under the touch of my tongue. I apply myself to giving her the greatest pleasure, laying my tongue flat and lapping her with firm, wet strokes, then increasing my speed as I feel her excitement grow, fluttering back and forth quickly over her thickened nub. She strains against me, lifting her pelvis into my mouth, silently begging for more. And I give it to her, with every ounce of energy left in me. I lick her over and over, taking my time, allowing her to climb towards that peak of pleasure once more. I lose consciousness of time, buried in the silken musk of her folds. It could be minutes or an hour; I do not know. Time has no measure when one is in heaven.

I feel her pleasure build, the nub beneath my tongue swelling. She gives a little cry as she climaxes, a small gush of her juices dripping into my welcoming mouth. When she is done, I stand quickly and notch my cock to her opening, wanting to feel her still pulsing cunt around me. I thrust, and I am into her deep. Holding her ankles to my chest, I start fucking my wife with all my might. I am feral in my need, wanting to plant my seed into her womb and make her heavy with my child. I do not last very long, such is my need. I grunt with each hard thrust and hear her echoing moans as I fill her with my thick length. And then, with a deep rumbling growl, I come, spurting my release inside her and shaking with the intense pleasure of it.

Eventually, I regain my senses and withdraw from her gently, going to fetch a damp cloth to clean ourselves with. Once that is done, we settle back in the bed, tucking the covers around us. She yawns delicately, nestling into my body for the night. "I do not know what comes over you, Benedict. It is like you are a man possessed." She giggles and adds, "But I like it!"

"I do not know what comes over me either, but I am glad it pleases you. Goodnight, my darling."

"Goodnight."

I reach over to extinguish the lamp, and soon we both fall into contented slumber.

GRACE

A year later

I CRADLE MY son to my breast as he finishes his first feed of the day. His brown eyes, already so like his father's, gaze at me solemnly, his little hands squeezing into fists. "Good morning, dearest one," I whisper softly. I tickle his tummy and give him a wide smile, wanting to elicit one from him in response. He stares some more, then I hear a little gurgle of laughter as his baby lips crease into a sweet smile. My chest tightens with emotion. I know that smile.

We have named our son Henry Walter Sedgwick, after both of his grandfathers. Thankfully, this second labour was nothing like the first. Benedict was so anxious about it, his face drawn from sleepless nights as the day of my delivery approached. But it turned out well, my sweet little boy entering the world eight hours after the beginning of my labour, in perfect health and giving a cry with his sturdy lungs. I have written home with the good news, and by now, my letter should have reached its destination and brought some cheer to my family. In Aunt Charlotte's last letter, which arrived only a week ago, she told of Benjamin's return from battle, sound in body but bruised and battered in spirit. This dreadful war, now finally over, has taken its toll on the country and our family. How I long to see them again. It has been nearly five years since they left.

My husband enters the bedroom, dressed and freshly shaved. He comes over to the bed with his sweet familiar smile. "And how is my darling boy today?" he asks as he lifts the baby in his arms.

"He is well fed and rested. Will you hold him, Benedict, while I get myself dressed?"

Benedict leans over to kiss me. "Of course. I shall take him down to see his grandpa." With another smile, he leaves the room. I stretch my arms above my head and give another yawn, then get myself out of bed to wash and dress. I'm keen to go down to the stable this morning to see our new mare, Treasure, who has been bred by Midnight and should be dropping her foal any day now. We have three mares, all of them having bred successfully with our prized stallion. Butterscotch has birthed two foals, and Honeydew gave birth to a sweet little filly last year. We have quite a family in our stable now.

On my way out, I stop by the kitchen and snatch a few treats to put into the pocket of my dress, then I'm hurrying out the side door towards the stable. I greet John Saunders, our groom, and go to Butterscotch first. "Good morning, sweetie. Look what I've got for you today," I say as I draw a carrot out of my pocket. She takes it between her teeth and munches on it good naturedly.

Outside, there's the clatter of hooves as a horse canters towards us. I glance out the open stable door curiously and see it's my cousin Daniel, Viscount Stanton. He comes to a stop and jumps down gracefully, taking hold of the reins to lead his horse into an empty stall.

"To what do we owe this unexpected visit?" I ask him mockingly.

He smirks. "Do I need any reason to visit family?" His horse tethered, he strides over to me and gives me a careless kiss on the cheek. "You look well, Gracie," he says. "Motherhood suits you."

"Yes," I smile. "I believe it does. Come join us for breakfast if you have not yet eaten."

"I have, but I will drink a coffee and take one of Cook's delicious buns if there is one."

I laugh. "You may be in luck, come along."

Together, we walk the short path towards the side door of the house, neither of us standing on ceremony. I stop to wash my hands with soap in the small sink by the kitchen, the habit now deeply ingrained. Daniel follows suit and then walks with me to the dining room where we find Benedict with Henry swaddled in his arms, together with Walter. They look up in surprise and get to their feet on seeing Daniel.

"Well this is a pleasant surprise," says Benedict. "Do come and join us, Daniel. May I tempt you with a fresh bun?"

"You may," grins my cousin as he takes his seat. I pass him a cup of coffee, which he takes with a grateful smile. After a few sips, he places it down on the saucer. "You may be wondering why I am here," he begins.

"I am sure you are about to enlighten us," I reply tartly.

He laughs, but soon his expression turns serious. "I have been mulling things over ever since I got this last letter from Mama. Now that Benjamin is back from the war, I am anxious to see him, and everyone else of course. I've spoken to Bella about this, and we're both agreed that we should travel to Ohio as soon as it is possible. I've asked about it, and ships have resumed passages to New York, so I'm proposing to go today to the nearest booking office in London and book us both a passage." He paused. "I was wondering if perhaps, you might like to come along too."

At his words, my heart leaps with excitement. Yes, I very much would like to go home and see everyone again. I glance across at Benedict and am surprised to see him grinning from ear to ear. He passes me a letter, which was lying on the salver. I take it and unfold the sheet, perusing it quickly. It is from Mr Lowe, accepting the temporary position of curate for three months while Benedict takes a leave of absence from his duties as vicar in order to travel to America. I look up at him in surprise, but it is Walter that speaks first.

"Benedict thought it would be the perfect birthday gift to take you on a trip back to your old home, so he wrote last week to Mr Lowe, to ask him if he could take over parish duties in his absence."

"Oh, Benedict," I murmur, lost for words.

"Your cousin's visit has unfortunately let the cat out the bag, for I meant to tell you on your birthday," says Benedict, handing over the baby to his father so he can come to me. He places his arms around me. "But now is as good a time as any." He glances across at Daniel. "Mr Lowe is arriving here a week from today, so yes, we would love to accompany you on your travels."

"And me too," interjects Walter. "I have never been as far afield as America and would love to explore this continent, if you will have me along for the ride."

"Of course!" I exclaim, too excited for words.

Daniel finishes up the bun he has been eating, takes a final sip of his coffee and stands. "Well, I am glad to hear it. I shall be off now and booking a passage for all of us. I'll stop by and see Mr Ridley too, so he can release the necessary funds for the journey." On seeing Benedict about to protest, he quickly pre-empts him, "No, Benedict. We all know you have no designs on Grace's wealth, so please, let us pay for it this time."

It is Walter who then sounds a protest. "Oh, but I cannot allow you to incur this cost on my account. Please send me a bill for my share of the passage and I shall settle it."

"No, Walter, I will not have it," I say stubbornly. "Please do not argue with me on this matter for my mind is made up. There is more than enough money sitting in my account and going to waste, and what better way to spend it than to have us all travel together to America?"

Benedict's arms around me tighten, and he bends his head to kiss my cheek. "Very well, darling. The important thing is that we make this journey, for I know how much you long to see your family."

Just then, the door opens and Anna runs in followed by her nurse. "Uncle Daniel!" she cries, rushing over to him.

He bends to pick her up and throw her into the air, much to her glee. "And how is Anna today?" he asks.

"Well, thank you," she says primly.

"I have good news for you. Can you guess what it is?"

Anna scrunches her face in concentration. "You have a new horse?"

"No. Even better than a horse. We are all going on a journey to see your grandma and grandpa in America. We'll be taking a train and then a very big ship. What do you think about that?"

She gapes at him in astonishment then turns her face to us. "It's true," smiles Benedict. "We're all going on a very exciting adventure, and Grandpa Walter is coming too."

"A train! We're going on a train!" she shrieks, overcome with excitement.

She runs over to us and Benedict lifts her into his arms. "And a ship too, don't forget," he reminds her gently. "It's going to be our best adventure yet."

"Yes," I murmur, overcome with happiness. "Our best adventure yet."

HISTORICAL NOTE

The Vixen's Unlikely Marriage is of course a work of fiction, but I have tried to make the time and events it describes as accurate as possible. There are though, a few instances where I have used artistic license to suit the purposes of the story. So for instance, the Stantons would not have been able to receive a telegram from England in 1860. While the invention of the telegraph and the sending of telegrams began in the mid-1840s, it was not until 1866 that a durable cable was laid across the Atlantic Ocean, connecting the two continents.

There are also a few time discrepancies with regards to two other individuals. Louis Pasteur wrote his paper on germ theory in 1862, a year after the events of the story. His paper was read with interest by a surgeon named Joseph Lister, who in 1864 began the practice of using dressings soaked in carbolic acid to cover his patients' wounds, as well as hand washing and sterilising instruments in a carbolic solution. As a result, the rate of deaths in his hospital ward dropped significantly.

While these two pioneers of germ theory were at work, the vast majority of the medical establishment still continued to believe that disease was caused by spontaneous generation—the theory that life arose from non-living matter—and it was not until the end of the 19th century that the consensus finally changed. I would like to believe though that Benedict, with his enquiring mind, would have come across germ theory in his reading and conducted his own experiments to verify the truth of that theory. It is not too much of a stretch, I hope, to imagine that he understood the need for sterilising instruments during his wife's labour.

We now come to the issue of Caesarean sections, and here, the results of my research proved to be surprising. I had assumed that C-sections were unheard of in the 19th century, or that they were mostly always fatal to the mother, but that is not the case. These operations were uncommon though, and as such, there was coverage of them in the newspapers of the time, usually in the form of a brief paragraph. Scanning through newspaper archives of the mid-1800s, I came across several accounts of C-section births where both the mother and child were saved.

I also found a very interesting set of statistics in a newspaper article (The Leeds Intelligencer and Yorkshire General Advertiser – 12th June 1847) which claimed—and I have no way of verifying the truth of these claims—that there were 378 known cases of the C-section operation being performed. "In 145 of these cases the women recovered... or the recoveries were in the proportion of 38 per cent... The fate of 318 children is mentioned, of whom 219 were saved... or the child survived in 68 per cent [of the cases]." These are still appalling statistics by modern day standards, but for 1847, surprisingly high given the lack of understanding with regards to hygiene. So while my story may stretch the imagination in having Benedict perform such a surgery, I hope it does not stretch it beyond the bounds of possibility.

It is worth noting that in today's world, C-sections are often the preferred action when a baby presents in the breech position and doctors are unable to get it to turn.

AFTERWORD

Dear reader,

I hope you enjoyed *The Vixen's Unlikely Marriage*, the second book in the series, *The Stanton Legacy*, which follows the lives and loves of the Stanton family. Book 3 of the series is a friends-to-lovers romance featuring Benjamin Stanton and Sarah Cranshaw. Read an excerpt in the following pages from *The Bluestocking's Secret Obsession*.

May I ask you for a small favour?

Reviews are the life blood of independent authors. Please could you help spread the word about this book by submitting a review on **Amazon**, **Goodreads** or any other book reader platform. Stay tuned for my latest book release news by subscribing to my newsletter on **mmwakeford.substack.com**. You'll also get access to exclusive freebies and discounts as well as some great book recommendations.

M.M. Wakeford

THE BLUESTOCKING'S SECRET OBSESSION

A HISTORICAL FRIENDS-TO-LOVERS ROMANCE

(AN EXCERPT)

THE STANTON LEGACY
– BOOK 3 –

PROLOGUE

BENJAMIN

"If any man cannot feel the power of God when he looks upon the stars, then I doubt whether he is capable of any feeling at all."
— *Horace*

December 1860, Oxfordshire, England
EVERYONE WAS GATHERED OUTSIDE TO witness the magnificent fireworks being put on display at the Stanton Hall Christmas ball. Everyone, that is, except for himself. Only a minute ago, Benjamin Stanton had sneaked back into the great house that belonged to his grandfather, the Earl of Stanton.

Now, he flew up the servants' staircase, not wanting to call attention to his movements, and made his way rapidly down the long corridor which led to the library. He had plans for tonight. While everyone was distracted by the lavish entertainment outside, he was to have an assignation with Daphne Phipps. He had met her on his arrival in England two weeks ago. She had sat to his right at church, and they had exchanged discreet glances throughout the service.

He had subsequently made it his business to find out who she was and to pursue her acquaintance. Great had been his delight to discover that Daphne, daughter of the village draper, was far from being an angel. A pretty little thing with a pert nose and comely curves, she had welcomed his advances with sly smiles and coy flutters of her eyelashes. In the ensuing weeks, Benjamin had made several visits to the draper's under false pretexts and flirted with Daphne, culminating in a quick fumble with her behind a wooden screen one day when they found themselves alone in the shop. It was then that he had proposed she meet him in the library on the night of the Stanton ball, when everyone else would be engaged in watching the fireworks outside.

He slowed his footsteps as he approached the library door. Very quietly, he pushed it open. It was dim inside, the only light coming from a small oil lamp on a side table. He looked around for Daphne and smiled as he spied a figure seated in the far corner by the window. He shut the door behind him and without a sound, tiptoed into the room. The closer he got to the seated figure, however, the more obvious it became that this was not Daphne. This person was tall, perhaps a foot taller than the draper's daughter, and her hair was dark, arranged in an artful bun on her head, not in blonde ringlets. He saw that she had her face in her hands and that her shoulders heaved.

What could be the matter? And who was this mysterious lady? He cleared his throat, not knowing what to say. At the sound, she froze then dropped her hands to her lap, revealing a tear-stained face and luminous grey eyes. All at once, he recognised her. It was Miss Cranshaw. He had met her once when she had accompanied her brother, the Earl of Stanton's land manager, on a visit to Stanton Hall.

"Are you quite alright?" he asked, then rebuked himself for the stupidity of that question. Of course she was not alright.

"I–I shall be," she stammered, dabbing at her eyes.

"Here, take this," he said, handing her his handkerchief.

She took it and wiped her tears. "Thank you," she murmured.

She made as if to return it to him, but he demurred. "No, no, do keep it," he said. He went to sit on the chair facing her, leaning forwards on his elbows. "Will you tell me what is troubling you?" he asked gently.

She used the handkerchief once more to wipe at her eyes then put it down in her lap with a self-derisive huff. "Mere foolishness on my part, I'm afraid."

He waited for her to continue. When she did not speak, he enquired with stubborn persistence: "What sort of foolishness?"

She sighed and looked away. It did not look like she would answer him, so he was surprised when she said: "The foolishness of hankering for someone who does not merit or return such sentiments."

"Ah. I begin to see." He eyed her with sympathy. "I have not myself ever been in love, but I am sure it must be painful to have unrequited feelings for another." At the tender age of twenty-two, Benjamin had not yet met any female that set his heart aflutter and whom he could imagine falling in love with in the way that his father and mother loved each other. He supposed, if ever he took the time to wonder about such things, that someday he would meet this person. There was plenty of time still for that, and he was in no hurry.

His was a carefree and happy existence, having grown up on the prosperous farming estate in Ohio that his father and uncle had built with their own hands after leaving England to seek their fortunes in America. They had done so to break free from the authoritarian Earl of Stanton, their father, who had used the enormous wealth at his disposal to exert control over his sons. Naturally, this exodus had caused a rift with the earl, which took many years to mend. Now, however, they were all back in England to attend to his grandfather, who was gravely ill. Notwithstanding his illness, the earl had decided to hold a sumptuous Christmas ball, keen to celebrate the return of his family, temporary though it might be.

Benjamin was brought back to the matter at hand by Miss Cranshaw's voice, which wobbled ever so slightly. "Then you should consider yourself fortunate not to have lost your heart to another, for I cannot recommend it."

"Was there something in particular that occurred tonight to upset you so?" He was curious to know what could have sent the outwardly sensible Miss Cranshaw to hide in the library and cry.

She toyed with the handkerchief in her hands as she spoke: "I went out earlier for a walk in the gardens accompanied by Mr Sedgwick, who as well as being the curate of this parish is a childhood friend of mine. We were there to observe the sky in the hope of seeing a meteor shower — astronomy is a particular pursuit of mine, you see. Instead, we came upon the person who holds my affections in a passionate embrace with a lady. You will pardon me if I do not name the individuals. I promised Mr Sedgwick that I would not spread any gossip."

"No, of course. Quite right." Benjamin nodded in understanding, though his curiosity had been aroused. "I suppose this encounter tonight has dashed any hopes you may have had with regards to this person you hold dear."

"Oh, I have long known it to be hopeless," she smiled sadly. "And yet it makes no difference. I continue to yearn for him."

Benjamin could not imagine how one could persevere in harbouring a passion for someone in the face of evidence that it was hopeless. In his experience, if a girl showed no interest in his flirting, it was best to move on to greener pastures. After all, there was no shortage of pretty girls in the universe. What was the point in wasting one's time and effort on someone who did not deserve such attention?

There again, he had never been in love. Perhaps, it was different when the heart was engaged. He tried to think of something useful to say, searching through his mind for a pertinent proverb. His mother often quoted maxims from her beloved classical philosophers, and they had become as familiar to him as they were to her. In the end, he settled on reciting this from Seneca the Younger: "True happiness is to enjoy the present without anxious dependence on the future."

At Miss Cranshaw's blank look, he elaborated. "You say you yearn for him. Perhaps you dream of a rosy future in the loving embrace of this person who has captured your heart. You may imagine yourself carrying his name and bearing his children, if only he could have a change of heart and truly see you. In all truth, nobody can say what will come to pass. It could be that this person is destined for you, and it could be that he is not. None of it matters though, because you do not live in the future, but in the here and now." He laughed a little self-consciously, all too aware that he was beginning to sound like a bore. "What I am trying most inelegantly to say is that happiness does not come from dwelling in the past or the future, but in enjoying the present moment."

"I suppose so," said Miss Cranshaw looking doubtful.

"Take me, for example. I will have you know, Miss Cranshaw, that I came up to the library for an assignation with a young lady who shall remain nameless. Instead of encountering that lady and enjoying a glorious embrace with her, I came across your good self. I could be forgiven for feeling some disappointment that my plans have gone awry, but there is no joy in dwelling resentfully on what could have been. So next, I ask myself, what would make me happy at this present moment? And the answer is simple. It would bring me joy to wipe that sad expression from your face and make you smile."

At this, she huffed and pressed her lips together, though he detected the glimmer of a smile. "What is it with all these secret assignations?" she grumbled. "I am tempted to believe that everyone but me is engaging in illicit activities when no one is looking."

"Maybe not everyone, but I would not be surprised if there are a good many people doing things in private that would be very much frowned upon in public. It is the way of the world."

She studied him. "Mr Stanton, you are a cynic."

He laughed. "Call me Benjamin, or Ben. No, I do not think I am a cynic, merely a realist." He stood and held out his hands to her. She took them and allowed him to help her to her feet. He looked down at her with a smile. "So now, we come to you, Miss Cranshaw—"

"Sarah," she interjected. "If I am to call you by your given name, then you must do the same with me."

He inclined his head. "Very well. So now, we come to you, Sarah. Put aside your woes about the past or the future and bring your attention to what would bring you joy this very minute." He held up a hand. "And before you say it, something other than having a certain man fall to his knees before you avowing his undying love."

Sarah's face took on a faraway expression. He presumed she was imagining that very thing happening. In an instant, it was gone. She took a steadying breath, murmuring, "Here and now, what would make me happy?" She was quiet, thinking about it.

Benjamin observed her as she furrowed a brow, contemplating the matter. She was tall and angular with smooth, pale skin, not the buxom shape he usually favoured. His gaze fell momentarily to her cleavage, covered in the pale blue silk of her gown. He discerned the slight outline of her breasts and pictured them in his mind—small nubs that would easily fit inside his hands. He felt himself grow hard at the thought. *Damnation! What was the matter with him?*

With an effort, he dispelled these unruly thoughts just as she looked back up at him and said, "I believe, right this minute, seeing a meteor shower would bring me joy. I was so sure my calculations were right and that there would be one tonight."

"Well, I cannot promise you a meteor shower, Sarah, but the next best thing. I hear no expense has been spared for tonight's fireworks display which is about to begin. How about we go out and watch?"

She touched a finger to her still-puffy eyes. "I am not sure I am in a fit state yet to be seen," she prevaricated.

"That is not a problem," he said swiftly. "Come with me." He held out his arm, and reluctantly, she placed a hand on it.

He led her out of the library and walked her to the end of the corridor. There, he proceeded to pull open the large sash window, glancing back at her with a grin. "Do you trust me to keep you safe, Sarah?"

"No," she responded reflexively.

He gave her a reproachful look, but continued undeterred, "Outside this window is a wide ledge that leads to a flat part of the roof. There is, I have discovered, a spot where the curvature of the slate tiles is such as to form a bench of sorts. I have been out there a time or two and enjoyed a marvellous vista of the grounds below. From there, we will have an uninterrupted and private view of the fireworks. Do come."

Without waiting for her reply, he swung one leg over the window sill and stepped out onto the ledge. He turned to face her, holding out his hand and speaking reassuringly, "The ledge is wide enough to stand on comfortably, and I shall keep hold of you at all times. Do not be afraid."

She shook her head. "This is madness."

"Don't think, just do," smiled Benjamin, citing another of his mother's philosophers.

"And now you are quoting Horace at me," replied Sarah. "Next, you shall be telling me to seize the day and put the least possible trust in tomorrow."

Benjamin's grin grew wider. "Seize the day, Sarah."

"Oh, very well," she huffed. Carefully, she pulled up the skirt of her dress and lifted a slim, stocking-clad leg over the window sill. With his assistance, she came to stand on the ledge. It was indeed quite wide, though she appeared to avoid looking below to see how far she might fall were she to lose her balance.

"It is but two steps to the right," said Benjamin. "Keep hold of my hand." Slowly, he guided her off the ledge to the flat part of the roof, then walked her carefully to the spot he had described. It was indeed shaped in such a way as to provide an unorthodox seat. Cautiously, she lowered herself down to it, shivering slightly at the cold feel of the tiles beneath her.

Benjamin settled himself at her side and noticed the shiver. "I am sorry," he murmured. "I should have thought to bring a blanket. Are you so very cold?"

She shivered again but replied, "No, I will be fine for a short while."

"You are a very poor liar, Sarah," mused Benjamin. He unbuttoned his top coat and draped it around her shoulders just as a loud bang was heard, followed by a flash of bright colours. Together, they watched the fireworks light up the dark winter sky. A minute into this, something extraordinary happened. Above them, a dot of bright light zoomed across the sky. Then it happened again and again.

"What was that?" asked Benjamin.

"A meteor shower." Sarah's voice exuded awed satisfaction at having her wish granted. For several minutes, they were silent, observing the show nature put on for them, nearly forgetting the man-made entertainments that were occurring concurrently.

"Incredible," murmured Benjamin.

"People call them shooting stars, but that is not really what they are. They are meteoroids or rocks in space falling towards Earth and burning up as they hurtle through the sky."

Benjamin turned his gaze towards her. "You seem peculiarly well informed," he remarked.

"Did I not tell you that astronomy is a particular pursuit of mine? I have what some would call an unladylike interest in science and engineering. On various occasions, I have been called an eccentric, 'an odd one' or a bluestocking by the good people of Stanton Harcourt."

He continued to observe her curiously. "Well, you are a little odd, but in a good way. It reminds me of Mama, who is herself considered something of a bluestocking. She likes nothing better than to bury herself in a book and quote classical philosophers at us whenever the situation demands it."

"Aha! That explains why you've been spouting Seneca and Horace at me this evening," exclaimed Sarah.

"Yes, it does rather. And though I am not quite as wont to do so as Mama, I do think that these philosophers have a thing or two to teach us. Aren't you glad now that you seized the day and came out onto the rooftop with me?"

She smiled. "Yes, I am, improper though it may have been."

"And I would hazard a guess that you forgot about the man that broke your heart for a least a few minutes."

A shutter came down over her expression. "I suppose I did."

"Stupid me! Now I have reminded you of your heartbreak when I was striving for the opposite."

She rested a hand on his arm. "You did help to distract me from my woes, and for that, I thank you."

"I am glad. Now, I can see you are still shivering, so I think it best we head back inside." He stood and held his hand out to her. She took it and got to her feet, handing him back his topcoat, which he quickly shrugged back on. Together, they stepped carefully back towards the window and climbed inside the house. Once they were in, Benjamin brought the window sash down again and turned to her. "Are you ready now to rejoin the ball?" he asked.

She nodded. "Yes, I am sure my brother, Ambrose, is wondering where I am."

"I shall let you go down first, lest our presence together occasions any gossip. Before you go though, I want to thank you for keeping me company this evening."

She could not help but laugh. "Surely it is I who should be thanking you? You have been excellent company, Benjamin, and a true friend."

"Good. I like the idea of us being friends. I do not think I have had any other female friends since growing into manhood, apart from my cousins. Will you allow me to call on you, as a friend, in the days to come?"

She bit her bottom lip in concentration. He noticed it was fuller than the top. "I would not like to call undue attention to myself," she said finally.

"You live in the cottage that lies at the edge of this estate, do you not?"

"Yes, Ivy Cottage."

"Well, if I should walk from the main house to you, I am hardly likely to encounter any gossips from the village. The grounds of Stanton Hall are extensive, so we should be able to take long and private walks together. That is, if you do not mind more of my company? You would be doing me a great favour, Sarah, for life here is rather dull, what with Grandpa being ill."

"Will you not be needed to attend to the earl?"

He shrugged. "Only some of the time. It is mainly Papa and Uncle Jasper who spend their days with Grandpa, and he tires easily, so there is not much for me to do. Will you take pity on me?"

Her lips quirked into a faint smile. "Very well. Goodnight, Benjamin."

"Goodnight, Sarah."

He watched her go, a strange feeling of elation blossoming in his chest. True, he had not had the pleasure of an illicit romp with Daphne Phipps tonight. But he had made a new friend, and was that not better than the fleeting pleasure of a carnal encounter?

ABOUT THE AUTHOR

M.M. Wakeford lives with her husband and son in a London terraced house that gathers dust while she loses herself in her writing. A lifelong reader of romantic novels, she writes in many genres including contemporary, sci-fi and historical romance. All her stories strive to capture that heady feeling of falling in love, with authentic characters whose journey to a happily ever after is lined with dilemmas to overcome. If you're looking for a page turning romance with high emotion and a good dose of spice, you've come to the right place.

ALSO BY THIS AUTHOR

MY CAPTIVE DUCHESS
Book 1 – The Reeves of Reeves Hall

"You cannot leave Reeves Hall again. Here you will remain."

Recently widowed, Jane, Duchess of Coleford, has moved to an isolated part of Cornwall with her young daughter. There she meets her nearest neighbour, Brook Reeves, a man with a seemingly permanent scowl on his handsome face who soon makes it clear that he wants her gone. Despite his many offers to purchase the crumbling house she inherited from her late husband, she stubbornly insists on staying.

It is not long before the two become adversaries, both determined to ignore the attraction that has flared between them. Until one day, Jane ventures uninvited into his domain and sees things she must never tell the world about. There is

only one solution. At Reeves Hall she must remain, his captive
duchess.

What you will get in this book:
- Forced proximity
- Enemies-to-lovers
- Grumpy/sunshine
- Mr Rochester/Jane Eyre vibes
- Slow-burn but steamy
- Regency romance with a sci-fi twist

My Captive Duchess is book one of the series, The Reeves of Reeves
Hall, set around the mysterious Reeves family who are not what they
seem. It can also be read and enjoyed as a standalone as each book in
the series has its own featured hero/heroine and HEA. If you're
looking for page-turning, heart-stopping romance with an original,
fresh twist, then this story is for you.

Praise for My Captive Duchess:

*"Absolutely outstanding writing... Original story with
uncompromising storytelling that you will have difficulty putting
down once you start reading."* ★★★★★ Goodreads review

*"I couldn't put this book down! It was a good story with steam and
great characters... This is going to be an interesting series."* ★★★★★
Goodreads review

*"The most fascinating story I have read in a long while... a wonderful
read!"* ★★★★★ Goodreads review

"I found the story so engaging I couldn't put it down." ★★★★★
Goodreads review

*"I applaud the clever plot in this story. I adore both Regency and Sci-
Fi, but never expected to see a combination of my two favorites! Well
done!"* ★★★★★ Goodreads review

KRANTOR'S MATE

Book 1 – The Venorians and Krovatians

One day, on a planet far from Earth, I meet my fated mate.
The only problem is, he's in love with someone else.

Martha has enrolled on a six-month exchange program to the planet Ven, whose people have recently made first contact with Earth. Newly single and broke, Martha looks forward to this once-in-a-lifetime opportunity to find out more about the Venorians, an intriguing humanoid race of massive bronze-skinned people.

As the son and heir of the Kran, planet Ven's ruler, Krantor has four somars—men who are his lifelong bodyguards and companions. He loves them all dearly, but one of them, Prilor, he loves best of all. Krantor knows he's destined to meet his fated mate one day, but it's Prilor he wants to spend his days and nights with. And he certainly hadn't banked on his fated mate being a human!

Will Martha give up her life on Earth for a fated mate who already loves another? And what of the feelings she has developed for Shanbri, another of Krantor's somars?

Author's note: this is a standalone sci-fi romance with steam and spice aplenty, featuring FM, MM, and MFM relationships, and a guaranteed HEA for all.

Praise for Krantor's Mate:

"Trope busting. Loved it... M. M. Wakeford offers a completely new take on fated mates. With all the expectations that are set with a trope, the author blows it out of the water with her fabulous storytelling. I completely enjoyed this take on RH, fated mates, and deep-abiding love." ★★★★★ Goodreads review

"What a phenomenal read. The worlds, cultures, and species created were diverse and detailed. The characters were rich, vivid, and beautifully flawed. I went on such an emotional ride with this book." ★★★★★ Goodreads review

"An interesting and original approach to the reverse harem and fated mate tropes... Thought-provoking and provocative, with high heat throughout." ★★★★★ Goodreads review

"Ultra-hot and steamy... An interesting fated mate RH menage that explores individual pairings within the group, as well as a new partner trying to fit in and find their place within an existing strong and loving relationship." ★★★★★ Goodreads review

"This is a fantastic sci-fi romance... Fantastic story. I loved it and the characters and I highly recommend this book." ★★★★★ Goodreads review

"Loved it! This book takes a unique twist on polyamorous relationships AND fated mates... definitely give this a read!" ★★★★★ Amazon review

"An interesting and original approach to the reverse harem and fated mate tropes… Thought-provoking and provocative, with high heat throughout." ★★★★★ Amazon review

*"I really enjoyed this book. Great world building. I loved the different and connected relationships in this book between the males together and with Martha… Lots of yummy steamy scenes to keep me happy, too. *wink*"* ★★★★★ Amazon review

"What a phenomenal read. The worlds, cultures, and species created were diverse and detailed. The characters were rich, vivid, and beautifully flawed. I went on such an emotional ride with this book. It is so amazing to watch this talented author weave such a magical journey with such a balance of realism and fantasy. I can see myself turning back to this book time and time again." ★★★★★ Amazon review